HER MOTHER'S DAUGHTER

Her Mother's Daughter

Cara Saylor Polk

CROWN PUBLISHERS, INC.   NEW YORK

Copyright © 1982 by Cara Saylor Polk

All rights reserved. No part of this book may be reproduced

or utilized in any form or by any means,

electronic or mechanical, including photocopying, recording,

or by any information storage and retrieval system,

without permission in writing from the publisher.

Inquiries should be addressed to Crown Publishers, Inc.,

One Park Avenue, New York, New York 10016

Printed in the United States of America

Published simultaneously in Canada

by General Publishing Company Limited

Library of Congress Cataloging in Publication Data

Polk, Cara Saylor.

Her mother's daughter.

I. Title.

PS3566.0475H4 1982   813'.54   82-9933

ISBN 0-517-54727-9   AACR2

Designed by Camilla Filancia

10 9 8 7 6 5 4 3 2 1

First Edition

To my mother, Betty, for bearing me in,

To my father, Harold, for bailing me out,

To my husband, Jim, for humoring me well,

To our dog, T, for allowing me time off to write.

Prologue

"Miss B, Miss B, where are you? I found the book!" Five-year-old Rosalind Connolly ignored her pink rabbit-toed slippers and padded barefoot into the hall.

"Mummy!" She spied her mother down the hall, sitting in the family breakfast room, talking with Miss B, Rosalind's and her brothers' nurse. Other people were there, but Rosalind saw only her mother and Miss B. "You're home!" she accused her mother. "Is *my* father home?"

"Rosie." Dianne Connolly blinked back tears. "You're supposed to be in bed."

Miss B swung around. "Miss Rosalind, you march yourself right back to your bedroom. And where are your slippers?"

"You promised to read to me." She held up her story book and stood her ground. "You promised."

"Me too!" The eager face of Rosalind's brother, Billy who was almost three years old, appeared from behind his sister's dark curls.

"Me too!" echoed Timothy, Billy's twin, as he emerged into the hall, blinking at the light.

"Very well. Come along, all of you," the Scottish nanny said firmly.

"Miss B!" Dianne's whisper halted the procession for a moment.

"Yes, Mrs. Connolly?"

"You'll have to do it, Miss B. I simply . . . can't."

"What can't Mummy do?" Rosalind asked as the twins sandwiched Miss B on the overstuffed nursery couch. Rosalind cuddled up beside Timothy, her dark head contrasting with the cherubic gold of her little brother's. "Miss B," she repeated. "What can't Mummy do?"

"Hmph." Miss B cleared her throat and opened the story book. "She can't bear to comb your hair because you scream so at the tangles. And you know that doesn't bother me a mite."

Rosalind frowned. "Miss B, you lied to me. You said she and *my* father were out, but she's here."

"I did not lie to you. They were out, but she got back early. She was . . . tired."

"Will Mummy come say good-night?" asked Billy.

"Will she?" Timothy fixed his wide blue eyes on the nurse.

"I don't know. She has visitors now." Miss B stared at the whimsical book illustrations for a moment. Then she dropped the book and hugged the twins to her lean breast. "I don't know, my poor babies. I don't know."

Billy fought for air and Timothy slipped free. Rosalind studied Miss B, sensing something wrong. "Why was Mummy crying?"

The twins frowned at Rosalind.

"She was crying. I saw." Rosalind spoke firmly.

"Maybe she fell down and went boom." Billy giggled.

"Boom!" Timothy laughed.

Rosalind's attention remained on Miss B. "Is *my* father home too? I didn't see him but he promised I could make him breakfast tomorrow on my little electric stove. Tiny, tiny little pancakes with lots and lots of syrup. He likes syrup."

"Me too! Me too!" chirped the twins.

Then the children fell silent at the sight of Miss B clutching their book to her breast, tears streaming down her face.

"Miss B, don't cry." Billy clutched her arm with his small hands.

Timothy touched Miss B's cheek softly, feeling the tears.

"What's wrong?" Rosalind was frightened. She had never seen her nurse cry before.

Miss B sniffed, pulled a white cambric handerchief from her

bosom, dabbed at her eyes and pulled herself together. "Children, a terrible thing has happened. Your father took very, very sick today. . . ."

"Daddy's sick?" Billy frowned at Timothy.

"Suddenly dreadfully sick," Miss B nodded. "He had something called a heart attack. And he collapsed in the middle of a speech. . . ." She paused, wondering if the children understood at all and searching for the words and strength to continue. "They took him to the hospital, but it was too late for the doctors to help him. I'm afraid," her voice choked, "he won't be back ever again, because he died and went to heaven."

"Heaven?" Billy blinked at Miss B.

"Will he come home soon when he's better?" asked Timothy.

"No, Timmy," Rosalind spoke gravely. "Daddy can't come back if Miss B's telling us the truth." She faced Miss B sternly. "Miss B, are you telling us the truth?" Her tone parodied Miss B's when she asked the children the same question.

"Oh, Miss Rosie, I never lie to you and I certainly wouldn't lie about this. I would never joke about your wonderful father."

"But where is he?" Billy persisted.

"Daddy's dead, Billy," Rosalind intoned, suddenly feeling she had to play mother to her brothers. "Remember when Flipper, our goldfish died? And Miss B helped us bury him beside the rose garden and we said prayers? You can't come back if you die. You get put in the ground . . . like Flipper." The little girl sobbed as the truth of her own words sank into her heart.

"Your father's in heaven now, lambies." Miss B's voice quavered. "He'll look after you from up there now."

Timothy, watching Rosalind, began to cry too. Then all three children were sobbing together.

"I know it will be hard for you—for all of us—without him, but I am certain he would want you all to be very brave and strong children now."

"I'm big," sniffed Billy.

"And brave," gulped Timothy.

"I'll be six soon," Rosalind whispered.

"Use your handkerchiefs," Miss B spoke automatically, forgetting the children were in nightclothes. "Poor dears," she murmured, recognizing their lack and wiping their small noses and cheeks. "It's going to be very difficult for your mummy without your father. She will need all three of you very much right now. You're all she has."

"But there's Grandma Jane and Uncle Herbie and Uncle Sean and Grandma Bea and . . ." Rosalind began the list.

"They're not around all the time. You are, so you'll have to be her very best friends now. And that means being very brave and good and helpful."

"I'll take care of her." Rosalind's tiny lips quavered. "*My* father says I'm getting to be a big girl."

"We're big, too," Billy spoke for the twins.

Rosalind turned to her brothers. "You must both try to be extra good, because Mummy needs you to. Isn't that right, Miss B?" Rosalind gripped the book with sudden intensity, remembering that her father had given it to her.

"Yes, boys. For the next few days you'll have to dress up and go places with your mummy and sister and be on your very best behavior."

Billy pulled his small, round body erect. His chin trembled as he gave Miss B the military salute a visiting general had taught them. "Yes, ma'am. We'll be good."

Timothy seconded the salute.

"You're all very good." Miss B reached out and pulled all three children into an embrace. This time the boys did not protest as they found momentary comfort resting against her strong heartbeat and Miss B's tears fell on one dark and two fair heads.

Her spur dug into Rajah's well-bred belly. She felt the stallion's strides lengthen as they pounded toward the triple jump. Adrenaline surged and she savored the fine edge of controlled abandon.

Rajah took the first jump with perfect form and made the second with ease. Dianne leaned forward intently, accidentally spurring him again as they raced toward the third, forcing a late jump and tipping the rail.

"Damn!" she shouted into the wind. Rajah quickly recovered stride. "Good boy," she whispered into his powerful neck. "You're the best ever."

Dianne delighted in this first great-grandson of Rami, the Arabian mare given to her by the Saudi king fifteen years before.

Her attention was diverted from her steed as Leda, the children's Norwegian elkhound, came hurtling across the field toward her like a fat black missile. Rajah gave the dog an imperious glance and turned his head toward Dianne.

She patted his neck. "Don't worry. You're my number one." She glanced at Leda and laughed as the dog picked up a stick and raced away, daring her to follow. Then her laughter faded and the scene felt empty as she thought of Rosalind and the twins. They should be there, she thought, to ride with her and play with Leda.

Her gaze swept past her stables and hovered on the faraway miniature white buildings of the neighboring estates. The panorama resembled a nineteenth-century landscape. She realized that her own buildings looked the same from her neighbors' perspectives. Protective coloration. Here at Walnut Hill she was undisturbed, with properly indifferent neighbors whose world was that of the landed gentry, more concerned with pedigrees than politics.

There had been years when she had not come near Walnut Hill, but she had held on to it. She needed to know it was there. Sometimes she wondered why she had never gathered up Billy, Timothy and Rosalind and moved inside its protective fences for good.

She shivered at the thought in the early November morning. There could be too much quiet here. One could dry up like a walnut left outside for the winter—the shell remains intact, but the meat withers inside.

Quickly, she handed Rajah to the groom and headed inside to change. Leda raced toward the limousine, conditioned to expect imminent departure when the ride was over.

As Dianne peeled off her riding clothes, she examined herself in the mirror. Thanks to her father's marvelous cheekbones, the face was holding up well. And her few gray hairs highlighted the natural blond with a touch better than her hairdresser's. Years of suppressing appetites had kept the flesh taut on her frame, skin molding gently over the outlines of her rib cage. The mere thought of her perpetual diet made her ravenous, but every hungry minute was worth it. One couldn't be too thin. Not at forty-plus, plus. She slipped into a soft blue cashmere that matched her eyes and picked up flecks of blue in the tweed slacks, then analyzed the effect.

Had she forgotten anything? She glanced around the bedroom, the same bedroom she had shared with Bill Connolly on occasional weekends. Almost fifteen years—it didn't seem that long ago, sometimes.

This was not the moment for nostalgia. She grabbed her coat and rushed out to the waiting limousine. Back to Manhattan. She needed some leisurely hours to get into top form for Tony. She pressed her fingers into the tense muscles at the back of her neck and willed them to relax.

After three weeks of businesslike secondhand messages from the Marino offices, Tony himself had called that morning, urging her to meet him in the city for dinner with some business friends. "Please, Dianne, I'm eager to have you with me," he had said.

At the word *eager* she had felt momentary hope for some change in her husband's attitude. More likely he's eager for his resident celebrity to help the business deal. His little starlets don't have the same clout.

In the early days of their marriage, Tony had paraded her around like a dancing bear, blithely brushing off her objections to the swarms of reporters and paparazzi. "We have our fun," he had insisted. "Let them have theirs." When a photograph of her sunning nude was published he took no offense, but admired the picture. Their fun was his fun. Crass. She should have seen it sooner.

Publicity in itself wasn't objectionable, if garnered in conjunction with the right makeup, clothes and timing. Then it equaled the high of an opening night, but being on call on the press's terms was intrusive. And her second husband, her so-called protector, was cut from the same shabby cloth as the Fourth Estate.

Her defense had been to back off, plead migraines or mythical "other plans." Tony responded harshly and accused her of not "living up to the terms," revealing his total insensitivity. No terms had been codified as far as she was concerned, except in Tony's warped mind.

It had been the same with Bill. As she had told Angus Benninger, her psychiatrist, she always felt punished for not living up to other people's interpretations of agreements, written or unwritten.

She let out a sigh of disgust. Would she never stop sifting through memories like a compromised vestal virgin who prays the sieve will hold water?

She glanced at the Cartier tank watch, noting the time. She would have to switch it for the flashy diamond pavé number Tony had given her. Chewing at her thumbnail, she wished she could stop biting her nails. Tony had pointedly complimented a woman's beautiful hands and nails at a dinner party recently.

She stared out the window at the median. It was impossible to distinguish where they were—California, Ohio, New Jersey or Missouri. Turnpikes are the arteries of American anonymity.

She pulled off her dark glasses and propped the velvet pillow that coordinated with the car's pale interior against the door, exhausted from contemplating her encounter with Tony. Leda was curled up, asleep like a giant black caterpillar in the passenger's seat beside the chauffeur. So simple for a dog, Dianne thought—to sleep, to eat, to be loved, brushed and petted. Were her own needs so much more complicated? She closed her eyes. Perhaps things would be different when she opened them.

๛   ๛   ๛

Dianne's blue eyes came into focus on the colorful Pissarro above the creme-colored couch. She preferred the one she had donated to the permanent White House collection when she had left it as the widow Connolly.

If it weren't for the Connollys she might attempt a quiet swap. Unfortunately, if the press got wind of it, it would upset Bea, her former mother-in-law. And, despite her controversial remarriage, the Connollys remained her safest port in storms.

"It's not easy to be extremely rich, terribly famous and the symbol of a nation's grief." Dianne could hear Bea's clear aristocratic voice counseling her. "That's why we need each other so very much now, to move forward together with style—and God, of course."

Dianne frowned. She didn't want to dwell on the past; she had enough problems with the present.

She eased herself into a more comfortable position on the velvet couch, noting with satisfaction that her pale silk dress harmonized with the salmon shades in the Pissarro. She gave herself an extra ten points for being ready before Tony arrived. At least he can't bitch about that for a change, she thought as she mentally rehearsed the special petition she had planned for him.

The champagne was iced and waiting and the hors d'oeurvres were perfectly arranged. She had sent the cook, Marie, out to walk Leda for at least an hour. She wanted optimum privacy.

She crossed the room and put Tony's favorite Sinatra tape on the stereo. As she adjusted the volume, she heard Tony stride into the room, rattling the Steuben ashtrays on the glass-topped tables. She swirled around, salmon-colored panels floating.

"Ah!" His resonant baritone pierced the pastels of the room. "What is this? A celebration? What is the occasion?"

"The occasion is having you home. It's been weeks." Dianne spoke huskily with a tinge of reproach.

"Business. It is all business that keeps me flying from one corner of the world to the other!" He gripped her shoulders with his short powerful hands and leaned up slightly to kiss her cheek. His hand reached behind her head and turned her mouth toward his.

The business of starlets, she thought, pulling away. Then she remembered her special mission and turned her mouth back to meet his.

"It is a shame we have people to meet so soon, yes? Otherwise . . ." He punctuated his remark with a playful slap on her rump.

Dianne smiled a bright hostess smile and moved to pour champagne for him.

He downed a glassful in one gulp and held out his goblet for a refill. "So," he changed the subject. "My secretary tells me you have important matters to discuss. Let us discuss it now. Serious business ruins my digestion. Let me guess." He rolled his eyes toward the ceiling. "Ah! It must be money if it is an important matter for Dianne." He laughed and reached for the champagne bottle.

Dianne shivered. Tony always second-guessed her like an Italian psychic. She was not yet ready to begin her plea. Nervously she sipped at her champagne, sniffing as the tiny bubbles burst in her nose. Tony was so crude. Of course money was important to her; she had grown up dirt poor. So had he. He had a lot of gall to fault her on the subject. His own lust for multibillionaire status was obsessive, as compulsive as his quest for fame and social position. He was now leaning on the fulcrum of their marital trade-off—her social status for his money. Her hand trembled as she reached for a cigarette. Tony had his international fame, thanks to her, but her share of the tacit contract, absolute financial security, remained unfulfilled.

"Well," Tony prodded. "Let's hear about it."

"When you married me," Dianne began airily, "you offered me the world, everything you had, anything to make me happy. . . ." She rattled off the clichés and paused expectantly.

Tony silently folded his arms, watching her face.

Unnerved, she plunged ahead. "I don't know how to phrase this. I find it all so . . . embarrassing."

He let her squirm.

"Well . . ." Dianne raised a finger to chew, caught herself

and folded her hands with an uneasy giggle. "Your office says you can't increase my allowance. Of course that's absurd. It must be that my messages aren't getting through."

Tony held his pose and his silence.

"Tony, with inflation and all the pressures, there is no way on earth that I can continue supporting Walnut Hill, this place and everything in style. Kiki can show you the books. It's awful—salaries, supplies, the stable upkeep . . ." She trailed off.

"Ah!" Tony's hands flew up into the air. "When you want clothes, you can charge, yes? When you want to fly away with your artsy-fartsy friends, my planes take you there for free, yes? I give you fifty times what the average family lives on—and you have no rent, no transportation, clothing or child-rearing costs!"

"But there is the staff here and at Walnut Hill and supplies, food, liquor, clothes, gifts, phones, security and . . ."

"And your allowance is more than sufficient along with what I give you for each of the children even though their mother won't teach them the proper respect for the stepfather who provides. Your allowance is more than generous. It is completely stupid and extravagant on my part." Tony's eyes were cold as Italian marble.

Dianne shuddered and dropped her eyes. "Oh, Tony," she said in a breathy little-girl voice. "Last month I had to send Kiki to a thrift shop with some of my old clothes to get spending money. Do you want that?"

Tony noted her cool blond beauty dispassionately. "I don't give a damn how you manage your money or what you do with your clothes. If you can't live on forty-five thousand dollars a month, sell Walnut Hill."

"Oh!" The cry escaped Dianne.

"Or sell one of the rings you have locked away in a vault where no one can see my terrible taste. You get a lot for nothing. If you were an employee, you wouldn't last a day. What do I ask in return for my money?" He held out empty hands. "I'm not around much to bother you."

"Never around is closer to the truth," snapped Dianne. "A fine husband."

"It takes a loving wife to create a fine husband. Perhaps the next time we entertain friends you'll attempt to be less than two hours late like last time . . . and the time before . . . and the time before . . . and the time before."

Dianne twisted a skirt panel nervously. This selfish man raging at her wasn't the warm protector she thought she had married. That man would have understood her need for time to prepare for things, emotionally as well as cosmetically. This dark stranger was a lump, a peasant.

Tony watched Dianne's blue eyes glaze as she drifted into her own thoughts. Once he had found her inner retreats intriguing. Now they bored him.

"You need money?" he broke in, pulling her from the couch. "Come to bed."

"What?" She blinked and froze.

"Maybe your high-class head doctor has taught you to handle giving me my money's worth." He grappled at the front of her dress, reaching for a breast. "How are you doing? How much do you think you're worth by now?"

She met his grasp with stiff arms, shoving him as hard as she could. He stood firm, raised his palms in a surrender sign, threw back his head and brayed with laughter. Her fists clenched as her voice lost its breathy quality.

"How dare you? What do you think I am? One of your Hollywood whores?"

"At least whores are honest about it. They give me service for my dollars."

Dianne bit her lower lip. Everything was twisting. Hadn't she planned to seduce him, knowing it was the only way? But not in such a blatant exchange. She shuddered.

Tony opened his arms invitingly in the way that had once endeared him to her. "Come on, little Mama. You might enjoy our pillow deal."

"No, Tony, no," she whispered as she hurried across the room to the mirror to rearrange her hair and regain her composure. She looked at his face in the reflection. "Besides, Tony,"— she attempted a smile—"don't we have to meet the Randalls in half an hour?"

His hands dropped, the invitation withdrawn. "Since when do you care about time? Or anything, except yourself and maybe your goddamn children."

"You're revolting." She sat heavily on the couch. "The children are both off at school and this house is always open to you." She stopped. She would not stoop to defend herself. "We can discuss this after dinner." She gave him a vague smile.

"I've lost my appetite." He reached for the overcoat the

maid had laid out for him. "I'm going to the office and do some worthwhile work. Maybe I'll have time to call you from Zurich tomorrow."

"Zurich? Tomorrow? But what about the Randalls, tonight? You invited them."

"Tell them I was called out of town. Tell them I ran off with a starlet who could deliver. I don't give a fuck what you tell them." He turned and was gone.

Dianne sat frozen, a work of sculpture in her carefully designed room.

What had she wanted from Tony? A Pygmalion who would bring her to life again with flowers and gems and beautiful people? But in her case, the myth was inverted. She wasn't running away. He was.

The marriage had begun with such promise. He had given her a devotion and a feeling of security she had never experienced. If the slightest argument had inspired one of his stormy Mediterranean exits, he returned within an hour, breathing passion and bearing gifts.

And with the gifts had come apologies, wine and lovemaking. As she allowed her mind to drift to those warmer days, a deep loneliness suffused her. She had been lonely before Tony had charged into her life, lonely too soon again while he was there, and now, even lonelier. She had been lonely during the years with Bill, too. Always walls. Always on the edge of estrangement. *Estranged.* She rolled the word around in her mind. In spite of being sought after by so many, she was close to so few.

For as long as she could remember, she had known consistent closeness only with her children. Now the twins and Rosalind were away at school. And Rosalind at nineteen was drawing away from her. Dianne recognized the signs of emotional separation as echoes of her own adolescence. She didn't like them.

She heard Leda bark and the rear entrance door slam shut. Marie was back. Dianne buzzed Marie to say she planned to dine in. Then she dialed Rosalind's number at Smith College. After twelve tinny rings, she gave up and dialed the Secret Service signal board with an emergency request for Rosalind's agents to have her call home immediately.

Next, she called Harvey Fineman, the season's leading playwright and persuaded him to cancel his date and take her to dinner with the Randalls. She had no inkling of what deal Tony

12

was brewing with Isaac Randall, but she was well aware, as was Harvey, that he was a heavyweight Broadway producer. She felt better as she buzzed Marie to say she would be dining out after all.

Rosalind threw her bookbag on the tartan spread. "Damn it, they're in collusion again."

Cynthia Swift, daughter of a solid Democratic canning family from Chicago, barely glanced up from her notebook. "Who? The press?"

"No, the Secret Service and Dianne, that's who! I wonder if a mother using U.S. agents to force messages on daughters constitutes invasion of privacy. Or misuse of public funds. Maybe I should initiate a case. Class action with Julie Nixon and Caroline Kennedy."

"Don't forget Susan Ford," added Cynthia. "She's good with agents."

Rosalind aimed her jacket at a chair. "Shit!" She picked up a brush and began to fight the tangles in her fine dark curls. Her tall slender body was casually dressed in a pair of tight jeans and a handwoven fisherman's sweater.

Cynthia waited silently, not pushing. If she probed, Rosalind might clam up for hours.

"Imagine . . ." Rosalind swirled around, brush in hand. "I am to call her immediately, but before eight at all costs. Probably because she's going out. It's bad enough to have perpetual bodyguards, but the way she uses them makes me feel hounded! If she hadn't had that stupid special bill passed by all her phony friends in Congress, I'd have been rid of them all last year. Now she can keep getting her little spy reports and track me down any minute she feels like it until I'm twenty-one. It's not fair. The Kennedy children got rid of their Secret Service guard at sixteen. She treats me and the twins like perpetual babies!"

Cynthia squirmed, uncertain how to respond.

"She could leave a message with the desk," Rosalind steamed, "like any other reasonable person would."

"Maybe it's an emergency, a real one."

"I doubt it. If it really were an emergency, she would have a helicopter outside the window with a sky hook. I just wish she wouldn't use the Secret Service to spy on me. I know she talks to them all the time. Just a friendly chat to see how I am." Rosalind dropped the brush on the old bureau and frowned at the results. "I wish my hair had more body. It's like her— unmanageable."

"Come on, Roz, she's your mother."

"But all mothers don't bring in the Secret Service. Her great liturgies about giving Billy, Timothy and me normal childhoods have a hollow ring at moments like this."

"True." Cynthia tried to look sympathetic, although she personally thought having the Secret Service in tow was romantic.

Deliberately Rosalind shifted moods. "Let's skip dinner to-night—it's chicken and corn, ugh—and go to Green Street for a burger and fries." A mischievous smile lifted the corners of her wide mouth. "My agents hate Green Street, especially Gino's."

Cynthia liked chicken, but she loved being part of the Connolly entourage. "Good idea." Cynthia grinned. "Let me find my boots."

They bundled up for the December chill and hurried out of their dorm, across the quad.

When Rosalind was in a good mood, she liked to chat with her "men in gray," as she called them. Other times she would stride forward quickly, leaving them to maintain a discreet distance. Rosalind had advised them to dress like Smith professors, mismatched and tweedy. Colin McReady took to the idea in his casual soul, but Thelonious "T" Smith, black, vested and newly conservative, resisted.

15

With frozen breath to lead them, the two men walked in tandem, keeping sight of their quarry who was setting a rapid pace.

"She says she's not athletic," grumbled T, "but that's only because Smith doesn't have a track team! And this Smith, namely me, is glad she can't get any training in it here. She's fast enough."

"It's genetic, T," Colin spoke between his teeth to keep out as much cold as possible. "Her father was quite an athlete. And one of the twins is on the track team at Andover."

"And you can't say she doesn't have Connolly spunk," T added. "Look at the way she jerks our chains . . . and her mother's."

It seemed to Colin that T had the last bit backward, but he only asked, "Do you think she's returned the call yet?"

T shrugged. "Who knows?"

Both men were aware of the growing communication problem between the former first lady and her daughter. They had recognized the signs a couple of years before when sarcasm entered Rosalind's conversations about Dianne.

The snow crunched beneath their shoes and the iced branches gleamed like crystal against the rosy tones of dusk.

"Colin," T broke the reverie. "They're moving out."

Colin narrowed his eyes against the wind and watched the girls break into a run. He and T had to dash.

The girls stopped short inside the small, dank coffee shop, gasping for breath.

"We could slip out the back way and go downtown for dinner." Rosalind grinned roguishly.

"If they couldn't find us, it might become national news," Cynthia spoke hopefully, finding visions of headlines appealing.

"No way." Rosalind shook her head. "According to Dianne, their prime job is to keep publicity away at all costs. Alerting the press is the last thing they'd do. Anyway, it's academic at this point."

A red-cheeked Colin McReady filled the doorway to the smoky, cramped room. T followed with a cough, his dark skin camouflaging any winter ruddiness. They walked past the two girls who had unthawed enough to start shedding jackets.

"Gino! Two coffees, please," Colin called. Then he turned to smile at the would-be conspirators. "Would you young ladies like to join us?"

Had Rosalind been alone, she would have accepted instantly. She despised eating alone. But with Cynthia for support, she blithely sat down at a different table. "You shouldn't try to pick up innocent young ladies. You know you could be put on report." She tossed back her dark curls and motioned for Cynthia to join her.

"Young, maybe," muttered Smith. He added cream to his coffee until it matched his skin tone.

Aware of the identities of his customers, Gino remained impassive, waiting for the girls to order.

"Double burger, fries, chocolate malted with vanilla ice cream," intoned Rosalind. Cynthia seconded the order. As they waited for their greasy fare, Cynthia lighted a menthol cigarette and offered one to Rosalind who declined as usual.

"You've never tried smoking, have you?"

"Dianne smokes enough for all of us," Rosalind said ruefully. "It doesn't matter how much the twins or I object; she won't cut down. She calls it her one untrammeled personal pleasure."

"You're lucky. I wish my mother smoked. I get one of her really-Cynthia-must-you looks every time I light up. And if my grandmother's home for a visit, smoking is verboten." Cynthia sighed. "It's the only thing that puts a pall on Christmas. No after-dinner cigarette unless I smoke in the john or garage."

"I don't want to think about it—Christmas, that is." Rosalind directed her attention to the burgers at hand.

"Why? Why not?" asked Cynthia between hungry bites.

"St. John's Island and the mad Marinos, that's why. Last year, with his weird children, was a disaster." She did not elucidate as she dug into her fries. "And from what I can sense on the Connolly side of the clan, Uncle Sean and wife Laura are in the middle of enough strain to make an East Hampton or Palm Springs Christmas rheumy gloomy." She found herself wishing this Christmas could be Dianne, Billy, Timothy and herself, period, the way it had been before Tony. But you can't wipe things out and go back, she thought; only for a moment in your mind.

Cynthia suggested Rosalind come home with her to Chicago for the holidays. "You'd love it. And if we wanted to, we could go to Delray Beach in Florida with my grandmother for a week or so. Really, you'd have a great time."

Rosalind felt a twinge of longing for something so all-American normal. "I'm sure I would, but holidays are too important to Dianne."

"If she needs you, I understand." Cynthia drowned her gray burger in catsup.

Rosalind wasn't sure she understood herself. For as long as she could remember, everyone, including her brothers and herself, had constantly worried about how Dianne felt and what Dianne wanted to do. Everything seemed to be geared to preventing Dianne from ever feeling bad. And Dianne encouraged it. "It would make Mummy so happy if we all went to the beach." "Let's go to the zoo. I just adore the zoo." "We'll go shopping. I want to buy you some new dresses; I just love to find pretty things for you and me."

Shopping seemed to work well for filling the emptiness in Dianne's life. Rosalind had compared Dianne's behavior with some of the case studies in her psychology books. As she analyzed her shadowy memories of their life after her father's sudden death, Rosalind perceived that she and the twins had been Dianne's therapy. Along with the shopping sprees and travel, they filled in the blanks. They were her base, her touchstone with reality. When the parties and trips ran thin, she had come running home to them and their nurses to be their "Mummy who is your best friend in the world."

"Are you my bestest friend in the world?" she would ask breathlessly. The image of her mother's wide-eyed expectancy was vivid in Rosalind's mind. So childlike. Sometimes Rosalind felt as though she were bringing up her mother. Other times, the child in her had yearned for something solid and she had reached out to a nurse, Timothy or Billy or the photos of her father that she had plastered on her bedroom walls.

The little restaurant was quiet as Smith and McReady shared the sports section of the Springfield paper. Cynthia's straw slurped noisily as she reached malt bottom.

"I shouldn't drink this thing. I've already gained fifteen pounds this year—the sophomore spread."

"It doesn't show that much," consoled Rosalind.

"Not in a skirt, but I can't squeeze into a single pair of my jeans anymore." She surveyed her slender friend munching on fries. "You don't have to worry. You never gain an ounce."

"It's genetic. I take after my father."

"But your mother's like a willow!"

"A willow on a constant diet." Rosalind grinned.

Cynthia changed the subject. Dieting did not fit with her image of Dianne. "So what do you think about Christmas?"

"I'll probably be in St. John's and you'll be in Chicago," predicted Rosalind. "Why don't you come with me? We'll get a better tan in St. John's."

"No, I really have to be home for Christmas."

"Then come the week after. Tony could send a plane for you. He just loves to make that kind of gesture." She spoke with a touch of contempt. "Let's go!" She pushed back her chair and rose.

"We'll see," Cynthia said dubiously.

They retraced their shadowy route, moving from one pool of light to another under the old-fashioned streetlamps, crossing the main campus until they reached the quad and their dorm, Martha Wilson House, positioned at the far side of the quad.

As soon as the large doors closed behind the girls, McReady stationed himself at the main entrance inside the quad while Smith moved around to the back entrance facing the street. They would remain in position until midnight when the house was locked, then retire to the Northampton Inn to return at four in the afternoon to relieve the morning shift. Hardly high-risk duty.

♫ ♫ ♫

Dinner was breaking up as Rosalind and Cynthia raced upstairs to their third-floor room, hoping to avoid the house mother's "Oh-oh-oh-my-dears-where-have-you-been?" A buxom six feet in stocking feet, Mrs. Tinkler was awesome to the eye, but vague in dealing with her charges. As long as they stayed out of her limited line of sight, she made no effort to search them out. Aside from meals and tea, they saw little of each other.

Rosalind glanced at the clock. There was still time to call her mother, who never dined before eight. She chewed on her bottom lip and braced herself for the call she hoped would be a casual "Hello."

"Oh, good, Miss Rosalind," answered Ardyth, the maid. " Your mother's been expecting your call."

The statement irritated Rosalind—Dianne was so certain the Secret Service would get her to return the call.

"Oh, good, darling, you got my message," Dianne began breathily. "I was so hoping you would . . . before I went out."

Rosalind waited silently.

"I wouldn't have tracked you down that way if it weren't so desperately important."

Accustomed to her mother's style, Rosalind wasn't alarmed. If one of the twins were hurt or it were serious, Dianne's tone would be less gushy.

"Don't you want to know what's so important? Well," Dianne rattled on, "we have the most marvelous opportunity to visit Saudi Arabia at the invitation of the royal family and the king, himself. You'll only have to take a few weeks off at the most. And it should be marvelously educational."

"When?"

"In about ten days—right after the dedication ceremony for your father's memorial. We'll have to scamper to get organized!"

"Mother, what's gotten into you?" Rosalind's voice registered disbelief. "We have less than a month before term finals. And those *are* educational!"

"But darling, it's so important to me. And I can't stand to go alone. I need you."

"Why not have Tony go with you?" Rosalind asked with superficial innocence. She had read the recent stories in the *National Enquirer* about Tony and his girlfriends, especially Nicole Turrell, the French film star. It seemed to Rosalind that Dianne's maternal needs and calls increased in direct ratio to the number of such articles.

"Tony's so busy." Dianne hesitated, then continued in a near whisper, sadly, "Actually, Rosie, he's the teeniest bit angry with me. Imagine! With all his money and all those companies and all that oil spilling out of the ground, we had a fight over my budget." Her laugh grated in Rosalind's ear. "He'll get over it," she reassured them both, "but right now things are difficult."

"I'm sorry," Rosalind said sincerely. "But you shouldn't let Tony worry you. Let him go his own way and . . ."

"So you can see," Dianne interrupted, "why I need you right now. I can call your dean tomorrow and explain this wonderful opportunity . . . "

"Why can't you wait until my holiday break? An Arabian junket would be wonderful after exams."

"But I have to get away from things now. . . ." Dianne caught herself. "We are invited for the week after next."

"I doubt if the dean will go along with it." Rosalind hoped she was making her point. Her commitments to herself should be at least as important as Dianne's were to herself.

"Well, I can try, can't I? I'm pretty good when I try."

Rosalind could picture Dianne's triumphant smile. She wondered if it would help to go to Dean Fisher first thing in the morning and beg her not to give permission. But if the dean held firm, Dianne would only call the college president. And if she did go, she would have to take all her exams after they returned. It would destroy her chances for decent grades and if she failed a course, Dianne might get indignant and insist she change schools. Either way, it would be hell.

"Why don't you take the twins? They say Middle Easterners go wild for blue-eyed blonds—the three of you would be a sensation."

"I'm not in the mood for their hijinks, darling. And I'd like us to share some mother-daughter time. Now, I must dash off to dinner, but I promise I'll call your dean in the morning."

"But, Mummy, I . . ."

Rosalind stared at the now-silent receiver, trying to keep her emotions under control and remain rational, an art at which she was normally proficient. She attempted to divert herself, to think about anything else, but tears of frustration spilled down her cheeks. Why did there have to be battles? Angrily she brushed at the tears. She had to get out of the room before Cynthia returned. She was in no mood to listen to her roommate defend Dianne. She grabbed her coat and ran down the hall. As she made the turn down the stairs, she heard Cynthia call after her.

"Roz! Where are you going?"

"The library!" she called over her shoulder as she ran down the stairs and out the door, tears still streaming. She raced across the quad blindly. She didn't hear the footsteps chasing her. Then she felt a hand close on her arm and pull her to a stop. "No!" She pulled away, then stopped short as she turned to see Colin's familiar face.

"Hey," he spoke gently.

"Oh, Colin, it's . . ." She choked and looked teary-eyed at the man who had been her protector since she was thirteen. Then she was sobbing in his arms.

"Come on, Rosie, calm down. It can't be that bad."

"Can't it?" She hiccuped. "You don't know!"

"How about coming to the inn, having a drink and getting it off your chest?"

She sniffled.

"It's too cold out here for tears. You'll turn into an ice maiden."

She gave him a halfhearted smile and reached in her pocket for a handkerchief that wasn't there.

"Here." Colin offered a neatly folded white square. "Ever notice that since women's lib came in, women have stopped carrying handkerchiefs? What do you suppose that means?"

Rosalind was too busy taking advantage of that fact to reply.

"My car's a block away. I'll drive you to the inn. Okay?"

She nodded and let him take her hand. She felt safe and warm as he tucked it in his pocket beside his own.

He rejected the thought of beeping Smith on the walkie-talkie to report where they were going. Smith was fine where he was. And Rosalind needed some quiet consolation, not the usual Smith-McReady comedy routine.

As Colin held open the car door for her, Rosalind paused and looked up at him, the hint of a question on her troubled face. The streetlight caught the sea green tones of her eyes. To Colin she looked like a beautiful young waif—and not so young at that. He was disconcerted by his thoughts. Rosalind was only a teenager, full of pranks and wisecracks the way she had been for the past six years, nothing more. The thought lacked conviction: he couldn't discount the knowledge that she would be twenty in March.

He silently navigated the dark and peaceful streets of Northampton, tires crunching on the frozen surface. Rosalind slid close to Colin, drawing on his solid warmth. She felt the tension flow out of her and began to study him. She had always considered him the most good-humored of her watchdogs, but thought Cynthia's evaluation of "gorgeous" extreme. Yet, his eyes were Paul Newman blue; periwinkle blue, Grandma Bea would call them. Except for the dark beard shadow, his skin was creamy and smooth. His hair was dark, almost blue-black—an Irish look. Although her Irish father had not fit the "Black Irish" model, Rosalind felt comforted by the comparison.

At the inn's parking lot, Colin opened the door and reached for Rosalind's hand; a spark snapped between their fingers.

"It's the upholstery," Colin explained. "It always does that."

She slipped her arm through his as they entered the lobby in unconscious imitation of Dianne's entrance style. They passed the candlelit eighteenth-century hunting scenes on the walls and entered the oak-paneled bar. Here they called it a pub.

22

Through habit Colin took the chair against the wall facing the door while Rosalind faced him, providing newcomers with a view of her back. Unlike Dianne, who usually positioned herself to be seen, Rosalind relished moments in public as a private person. Perhaps the years of listening to Dianne plead for their privacy had taken effect. Do as she says, not as she does.

"What are you drinking, my dear? A glass of wine?" asked Colin.

"A double scotch on the rocks—with a twist."

Colin raised dark eyebrows. "Isn't that a pretty heavy potion for a young lady?" He debated over allowing her a double. But she had been terribly upset; it might help her relax. He ordered two double scotches from the waitress who was watching Rosalind with more than casual interest.

"She didn't even card me!" whispered Rosalind with great satisfaction as the waitress walked away. She watched Colin return her smile, wishing he would take her hand again. Touching him made her feel warm and . . . it made her want to be closer still. The embrace in the quad had been too tearful for more than comfort. She looked at him with an unformed question.

In the quiet bar, they heard the waitress place their order with the bartender and add, "That's Rosalind Connolly; I'm sure of it."

The two businessmen sitting at the bar rubbernecked at her.

"See? I can't take you anywhere." Colin tried to lighten the moment.

Rosalind deflated. "This is no place to talk. It will all end up misquoted in a newspaper column." She looked ready to burst into tears again.

"Tell you what." Colin patted her hand, attempting to do it paternally. "I have a bottle of scotch in my room." He couldn't help noticing her long slender fingers. "We can pay for these drinks"—her skin was soft and smooth—"and talk upstairs." He cleared his throat. "If you'd like to."

Rosalind chewed on her lower lip a moment and looked at him. She nodded.

Dropping a ten-dollar bill on the table, Colin led Rosalind from the bar toward the elevator. A nervous giggle escaped. "Mummy would have a cat fit."

Colin felt a twinge of guilt. Less than two weeks ago Dianne had fixed her wide blue gaze on him and gushed, "Mr. McReady, you have no idea how secure it makes me feel to know you are watching out for my Rosalind."

∽   ∽   ∽

Colin's room in the old inn was spacious and comfortable, with a desk and sitting area to the right of the door and a large bed and mellowed oak bureau to the left.

"Don't you rate a suite?" asked Rosalind.

"T has the only suite available for long-term rental. And he has seniority."

"But that's not fair!" she protested. "You have to be here all year long, too." She plopped down on the corner of the bed closest to the door. "But it's not bad, really. It's a nice room."

Colin picked up the phone and called room service for ice. "Want anything to snack on? Chips? Cake? Indian pudding?"

Rosalind shook her head. She wasn't hungry.

While they waited for the ice, Rosalind avoided discussing what was bothering her. She asked Colin about the Secret Service and the FBI job he had had before, half listening to his replies. She was too busy willing him to sit closer to her. "Do you really like the Secret Service better than the FBI?" He seemed strong and confident, not like the preppies she dated. He wasn't the kind of man who teased—or liked to be teased. Still she wanted him to move closer.

The bell rang. Colin neatly fielded the bellman outside the door and quickly fixed them both a healthy scotch.

"Here's to you." He raised an inelegant tumbler.

"And to you," she echoed, taking a deep swallow. She choked and sputtered.

Colin chuckled. It was fine twenty-year-old scotch, his luxury in the outlands.

Rosalind fixed him with a black look. "It went down the wrong throat. It's very good scotch," she added with a connoisseur's air.

A faint smile creased Colin's face. He straddled the desk chair, turned backwards so he could rest his arms while looking at her. He couldn't resist openly admiring the lithe young woman in her bulky sweater.

"What are you staring at?"

His smile widened. "Only the most beautiful young lady in western Massachusetts."

"Oh." She stared at her ice cubes. She had no words.

Colin pulled himself back, ready to play the protector. "Okay, what has you so upset tonight? Let's get it out in the open."

She closed her eyes for a second. "Dianne is into one of her massive manipulations again. No one is safe when she gets moving—especially me. I mean, she is totally incapable of seeing any perspective except her own. When she and Tony were gallivanting around the world, things were fine; she left me alone. . . . What am I trying to say?" She took a drink, swallowing hard to avoid a cough.

"Whenever she feels at loose ends," Rosalind continued, "she comes running to us, me and the twins. All we have to do is let her play Magic Mummy and everything is fine for her. For a while. And if we don't come running when she needs us, she makes us feel guilty. At least I feel guilty. Even when I know it's a silly thing that she'll get over, I can't help feeling guilty."

"You have your own life, Rosie. You're almost twenty."

"Sure. She sings that song too, but with her own tune. 'You're getting so grown up; now we can be real friends and travel and shop together. You have your own beautiful life to live.' It sounds independent, but it's the same old game."

"I still don't understand what happened tonight. What did she do now?"

Rosalind's chin came up squared. "She wants me to take off before exams and go to Saudi Arabia with her. And if I do, I'll flunk out . . . I can't even talk about it," she sniffed, starting to cry again.

Quickly Colin moved to the side of the bed and gathered her into a hug. It only made Rosalind cry harder.

"Rosie, Rosie, it's not the end of the world. That's the way she is, but she does love you. You don't have to take the trip. Say no. You've done it before."

"Only to Tony," came the muffled reply. "Not to her. It makes her so unhappy when I don't go along with her. . . ."

Colin leaned down and kissed a tear suspended on her cheekbone. "But you have a right to be happy too. It's important . . . because you're important."

Rosalind looked up, startled. Did he really think she was important? She saw the blueness of his eyes as he leaned closer and gently kissed her lips, a feather brush.

She pulled him beside her on the edge of the bed and held

on to his hand. She wanted him to stay close to her. "Colin?" she whispered, unable to put her questions into words. Did he feel the same trembling? Did he want her—as a woman—or was he only doing his good deed for the day? And if he wanted her, could she . . . ?

He leaned down and gave her a long, soft kiss that evolved into a long, hard kiss. She sank back on the bed. Her throat was dry and her entire body was swimming.

Rosalind had let boys kiss and fondle her before, but she had never felt such intense physical excitement. She wanted to melt into him. He had to want her or he couldn't kiss her that way, make her feel that way. A shadow of apprehension passed over her. Should she? He smiled as she looked up at him. Yes, she silently answered her question. This night, this man.

He stretched beside her, molding his body against her. Rosalind inched closer, wondering if the sensations that seemed to come from inside her skin would be more intense without clothes. Then she let her thoughts go and gave in to his kisses, sinking closer still.

An alarm went off in the professional section of Colin's mind. This is Rosalind Connolly, he thought. He rolled away, fighting for control.

"Colin . . . is anything wrong?"

"I'm supposed to protect you." His voice was hoarse. "Not molest you."

She rested against his soft sweater. "You're supposed to take care of me."

"Rosalind, I'm a lot older than . . ."

"Shh . . ." She found his lips again. Strong in her desire and in her need not to be treated like a little girl, she silenced his objections with deep kisses, like a woman.

"Colin . . ." She shivered as his hand reached under her sweater. His touch sent delicious sparks across her skin. She slipped off her sweater, then her jeans and the rest. "Hold me," she whispered.

"You're lovely," he said softly.

She felt shy, exposed. She had never been completely nude with a man. Sweaterless, skirtless, braless, yes, but not all at one time, not all the way. "Warm me, Colin."

He gathered her into an embrace. She could feel his hardness before he backed away. "Don't stop."

26

"I'll be back." He smiled.

She watched him swiftly disrobe in the dim light. His body was trim and tan. He could be a suntan lotion ad, she thought as he hesitated beside the bed, obviously aroused, whatever his reservations.

She reached up to him, wanting to feel his naked hardness against her. Inside me, she thought with a tremble as he gently ran his hand along the curve of her waist up to her firm young breasts. She shivered with kinesthetic delight. If the foreplay drove her up the wall, what would real lovemaking do?

The image of Dianne flitted into her mind, unwelcome but inevitable. How would Dianne react if she knew? She would probably have Colin fired. But it didn't matter, because Dianne would never find out. Then Rosalind buried Dianne along with the Arabian itinerary as Colin's tongue caressed her aroused nipples. She felt building in her loins a heat she had never experienced before. She moaned and pressed her body against his, grinding.

"Easy," he whispered. "Easy."

Skin next to skin, no clothes to fumble with, no probing hands that triggered resistance. His touch was sure. Rosalind wanted it to happen, whatever it was. She turned her breasts against his muscled chest, luxuriating in the feel and the sense of freedom. For the first time in her limited years of restricted lovemaking, there was no question of when to stop—no roles, no rules.

His tongue slipped between her teeth and found hers, sending still another tingle across her body, intensifying the peculiar aching sensations she felt. Building, rising sensations mounted sharply. She felt the hot hardness between her thighs and opened to him. This is what it is, she thought dizzily as she felt him enter her. It doesn't fit, flashed in panic through her mind as she felt her body's resistance to his thrust.

Colin groaned and pushed. She tried to back away from the pain, but there was nowhere to retreat on the firm mattress. Then he withdrew, massaging the round center of her nerve endings to make juices flow and hips undulate with a newly discovered age-old tempo. As she felt his fingers inside her, touching the inner walls, she reached down with shaking fascination to touch him. Her touch elicited a groan from Colin and he moved to enter her again. Slowly he slid inside, inching deeper and deeper, back and forth. Then he seemed to let go, moving faster and faster with each thrust. She felt a searing flash of pain and he was inside her—deep inside her now.

From far away, she heard him cry, "Now, now, now!" and she felt his weight relax against her. The pain left a throb, but the mounting ache inside had been slaked. I've done it, she thought. She pushed aside a shadowy feeling of loss and smiled to herself as a woman.

Colin lay back in their dampness, replete. Rosalind searched his face. Had she been good for him? She moved back into his embrace. His arms automatically tightened around her and a frown etched itself between his brows.

"What's wrong?" she asked.

The frown deepened. "Was that your first time?"

A dimple appeared at the corner of her mouth. "Mmm-hmm."

"Good Lord!"

"I was waiting for you, but I didn't know it was you, if you know what I mean." She stretched in sleek contentment against him.

He was incredulous. "But Rosie, what about that November weekend you spent at that frat house at Dartmouth?"

She traced the outline of a muscle in his forearm. "It's obvious I was only messing around, isn't it?"

"And T and I were certain you had an affair with that Yale boat freak last year. You stayed in his apartment all the time."

The situation began to amuse Rosalind. She planted a kiss on the tip of his nose. "Appearances are deceiving. I can't account for your salacious thoughts."

"But I saw that kid from Amherst all over you a couple of weekends ago, and you stayed overnight there, too!"

"You certainly have kept an eye on me."

"That's my job." He smiled. "And I try to do it well."

"I'd say you do it well." She returned the smile.

"And considering your lack of experience, you do it fantastically well," he retorted, his good humor back in place.

"You mean you took me to bed only because you thought I slept around anyway?" she asked melodramatically.

"Believe that and you'll believe anything. If anyone had told me this morning that we would be here like this tonight, I would have had them committed."

"Then it was a complete surprise to you, too?"

"Understatement."

"I'd never thought of you like this, either."

Colin nodded and stroked her hair. "Did I hurt you? Are you sorry?"

"I wanted you so much I hardly felt it happen." She gave him a half truth, not wanting to describe the pain. "And I'm not sorry. After all, this makes me older and wiser, right?" She smiled. "And they say the second time is even better. Is that true?"

Colin took a deep breath. "No second time tonight. No second time, period, until you have some protection."

"You're my protection. It's your job."

"From kidnappers, cranks and reporters, maybe, but not from accidents that put ten pounds of baby in your tummy."

"Do you have to be so serious?" She wanted to laugh and cuddle with him, maybe make love again and see how it was. A birth-control discussion was hardly romantic. But he probably was right: she couldn't deal with getting pregnant. Diane would . . . She left the thought unfinished as a tremor of panic ran through her. What if she were already . . . ? She knew nothing about the right or wrong timing.

Colin dug into her ribs, interrupting her misgivings and sending her into shrieks of laughter among the twisted sheets and discarded clothes.

She hugged a pillow with a smile. "If I call Cynthia, she could sneak downstairs and add my name to the sign-out book for an overnight."

Colin picked up the strewn clothes and began dividing them into his and her piles. "There is nothing in the world I would like better than to have you spend the night." He tossed Rosalind her pile. "But I must coordinate with T for the midnight sign-off. We usually have a drink after that. Unless you want to make it a threesome, I'd better content myself with seeing you first thing in the morning. I'll trade for the eight-to-four shift. That's my personal sacrifice just to make sure you're okay."

"Good!" Rosalind's eyes sparkled. "Then maybe we can do something tomorrow night. Catch a movie or something."

Colin watched her face fall as he shook his head. He sat on the bed and hugged her to him. "If you want to see me—and believe me, I do want to see more of you—it's not going to be simple. If my superiors thought we were together like this, I'd be pulled back to D.C. in a flash."

"But . . ."

"I'm only telling you how they would view it." He kissed her fingertips one at a time. "And if Dianne got suspicious . . ." Colin drew her hand across his throat.

"She'd hire Pinkerton to keep an eye on the Secret Service." Rosalind laughed despite a growing awareness of the nature of the situation they were creating. She felt a freedom, inside and out, with Colin. She wasn't *the* Rosalind Connolly her dates squired. She had no mystique, no mask, with him. He was practically family; if anything, the relationship felt a bit incestuous. And aside from the moments of pain, she had never felt such strong feelings of closeness. She wanted to feel them again and again.

"All right," she agreed. "I'll get dressed, ready for my 'return from the library.' You don't have an extra book around, do you?"

"Only paperbacks and the Gideon Bible."

She laughed and stretched contentedly without inhibition.

Watching her slim body grow taut, Colin put down a shoe before it reached his foot. "Looking like that, you could destroy my resolve for discretion, young lady."

Rosalind reached for her clothes. "I could contend with Uncle Sam getting upset, but not Dianne." She searched her mind for a trace of guilt over finally giving in after all those nights she had resisted eager hands and bodies. It wasn't that she had thought lovemaking was wrong: Dianne had implanted no strong guilts; she had never openly discussed sex, only passed out vague "Be goods." But Rosalind had not wanted to make love with those young men.

"Have you seen my belt?" asked Colin.

She watched him retrieve it from the floor beside the bed. No, she had no regrets, only a certainty that she wanted to make love with him again. If that meant subterfuge and complications, so be it. Eluding other agents and Dianne had its own perverse appeal.

Dressed, Rosalind moved reluctantly toward the door. The room held freedom and warmth for her. It occurred to her that now they would be less free than when they had entered. She wondered how they would react tomorrow.

"Ready?" Colin was beside her with a hug. He held on for a long moment. He wanted the full night and the morning hours with her—falling asleep in the afterglow was one of the best things in life. He settled for one long last moment.

30

Snow began falling as they reached the front steps of Martha Wilson House. Rosalind reached up to the flakes. "Beautiful! It's the second snow already. I hope it means great skiing!"

"Let's cross our fingers." Colin caught a tiny white flake. "Do you ski?"

"Like a renegade Irishman—fast and furious. And far better than you do," he added mischievously. "You didn't notice last year in Aspen?"

"I'm afraid not." Her attention had been on skiing in a pack with Uncle Sean, her brothers and the cousins. "Considering how long I've known you, I don't know much about you."

"True," he spoke solemnly above a twinkle. "You've only known me about seven years."

"No. One night."

"Yes." He touched her cheek, noticing that the snow falling on her head was creating a virginal lace cap on her dark curls. "One night which is getting late." He glanced around the empty quad and opened his arms. "One last hug before T comes."

She moved into his arms quickly. "Sleep tight," she whispered before whirling around and racing up the steps and inside. Her mind floated with the feelings and sensations of the evening. He hadn't said when they could see each other alone again. He had to want to. Was he really afraid of what Dianne would do if she discovered the affair? Was it too soon to call it an affair? She didn't care if Dianne knew as long as Colin wasn't transferred. Would Dianne have him transferred if she knew? Rosalind didn't want to put it to a test. She laughed at her old fears over losing her virginity. Colin had been gentle, building her up to it. Did she love him? She wanted to be with him again. It was too new to analyze.

To her relief, Cynthia was sleeping when she tiptoed into the room. She wasn't ready to share her evening. She slipped out of her clothes and pulled on a flannel nightie. Then she left her underpants in a bowl of cold water to soak overnight and climbed into bed.

Dianne pulled down her sleeping mask. She should have had more to drink with dinner. Three-thirty in the morning. Why had she napped in the car coming back from Walnut Hill? She should not have allowed Tony to upset her. If she had played on his ego the way she used to, he might have been more receptive to her plea. No. She could not play that game, not with the way he behaved, not with his total disregard for her feelings.

Everyone seemed unreachable. Sean had been in meetings all day. She doubted if his secretary had even given him her message. She would talk to him about that; maybe the girl should be fired. Rosalind didn't sound excited about the trip. She was becoming impossible. Billy and Timothy had sounded cheerful, but they seemed distant too, caught up with their friends and activities.

She shuddered to think she had almost slept with Harvey Fineman . . . out of loneliness. But never with Harvey; he was a switch-hitter. As much as she found the thought of her husbands sleeping with other women repugnant, the image of a man with another man completely turned her stomach. She had tried making love once with a designer friend known for his prowess with "the boys," but every time he touched her, her mind had filled with images of him in strange positions with young Adonis types. It hadn't worked.

As the gossip had grown with Bill and Tony, so had her frigidity. She would smell other perfumes on them, imagine the other women. With Bill, it had been tolerable. He had been so fast—five minutes and he would let her alone. But Tony prided himself on his Italian talent for lovemaking, long sensual techniques that had touched wellsprings of response in the early months. She wondered where Tony was bedding tonight, and with whom.

She reached for her barbiturates. Two were supposed to be enough, but two hadn't worked. Tony—Tony never took pills. He viewed them as signs of guilt, of which he had none—it took conscience to feel guilt—so he didn't need pills.

"Go to sleep," she ordered her mind as she downed two more pills. The chinchilla spread felt soft under her fingers. "A wonderful nestling thing" she had called it when Tony wrote the five-figure check for it.

Her head throbbed. She wondered what aspirins would do on top of the barbiturates—probably give her dark circles in the morning. She crawled out of bed and shuffled to the bathroom, groping in the cabinet for aspirin. She shook out three. That should do it. After these, she would not take another pill if it killed her. Because it might.

As she swallowed the large white pills, she wondered if Rosalind's hostility toward Tony should have warned her away from him, right at the beginning, at the first explosion. Her thoughts drifted back through the years as she returned to bed.

The week had begun with enthusiasm for Tony and the twins. Dianne had anticipated a delightful sun-filled week and Rosalind had been quiet as a whisper. The crucial incident remained vivid in Dianne's memory. One of the crew suggested Rosalind try sailfishing. Rosalind became intrigued, asking about the size of sailfish and whether she could have one stuffed for her wall if she caught it. Tony tuned in on the scene and characteristically came over to play expert.

"That's all right," Rosalind began mildly enough. "Roger's explaining it to me." But Tony ignored the brush-off and continued to rattle off a stream of advice.

With beginner's luck, Rosalind had barely cast her line when she had a strike. Everyone, especially Tony, was excited. He screamed encouragement, dancing around Rosalind, waving and gesturing. Finally, unable to restrain himself, he grabbed the rod from Rosalind and began to play the fish in earnest.

Rosalind's face turned red with anger. "Give me back my fish! You have no right! You're not my father! I hate you!" The words still echoed across the years.

Eyes on the sea and the fight at hand, Tony paid scant attention. "What are you talking about? I'm your stepfather."

"I never said you could be my stepfather! I wish my mother had never married you!"

Then Rosalind kicked the can of bait, spilling brackish water and tiny, flipping silver fish all over the deck before running down the stairs to her stateroom. Dianne would never forget the sound of the door's slam.

She had been an audience frozen beneath the sun until that slam. Then she walked over to accuse Tony. "You took Rosalind's fish, Tony."

"Nonsense. She's a little girl. She couldn't handle this one alone. It's a beauty. After I bring it in, I'll give it to her. I'll have it mounted as a present from her papa. What ever happened to Papa, anyway? They are supposed to call me Papa. And she shouldn't talk back to me like that. What kind of a mother are you that your daughter can't treat me with respect?"

"You made her angry," Dianne chided softly, more upset than she wanted to admit over Rosalind's open hostility.

"Move, move. You're getting in the way of my fish. If she's upset, go straighten her out." He turned his graying head so she could see herself reflected in his sunglasses. "Tonight I shall be especially nice to our Rosie, yes? Cook shall prepare a special party to celebrate her great fish. And there will be a big present for her mama, too. Now go!" He gave her a careless pat on her bottom and Dianne kissed the tan, weathered cheek and went below.

In the cheerful little-girl decor of the stateroom, Rosalind lay on her stomach, pounding her fists on the bed, hissing, "Hate him, hate him, hate him, hate him," through her sobs. Dianne gently pulled her up to wipe the tears on the still-round cheeks.

"Rosie, Tony only wanted to help."

"He's a bully," the child spat. "Roger was helping. That

was enough help. He's not my father and *my* father would never have stolen my fish."

"He's your stepfather, your papa. He's very good to us."

"No, he isn't. He tries to buy us and make us belong to him because he married you and has you . . . and I hate him . . . the old, old hypocrite!"

Dianne was startled to hear the words coming from her ten-year-old. But she couldn't allow Rosalind to treat Tony that way. It was too uncomfortable. "Stop it!" She slapped Rosalind across the face. "I don't care how you feel now or any other time; you must be polite to Tony."

That was the first time Dianne had ever hit Rosalind, and the pain had come between them because of Tony.

Tony succeeded in landing Rosalind's sailfish with style. The small orchestra played and the great fish was brought forth on a massive sterling platter, custom-designed for Tony's catches. The cold dead fish lay in crushed ice awaiting its journey to the taxidermist's.

Her brothers were enraptured. Rosalind's gaze matched the fish's; she announced that the twins were welcome to it. "Eight-year-olds appreciate things like that."

(Stuffed and properly mounted, the sailfish still hung on the boys' wall, surmounting their trophies. Rosalind had never stopped hating the sight of it.)

Tucking a subdued Rosalind into bed that night, Dianne admitted Tony had been unfair but she still insisted that Rosalind forgive him. "Men get carried away by fish, my darling; it's the way they are."

The child reached up and pulled Dianne close for a hug. "You're still my bestest friend in the world, Mummy," she had whispered without referring to Tony at all.

Dianne wondered if Rosalind's memory of that day was as vivid as her own.

Less than a week after the incident, Tony had appeared with a puppy for the children, the Norwegian elkhound Rosalind had named Leda, after Leda who was the mother of Castor and Pollux—the Gemini twins—and Helen of Troy. Tony had given the children Leda to lessen the effect of Dianne's absence as he had whisked Dianne away for a four-month trip to South America. Rosalind's class had been studying Greek myths at the time. Had Rosalind looked upon Leda as a substitute mother too?

Dianne clapped three times and heard the jingle of Leda's dog tags as the old elkhound padded down the carpeted hall into Dianne's bedroom. Leda yawned and blinked at the light before plopping down beside the white bed with a sigh. Leda was getting old, Dianne realized, nearly seventy in human years. Like Tony. She pictured Tony's eager face as he had handed Leda to Rosalind, hoping for a spark of affection from the child. But Rosalind's expression had been closed to Tony, although Roasalind's and the twins' hearts immediately opened to the dog.

Dianne pulled herself back to present time, thinking her "bestest friend" hadn't sounded very enthusiastic about a trip to Saudi Arabia. Perhaps once they were on the way, sharing the adventure . . . Dianne thought, getting groggy. She wanted to do something to bridge the growing distance she felt from Rosalind. She didn't want her daughter to withdraw into the cool politeness the girl had directed toward Tony for years.

She constantly told her children how important it was to be independent—the way she had been from her own parents. Parent, she corrected herself. Her father was dead; so was theirs. Self-reliance was important. She had sent them to camps and on expeditions with their cousins. There were so many times she had had to go places with Bill and then Tony and others where they could not come along. They needed their own interests.

But right now, Dianne needed her best friend, her daughter, who had grown up too fast. She needed the security of those young arms around her neck. Her thoughts grayed out into a leaden sleep. Leda snored on the floor beside her and the black ruffled sleeping mask twisted as Dianne rolled into a more comfortable position.

ตา   ตา   ตา

At ten the next morning, aided by pots of black coffee, Dianne was double-checking Kiki's Saudi arrangements for them. She contemplated having Kiki call Dean Fisher to arrange for Rosalind's permission, then decided the personal touch would carry more weight and placed the call herself.

As she finished speaking to the dean, Dianne made a face.

"What's wrong?" asked her friend and secretary. "What's the verdict?"

"The court has determined that the verdict must be Rosalind's. If she can handle both the exams and the trip, there's no problem. Two of the weeks we're gone are open study time and there is a week of exams before the holiday break." Dianne replaced her glasses and studied the itinerary. "She'll only miss three days of class at the start of the new term."

"That seems to solve it, doesn't it?" Kiki smiled.

"I hope so," murmured Dianne. She hadn't told Kiki that Rosalind would have to take all her exams for this term the same week the new term began.

Dianne leaned back and pulled off her glasses. She despised having to wear them; it was an admission of age as well as an inconvenience. Sunglasses disguised the prescription outdoors, but they didn't work for indoor reading. The best she could do there was pale gray lenses in large tortoiseshell frames.

Kiki waited. She had learned decades ago at Wellesley that pushing for information only sent Dianne into deep zones of silence.

This time Dianne completely avoided further discussion by asking Kiki to type a clean inventory list of clothing for the trip. Dianne fiddled with the draft lists and wondered aloud if she should take jewels out of the vault for the royal family's special reception in her honor. A few, perhaps. Enough to be polite, but not too many to discourage the normally generous Saudi king from presenting her with a few more wonderful stones for her collection.

She reached for the telephone and stopped. No, she would wait until after her luncheon date to call Rosalind, uncomfortably aware that she faced a task of persuasion.

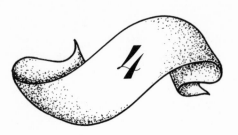

Rosalind bounded out of the house into five beautiful inches of new powder. She skidded to a halt beside Colin and T, turning her shining eyes to Colin. "G'morning, gentlemen. Isn't it marvelous? Don't you just love this snow?"

"Cold enough," grunted T.

Colin grinned at her. She looked so cheerful in her lollipop-red parka he would have hugged her if T hadn't interrupted their silent signals and asked, "Where are we off to this morning?"

"Religion. Can't you guys ever get my schedule straight? How can you report to Dianne when I cut a class?"

"Very funny." T coughed. "You know, this isn't our usual shift. Why Colin talked me into taking the morning one today, I'll never know! I'd forgotten how much colder it is in the morning. Why couldn't you go to Stanford or the University of Miami like a civilized person?"

"Because . . ." Rosalind threw her arms open wide. "I love snow! If there were two more inches or a decent base, I'd cut afternoon classes and we would all go skiing." She laughed at T's groan and strode across the quad toward the classroom buildings, keeping in step with T and Colin.

"Hey!" T gave her a curious look. "What's with you this morning? No hide-and-seek. No race."

She wondered what T would say if she replied she wanted to stay as close as possible to Colin, that she was so happy the vibes were still there this morning that she could do cartwheels in the snow. She couldn't even look at Colin without thinking about lovemaking. She had been nervous before she had run outside, afraid she might feel strange or embarrassed. But she only felt wonderful.

"It's too nice a day to rush and give myself a heart attack." She looped an arm inside Colin's, ignoring the warning shake of his head. She laughed as he started pulling his arm away, held on tightly and slipped her other arm through T's.

Walking on her right side T was hit by her swinging bookbag with every step. "This is all very nice and chummy," he protested, "but I'm getting academically pelted by your books!"

Seizing her moment, Rosalind slid her arm away from T and moved closer to Colin. "If you can't take it, Mr. Agent, I withdraw. How 'bout you, Mr. McReady?"

"Oh, I'm big and strong," he said casually. "I can take it."

"You're both nuts this morning," T muttered as they reached the theology building.

She gave Colin's arm a quick squeeze as they entered the building.

"I'll be in the third room to the left, in case you need me." She winked.

"Got it." Colin winked back. "Third door to the left, in case Dianne calls," he said to her slim-jeaned retreat.

"What's with her? Last night she was seething about having to call Dianne. This morning we have Miss Sunshine."

"She's becoming a woman, T, and women are unpredictable."

"Thanks for the new insight, pal." T opened his briefcase. "Want the sports section or the crossword?"

"Got my own for a change. Got up with the birds." Colin dug into his own briefcase, checked his beeper and settled down to see how the Caps were doing. By the time Rosalind reappeared, he had figured out what three-letter English town would complete the crossword.

As the trio trekked back across the snowy paths toward Martha Wilson House, Rosalind teasingly asked Colin if he would buy her lunch at Gino's.

His forehead tensed. She couldn't keep this up—T was no dummy.

But suddenly Rosalind remembered her lunchtime mission and sprinted away from them. She had to talk to Cynthia. "Let's race!" she called.

"Christ, I'm going to get gray hair and a peptic ulcer before I'm fifty," groaned T, lengthening his stride to keep her in sight.

ை ை ை

Rosalind charged into the hall and raced up the two flights, two steps at a time, giving thanks she wasn't an elephant like Maria Brockton who made great clomping sounds walking up, let alone running. The stairs grew creakier as she reached the last landing. On nights they wanted to sneak out of the house, those stairs caused waking nightmares, visions of Mrs. Tinkler at the foot. Today, they were only old and friendly, leading Rosalind to Cynthia—she hoped.

"Cynthia! Cindy!" she shouted as she charged down the hall, pulling off her jacket as she ran. "Where are you?"

Cynthia's dark curly head popped out of their doorway. "Hi! Ready for lunch?"

"Yes. No. Wait." Rosalind ran into the room and slammed the door behind them. "I have to talk to you."

"Me too." Cynthia grinned elfinly and held up a deep blue velvet dress of Rosalind's. "Would you lend me this for the weekend? Andy called and said there's a Harvard faculty reception and everything I have is either too much or not enough."

"Sure." Rosalind shrugged off the request. "You know you don't have to ask. Take what you like." Designer clothes simply hung in Rosalind's closets. She preferred casual things, but Dianne insisted on buying special "party outfits"; her idea of college parties had atrophied somewhere in the 1950s. Rosalind succumbed to Dianne's wardrobe choices to keep her mother happy. Personally, she would have liked that velvet dress better in green, but the blue would look wonderful on Cynthia, matching her eyes and flattering her pale complexion. But this was no time to analyze Cynthia's coloring.

She watched Cynthia carefully fold the velvet dress in the suitcase. "I need to talk to you about protection."

"What?" Cynthia forgot about the dress.

"Birth control. What do you do?" Nervously Rosalind picked at the bedspread.

"Ha. You are answering the question you have always avoided," Cynthia noted with friendly satisfaction. Rosalind had always been enigmatic on the subject of her virginity, sometimes implying a wealth of experience, other times dropping virginal remarks.

As Rosalind began asking questions, Cynthia was amazed at her lack of knowledge. "Didn't your mother tell you anything?"

"She tells me I'm too young to get serious. I think she means sex when she says that, but she's never been explicit." Rosalind felt the first faint twinge of guilt as she spoke. "She's really very broad-minded about things. She goes drinking with me and the cousins, swears with us. That's pretty liberal. Okay"—Rosalind moved away from thinking about Dianne—"what do you know about the campus doctor? Are you sure he won't broadcast things?"

"No. I'm not even sure he'll prescribe anything for you there. I get mine in Chicago. I think you better go to a town doctor."

It seemed so complicated suddenly. What did she want? Pills, diaphragm, IUD? Condoms for Colin? She wondered what Dianne used or what she would suggest if she didn't throw a screaming tirade about it. There was no way she could ask her. Rosalind only hoped she could find a discreet doctor in town.

"If you don't want to go alone| . . ." Cynthia began.

"Oh, I'm never alone. Remember?"

"God, they'll follow you right to the door: Ob-Gyn." Cynthia closed her eyes at the image.

"Hand me the Yellow Pages before I lose courage," begged Rosalind.

Together, they pored through the listings until they came to a Robert Sorokin, M.D., Ob-Gyn, on State Street.

"It's only a few blocks away and there aren't any shops or restaurants," Rosalind noted. "It's unlikely I'd bump into anyone I know." She jotted down the number and reached for the phone, fingers trembling.

"You're really uptight about this, aren't you?"

"A little," admitted Rosalind. She could feel the phone ringing in the pit of her stomach.

"Doctor Sorokin's office," answered a voice that sounded like a sweet old lady's.

"Hello," Rosalind's voice cracked. "Is it possible to have an appointment this afternoon?"

"Is it an emergency?" The standard question . . .

Rosalind wondered why she would ask that? Was Sorokin an abortion quack? She almost hung up, then pushed herself to continue. "Not really, but I would like to see the doctor as soon as possible."

"Are you a patient of the doctor's?"

Rosalind shook her head.

"Excuse me, dear, but are you a current patient or will you be a new patient?"

"New patient," Rosalind blurted.

"Could I have your name, please."

"Uh . . . Cynthia Connolly." Rosalind panicked.

Cynthia giggled. Somehow the background giggle comforted Rosalind enough to emerge from the phone conversation with a three-thirty appointment, thanks to a last minute cancellation.

"Cynthia Connolly." Cynthia shook her head. "No one in the world could possibly track you down with that one."

"Damn." Rosalind grinned. "It was all I could think of. But as long as it prevents the doctor from calling some reporter friend and announcing it in the *National Enquirer*, it's good enough."

"Aren't you being a little paranoid?"

"Dianne goes up the wall over articles about nothing! Imagine how she'd react about an article mentioning my birth-control pills! Come on, let's go to lunch. I'm starving."

✍ ✍ ✍

Rosalind gave Colin a few penetrating looks between classes, but she couldn't find a way to get him alone long enough to report. He would find out soon enough when they reached the doctor's office. So would T. What if T told Dianne? All she could do was hope he wouldn't. She had to go through with it.

Dr. Sorokin turned out to be a tall, thin man in his mid-fifties, old enough to have a daughter Rosalind's age. With his thatch of straight gray hair that fell across his forehead and brushed his silver-rimmed glasses, and because of his long, pointed nose, Rosalind silently dubbed him "Dr. Crane."

A stern-faced nurse helped her prepare for the examination. Rosalind fought down embarrassment. The examination gave her more discomfort than losing her virginity had.

The physical torture completed, Dr. Sorokin discussed the alternative methods of birth control. He added a brief lecture on promiscuity and veneral diseases. Then he gave her a few minutes to think about which type of contraception she preferred—and if she really wanted it. "The lack of protection, for a bright young woman, can sometimes be the best deterrent against rash, inconsequential relationships."

"It's not rash," she whispered.

"Think about it." Wispy hair fell across his glasses as he nodded wisely. Then he changed gear and took a brief medical history. Amid the questions on tonsils and measles, he asked for the address of her parents, for emergency purposes.

Rosalind stared at the floor. The crane doctor was coming on like a priest, but this time she couldn't rattle off, "I was inconsiderate with Mummy and selfish with my brothers."

The doctor broke the silence with a chuckle. "You wouldn't be Bill Connolly's daughter, would you? I read she was at Smith."

Rosalind felt a mixture of relief and betrayal. It was her own fault. She had used the name Connolly and hadn't prepared for standard questions. Still, the crane seemed sympathetic enough in his dry way. "Yes, sir. But the name is Rosalind, not Cynthia. I was afraid it might get in the papers if I used my own name."

"I'm a doctor, not a press agent, young lady," chided Dr. Sorokin, pushing his glasses firmly back into position. "I was a strong supporter of your father, but if you were the daughter of the milkman, I would still observe professional standards."

Feeling more secure with his Yankee sense of discretion, she answered his questions quickly, concluding by announcing a decision for pills.

Dr. Sorokin pulled out a prescription pad and scribbled indecipherable marks on it.

"Oh, please!" cried Rosalind.

"Please what?" He looked up over his glasses and frowned. "I'm prescribing birth-control pills for you."

"But I can't possibly go to the drugstore, not with my own name on it!"

The good doctor thought Rosalind was overreacting. Certainly the Connollys were targets for the press, but no Northampton pharmacist would call the *Boston Globe* about Rosalind's prescription. And if some fool did, the *Globe* would never print it. Still, if she were involved with some boy, she needed protection. "I may have some samples in the back."

He returned shortly with two small pink disks. "These are a full two months' supply. Come back in six weeks and give me a full report on how you're doing—any weight gain or adverse reactions. And if you have any problems in the meantime, call."

He refused to accept any payment for the samples, only for the office visit. "I don't pay for them," he said. "Why should you?"

As she left the office, she was acutely aware of the pills in her purse. When she glanced at her purse, she could "see" them and imagined she could feel their weight. Would Colin sense them, too?

T and Colin were waiting outside, arms clasped around their chests against the cold. She had refused to let them wait inside when she had noticed with relief that the doctor's shingle outside simply stated "Robert Sorokin, M.D." She preferred that T not become aware of Dr. Sorokin's specialty.

"Everything okay?" Colin asked with concern.

Her smile warmed ten degrees. "Yes, just fine."

Colin walked silently. He had gone inside for a minute to answer his beeper by calling headquarters and noticed the "Obstetrics and Gynecology" on Sorokin's cards. She was taking his advice, obviously serious about continuing their relationship. He wanted more than a taste of her, but he was nervous about having the whole loaf.

The phone call!

"Rosalind, I almost forgot. Dianne called. The message said to call her back tonight. Important."

"You didn't tell her where I was, did you?" The possibility hit Rosalind in the solar plexus.

"I didn't talk to her. She left word."

Rosalind's relief turned to irritation. "Yuk. She probably wants to discuss life in the Saudi desert again. I wonder what the dean said."

T rubbed his gloved hands together and gave her a toothy grin. "I hope it was 'Go get it, gal.' It's a lot warmer over there."

Rosalind glanced at Colin. Not necessarily, she thought.

At the back door of Martha Wilson House, Rosalind asked

with studied casualness, "In case I need you guys later, where will you be?"

"I'm sad to say that Colin's got the street side, nice and cozy in his car. I've got the quad side in my long johns." T sadly shook his head.

"Bad break." Her smile was warm for Colin.

As she relaxed, the bitter cold pierced her jacket. She shivered, waved and scampered into the house.

Colin positioned his car on the street, twenty feet from the back door. He was sorry Rosalind had had a difficult session with the doctor. Her discomfiture had been obvious. But as the old saw went, better safe than sorry. He'd gleaned from their conversation the night before that she had known little about birth control and educators acted as though only poor children's parents didn't clue them in to the modern variations on the birds and the bees.

ᔕ ᔕ ᔕ

Cynthia greeted Rosalind with a conspiratorial smile. "Well?"

"God, you should have warned me about that table. It belongs in a chamber of horrors. And that nasty little probe. I don't see how gynecologists can make love themselves after doing that all day long."

"They're supposed to be the worst. I mean the sexiest," Cynthia said, echoing a remark made by her sister, who was a registered nurse.

Rosalind proudly displayed her pills and was delighted to discover they were identical to Cynthia's. It made them seem less sordid.

"Okay. Now you've got to tell me who the mystery man is."

The phone rang before Rosalind could reply.

"Oh." Cynthia gave Rosalind a guilty look. "That's probably your mother. I promised to have you call the second you came in."

"Don't worry about it. I think your priorities are doing fine." Rosalind picked up the phone, pills in hand.

It was Dianne, playing the martyred mother. She understood how busy Rosalind was, but she had been waiting by the phone for two hours. Rosalind's grumbling responses inspired Dianne to switch tactics, becoming the "good buddy". Wasn't it wonderful? The dean had recognized the merits of a Middle Eastern trip and agreed with Dianne that it would be a wonderful experience for Rosalind.

"The dean agreed I should go?" Rosalind was incredulous.

"Well," Dianne hedged. "She didn't actually say you should go . . . exactly. She said if you wanted to and felt you could handle your exams after we got back, you could. Fortunately, two of the weeks in question are open study time."

"But I need that study time!"

"You can bring your books along. It will be the same thing— open study time—but in a different climate."

"Sure. No distractions, except a few dozen shopping excursions and a stream of luncheons and dinners. Mother, it isn't the same thing and you know it. I am not going trekking off to Saudi Arabia to watch you party it up with everyone."

"You're invited to everything I am, Rosie. After all, you're practically grown up."

"Right." Rosalind gripped her pillbox for support. "I'm grown up enough to know that if I am to take school seriously, I must attend—and study."

Dianne protested less vigorously than she would have an hour before, before Kiki had volunteered to come along with her husband George—and George would pay their expenses. He had always wanted to see Riyadh. She would not be unattended, but that did nothing to help bring Rosalind closer. She needed to spend more time with her daughter.

Rosalind did agree to come to New York the following Friday to spend the weekend with Dianne before the Sunday ceremonies for the William J. Connolly Memorial dedication in Washington. But that had been on the schedule for all of them for months.

Cynthia watched as Rosalind slowly replaced the receiver in its cradle. "You look like you just picked up the weight of the world. Do you have to go?"

"No." Rosalind shook out one tiny pill and placed the case in her top dresser drawer under her panties. "No. Kiki and George are going." She pulled off the heavy rust pullover and exchanged it for a soft green blouse that accented the color of her eyes.

"I think it must be difficult for all children with a single parent," Rosalind mused as she brushed her short dark hair, staring in the mirror. "They have to take the brunt of all that mothering or fathering. Psychologists talk about how difficult it is for the parent all the time, but I think it's at least as hard on the children. The parent thinks he or she has to be everything. So you get spurts of discipline and concern and companionship and whatever. And when the parent isn't getting whatever he or she wants, they pull it out of the children. It's too much pressure."

This third-person stream was the closest Rosalind had come to discussing seriously her feelings about Dianne. Speaking abstractly prevented it from really getting down to painful specifics. Often, the wisecracks were more revealing.

"Well, I'm glad you don't have to go steaming off to the desert, worrying about exams." Cynthia rose. "Ready to go down to dinner?"

"No. I'll grab something later or eat some of the tea cakes we stashed away Friday. I forgot a book at the library."

"You certainly have become a library fiend lately. Are you having an affair with a graduate researcher?"

"Right." Rosalind laughed. "You can find us under the reference table, analyzing the rise and fall of . . . something or other."

"Sure." Cynthia smiled. "See you later."

Rosalind bundled up again for the cold. She ran down the stairs and turned toward the library. She chuckled to herself. Her white lies were getting good if she believed them herself. She switched direction and exited out the back doors.

A flicker of flame in the front seat of Colin's car assured her he was in position, lighting a cigarette. She ran over to the passenger side and slid in beside him. "I deserve a hug. A big one."

"If you did what I think you did, you deserve more than that."

"Nobody's around." She took his hand.

"T is due back from dinner in about ten minutes. I suggest you pop back inside for half an hour before we go anywhere, give him time to check in and get positioned inside the quad. Have dinner," he added, noting the time.

"You mean you aren't even going to take me to dinner to celebrate?" Her eyes flashed green sparks.

"Okay." He smiled. "We'll have a nice dinner at the inn on my dinner hour—from seven to eight."

"But then you'll have to come back and check with T!"

"Only for a few minutes."

Happily, she got the message. He didn't need to explain further.

With that simple conversation, the pattern was set. Privately, they would slip out for dinners at the local inns and small Italian restaurants tucked away in the white clapboard side streets. They caught a movie at Deerfield, a small town nearby. Physically, they delighted in each other. Colin made an excellent teacher for his enthusiastic pupil. And Rosalind found him as satisfying a confidant as a lover. Yet, in public, she treated him with the same lighthearted banter as T. It required concentration and caution.

On this Wednesday night, Rosalind lay across Colin's bed, staring at the faint water marks on the ceiling. "There's no way I can get out of this weekend with her in New York, is there?" The question was rhetorical.

"It won't be so bad. Three or four days, counting Washington."

"If she tries to make me feel guilty for not going to Saudi Arabia, I'll explode and regret it. It always happens."

"And you always survive. So does she." He pulled off his tie. "Why bother making a scene? You've made your position clear. Just make sure she knows it's the trip you're rejecting and not her."

No, she thought, she didn't want to reject Dianne, just keep her at a distance. Too much of Dianne became claustrophobic. "You're right. I'm not being swooped off to the desert. I might as well be pleasant." She punctuated the remark with a hug. "You are not only a marvelous lover, but you make a great father confessor and lay analyst!"

"I like that phrase"—Colin chuckled—"lay analyst. I accept the job." He leaned down to kiss her. "Is this how a lay analyst begins?"

"I think you have to get a little deeper into things."

"Don't worry. I'm equipped for that." He proceeded to prove it.

The New York weekend began in disorder. A heavy morning snow made the trip to Connecticut's Bradley Field longer than usual. If the flight had not been delayed by the weather, they would have missed it. Rosalind didn't have the heart for her usual banter with her agents. Colin was off duty for the weekend and had left for Washington the night before.

She sat back, letting people and events swirl by, and buried her nose in *The Major Poets* which she had brought along to work on an English essay.

La Guardia was equally disorganized in what now was freezing rain. Dianne's limousine was nowhere in sight. Rosalind and her agents were forced to wait in line to scramble for a cab, which inched its way toward Fifth Avenue through the jam of Friday night commuters. I don't need this, she thought, reminding herself to make a remark about missing Dianne as soon as she was inside the door to avoid her mother's favorite martyr's question, "Didn't you miss me? You haven't told me you did." Rosalind really didn't need to hear that tonight.

Dianne surprised her by being all cheer and radiant smiles, rattling on about the weekend plans before Rosalind had her coat off. The twins would not join them until Sunday for the

Washington ceremonies. Dianne was sorry Rosalind wouldn't be going to the Middle East with her, but she was delighted her daughter was here to help with the last-minute shopping. "It's much more fun when you're with me, Rosie. You always know what looks best on me."

Relieved to be off the travel hook, Rosalind prepared to enjoy New York with her mother. As soon as she changed into the requested "city dress," Dianne whisked her off to meet some couple and their pimply teenaged son.

George Neidermeier, Sr., was involved with a diamond-trading operation. Rosalind paid scant attention as her mother raptly drank in his description of fifty-carat discoveries. Rosalind sensed that Mrs. Neidermeier would have been happier if Dianne had been less rapt. But Dianne never seemed aware of the other women's reactions—or other women, for that matter.

Rosalind half listened to owl-eyed George, Jr., talk anthropology as she glanced around the Neidermeier dining room, polished into the deep lusters that only fine wood could acquire. Quiet Old-World elegance. It was almost un-American. She emerged from her musing long enough to say "How nice" to George, Jr., as he touted his sizable skull collection.

"Would you like to see it?" he asked eagerly.

Poor thing. He was trying so hard to be nice. She almost felt maternal. But Rosalind had no time to reply as George, Sr., announced that coffee and after-dinner drinks would be served in the screening room.

Dianne threw her a conspiratorial smile. Surprise time. Rosalind soon realized that George, Sr., had been to Saudi Arabia several months before, taking a professional cinematographer with him.

"The movies I take myself could never live up to my screening room," George, Sr., explained as he positioned himself beside the wide screen for his narration.

"This is so wonderful! I wish we could afford something this grand, don't you, Rosalind?" Dianne, in her de la Renta original, attempted to give George, Sr., a poor-little-match-girl look. Perhaps George, Sr., felt sympathy; Rosalind felt slightly embarrassed for her mother.

Dianne pulled a dime-store notebook from her cut-velvet purse, ready to take notes. Rosalind had wondered earlier why they had been invited here for dinner. She had never heard of the Neidermeiers before and she couldn't believe that Dianne would try to fix her up with George, Jr. Trust Dianne to pull people out of the bushes for whatever she needed. Rosalind would have settled for a *Time-Life* travel book, herself.

Tan and athletic, George, Sr., began his narration by saying he had first developed his interest in Saudi Arabia and the Middle East while at Colgate. Rosalind's ears pricked up. Colin had gone to Colgate. She took a closer look at George, Sr., and realized he wasn't much older than Colin. It gave her a strange feeling.

The footage was wonderful and George, Sr.'s travelogue entertaining.

"You've been so helpful, darling." Dianne beamed at George, Sr. "Now the Saudi king won't think I'm a total fool."

"No one could ever say that," George, Sr., protested. "But you realize now you owe me a complete report when you return."

"Oh, yes." Dianne rested her hand on his arm. "We shall have a wonderful lunch and I'll tell all. That would be such fun." She gave him a 150-watt smile. "Thank you again, George, for inviting us tonight. It was so helpful."

"It was my pleasure," he replied as he personally escorted them to the door.

"Good night, Mrs. Neidermeier," Rosalind called down the hall to her hostess, attempting to cover her mother's omission.

"Good night, dear," murmured the quiet, slender woman standing a few feet behind her husband.

"I never got to show her my skulls. You said I could." George, Jr.'s complaint followed them out the door toward the limousine.

✍ ✍ ✍

Saturday morning began with a whirlwind tour of Bonwit's, Bergdorf's, Halston's Boutique and Bloomingdale's. Dianne always claimed she was "out of everything." Rosalind knew that wasn't true. Dianne was a keeper and the spare rooms' closets were jammed.

"Don't you love your things?" asked Dianne. "Aren't we having a marvelous morning?"

"It is fun." Rosalind grinned back, thinking she would wear at least two of the turtlenecks and Cynthia would love the blue print Halston.

"And tonight—" Dianne clapped her hands in excitement. "I have tickets for the new Bob Fosse show. On two days' notice!"

"Mother, that's a miracle!" Rosalind was genuinely pleased. She knew the normal wait for tickets was over six months.

"It helps to know the producer," Dianne confided. "Tony's putting money into his next play, too."

The thought that she owed this favor to Tony deflated Rosalind's enthusiasm. "Why did you have to bring him into it?" she grumbled.

"Because he's involved. He is still part of my life—and yours." Dianne hated confrontations, but Angus kept telling her to get things out into the air. "Rosalind, I know you still resent Tony but he is my husband."

"But he's not my father and he never will be," she said stubbornly.

"No one could take the place of your father, Rosie," Dianne replied softly. "Not for me, either. But Tony should have a place of his own in all our lives."

It was sounding too soupy for Rosalind to handle well. "Where is he these days, if he's such a wonderful husband?" she asked nastily, hoping to inspire a subject change.

"On a business trip. So much of his life is business." Dianne sighed.

"And the rest is bullshit," quipped Rosalind.

Dianne refused to be ruffled. "Some of it, yes. But life is that way for all of us sometimes."

"I never did know what you found so attractive about Tony." Rosalind had never had the courage to pose that question before.

Dianne tried to be open. "I know Tony doesn't win any beauty contest, but he's very strong—and he gave me a place to rest, a haven, when I desperately needed one. And he can be dynamic, articulate, exciting, even romantic . . ." She stopped, searching for her bearings, somewhere between the past and the present.

"I still can't see it. My father was dynamic and articulate, too. But he didn't look as though he just came off the boat."

"Tony has a different build," Dianne countered as they turned north on Fifth Avenue. "And your father was dead. I had needs . . ." Perhaps Rosalind was too young to understand, or perhaps she was too determined not to. Dianne lit a cigarette

and brightened. "Let's decide what to wear to the theater tonight."

"That's hours away."

"True. Then let's discuss your summer plans. I think you
should spend this summer with me and intern in Washington
next summer." Angus had stressed that if she wanted a closer
relationship with Rosalind, they had to spend more time together.

"Mother! It is all arranged. And Congressman O'Brian needs
me for his senate campaign. And I promised Uncle Sean I would
do it!"

"Anything that's arranged can be unarranged. I need you
with me this summer. Tony has a terrible project going in Central
America and I simply cannot spend the summer sweltering
down there with him. Besides, New York is the center of theater
and you've decided to major in theater, right?"

Rosalind nodded slowly. Dianne had let her off the Saudi
hook only to toss out a larger one.

Dianne rambled on about seeing every play on Broadway,
spending some time in the Hamptons and taking a few weeks
in Europe. She promised it would be a delightful summer for
them.

A tiny light switched on in Rosalind's brain. Peggy Linde,
a classmate, had been talking about an off-Broadway group
that was looking for summer interns. She would check with
Peggy about the place. She needed some project besides Dianne
or she would go crazy.

Dianne held up both ends of their conversation. "Theater
is such a marvelous, wicked thing. I know I've told you all
about my days as an apprentice with ANTA, the Washington
repertory company, where I was working when I met your
father. Even though I only appeared in a couple of walk-ons,
my mother was scandalized—although she never said so directly.
She was of the old school where it was considered tacky to go
onstage as a 'hired professional.' Sometimes I think I should
have stayed with it. Half the time I'm onstage as it is. I might
as well get paid for it." She laughed merrily. "I'm only joking,
darling. There is no way on earth I would ever give a paid
performance again and face all the publicity and critics.

"As my father used to say, Rosie, 'When you have it, you
know it, and you don't have to strip yourself before the whole
world to prove it.' Oh, I wish you could have known him."

Dianne glowed softly with her recollection. "He would say, 'Be the mysterious lady arriving at her own hour, on her own terms, dressed like a princess, a glove length away, and they'll treat you like a queen.' He was so sure of himself, so positive— with the most marvelous sense of humor. He could always laugh me out of my black-and-blues."

Dianne was eulogizing the man Grandma Jane coldy referred to as "Dianne's father." Rosalind had overheard her grandmother describe his dissolution. Grandfather Van Druten had died of cirrhosis before she or the twins had been born. Rosalind held her tongue, inured to Dianne's coloring personal realities—past and present—all rosy or all black. Rosalind reacted by making an attempt to see things as they really were, when she could.

Dianne implied to the world and her children that her background was with the elite—*The* Van Drutens of Manhattan and *The* Wards of Connecticut. Dianne spoke casually of her grand Southampton debut that acknowledged the moneyed status of the Wards, her stepfather's family, and of her graduations from Miss Potter's and Wellesley. She ascribed the term "genteel" to her father's side and "old-family Irish" to her mother's, euphemisms for "former money" and "shanty Irish immigrant," a reality she rarely admitted, even to herself.

In a now-regretted burst of confidence during a quiet evening early in their courtship, she had shared her dark childhood secrets with Tony, relating the little-girl worries that her mother wouldn't have enough money. New clothes had been for other people. She still remembered the cardboard in her shoes to make them last longer—a five-year-old's shame. Dianne carefully kept her distance from relatives other than her mother and stepfather's family, avoiding direct confrontation with the others' shopworn realities.

Her father, a blond, blue-eyed Adonis of the Roaring Twenties, was born the son of a Van Druten, one of the Dutch founding families of New York. Robert Van Druten, Sr., had poured the family fortunes into the glittering pits of Wall Street. Robert, Jr.—"Little Bob" as he had been dubbed in New Haven to parody his tall, powerful physique—was a junior at Yale when the market crashed.

Robert, Sr., was unable to cover the unauthorized loans he had made from customer accounts, and his personal fortune had turned to ticker tape IOUs overnight. He opted for suicide over charges of embezzlement.

With Catholic sensitivity, the overdose was officially reported as "heart failure," or, as Dianne's mother, Jane, told it, "He didn't have the heart to face the music . . . his own composition, it was."

Jane's immigrant family had arrived in Brooklyn in 1920 with the clothing on their backs and ambition in their souls. But the Cleary philosophy valued work over education and all six Cleary children were put to work before the age of ten. Jane's father and brothers labored in the shipyards and her mother took in the traditional laundry. Jane, the only girl of the six, stayed home ironing and mending until she was sent uptown in 1927 at fifteen as the upstairs maid for the Van Drutens.

By 1928, Little Bob had fallen in love with the pert Irish girl with the ready laugh and the eager desire to learn. "No plain Jane, you," he would tease her as he tutored her in reading, his ego thrilling to watch her blue eyes turn to saucers as he talked of America, their land of endless opportunity.

Stolen kisses were not enough for Little Bob, and his iron-willed maiden would give him no more without "makin' it proper." But Robert, Sr., was adamant. The Cleary lass, the little maid, was no proper match for his Van Druten son.

His emphatic "Over my dead body!" echoed ironically at the 1929 wedding of Little Bob and Jane. Their honeymoon was spent getting the summer estate in Newport ready to sell to pay legal fees and provide sparse support for Little Bob's mother and two younger sisters.

Little Bob and Jane stayed in the spacious Park Avenue cooperative with his family and Little Bob went to work as an insurance agent. His quick humor, beauty and intelligence had always oiled the doors of his life, but he lacked the spirit of competition in which "no" serves as incentive. When he encountered the mildest sales resistance, he would take his would-be client to a speakeasy to "talk things over." And by the time he had overcome any real or imagined resistance, he was too juiced to care about closing the deal.

Barely breaking even in the insurance game, Little Bob turned to Wall Street and family tradition. A great-uncle who had preserved his seat on the Exchange offered him a clerkship. Under pressure to earn a reasonable living, Little Bob took his six feet and two beautiful inches to Wall Street.

He detested the claustrophobic office and the open confusion of the floor. And regardless of what profits he made for his great-uncle's clients, he only received his meager salary. Uncle Horace called it "serving a traditional apprenticeship." Little Bob called it family usury.

Aware of her husband's discontent, Jane quietly arranged a teaching job for him at the local high school. He turned on her, raging that he would never earn any real money stuck in a red-brick prison working for peanuts. A Van Druten was worth more than that.

By this time, Dianne was part of the domestic tension—another mouth to feed. Little Bob refused to worry, delighting in his "fairy princess," showering her with expensive stuffed animals and toys, while Jane fought to stretch the stew meat, soup bones and potatoes.

In desperation, Jane took a job as a waitress in a restaurant a crash victim was opening in a once-elegant townhouse down the block. Little Bob was furious: it was demeaning for a Van Druten. When she ignored his protests with a saucy "It's more demeaning for a Van Druten to starve," Bob took his wounded ego to visit school friends on Long Island, playing a mysterious Great Gatsby role for the seduction of willing female houseguests.

Perfumed handkerchiefs, letters and lipstick stains on the collars she scrubbed left little question in Jane's mind, but she was too tired to argue. Tears fell into the washtub and her respect, and love, ran dry.

With strawberry-red curls, bright blue eyes and a willing heart, twenty-one-year old Jane was soon a favorite at the restaurant. Within a year, thanks to her sister-in-law's tutelage in math and accounting, she was promoted to hostess and assistant manager.

As Little Bob's waistline grew, so did his name. Friends now called him "Big Bob." He ate, drank and was frenetically merry with his pals, joking his hours away between girlfriends' homes and the many newly opened pubs and clubs, making a career of celebrating the repeal of Prohibition. The marriage dissipated along with Big Bob.

A regular customer who served on the board of the elite Miss Potter's finishing school in Connecticut told Jane about an opening for an assistant housekeeper at the school. When the school's director agreed to free enrollment for Dianne and a small house on the school's property for them to live in, Jane quickly made the break, shocking Catholic families at both ends of Manhattan society with the divorce and litigation for child support.

Big Bob continued his stabs at the market, oil futures and land deals—always waiting for the big deal that would make his fortune, always the "next one," while Jane waited for her support checks, usually months in arrears. She thanked her lucky stars that the job included food and shelter for them. Otherwise, they would have been hungry and cold as well as threadbare.

Despite her lack of formal education, Jane's instincts were good and her ambition strong. As she taught her small daughter to read, write and speak correctly, she improved her own skills. She watched the visiting mothers and with increasing assurance altered and softened her own style. She eyed the students like an Irish hawk, analyzing designs and colors to sew copies by hand for her daughter. Miss Potter's was an ideal place to cull standards from the oldest and wealthiest families in America.

By the time Dianne officially entered Miss Potter's at seven, there was no more cardboard in her shoes. Jane's salary had risen with her position. Little Janie Cleary, so lately of Dublin, gave a creditable performance as Mrs. Jane Van Druten, head housekeeper of Miss Potter's.

Although she had clothing that looked interchangeable with the other girls', identical inflections, grades well above the mean and blond hair worn straight and long with a proper WASPish center part, in her heart Dianne thought of herself as "only the housekeeper's daughter." Religiously, she aped the mannerisms of her classmates, not daring to act or appear different, but she felt like a pretender among them. She was ashamed when her beautiful, neatly dressed mother would encounter her with classmates in the hall, occasionally slipping into brogue as she passed the time of day with them.

Dianne never shared these feelings with Jane. She knew her mother with her fierce Irish pride would be angry and hurt.

Not until Dianne was mistress of the White House, did she have the confidence to change the regulation WASP part in her hair and allow hairdressers the freedom of curls and bouffants. By then she believed she had shown all her "snobby friends"— and herself—that Dianne Van Druten Connolly was as rich and estalished as they were. She hired old classmates as secretaries and assistants. Having them work for her gave her constant affirmation that she had made it to the top of Miss Potter's heap and therefore the world's. She could accept the fact that she deserved being first lady.

But during those darker years with her mother in the courtesy cottage, Dianne's world had been restricted. Without a summer house or winter retreat of their own, Dianne's vacations were at the mercy of others' invitations. Dianne never resented generous offers of sailing weekends or summer excursions to Europe with friends and their parents but relished the opportunities. For the rest of her life, she would always find greater pleasure in "free" outings than in ones she had to finance herself.

The Cleary relatives were off limits for the daughter Jane was carefully molding. Dutifully, Jane corresponded with her family and made brief visits to Brooklyn when Dianne was away, but she was determined to insulate her from the "common laborer" element. The Cleary clan considered success as having two of the five sons on the police force and the other three dock supervisors.

Big Bob and the Van Drutens were permitted to see Dianne on weekends, but only because the court had so ordered. Until Dianne was fourteen, Big Bob picked her up every other month and took her to New York, treating her like his "best date," dining her at "21" and the Stork Club and renting horses at Central Park stables, indifferent to the worn-out Orientals in the Van Druten apartment and the delinquent support checks.

The angry scene Jane had thrown over an expensive riding habit and a pair of soft, elegant boots was forever etched in Dianne's memory. Dianne had needed a winter coat and the support payments were five months in arrears. But at ten, Dianne hadn't cared about winter coats or impersonal checks. She had beautiful riding clothes and Big Bob had given her a wonderful time. She adored him. He assured her that she was beautiful and important. He never nagged her about her hair, fingernails, grammar or eating chocolate. As far as Dianne was concerned, Jane did more than enough of that for two people.

In Dianne's fourteenth summer, the Van Druten circus closed and the tent tumbled. Big Bob was sent to a sanatorium, putting a halt to both the merry weekends and the sporadic support checks. The family discussed his ravaged lungs but not his diseased liver.

Several years later, the weekends resumed irregularly, but

Big Bob, still fighting to find a place for himself in his world, rang hollow. The support checks never resumed.

As the years passed, Jane fretted about finding money to send Dianne to a good college. Jane's Gaelic prayers were answered in the guise of a kind middle-aged widower, Hebert C. Ward IV. Enchanted by Jane the day he enrolled his twelve-year-old daughter in Miss Potter's school, he courted her with wonderful manners, quiet, generous charm and persistence. Jane was fond of him and what was more important, she recognized that she could do more for her daughter with him than alone.

Herbert, soon known as "Uncle Herbie," genuinely liked Dianne and she found both him and his daughter "Babs" enjoyable companions. Before the school year was out, Jane and Uncle Herbie were married.

Jane immediately retired and established herself at his Westport estate, delighted finally to have the money to match the taste she had so carefully developed. She mellowed and blossomed under the mantle of real security and entrenched class, becoming involved with charities and community projects. She was easily accepted, well liked for her genuine interest in others and their happiness. Herbert seemed equally content with his new wife and her daughter. And Dianne, no longer the housekeeper's daughter, finished Miss Potter's in better style.

Even now, as Tony's wife, all illusions sullied, Dianne still wanted to believe in Cinderella marriages, where people lived happily—or at least, contentedly—ever after, like Jane and Uncle Herbie. She never wondered whether Jane had ever held back dark moments from her as Dianne did so often with her own children.

～ ～ ～

Saturday afternoon flew by with a last-minute dash to I. Miller's for sandals and a VIP visit to Dianne's vault for jewels. Then, after a flurried change into evening clothes, they dined at "21" and arrived only ten minutes late for the musical comedy at the theater.

Emotionally, the weekend was its own kind of dance for Rosalind. One minute she was laughing with Dianne; the next, judging, distancing. Dianne seemed too busy juggling things in her suitcases to notice. She added and subtracted from lists, searching for the perfect wardrobe equation.

They both slept late Sunday morning and hurried to board the Marino jet at La Guardia. First they would pick up the twins at Bradley Field, then continue on to National Airport in Washington.

The takeoff was smooth. Rosalind sipped coffee and wondered what the ceremony would be like. Dianne made the tactical error of chattering about Tony and how wonderful it was to have his jet at their beck and call.

Rosalind was irritated. Dianne shouldn't be dwelling on Tony during their pilgrimage to commemorate her father's death. By the time they landed at Bradley Field, Rosalind had retreated away from Dianne into the *New York Times*.

∽ ∽ ∽

The participants gathered at the top of the hill for the ceremony to dedicate the William J. Connolly obelisk. Immediately, Rosalind focused on her Uncle Sean, watching the VIPs mill around until Dianne sent an agent over to lead her to her seat between Dianne and the twins.

"Rosalind"—Dianne sighed as her daughter sank down beside her—"this is our history much more than the rest of the country's. We should be together, the way we were fifteen years ago."

"But we weren't together then. The twins and I weren't told for nearly a day. And if it was so important, why did you leave it to Miss B to tell us *my* father was dead?" Rosalind unconsciously emphasized the *my*, using her childhood inflection. She viewed her experience at five from a nineteen-year-old's perspective and felt cheated.

Dianne's lips tightened. This was no time for an encounter session. She had not been aware Rosalind knew the sequence of events that day so precisely. She must have read it in that nanny's trashy memoirs the lawyers couldn't stop.

The ceremonies began. Dianne turned away from Rosalind to watch Sean, the handsome surviving brother, read the dedication. She still thought of him as more than a brother-in-law, nearly a brother, although they no longer shared the Connolly surname.

"The Connolly vision of bright and shining youth . . ." Sean's words, in an echo of Bill's voice, reverberated among the graves, aided by loudspeakers. Dianne remembered the students lining the streets to see and touch the author of their vision, a vision Bill had called privately, "Conviction like the Hitler *Jungen* minus the militancy and bigotry." They had loved him in throngs and Dianne had found it unnerving.

Today, no "Connolly Youth" covered the hillsides; they were in their thirties now, she thought with surprise. His vision is gone. He is gone.

Had it been worth it for him? He had joked about being born on the path to the presidency with a Gallup poll on his silver spoon; he had no other path to take.

Dianne stared out across the rows and rows and rows of Arlington tombstones. She detested funerals and cemeteries, which always reminded her of the painful day they had buried her father in a seedy, threadbare affair, his insurance policies having been cashed during his lifetime.

Ill paid as a theatrical apprentice, Dianne had had no money of her own with which to help. Jane deemed it inappropriate for the Wards to contribute money and dismissed Dianne's pleas on grounds of "bad taste."

Jane did attend the funeral with her daughter, standing back, cool and pleasant, deliberately outclassing the family she had once served as the upstairs maid.

Dianne cried for her father, cried for his final illness and the lack of respect—cried because if Jane had been the spine of her disciplined life, he had been the joy. The second-hand coffin hurt.

Someday, she promised herself that afternoon, she would have it changed for a wonderful brass one, worthy of the historic Van Druten mausoleum and Big Bob's exuberant spirit. Someday, when she was rich. And she would be, God help her, she would be rich . . . the vow was not a new one.

When Bill Connolly's estate had been signed over to Dianne, one of her first expenditures was a new brass casket for Big Bob's remains. It was ironic to her that Bill's death had made it possible as she had requested a new casket for her father as a first anniversary gift from Bill. He had laughed at her. "Let sleeping Irish renegades lie," he had quipped before presenting her with a ruby bracelet. She had considered selling the bracelet or skimming money from the household budget, but that never seemed right—it had to be a straightforward action. Then Bill's money became hers and the argument was settled.

Bill the strong, the beautiful, the political, the driven. It seemed a thousand lifetimes ago—and a day before at the same time. She remembered their first date as if it had been last week. She had scarcely taken a taste of onion soup before he asked if she would like to be first lady. It was so clear in her mind. She had worn a pink Anne Klein dress and her mother's pearls.

"Well, it's a nice house." She had laughed softly. "But it does need work. The decor is simply a podgehodge of a hodge-podge."

He had replied matter of factly, "No problem. You can redecorate it, if you like."

She had loved his reply and had fallen in love then and there with the glamour and energy of the young senator from New York. And her fairy tale had come true for a while . . . such a little while. It had shattered long before he collapsed in the middle of that last impassioned speech, leaving her a widow so unexpectedly. She could still feel his cold lips as she had kneeled frantically beside him, trying to breathe life back into him.

She shivered and closed her eyes, overcome by images of the days after the so-called coronary. She had been racked by guilts and fears and so many questions. His heart had been strong: Was it a real heart attack? He had so many enemies; he had been too strong a president. Her mind had refused to accept natural causes. Others agreed and investigative committees mushroomed in the House and Senate, creating headlines, not answers.

Sean's voice intruded into her distressed reverie. She had needed Sean in those days, needed his shoulder and handkerchiefs and firm decision-making. He resembled Bill enough to give her life a shadow of continuity . . . only a shadow.

She opened her eyes to the obelisk. Bill. The great phallic symbol, erect and gleaming. "Shiny white and noble," she had instructed the architect. In the days of the monument's inception, the grieving nation had been unaware that the young president they mourned deserved a medal for his carnal exploits as well. Now the obelisk could do double duty.

She pushed the thought away. Today was a day to remember Bill's good qualities. Beyond his insensitivities and infidelities as a husband, Bill had been a good father. He had carved out midday moments with the children in the Oval Office and they had adored him. She had adored him, too—in the beginning. Was a single good relationship impossible for her? Tony flashed in her thoughts like a sigh. At least she and the children were finally secure.

As her thoughts roamed, Dianne sat motionless, golden hair perfectly in place, the black Balenciaga suit and coat elegant and appropriate, eyes on Sean, but not quite focused.

Rosalind noted her mother's blank stare. She wondered if Dianne felt any loss, if she had ever felt a real loss. Rosalind blocked out past images of Dianne sitting quietly at her desk, tears streaming as she whispered to five-year-old Rosie, "Oh, what shall we do without Daddy?"

Sean's voice, sounding so much like her father's, which Rosalind knew best from tapes and TV clips, grew stronger. "I cannot—and you must not—forget—William J. Connolly, my brother Bill, and his vision of a strong, dynamic, compassionate America."

Rosalind looked around at the crowd as the current president stepped to the podium. Many gazed at the floodlit obelisk. It was gaining drama as the sky darkened, rising needlelike above the tomb-dotted hills of Arlington, set above the Kennedy Memorial's eternal flame. They're running out of room, she thought irreverently. The Secret Service better tighten their act.

"Rosalind," Dianne whispered the cue. It was time for the twins and Rosalind to play their roles.

It was all so formal, nothing like the fantasies of warm hugs Rosalind coveted in her shadowed memory. Former president. My father.

Dianne watched the children solemnly carry dark red roses to the foot of the obelisk. Billy and Timothy looked so grown in their navy blazers. They were already an inch taller than their sister. It had all happened so quickly.

The lights from the TV cameras turned on the waiting limousines. Dianne shook herself; the ceremony was over. She moved toward the cars, idly chatting with the other participants. It occurred to her that no one was asking about Tony. But why should they here? If they read the scandal sheets, laced with too much truth for comfort, they would know her marriage to Tony was another fairy tale gone to hell.

Rosalind was carefully silent as she received people with her mother beside the limousine. She nodded "Mmm" to pleasantries while Dianne whispered, "Yes, it's beautiful," "How nice to see you again" and "So glad you could come."

Rosalind was hypersensitive that day to Dianne's not being

a Connolly anymore. She was a Marino. And Tony Marino might be one of the world's richest men, but he had no place on her father's hill. In some ways Rosalind felt that his wife, her mother, albeit Bill Connolly's widow, didn't quite belong here.

Billy came up from behind Rosalind's right and Timothy closed in the ranks on Dianne's left, uncoached by the photographers who delighted in the spontaneous family portrait.

Dianne rewarded her sons with a radiant smile that made the front page of the *Washington Post* the next morning. "Your father would have loved the effect of the obelisk above the graves," she said softly.

Rosalind bit her tongue, restraining herself from asking if their father would have loved Dianne's new last name. At least Dianne had the class not to have dragged Tony along. Then she spied Uncle Sean and broke away from Dianne and her brothers to run into his arms for a shared hug.

"Hey, Rosie." He laughed. "Was I that good?"

"Better," she said. "Are you riding with us?"

Such an emotional outburst was unusual for Rosalind, he thought. Perhaps she was having a row with her mother. From Dianne's recent reports, it seemed possible. "Sure," he quickly agreed. "I always go where I'm wanted."

"You're wanted." She returned his grin, the family resemblance evident. "You are our favorite uncle."

"Then as your only uncle, I accept," he retorted.

"Hey," he changed the subject. "Remember our talk about your working for Congressman O'Brian as an intern next summer? Are you still for it? He could use you, that's for sure. We have to keep up the Irish representation—it's a family obligation," he winked.

"I would love to!" Rosalind turned to her mother. "Dianne?"

Dianne winced at Rosalind's use of her first name. "I thought we had settled that; I thought you were opting for a New York summer with me. But . . ." Rosalind looked so enthusiastic, she succumbed for a moment. "If you really want to and if Sean thinks he needs you, we'll see." Dianne looked at Sean; his muscular arm still enveloped Rosalind. She would discuss it with him privately.

"Rosie can stay with me in Great Falls." He smiled before sobering to add, "And Laura, of course. Oops, almost forgot.

Laura sends her love—and her apologies for not being here. She's at her mother's in Rye; she can't seem to shake a bad cold that's been plaguing her. I'm encouraging her to go to Palm Springs for a while."

"Yes, I could use some sun myself." Dianne's whispery voice filled with longing. "Perhaps in Saudi Arabia," she said as they climbed into the limousine, Sean satisfied that the press had had their fill of Connolly faces.

Grateful to be in the warm car, Rosalind settled back against the soft leather seat and became an observer while Sean, relieved of cermonial concerns, relaxed with Dianne by cutting up the manners and modes of the attendees.

"I wonder if Ralston gets his clothes from the AFL-CIO relief fund," Dianne said wickedly.

Sean laughed at the slur on the current president. "I hear he's in the pocket of labor."

"It wouldn't matter if he shopped at Brooks Brothers, Sean. Any suit would look thrift shop in five minutes on him. He's simply lumpy and bumpy."

"If old Lumpy and Bumpy could hear us now!" Sean was savoring chopping down the man he found incongruous sitting in the Oval Office. "He might pop one of his cheap buttons right off."

Rosalind never took offense when Sean and his politicronies wisecracked; their jokes had a good-humored edge. But when Dianne got into her dissections, Rosalind cringed at the venom. She had learned years before—at the tender age of eight—that the best way to cheer up Dianne was to initiate a catty conversation. "Mummy, did you like the dress Eleanor was wearing yesterday?" could work wonders. At times like that, she felt as though she were Dianne's mother, cajoling her into a better mood.

She stared out the window past the bridge lights at the Washington Monument gleaming in the evening sky. She craned her neck to see the newly lighted obelisk behind them, an echo to the Monument.

Sean was giving Dianne a family update. "Laura gets so tired just now. She really doesn't have the strength to entertain anymore." Sean tried to laugh. "And that's ninety percent of the lobbying game—staying entertaining. Looking after the children and keeping up with my hectic schedule gets to be too much for her, I guess."

The words rang false to Rosalind. She knew her uncle had a full-time housekeeper.

"I wish we had more time to help you entertain," Dianne responded. "Tony is just so, so busy with his companies."

Rosalind wanted to scream. Half the country knew that Sean and Laura were on the outs ever since Laura had given an interview discussing the lavish presents Sean's Japanese clients had given them and publicly complaining about Sean's late nights away from home. And the gossip columns were also filled with Dianne's and Tony's feudings. And on top of that, Rosalind was also certain that Dianne had no intention of letting her spend the summer in Washington with Sean. Sean was their closest relative. Why couldn't Dianne be honest with him and why couldn't he level with Dianne? Were all adults hypocrites? Would she be that way too in a couple of years?

Silence reigned for several minutes until Sean frowned and asked, "Where are the twins?"

Dianne twisted her head to see the headlights tailing them. "In the limousine behind us with Grandma Bea. I hope they're not driving her crazy with their nonsense."

Sean nodded. "I was afraid the ceremony would be tough on her, stir up all the old sadness. . . ."

"She seemed very pleased and proud." Dianne patted Sean's knee. "You're lucky to have such a marvelous mother."

"She's a tough old bird," he agreed.

"I'm so glad we have stayed close with Bea for all these years," Dianne spoke tenderly. "Tony is particularly fond of her. And she's fond of him."

Rosalind broke her vow of silence. "You can't account for people's taste all the time."

Dianne threw her daughter a dark look of reproach.

Sean had sensed for years that the children had reservations about Tony, although neither had ever spoken to him about it. He waited for Rosalind to say more.

Silenced by a glare from Dianne, Rosalind muttered, "Just a manner of speaking." Rosalind resented Grandma Bea's pro-Tony attitude and considered Bea's praise for Tony as a self-made man a slight to Bill Connolly, whose success had been supported by the Connolly millions.

Dianne rested her hand on Rosalind's knee, gently striking back. "Rosie, the skirt you have on is shabby. Why don't you give it to the Salvation Army or throw it away?"

"It's the Connolly tartan Uncle Sean gave me! I thought it was appropriate." She looked at Sean for help.

"Years ago, I suspect," he said diplomatically. "I'm surprised you can still get into it."

"I've gotten taller, not broader." She smiled.

"That's very sweet, darling, but you need a new one," Dianne said.

Sean tried to ease the situation. "I'll have a new one sent to her."

"That's so good of you," cooed Dianne. "I don't know what I'd do without you."

"You'd think of something." He laughed.

"Rosie, I almost forgot." Dianne rummaged in her Cardin purse and emerged with a small white box with a Cartier label. "Abracadabra!" She merrily waved it in one of her mercurial mood shifts. "What do you think this is?"

Rosalind decided to play the game, feigning excitement. "Oh! It must be an exotic breed of miniature turtle!" She shook the box.

Dianne giggled and shook her head.

"You try, Sean."

"A microfilm copy of your memoirs?" He joined the whimsy. "That would be worth a lot."

"I'll give you a clue. It's a present for Rosie from Tony!"

Rosalind was conscious of Dianne's eager surveillance. She decided not to react to the Tony allusion as she prodded her imagination. "I know. It's a freeze-dried housing development. It looks teeny, but you put it beside an ocean and *whoosh*—high rises."

"I wonder if I could freeze-dry voters for O'Brian," Sean asked dryly, adding a wink as Rosalind laughed.

"That's all the guesses you get." Dianne had saved the present for six months, waiting for a moment when she might need it. Now she wanted Rosalind to think of her with fondness while she was away.

"Tony was in Paris last week and thought of you. Isn't that nice? Open it!" Dianne urged, like a child at a party.

Rosalind looked from the box to Dianne. Dianne had not mentioned seeing Tony last week. She opened the box. A delicate butterfly pin rested on white velvet, gleaming with diamond, ruby and sapphire wings. She made a stab at enthusiasm.

As a thing in itself, the pin was interesting, but Rosalind

hated pins. Dianne knew she never wore them without protest. Not that it mattered. Dianne had all their jewelry stashed in the vault. Rosalind couldn't begin to remember all the inappropriate jewelry Tony had given her. Given? She amended the thought—bribed her with.

"Do you want to keep it while I'm in Saudi Arabia?" Dianne asked. "You'll have to be very careful—God knows what it's worth. Or shall I put it away for safekeeping?"

"Put it away." Rosalind started to hand back the box. "No." She pulled it back. "Let me keep it, in case there's a Christmas formal." Or an emergency, she added to herself. Her allowance of $150 a month was adequate rather than generous, since she had to buy books with it, too. Dianne liked to remind Rosalind that her own allowance had been only $50 a month. Rosalind made a mental note to research the inflation figures to compare.

Dianne sat back, content. Her little ruse with the butterfly Tony had given her was working. It really was a silly little thing and much too youthful for Dianne. And to think she had almost sold it.

"Tony is a generous man," commented Sean.

"Oh, yes. And now he's thinking of building more projects in South Africa. You know diamonds just grow on trees over there. It's wonderful."

Rosalind tapped her fingers on the window. When were they going to get out of the limousine? It had stopped five minutes ago. "Dianne, are you flying with us to Bradley or are we dropping you at La Guardia first?"

Again, Dianne winced at Rosalind's use of her first name. "It doesn't matter, darling. If you're in a hurry, I can drop you off first."

Sean caught the pained look. Trained by an old-fashioned matriarch, he believed in parental respect. "Rosalind," he began sternly, "sophistication can go too far. I don't think your mother appreciates your calling her Dianne."

Dianne flashed him a pathetically grateful smile. She wished she had the courage to confront Rosalind directly like that. She was at her best when she could keep things light and gay.

"Sorry, Mother. A lot of my friends call their parents by their first names."

"You know I want us to be pals, darling, but I would rather be your mummy in name."

"Okay, Mummy or Mother, if I give you my solemn oath not to call you Dianne, will you let me out of this limousine?" Rosalind laughed.

"We're here, aren't we?" Dianne blinked out at the parking lot of the charter terminal.

Rosalind burst from the limousine, flitting over to hug Timothy, Billy and Grandma Bea in turn, then dashing back to collect Dianne and hurry to the plane. Suddenly she realized that the twins were coming along and ran back to collect them.

"Boy, are you wired," said Timothy.

"What's the rush?" asked Billy.

She didn't reply as she herded them toward Dianne.

On the Marino jet, Rosalind spent most of the flight in the cockpit, discussing airline safety with the pilot, only returning to her seat in time to gulp down a club sandwich before they landed at Bradley Field.

Taxiing toward the colorless Connecticut airport, Dianne hugged the twins and then Rosalind. She promised Rosalind that she would get at least ten hours sleep a night all week so she wouldn't be too tired for her Arabian adventure. Rosalind hadn't said a word to elicit the promise.

Separate agents, separate limousines. Rosalind kissed Timothy and Billy good-bye and sent them off to Andover before she climbed into her own limousine and switched on the reading light, pulling out *The Major Poets* to discourage conversation with the agents.

Her eyes were caught on page 361 by the line "Tears, idle tears," from "The Princess" by Alfred Lord Tennyson. Where would I be if my father were still alive? she wondered, as she slowly read the nineteenth-century message:

Tears, idle tears,
I know not what they mean.
Tears from the depth of some divine despair
Rise in the heart, and gather to the eyes,
In looking on the happy autumn-fields,
And thinking of the days that are no more.

She chewed her lower lip, thinking of the days that were no more, and continued to the end.

Dear as remembered kisses after death,
And sweet as those by hopeless fancy feigned
On lips that are for others; deep as love,
Deep as first love, and wild with all regret;
O Death in Life, the days that are no more!

No, she wouldn't write her theme on "Idle Tears." It caught too fully the melancholy she felt when she thought of her father, a mood she had carefully cultivated for nearly fifteen years. She would search for a less personal subject.

She relaxed and contented herself with the thought of giving Colin a full report on the weekend over a late-night drink.

6

The grind of exam week was relieved by an extraordinary two-foot snowfall. Rosalind deserted her books for the afternoon and headed for the gentle slopes of neaby Mount Tom, giving her book-strained eyes a diversion.

"If I go blind by Christmas," she said to Colin as she adjusted her goggles, "will you put a red ribbon around your neck and be my seeing-eye agent?"

"How would you know if the ribbon was red?"

She pelted him with a snowball and raced him down the slope. He won easily, edging to a stop beside T who was waiting at the base of the run.

Rosalind skied to a stop beside them. "I won!"

Colin's brows shot up.

"You're standing at the bottom of the hill. You aren't even racing. So I must have won. Right, T?"

"Agree to take a break and I'll confirm anything."

"Sold. Let's get some hot apple cider." She undid her skis and led a plodding path to the ski hut.

"T—" Rosalind smiled up at him. "Please get us some hot cider. I'm freezing."

"Buttling is not part of my job description." He grinned, happy to be warm and cozy.

Colin laughed. "I'll get the cider while you two feud."

The line was short. Colin balanced the steaming Styrofoam cups carefully and made his clumsy way back to their table in time to hear the end of T's remark.

"You're turning into a hermit. Or maybe you're preparing to become a nun. I know it's easier for us when you lock yourself inside with your books all the time, but all work and no play, as they say . . ."

"Colin." Rosalind looked up with relief as Colin placed a cup in front of her. "T is getting on my case just because he hates skiing."

"Well, he has a point. You've been hitting the books for weeks without much relief."

She frowned at him. He was the only person who knew that wasn't true.

෨ ෨ ෨

Late that night, over hot toddies and room service burgers, Colin repeated T's remark about Rosalind turning into a nun.

"What does it matter if T thinks I'm a bookworm?" She bristled. "You don't think I'm a nun, do you?"

"Hardly." He stroked her hair. "Less every day."

She giggled. "I suppose I could say you were becoming a habit."

Colin groaned at the bad pun. "Next you'll tell me your real name is Rosary. But seriously, your hibernation is striking T as peculiar or he would never mention it. I think you should go out on a few dates with guys your own age."

"That's absurd. People can be young at eighty and old at twelve. Age is a state of mind."

"I'm talking about appearances, not psychology—or feelings. As long as things appear normal, T won't get too curious."

She made a moue. "The young men around here are about as exciting as my cousins. Dining clubs, preppie cars, fun and games. All they do is play around."

"That's how I started at Colgate, kiddo, all-around playboy."

"I thought you got married in college."

"Third year. Then I turned in my playboy credentials for diapers." And Ian, he thought. His sole offspring Ian was a freshman at the University of Dublin and was only a year younger than Rosalind. The thought of Ian made Colin feel every bit of his thirty-eight years. He traced his fingertip along the bridge of Rosalind's nose. "Anyway, my freckled Rosebud, T and the guys are getting curious. So go to a few parties."

"Why must I?" She tugged at his earlobe as though it would enhance his hearing. "Why do we have to sneak around all the time, anyway? Dianne's happy as a clam chasing camels with Kiki. They won't be back until after the holidays. Billy, Timothy and I are going to Grandma Bea's in Palm Springs. How does Christmas in Palm Springs sound?"

Colin glanced at his watch and reached for his clothes. "I could use the tan for me beautiful body, but I've promised to visit my old Irish parents in Cleveland."

Her thoughts jumped on as he spoke. If she didn't have an entire book to read for an 8 A.M. exam, she would have checked out for the night. Colin had such a beautiful body. She knew it so intimately she felt as though it was partially hers. Now it disconcerted her to think of him as having parents or family beyond a shadowy ex-wife in Cleveland and a son in Ireland. It ran against the grain of her belief that his time was hers, as her agent, her lover.

"I'll miss you," was all she said.

　　૭ಾ　૭ಾ　૭ಾ

Rosalind attended a few parties as the holiday spirit mingled with the finals crunch. Despite her protests to Colin that she despised immature gatherings, she loved the noisy parties that allowed her to blend into the crowd of dancers with a delicious anonymity. No one cared what Rosalind said or did; she was only one of a crowd.

　　૭ಾ　૭ಾ　૭ಾ

Christmas was warm in every respect. The ninety-degree sun beamed down on the lively poolside games with the cousins and Uncle Sean. Grandma Bea bustled about, organizing and reorganizing decorations, meals and the staff. The holiday spirit was in high gear in Palm Springs.

Dianne's calls, tinged with motherly guilt, came at all hours of the day and night Christmas week. She missed them all and longed for them to join her, but she skimmed past vague offers to fly them over. Lord Harley had joined their party, she reported, and they were having a marvelous time. Lord Harley had even promised to take them to see Jerusalem for Christmas. Kiki was so excited about it.

Well aware that Dianne was not mentioning Tony, none of her children asked.

The moment the Connolly clan sat down for Christmas Eve dinner, Dianne called to tell Rosalind and the twins that Tony was going to meet her in Paris for New Year's Eve.

It appeared that Tony was back on Dianne's "good" list, or vice versa. Rosalind crossed her fingers and hoped it wasn't so.

Grandma Bea couldn't help noticing the drop in Rosalind's energy as the conversation turned to Tony. Bea liked Tony and was sorry that the liaison with her late son's wife had not worked out better, but Dianne had always been difficult. She wasn't a real team player, and if nothing else, the Connollys were a team. Bea had hoped Tony and the children could develop a good, supportive relationship. Another false hope, she told herself with a sigh.

Bea watched the serious faces of the twins and Rosalind as they passed the phone to one another for the report to Dianne. Minutes before, Rosalind had been helping her cousin Terry paint a caricature of Sean while the irrepressible twins had been roughhousing with their cousins by the pool. Such complicated lives they have stumbled into, Bea thought, simply by being born. Perhaps the good Lord will help them find a smoother path than that of the past two generations. She crossed herself and retreated into the kitchen to check on the plum pudding one last time.

After dinner, Sean and Grandma Bea joined the cousins by the tree to open presents and pop champagne bottles. Bea sent the merry crowd to bed at midnight. Everyone had to get up with her for Christmas mass the next morning, without question. It was requisite for spending Christmas with Grandma Bea.

She smiled happily at her only surviving son and reached up to chuck him under the chin. "And that means you too, Sean Thomas Joseph Connolly."

"Yes, Mother." He nodded dutifully. He could have been ten.

∽ ∽ ∽

The good night's sleep was interrupted at three in the morning when Dianne called. She had just gotten back from a Christmas service in Jerusalem.

Bea, sleeping the light sleep of the aged, answered the telephone herself. With exaggerated politeness, she turned the call and Dianne over to the children. She crawled back into her bed, wondering if Dianne would ever learn any common sense.

Dianne wanted to know if they liked the presents she had sent. Billy was enthusiastic about the new skis and Timothy loved the scimitar. Rosalind was sleepily pleasant about the embroidered skirts and robes. "Perfect for parties," she said as she thought, costume parties.

Dutifully, they recited a liturgy of presents from the others. Distilling the warm family gifts to a factual list for Dianne to appraise seemed cold to Rosalind, but she went through with it. She didn't want to alter Dianne's good spirits; she was glad her mother was having a good time. She didn't miss her—with the constant phone calls, Dianne hadn't given them the space to miss her. As Timothy had quipped after yet another call, "She might as well be here. It would be cheaper to fly back for a day."

"Yeah," Billy answered. "I miss Leda more than Mum."

∽ ∽ ∽

Snow conditions in Aspen where they stopped with Uncle Sean for three days on the way back East were ideal. Rosalind even ventured down a diamond-marked expert trail behind her brothers. The boys were natural skiers; their instructor said if they had the discipline to match their ability, they would be champions. The instructor also said if Rosalind had the natural ability to match her discipline, she would be fantastic.

Stubbornness can only help so far, she thought as she watched her brothers' perfect parallels down the slope. She traversed her way behind them and wondered if they could outstrip Colin on the slopes. It would be close. She planned to punish Colin for Cleveland when they got back by telling him how wonderful the snow conditions had been and how perfect the weather.

She caught up with the boys outside the lodge.

"Hurry up, big sis, I'm starved!" Timothy urged.

"What took you so long?" added Billy. "It was an easy little trail."

They leaned their skis on a rack and plodded inside. Rosalind saw her uncle holding court at a round table, leaning close to a beautiful young woman. It struck Rosalind that the girl wasn't much older than she. She moved close enough to overhear the girl say, "Okay, call me then. I'm in room two-twelve at the inn."

Rosalind glanced at her brothers but they appeared to be studying the room. "Do you see Sean, Jr.?" Billy asked Timothy.

"He and Kevin were coming up the lift as we were skiing down. They're at least ten minutes behind us," Rosalind answered.

"Hi kids!" Sean waved them over. "Meet Sally Stevens, one of Jim O'Brian's senate campaigners from Manhattan. Sally, my niece Rosalind and my nephews Billy and Timothy—Connollys all."

Billy gave Sally a friendly hi.

Timothy grinned, "I'm the older one."

"Only by three minutes," protested Billy.

Rosalind and Sally assayed each other, female to female. Sally's brown eyes dropped first.

Arm still casually draped across Sally's shoulder, Sean didn't seem to notice. "The cousins still out on the slopes?"

Billy nodded. "They'll be in soon."

"Can we get a burger while we're waiting?" Timothy asked.

"It's getting close to dinner." Rosalind started playing mother to the twins, an old habit.

"Go ahead. It's vacation," Sean grinned. "And your mom and Aunt Laura aren't around to stop you."

The boys headed for the food line and Rosalind turned back to Sean. "How is Aunt Laura feeling?" she asked with what she hoped was innocence.

"Well, I have to run," Sally spoke too brightly.

"Okay." Sean squeezed her arm. "I'll talk to you later. I have to keep O'Brian's campaign rolling along."

"Nice meeting you," Sally said. Rosalind nodded shortly.

"To answer your question," Sean said as he watched Sally's rounded rump bounce from the room, "Laura said she was feeling better when I talked to her this morning. She was sorry she had to miss Palm Springs with us, but the doctor thought the excitement would be too much for her."

"I guess that's true," muttered Rosalind. Dianne would have made a sympathetic remark without conveying any real sympathy for Laura. Rosalind liked Laura and felt sympathy for more than her physical ills—but she loved Uncle Sean. The combination created mixed feelings.

Sean ordered Rosalind a hot-buttered rum to unthaw her toes. "Now, Rosie," he said seriously, "Grandma Bea tells me you're not coming to Washington this summer. What's up?"

Rosalind's face fell. "I'm sorry. I thought she . . . Dianne . . . would have told you. She said she would." But Dianne often avoided dealing with things she considered unpleasant. She worked hard at arranging that bad news or changes came from others. Rosalind was often left holding the bag. "She must have gotten caught up with her latest trip."

"Sure." Dianne called him twice a week religiously. "I thought it was settled." Sean seemed genuinely disappointed.

"I'm sorry, Uncle Sean. Truly I am. But I think she considers it a trade deal. She wanted me to go along to Saudi Arabia, but she let me out of it by insisting I spend the summer with her."

Sean chuckled in spite of his disappointment. He found Dianne's blatant manipulations amusing. "I'm afraid I understand, but if you change your mind, or she does, the offer is open, I'm certain. Jim O'Brian can always squeeze a bit and let you share his seat in his congressional office."

"In the Senate, too?"

"Maybe even in the White House, if things go right."

"It's all right. I've been," she retorted.

"Well, he hasn't," Sean laughed. "But his time could come. Remember, he has the support of the campaigning Connollys."

"Meanwhile," Rosalind looked meaningfully at the door where Sally had exited. "You have the O'Brian Senate race to . . . get rolling, right?"

If his niece meant what he thought she did, she was definitely growing up quickly. He hoped that was a good thing.

Peggy Linde halted dramatically in the center of the formal living room of Dianne's New York cooperative. "I knew it would be sensational, but it's better than that. It's quietly, luxuriously sensational. Swimming in taste, I would say."

Rosalind, playing spectator at the door, laughed. "Dianne phoned from Athens and won't be back until next week. She sends her apologies and asked if we needed a chaperone beyond the staff here."

"God!" The thought sent Peggy diving to the couch in laughter. "Chaperones! But I'm disappointed. I wanted to meet her."

Sure, so you could tell everyone you know Dianne Marino personally, thought Rosalind. Peggy was like that, but since she was Rosalind's contact for the summer job off-Broadway, Rosalind tolerated her. "You'll meet Mummy this summer."

"I just love the way you call her Mummy. It's so British, really."

Rosalind cringed, but was saved from having to respond as Leda wagged her way into the room and stopped short at the sight of Peggy, barking furiously at the intruder.

"God, we have to dash." Peggy jumped up, away from

Leda as Rosalind silenced the old dog with a hug. Rosalind smiled to herself. Peggy was obviously not a dog lover.

"By the time we wait for the Lexington Avenue subway and transfer at Fourteenth Street, we'll be late."

"That's okay, we'll take the limo."

Peggy's eyes sparkled as they climbed inside the limousine with the plush beige interior. She noted that Rosalind, who was sometimes ill at ease among their contemporaries, was totally assured in her dealings with maids and drivers. Poor little rich girl, Peggy thought enviously.

Rosalind glanced out the back to check for the Secret Service escort. Colin had the weekend off, but he was on his way to New York. The local agents assigned to her for the weekend were unknown to Colin. He had made certain of that. If the Service ran a routine check on her escort, they would get a benign report on poor pimply George Neidermeier, Jr. A free weekend with Colin—she savored the thought.

Putting up with Peggy had given her a good cover for Dianne, especially since Marie was away for the weekend. And Peggy had her own plans for a weekend with a boyfriend, far uptown, away from Rosalind.

The Eighth Street Theater was an unlikely place for a limousine. The marquee had been hand-painted in bright blue— a poor attempt at theatrical graffiti. Rosalind began to have second thoughts about the job. Then, as they scurried through the rain to the box office, she noticed a beautifully restored nineteenth-century ticket cage of highly polished brass. She felt better: it showed taste.

"They've done such a marvelous job with this place," Peggy gushed. "It's the most exciting off-Broadway theater in town."

Inside, everything sparkled in period, from the carved proscenium to the 1920s water fountains. The 150 seats had come from a turn-of-the-century theater and were newly upholstered in maroon velvet. Gold and maroon. It was charming.

A slender man in blue jeans and a red-checked flannel shirt emerged from backstage, crossed the dimly lit stage and easily hopped down to greet them. "Hi, girls. You're right on time. That's ten points already." He grinned.

"Hello, Mr. Wilde," Peggy spoke pertly. "One's always on time for the theater." She added, "I'm Peggy Linde."

"Right." Wilde brushed past the supercilious remark and looked at Rosalind. "And you must be Rosalind Connolly."

Rosalind froze. She always froze in the first moments of challenge until she became involved with the game or project. She reached for her voice. It sounded as breathy as Dianne's to her ears. "Yes, I'm Rosalind." She paused and added lamely, "Mr. Wilde."

"Everyone calls me Oscar." He grinned at her. "The name's really Arnold, but some joker started calling me Oscar years ago and it stuck."

She felt herself warming toward this man who seemed so casual, not at all what she expected of the producer and director of a New York theater—even off-Broadway.

Peggy resented being ignored. "I assume you got the letter from Cadge Martin at Stockbridge?" Oscar nodded and she rushed on. "Cadge had me doing everything from ushering to playing bit parts. I loved it, but I really want New York this summer."

Oscar nodded again. The letter from his old friend from Yale Drama School days indicated that Peggy was an eager worker, but she had overacted even in walk-ons. Oscar's company was small and his budget adequate, but tight. He needed his apprentices to be as versatile as possible. Still, the Linde girl had nice energy.

"You've had some good training." He smiled at Peggy. Then he turned back to Rosalind. "From Peggy's letter, all I know about you is that you have decided to major in theater. In which area?" He did not say that Peggy had written that Rosalind was *the* Rosalind Connolly. Oscar liked to consider himself a purist, but he couldn't help thinking about the box office draw if Rosalind proved even barely adequate for walk-ons. Competition was tough in the Village. He fought back those crass considerations: he would choose his apprentices on merit and potential alone.

Rosalind examined Oscar's lean face. He was close to Colin's age, she decided. "Acting and directing are my main interests. I'd love to be able to design sets, but I'm a terrible artist. I'm not bad with a camera, though. If you needed photo blowups, I could help. And I make good coffee." She grinned.

The grin was infectious. Oscar smiled back. Humor and some imagination, he thought. Not bad. A bit shy. There was no attempt to be glamorous, but she had an Irish wholesomeness with her curly dark hair, creamy white skin and green eyes.

They chatted about twenty minutes and Rosalind and Peggy filled out mimeographed application forms. Oscar escorted them outside, stopping to share the Chicago dance hall history of the brass ticket cage.

Quietly, the limousine pulled into position by the marquee. Oscar watched the chauffeur balance a black umbrella and ease the girls into the back seat. As he turned back toward his small theater, a line from Shakespeare ran through his mind, " 'Tis one thing to be tempted, another to fall."

Peggy chattered incessantly as they drove uptown. Wasn't Oscar marvelous? So brilliant and sinewy. Rosalind found him interesting and perceived that his dedication to the theater was genuine. She approved of his policies of mixing original works with classics and marketing for subscriptions rather than single-play audiences. She hoped she would get an offer for the job, but her experience, compared with Peggy's, was zero.

"I think he liked us, Roz, don't you?" Peggy intruded on Rosalind's stream of thought, finally seeming to require a response.

"I hope so," Rosalind said. She didn't want to admit that she craved an offer from Oscar. It would be the first project that Dianne had not arranged for her. She was afraid to hope.

"He really did like you, Roz. I could tell."

"We'll see soon enough." Rosalind tried to put the matter out of her mind. She was instinctively drawn to theatrical superstition: Don't think about it until it happens.

As they changed clothes for dinner, Peggy expressed her regret that she wouldn't have a chance to sleep in the "marvelous" guest room. She was planning to stay overnight in her boyfriend's apartment on the west side.

If Peggy's fishing for an invitation for two, she's fishing in the wrong pond, Rosalind thought. It had not been easy to convince Colin that a weekend together in New York was a reasonable request for her birthday present. She dropped Peggy off on West 79th Street with relief.

Back in the apartment, Leda gave a dolphin leap at the sight of Rosalind again. Leda was probably delighted that Peggy had not returned too, Rosalind thought. Dogs had a sixth sense about people.

Quickly, Rosalind double-checked Dianne's bedroom. Everything was in order. She ran her hand across the soft fur spread. It gave her a delicious thrill of subterfuge to contemplate sleeping there with Colin.

Time to get dressed. She pulled a pale green challis dress from the closet and realized she had never dressed up for him before. It felt good. She knew he had reservations for them at Windows on the World. Remembering that Colin and T often joked about being overworked and underpaid, she had protested that it would be too expensive—the first time she had ever considered the cost of an evening out. She had been pleased when he brushed aside her objection, proclaiming the end of her teens was a cause to celebrate.

When Colin arrived an hour later, she reached for the intercom to summon the car and driver. He stopped her; a cab was waiting. She felt content with him as he complimented her dress and helped her on with her white wool coat. "Have we met before?" She smiled. "I'm not certain I know you in your formal behavior."

"Once before, I think," Colin responded with playful solemnity. "On a snowy night in the north woods. You were the ice princess, if I recall."

"Yes! I remember. And you were the polar bear!"

He growled his reply, nuzzling her neck. "Polar bear hungry. Polar bear could stay and have ice princess for dinner, but then ice princess would starve."

"Perhaps not. She could have the polar bear for dinner."

"Let's discuss that later," he winked.

Leda awoke with a bark.

Colin started. "What's that?"

"You'll see," laughed Rosalind. "You are about to be given the real Connolly litmus test."

Leda eyed Colin, her curled tail wagging expectantly as she trotted over to him to receive homage.

"You've passed! She likes you."

"That's a relief. She's too big to have as an enemy."

Ardyth, the maid, appeared to ask if there was anything else Rosalind needed.

"No," snapped Rosalind, irritated at the interruption. "Don't wait up for me. And don't wake me in the morning. I want to sleep late. And I'll be using Dianne's room tonight. So don't knock on that door either."

"Very good," Ardyth replied with a sniff. "Have a good evening, Miss Rosalind."

"Thank you."

Colin gave Ardyth an apologetic smile. He waited until he was alone with Rosalind in the elevator to chide, "That was a bit snippy, don't you think?"

"What?" she asked honestly.

"The bit with the maid. Remember, I'm just as much part of the 'hired help' as she. We're only people doing our jobs."

"Colin, don't be silly." She thought about it for a second. "Besides, sometimes I'm snippy with you—when I'm in a hurry."

"Don't be coy. Our relationship is personal, not professional. Your maid was only trying to be helpful." His tone was paternal.

"That's the way Dianne talks to her all the time. She's used to it." Colin's disapproving look stopped her. "All right. I know what you mean, but you don't have to make a major issue out of it on my official birthday night." She pouted as they entered the cab, but soon the streetlights, neon and rain diverted her, creating a rainbow city on the pavement. She dropped her pout to share her pleasure with Colin. Her high spirits were restored by the time they reached the top of the World Trade tower.

Despite their reservations, they had to wait twenty minutes for a table. Dianne would have made certain Kiki had warned the manager to expect them. Rosalind liked their status as simple patrons tonight.

She nudged Colin with amusement as the fill-in Secret Service team tried to slide unobtrusively into seats at the bar. Colin attempted to share the humor.

"Mr. Neidermeier's party." The captain smiled. Colin stared at him blankly.

"Yes, thank you." Rosalind recovered first and rose to follow the captain.

"A fine secret agent you make," she whispered. "Can't even remember your name."

"I'm in security services, not the CIA."

"Good thing."

They were given window seats by luck rather than influence. Rosalind looked down at the miniature lights of Manhattan, thinking that every city in the world should have at least one hundred-story building so there could be a single place without litter or slums—all one had to do was rise above it.

As Rosalind took the last tender bite of her Steak Diane that she had ordered in honor of Dianne's absence, she heard a familiar laugh, full and deep. She turned and caught Tony's eye, several tables away. He was with a beautiful young woman whose rose dress did little to conceal her considerable assets, even while seated. She looked vaguely familiar to Rosalind who supposed she was some kind of actress or model.

Head thrown back in laughter that revealed perfect teeth, the young woman didn't notice Tony's attention shift from her. Tony gave Rosalind a polite nod and turned back to his companion, making another remark that rekindled her laughter. Since the young woman didn't even glance in their direction, Rosalind knew the remark was not about her.

"Well," said Colin at a loss for words. Tony knew he was Rosalind's agent.

Rosalind's thoughts were elsewhere. She felt a surge of outrage on Dianne's behalf. Tony was putting himself on display. No wonder Dianne stayed out of town; she would have been mortified by such a chance meeting. Rosalind sipped at her wine, careful to concentrate her attention on the view and Colin. Tony wasn't even putting on a front anymore. A year ago he would have come running over, insisting that they join him, introducing the girl as someone involved in a business deal. As Rosalind squeezed Colin's comforting hand, she thought it was better this way, less two-faced for all of them.

Colin was doubly relieved when Tony paid no further attention to them.

꿍 꿍 꿍

Making love with Colin in her mother's oversized bed was even better than Rosalind had envisioned. The precious luxuries of time and space were enhanced by the thrill of the implicitly forbidden.

As Colin took a fast shower, she straightened the sheets and smoothed the furry spread. She smiled as she heard him humming in the shower. She couldn't catch the tune, but it sounded happy. The photos on her mother's dresser were smiling, too. Billy and Timothy. Herself. Grandma Jane and Uncle Herb. Tony. It occurred to her that both she and Tony, each in their own ways, were cheating on Dianne that night.

"Hey, ex-teenager!" Colin called from the shower. "I'm saving you some soap!"

"Good!" she called back. "And I need a back rub from you, Coach," she added as she headed for the shower and Colin, shadows of guilt forgotten.

Leda sat silently on a teal velvet Queen Anne bedroom chair, patently ignoring the activity. Although she didn't appear to approve wholeheartedly, she could not report to Dianne.

Rosalind hurried into the house dining room, famished. The unseasonably warm April day had inspired her to drag her bike from the storage room in the basement and take a quick ride between classes.

"Hey!" Cynthia waved at her from the far corner of the dining room. "You're late."

Mrs. Tinkler's silver bell sounded and the dining room doors closed.

"I picked up our mail," Cynthia whispered as everyone rose for grace.

Rosalind stood solemnly behind the chair Cynthia had saved for her and bowed her head for Mrs. Tinkler's sonorous prayer. She glanced down at the envelopes beside Cynthia's water glass, focusing on the return address of the letter on top. The Eighth Street Theater. Before the amen had sounded, her hand had darted forward and secured the missive.

"Rosalind," hissed Cynthia, watching her friend tear open the envelope and digest the contents. "Mrs. Tinkler might see you." Reading mail at the lunch table was one of their house-mother's pet peeves. It could mean loss of tea privileges for two weeks.

Rosalind couldn't have cared less. Mr. Wilde had chosen her! She slid the letter in her pocket, the critical sentence etched in her mind: "I am happy to invite you to join our Eighth Street Theater group in the position of summer intern." She would even get paid $75 a week. It was wonderful! And Dianne had done nothing to help her get it. Dianne. She felt a tremor of misgiving.

"Rosalind!" Cynthia held out the platter of Welsh rarebit. "Where are you?"

"I got it, Cindy! I got the internship!"

"With the congressman in Washington? I thought you had that any time you wanted it." Cynthia looked puzzled.

"I'm sorry." Rosalind beamed at her friend. "I hadn't told you—or anyone. I didn't want to jinx it until I had a reply." She went on to explain.

"Does Dianne know?" asked Cynthia.

"No. No one does except Peggy and . . . except Peggy." Rosalind popped a cheesy square into her mouth and paused to chew. "Dianne wants me to spend the summer with her in New York. My internship won't interfere, I hope."

"Sounds logical."

Rosalind had almost mentioned the other person who knew—Colin. He had been encouraging, teasing her that the wanton spirit he knew in private turned to ice in public. He thought a summer in the theater might break down some of the public reserve, making it easier for her to handle speeches and interviews. Rosalind was also aware that in both subtle and manifest ways, Dianne encouraged that reserve in her daughter.

"Now it makes sense!" Cynthia said suddenly. She explained that Peggy Linde was in her English lit class and had come in late this morning, visibly upset. She had stopped by Cynthia's desk and whispered that she wanted to talk privately after class. The professor with the crisp British accent had asked Peggy to refrain from speaking unless she cared to teach the class that day. Peggy had burst into tears and run from the room. "I never saw her after class," said Cynthia, "but I'll bet she didn't get chosen."

Rosalind continued eating silently. She had steeled herself to putting up with Peggy's endless chatter and dramatizations if she were chosen but had never dreamed she could be selected without Peggy. Yet, Cynthia's report sounded as though that was what had happened. Rosalind felt a touch of relief which she quickly shoved aside. She would have to be terribly sympathetic to Peggy who, after all, had provided the entrée.

That night she shared her excitement with Colin, but she couldn't duck his questions concerning Dianne's reaction.

"It's going to be worse if you procrastinate," he advised.

"You're right, I know. She'll wonder why I didn't call her immediately. I can hardly say, 'Because I was terrified that you might spoil it.' "

"You might try it. Her response could be interesting." He gave her an encouraging hug.

"I know what she would say to that. 'Terrified of Mummy, your bestest friend in the world? Don't be silly, darling.' " Her mimicry of Dianne's breathy voice was uncanny.

Colin laughed. "However you handle it, it's better that you get it over with."

"Yeth, Uncle Colin," she lisped at him.

"I'll 'yeth' you." He rolled her back on the bed and changed the subject.

∽ ∽ ∽

At noon the following day, Rosalind stiffened her upper lip and dialed Dianne. Dianne was delighted by Rosalind's unsolicited call. She had news for Rosalind, too. Tony had summoned her to Rome—she had wanted to tell Rosalind right away, but she never knew when to find her in these days.

Rosalind was glad to find Dianne in a rush. It would make her task easier.

"Kiki's putting my itinerary with contact numbers in the mail today for you," Dianne hurried on. "And of course I'll call you."

Rosalind tried to keep the excitement out of her voice as she mentioned a possible apprenticeship for the summer in New York. "I am considering it only because we'll all be in New York anyway."

Dianne pulled her mind away from her packing lists. "But I was planning some special excursions for us."

"You can take the twins. The program doesn't last the entire summer."

"Well, it simply can't, that's all."

"Mother, it will be a good experience for me."

"If you really want to do it, but don't blame me when it cuts down your flexibility." Dianne sighed.

Rosalind had a fleeting precognition of conflicts between rehearsals and Hampton weekends or trips. But she had made it past the first hurdle; the rest could be dealt with later.

"Oh, Rosie, I don't know." Dianne breathily considered. "An off-Broadway theater is awfully tacky. It's one thing to study theater in school, but to go out and do it . . . I'm not certain it's the right thing for a Connolly to do."

Rosalind's toe beat a staccato on the old hardwood floor and she came a hair away from slamming down the phone. But she was beyond the childhood techniques of running from rooms and slamming doors to shut out Dianne and the world. Now she struggled to include Dianne as a part of her own growing world. "It's an educational program, an apprentice position. And why should it matter if it weren't? You had a job with a professional theater when you met my father, didn't you?"

Dianne paused in stacking her lingerie into neat pastel piles. She remembered how thrilled she had been by her three walk-on roles. Of course, she had never taken acting seriously. Moments of picturing her name in bold letters above marquees had been buried under new roles in the higher-level soap opera of her life.

"Mother?" Rosalind pressed. "Please."

"Well, I don't see how a summer can hurt and it could be fun." Dianne backed off. Still, she didn't relish the thought of her daughter parading herself before the public. "It is directing and writing that interests you, isn't it? Is that what you'll be learning?"

Rosalind laughed, knowing she had won the case. "I'll never get that far this summer. I'll be stuck with a can of paint, I'm sure. An apprentice is only a polite name for gofer."

There was silence as Dianne picked up her packing list sightlessly, remembering her own theatrical adventure as a semi-rebellion, with her father encouraging and her mother opposed. She didn't want Rosalind to feel toward her the way she had felt about her mother's acquired snobberies. She added enthusiasm to her voice. "You should learn a lot, darling—gofer or not. It will be exciting to work in a real theater, even a tiny one."

"That's how I feel. And you'll come to all the shows and see how wonderfully I can paint flats." Rosalind laughed happily. "I'm going to write Mr. Wilde right this minute, accepting."

"I don't suppose his first name is Oscar," Dianne said dryly.

"Not really, but it is his nickname. His real name is Arnold. It's on the letterhead."

"And the place is called the Eighth Street Theater?" Dianne reached for a pen.

"Yes." Rosalind could sense Dianne jotting it down to have Kiki check it out. But unless Oscar turned out as salacious as the original, which she doubted, Rosalind wasn't worried.

"I suppose it is time you spread your wings a bit. You are twenty. My teenage daughter is gone." Dianne's sigh wafted through the phone. "If I had known you wanted to work with a theater this summer, I could have gotten you a job with a producer uptown."

Rosalind didn't respond.

"But it was terribly mature of you to find this job all on your own. I'm terribly proud of you." The tone, fluctuating between soft rebuke and modulated enthusiasm, signaled Dianne's mixed emotions. "Now, I must get busy, darling. Is there anything special you'd like from Rome or Paris?"

"Nothing I can think of," Rosalind answered.

"Then I will have to surprise you. You know I love surprising you." Then Dianne said, "Good-bye to my bestest friend in the whole world," smiling as Rosalind dutifully said good-bye to her "bestest friend," too. Dianne hung up the receiver, blew it a kiss and returned to worrying whether her week with Tony would pass for better or for worse.

Rosalind let out a whoop of joy. It was time to celebrate. She had braved the dragon and won. She looked out at the early afternoon sun—another mild day, a picnic day. She knew Colin had the day off; he had muttered something about working on his taxes, but taxes could wait. He could always get an extension. She dialed the inn and asked for his room, fingers crossed.

"McReady here."

"Connolly here."

"What's happening in your funny little world, my little rose-bud?" he asked with a bad W. C. Fields imitation.

She gave him a glowing report of her conversation with Dianne. He was delighted.

"Now we must celebrate. I only have a dance class this afternoon. That's cuttable. And it must be seventy degrees outside by now. Perfect picnic weather."

"Rosie, I barely have my receipts together. I have hours of work," he began. "But I can always get . . ."

". . . An extension," they chorused.

"I'll sneak out the cellar window and meet you on State Street. You'll have to drive. I can't get my bike out the window."

"And we can stop by that little inn in Holyoke we've been talking about." Colin was getting into the spirit of the day.

~ ~ ~

Rosalind tiptoed down the cellar stairs. It was darker than she remembered. She laughed at herself and removed the large round sunglasses, a discarded pair of Dianne's. That was better. She walked past the row of chained bikes toward the window that looked awfully high and narrow. Carefully, she dragged two large trunks over and climbed on top of them. The window gave easily. She suspected this wasn't the first time it had served as an escape hatch.

The only bad moment came as she crossed about ten feet of open lawn before she could turn left, up State Street; she had to pass directly beside her agent's post. Luck was holding. The agent was sitting in the car, reading the morning paper. With a paisley scarf hiding her hair and in Cynthia's plaid coat, she wasn't recognized.

Colin was parked beside Dr. Sorokin's office. It had been the only address on State Street that they both remembered precisely. He chuckled to see the turbaned, spectacled figure approach and rolled down the window.

"Is that the latest look for well-dressed young Smithies?"

"The Mata Hari special." She grinned. "So be careful what you say. I have you bugged."

"So turn off the recorder and get in the car."

Mata Hari disappeared along with the coat, glasses and scarf. "First the market," Rosalind directed.

While the other agents guarded the house without a Rosalind, she and Colin carted bread, wine, cheese and fruit into the woods.

Rosalind lay back on a blanket confiscated from the inn munching on some grapes, with her head resting in Colin's lap as she watched the sun filter through the branches. "Colin, I still can't believe it. It only took about three minutes before she capitulated."

Colin brushed a tiny red spider from Rosalind's hair. "Relax and enjoy it. It's exactly what you want."

"I'll probably get some walk-ons. Oscar uses apprentices to fill in the crowd scenes. Do you promise not to laugh when you see me made up like an old crone?"

Colin laughed. "I'm afraid I'll have to miss it, but I admit I'd have to see you as an old crone to believe it."

"What do you mean, miss it?" She sat up. "No one can stop you from coming to my performances, on or off duty."

"That's not the issue." He stopped to watch the sun sparkle in the reds and golds of her hair. "My summer plans have been set for a year. I'm spending six weeks in Ireland with my son, Ian."

"And your ex-wife?" she asked between her teeth.

"She lives in Cleveland—teaches school there."

"Won't she be on vacation, too?"

"Immaterial. I'm taking Ian alone. It's important that I spend some time with him now. I haven't seen much of him in the past ten years."

"He's practically grown. You should have done that years ago, before I knew you." She stared away from him, into the shadows of the woods.

"You're right." Colin sighed. "But a man still has to try."

"You were the one who encouraged me to take this job and now you won't even be around." She felt as though she were being robbed. He had no right to leave her for six long weeks.

"I'll catch up with you in the middle of the summer when you've perfected your act." He leaned forward to kiss her.

She pulled back. "I think it's a rotten thing to do to me."

"Besides, it will give you the space to meet some new people, maybe even a new man. After all, you've only tried one. The second might be better." It hurt to say that. Colin hated the thought of her with someone else. But in his rational mind, he believed the affair could not last. Beyond the disparity in their ages, their life-styles were light-years apart. There were no McReady jets or estates; it was a different league.

"Don't be silly." She gave him a hurt look and reached out to touch the shadow of his beard. "I love you," she whispered, her eyes welling with tears.

"And I love you," he answered, pulling her close. He had never said it to her before. He had told her he loved her hair, her body, her skin, her clothes and her wit, but never simply "I love you." Perhaps, in departure, it felt safe.

They made an intense kind of love on the damp floor of the woods. Rosalind was acutely aware that he would be gone for six weeks, that he might be leaving her as a lover forever.

Their covert evenings for the next crowded weeks carried unspoken currents. The bantering continued, but their hearts were heavy. Colin was still Rosalind's touchstone, but one with a new ephemeral dimension. Rosalind felt torn between willing the weeks to pass quickly so she could begin her Eighth Street Theater adventure and praying they would move slowly so Colin would not disappear so soon.

The weeks passed at their own rate. Colin left for Ireland on the last day of May, while Rosalind was taking her final exam in European history.

9

Paintbrush in hand, Rosalind watched the auditions for Shaw's *Saint Joan* from the wings. It was obvious that Oscar was not pleased.

"No!" he shrieked at one auditioner. "Joan is not a coquette. This isn't a card party with the bishops, damn it!"

He glared at the eleven would-be martyrs. "Take ten. I can't stand looking at you right now." He took a noisy breath, wheeled around and moved stage right into the wings, nearly colliding with Rosalind.

"Well? Since you were watching, what do you think?" he demanded. He had already told her she would be used in some crowd scenes, relieved when she seem pleased. So far, she wasn't acting like a prima donna. In these first two weeks she had fitted in fine, polishing armor with the best of them. Oscar applauded his good judgment in hiring her.

"No one seems right yet," Rosalind began, looking at him with an open gaze. "Joan isn't that complicated, in my opinion. She is aware of the opposition against her, but she doesn't dwell on it. Her goal is simple. She must rally the troops to save France. Nothing, no priests or generals or politicians, can stand in the way of that mission. It's straight-line, goal-directed reasoning."

Oscar's brows lifted as he leaned against the edge of the proscenium. "Go on."

"She's not flippant or flirtatious. And even though she can rant and rave at the drop of a sword, she is not uncontrolled—stubborn in her loyalties and beliefs, yes, but controlled and singularly directed by her holy mission, to save France." Rosalind paused for breath.

Oscar's brows were rising toward the catwalk. He was surprised that Rosalind was capable of such impassioned analysis. He noted in greater detail her fair complexion, green eyes, curly almost blue-black hair and the generous mouth. Even in paint-splattered clothes, she held herself with a slender elegance reminiscent of a young Audrey Hepburn. A peasant with class.

"Do you disagree?" she asked to break the scrutiny.

He continued his silent surveillance while he debated with himself. So far his auditions had scored four weak possibles. It couldn't hurt to try. If by some miracle she could handle the part, the Connolly publicity could sell out subscriptions for the next two seasons. "Would you like to read for the part?"

"Of Joan?" She gasped. "Do you really think I could . . . do it?"

"I don't know. Have you ever done a full role before?"

"I played Margery Pinchwife in *The Country Wife*, but it was a college production."

"I can't seem to find anyone out there!" He made a theatrical gesture toward the stage. "I might as well search in my own backyard—or backstage, in this case." He grinned encouragement. "Want to give it a try?"

Rosalind nodded, not daring to try her voice.

"Now when you audition, Oscar coached, "don't try too hard to act. You can think about the traits and motivations you talked about just now, but all I want you to do is read it with understanding as Rosalind."

Rosalind nodded again, picked up a script and walked onstage to the row of chairs she had helped arrange for the audition. She swallowed and decided if the gods wanted her to do the role, they would help her keep down the bile. She was certain Joan would never have become a saint if she had thrown up on the bishops. She smiled to herself at the image. The first crisis was over.

Oscar asked her to read as soon as the break ended. She was grateful she wouldn't have to go through the agony of listening to the others' inflections and letting them influence her. This situation of competing with strangers was alien to her.

Oscar nodded for her to take center stage and begin. Twenty-four eyes fixed on Rosalind as she met an invisible Dunois and changed the direction of the wind to prove her power.

The scene flowed as Rosalind relaxed. Her competitors became an audience, unaware of her name. They only saw a young woman bring Shaw's words to life with youth and passion.

Rosalind finished the monologue and looked at Oscar for a reaction. He stood frozen; she couldn't read his expression.

"Is that all?" she croaked from center stage, back to being nervous Rosalind Connolly.

"You may sit down," he said.

Rosalind perched on the edge of a chair, carefully watching Oscar.

Oscar stared back at Rosalind. She wasn't polished. He would have to work his tail off smoothing the rough technique and the tendencey to wander and flail her arms. If she flailed with a script, she could be wild without one. But Rosalind did have youthful enthusiasm and a real spark. It would be a big gamble, but if she were good, she could be his ticket uptown, to produce and direct on Broadway. That dream had seen him through years of penny-ante summer stock, dinner theater and off-off Broadway. Rosalind could be his personal saint, his special angel.

Was he kidding himself? What was the worst thing that could happen? She could be terrible. So what? Jean Seberg had been dreadful as Saint Joan, but it hadn't hurt Otto Preminger's reputation. Rosalind could make Oscar and Oscar could make Rosalind more than the nondescript daughter of a dead president. Everyone could win.

Chairs creaked as the auditioners became restless.

"Auditions are closed," Oscar announced. "The final cast will be posted in the morning."

"I hope you get it," said a curly headed girl sitting beside Rosalind. "You should have no problem," she added, "being who you are."

"Thanks," Rosalind replied automatically. Then she frowned. Did the girl think Oscar would give her the role because she was Rosalind Connolly? That would be unfair.

Oscar crossed the stage, stopped a few feet away from her and silently appraised her. "Well . . ."

"Yes?" she asked.

"Yes," he echoed affirmatively. "Congratulations. You have been selected by both the director and the producer to play Saint Joan."

"Are you sure?" she gasped. "You aren't just giving me the part because of my . . . my name or anything, are you? I've only done college productions and everyone else is professional."

"You have the fresh naïveté and enthusiasm I want for Joan, but we will both have to work very hard to pull it off. Are you up to it?"

"All I can do is promise to put everything I have into it."

I hope that's enough, thought Oscar. Then he turned to business, explaining that she would have to join Equity, but her salary would go up, too.

Rosalind's first thought was to turn those technicalities over to Kiki. But she quickly resolved to keep this affair separate from her uptown existence. She gratefully accepted Oscar's help with the paper work and fees. He would pay them and take it out of her salary.

In concession to Dianne's fear about "that part of town," the limousine was waiting outside. Rosalind glanced at the Secret Service car parked behind it and thought of Colin. She didn't even have a telephone number for him in Ireland, and she couldn't track him down through the signal board. Too many people would become curious. But with him or without him, she wanted to celebrate the achievement of the impossible.

She looked at her watch. Four o'clock. She didn't remember if Dianne had any special plans for the evening. She hoped there weren't any people coming over or plans to go out. Rosalind wanted her celebration limited to Billy, Timothy and Dianne. It was too special to share with outsiders.

As she skipped into the apartment, Billy was pulling on a sweater getting ready to go out. "Where are you going?"

"Over to Gary's to play pool. Tim's already there. I'm going stir crazy around here. Tell Mummy I'll be back before dinner."

"Why don't you tell her yourself?"

"Because you're home and you'll save me a trip to the den."

"Lazy bones." Rosalind laughed. She could rarely get upset with the young men her plump little brothers had become.

"Just make sure you're both back in time for my celebration dinner!"

"What are you celebrating? It's not your birthday."

"Today, June eighteenth, I became a saint."

Billy convulsed in laughter. "A saint? Be serious, Roz."

"I did become a saint, in a way. Saint Joan. I am playing the lead in my theater's production of it."

"Hey, that's great! How are we going to celebrate? Burn a 'stake' or two?"

"You're close, little brother. I thought we four might eat a steak or four."

"Call us at Gary's when you have the schedule set and we'll come running back, but don't call before six. Gary and Tim and I are . . ." The elevator arrived midsentence.

Leda barked in protest at Billy's departure then plopped herself down on the hall carpet, chin flat on the floor between her paws, looking bereft. Rosalind laughed and gripped her copy of *Saint Joan* for moral support and headed for the den. Dianne, wearing slacks and a powder-blue T-shirt, was sprawled across the leather loveseat, reading a book on Russian icons. She grinned across her toes at Rosalind.

"Hi!" Rosalind grinned back.

Dianne sat up. "Okay, kiddo. Spill. I can see you're excited."

"You won't believe it! I still can't believe it! I was just standing there watching the auditions, holding a paintbrush—and the next thing I knew Oscar asked me to audition and now I have the lead in our first play. No more prop carrying!"

"Slow down." Dianne laughed. "What's the production and what's the part?"

"*Saint Joan* and Saint Joan." Rosalind smiled. "One and the same."

"Rosalind! That's a huge part!"

Rosalind's words tumbled over each other. "Oh, Mummy, I know, but I'm sure I can handle it. I know I can be good. I only hope I don't get stage fright with a real audience of strangers." She was sensitive about her own paralysis at political affairs, but then she was appearing as Rosalind Connolly who panicked in the pit of her stomach. Saint Joan wasn't the kind of person who was ever daunted.

Dianne drew back for a moment and watched a daughter who had dropped all barriers in her enthusiasm—she was seeing her "bestest friend" again. Now she congratulated herself. Her instincts had been right: a summer together was exactly what her special foursome needed. If the Eighth Street Theater and its crummy productions served her purpose by bringing them closer, it had been a wise decision.

"So?" Rosalind finished. "What are the plans for tonight?"

"I don't know about Billy and Timothy, but mine have just been canceled so I can help my bestest friend celebrate." Dianne leaned forward to give Rosalind a hug. "Where shall we go?"

Rosalind announced she was going to cook a feast for all four of them. They'd have Beef Wellington, if Marie would help with the puff pastry, and the boys' favorite dessert, Bananas Foster.

ᔕ ᔕ ᔕ

Marie grumbled lovingly as she hurried off to the grocery. Only for Rosie, she thought, would I do this. She liked helping Rosalind cook, believing in the depth of her provincial heart that Dianne's lack of interest in cooking was a major flaw. She suspected Dianne couldn't make a boiled egg if she had to. All that woman ever did was fuss with Marie's menus, changing things all the time. Marie pocketed her pique as she entered the gourmet grocery and shopped with care.

ᔕ ᔕ ᔕ

Dinner was a big success. Timothy pronounced it "Four Star" and Billy gave Rosalind a ten-for-ten on the Bananas Foster. Rosalind, knowing it would please Dianne, made a premiere appearance in one of the embroidered skirts Dianne had sent from the Middle East.

Dianne was pleased to have them all happy. She freely poured the Latour '69 which Tony had shipped by the case for special occasions. With each glass, the party grew merrier. Dianne's talent for mimicry appeared front and center as she aped the expressions and accents of everyone from Sean to Grandma Bea to Tony himself. She sent her children off to bed in smiles.

No need for barbiturates tonight, she purred to herself.

ᔕ ᔕ ᔕ

Rosalind proved to be a fast study. Although her role demanded memorizing 594 lines in the six scenes of the play and 95 in the Epilogue—approximately 7,000 words—she was past prompting by the end of the first week of rehearsal.

Oscar focused on other problems, especially blocking and timing. "When I tell you to range naturally, I don't mean run in circles!" he barked the second Monday. "And when I say be firm with the Dauphin, I don't mean scream in his face!"

At the end of the day, Rosalind equivocated between bursting into tears and telling Oscar to take his play and shove it. But he took her aside and assured her they were making wonderful progress. She would be a memorable Joan, he promised, adding an ambiguous, "One way or the other."

She arrived early and stayed late for rehearsals, wanting desperately to be good. It would be the first time Dianne would see her perform; she had missed all of Rosalind's school plays. Especially because she had gotten this job and part on her own, Rosalind had to succeed.

Her real "saving grace," as she called him, was Richard Stevens, cast as Charles VII, the Dauphin. An experienced actor who had been on Broadway as one of the children in *The King and I*, Richard joked that he had worked his way down to off-Broadway. Gifted, but short in stature, he found appropriate parts to be scarce. The role of the Dauphin suited him perfectly.

He spent many extra hours working with Rosalind, trying to make her movements firm but natural, teaching her how to come close to other actors' lines without stepping on them, and working on finding the pulse of scenes, the changes and the builds. Many of the good moments Oscar believed he had wrenched from Rosalind were courtesy of Rich.

Rich didn't mind; he was concerned with the end result. He also knew that preserving a director's ego was requisite for being a working actor.

As rehearsals reached the end of the second week, Oscar made a pilgrimage uptown to St. Thomas Church where he lit four candles—one for Rosalind, one for himself, one for Saint Joan and one for his dream of Broadway. It was the first time he had been inside a church since his father's funeral ten years before.

ல ல ல

At home, Rosalind had readily accepted Dianne's and the twins' offers to help. The days became balanced between serious rehearsals by day and merrier home versions at night. Billy and Timothy switched roles from Court Page to Charles VII to assorted priests and soldiers. Dianne played captains, the archbishop and townsfolk. Timmy and Billy dragged out Dianne's evening capes and furs for costumes. Dianne's protests were weak and amused until Timothy fastened a silver fox cape around Leda's neck and proclaimed her true heir to the throne. Both Leda's and Dianne's protests became serious and Dianne decreed her closets off limits for costumes. They would have to make do with the linen closet's contents.

Despite the costume incident, Dianne and the boys spent evenings at home to enjoy the new theatrical sport. They could find nothing in the world more entertaining than themselves.

Rehearsals moved into the third and final week and Rosalind's tension built. She didn't laugh as heartily at her brothers' cracks, such as "How are things going, hot lips?" On Tuesday night she announced that the home rehearsals must come to an end. Oscar had told her she must concentrate seriously from now on. Rosalind couldn't bring herself to share her frustration. One minute Oscar would tell her to "loosen up" and the next, he would be screaming, "Tighten up and concentrate." Only Rich's patient coaching after rehearsals gave her strength. She was grateful that many of her main scenes were with him.

    ∽ ∽ ∽

The afternoon of the preview, Dianne debated what to wear. She still had not seen the theater, but Kiki assured her it was charming in its own fashion. The red Givenchy was slated for opening night—with Tony. The preview wasn't formal, but she still might run into someone she knew and—it hit her like a flash—photographers. What if the press made a big deal over Rosalind starring in this silly little play? A faint line etched itself between her brows, and her blue eyes narrowed in thought. That was precisely why she hadn't wanted Rosalind to take the apprenticeship in the first place: fear that a day like this could get out of control. She reached for a flattering soft blue Halston, just in case her worst fears were realized.

At that moment, on the Eighth Street Theater's stage, Rosalind and Oscar were encircled by the very people worrying Dianne.

A reporter from the *Village Voice* was asking Rosalind if she intended to become a professional actress. "I'm not sure," she whispered.

"Miss Connolly," Oscar smoothly interpreted, "is only here for the summer in our apprentice program which is designed to give promising college students an opportunity to sample the delights of the theater and determine if it's right for them. First Miss Connolly must sip before she can judge the wine. Right?" He smiled at Rosalind.

"How did you prepare for the role of Saint Joan?" The cub reporter from the *Times* poised his pen.

Rosalind darted a panicked look at Oscar. How could she explain the hours and hours of drills and coaching? She didn't want to say that Oscar's intensity at rehearsals and his constant interruptions were overbearing and she was beginning to feel like his robot. She knew she had been woefully wooden at dress rehearsal the night before.

"Do you use any special technique? Stanislavski?"

Technique. Rosalind was weary of the word. "Your technique is rough," Oscar had said. "We must polish and refine." He practically positioned her fingers.

"We have developed the Connolly-Wilde technique," Oscar answered, despairing they would get an answer from his protégée. "Or perhaps," he added with a chuckle, "I should call it the Wilde-Connolly technique."

The reporters smiled politely. Rosalind was barely animated, let alone wild. She stumbled through the rest of the interview, increasingly tense under the personal scrutiny.

She was painfully aware that she was committing Dianne's cardinal sin by granting an interview. Dianne loved to remind people that there had not been a single interview granted since their White House days and there would be none. Rosalind tried to rationalize that it wasn't a personal interview; it was only part of the standard publicity for the production.

Oscar was surprised that someone who had spent all her life in the public eye would freeze in an interview. He trembled as he wondered what an audience might do to her performance. He had done everything he could think of in the three short weeks. Her performance was technically sound, but the spark of passion he had hoped to fan was now buried beneath a stiff, competent rendition of the role. She would neither flame them nor shame them, he had sadly rhymed to himself during dress rehearsal. Nonetheless, the heavyweights would attend and the Eighth Street Theater would headline the *Times* theater page. It wouldn't be a total loss. He took one more question and sent the reporters packing.

"Thank God that's over," muttered Rosalind.

Oscar hadn't believed her when she warned him that she was terrible at interviews, but she had been as truthful as the saint she played. It didn't really matter. The critics that counted would be there in a few hours. Then, they would see a different Rosalind, an actress, he prayed.

Rosalind grabbed his hand. "I'm sorry, Oscar."

Oscar tried to give her a reassuring smile. "The comparison can only make tonight seem better."

She blinked hard, fighting back tears of frustration. Oscar had worked so hard; so had Rich. What if she let them all down, forgot her lines, screamed too much or froze?

"Hey." Oscar gently patted her cheek. "You're the fearless Saint Joan, remember?" He had to do something to relax her before she fell apart on stage, on his stage. "You know all the things we've worked on? The walk, the hands, the feet, all of that?"

She nodded.

"You have those techniques down now. So I want you to stop worrying about any of that. Let yourself plunge into the role tonight; just let it flow. Let Joan do her play tonight."

He watched her walk away. Perhaps he was asking too much. Maybe all the pressure wasn't fair. But if she performed even as well as she had at dress rehearsal it would be all right. Rich and the others could carry her. As long as she didn't freeze, the publicity would be wonderful.

෴ ෴ ෴

Back in her dressing room, Rosalind tried to relax. The anticipation is the worst part, she thought. She fingered the armor she wore in the second scene. She liked the feel of the metal; it helped her keep the militant mood flashing as the lights sent steely sparks from her chest. She stretched her long, slender fingers out toward the dressing room light. As she surveyed the pale half-moons at the base of each nail, she considered letting them grow. Dianne preached that nice young ladies kept nails short and natural. When Rosalind had allowed hers to grow only a quarter inch the year before and painted them a subdued "vanilla orchid," Dianne had pointedly reminded her of its tastelessness. How old did she have to be? She had a sudden image of Dianne's chewed fingertips. Perhaps the motivation was jealousy rather than taste.

It was still too early to get dressed. She was too on edge to read. At breakfast she had insisted that her brothers and Dianne not arrive early or come backstage until after the performance. Now she longed for the twins' irreverent humor to divert her; on the other hand, Dianne's presence would be devastating at the moment.

As if on cue, Rich's tightly curled head appeared in the doorway. "Hi, there! Want to grab a bite?"

"Thanks, Rich, but I don't think I could eat a thing."

"Then how about a drink?" He persisted.

Rosalind grinned. "I feel like I could use a whole bottle, but I'd better not."

"As an old theater hand," he said as he leaned dramatically against the door, "it never helps to sit and stew. In fact, the last thing you should do is think about the play. Remember, my coaching can turn a frog into a queen. And since you are far better than a frog, now you are far better than a queen." He preened at himself in the mirror. "It takes one to know one," he added, grinning backward at her.

"I'm afraid the frog has lodged in my throat."

"Nothing but opening-night jitters, my dear. Dr. Richard prescribes that we get out of here as fast as possible. Come on. If we stay here, you'll go crazy . . . and we haven't rehearsed *The Madwoman of Chaillot*."

Rosalind liked Rich, gay in both senses of the word. In addition to being a resourceful drama coach, he was a safe and amiable companion. He was marvelously sensitive to moods and feelings.

"I must say, my dear, I far prefer it when you aren't wearing those awful Amazon clogs you have," he said as they crossed the back alley toward the local diner. "Not only are they noisy, but they're high. You are much closer to my ideal height when you wear the nice flat slippers you have on now."

"It doesn't matter, Rich. I'm still inches taller than you, even in bare feet. But I don't mind; I'm accustomed to being tall."

"You're not that tall," he noted sadly. "I'm just that small. Five-five even on the rack, but it means, like Charles the Seventh, I must overcome my lack of height with loftiness of spirit!" He turned to her, his baby face a study of intent. "Bow to me. Prove to me that I am king!"

She frowned at him for a second before she recognized that he had slipped into an improvisation.

"Bow!" he ordered again. "Bow, or I shall cut you down to size and thus be certain I am king."

"Oh, Richard, Richard!" She bowed in mock despair. "You must not cut me down, but rather you must preserve me from those who would." She looked up and grimaced. "Like the critics."

He laughed as they entered what had become the Eighth Street Theater's personal greasy spoon. "Fear not," Richard spoke with a flourish of an imaginary sword. "I am prepared to slit them from their guggles to their zatches, to quote Mr. Thurber."

Rosalind had relaxed enough to feel hungry and ordered oatmeal and a glass of milk to counteract the acid still churning inside.

ᔐ ᔐ ᔐ

"Ten-minute warning."

Backstage, in the simple garb of the Maid of Orleans, Rosalind was driving herself crazy. Was Dianne in the audience yet? Were Billy and Timothy there? She restrained herself from peeking through the curtain. It was verboten by both tradition and Oscar. She fingered her father's gold baby ring which Grandma Bea had given her on her sixteenth birthday. Too delicate to wear all the time, she slipped it on a gold chain at times like these, when she needed all the help she could muster.

What if she froze as on the afternoon she had been scheduled to give a speech to the Democratic Youth of Connecticut? Her tongue had become paralyzed. She had stared at the audience for the longest two minutes of her life and sat down again.

"Please, my father." She clutched the tiny ring. "If you're up there tuned in, *help*."

"Five minutes." The stage manager tapped on the door.

Where was Colin? She wondered exactly where he was right that second, but in a way she was glad not to have the extra pressure of another person she loved in the audience. Billy, Timothy and Dianne were enough.

Would Dianne like the performance? Rosalind would know in less than two hours. She licked her dry lips and applied lip gloss for the twentieth time.

_ల_ _ల_ _ల_

The dark limousine glided to the curb under the marquee. The alerted press lifted cameras and readied notebooks. The twins, tan and blond in their navy blazers, climbed out first, paving the way for Dianne and her friend Lady Eleanor Babcock. A TV reporter jammed a microphone in Dianne's face before she could get her smile in place. "How do you feel about your daughter wanting to be an actress?"

She made no comment as her chauffeur and the twins' agents forced a path for them through the media cluster.

Billy turned back to the newsmen and growled, "Stay away from us or we'll burn you at the stake."

"Just keep your distance," added Timothy.

The cameras kept rolling.

Dianne was stiff with anger as they were ushered to their fourth-row-center seats. Lady Eleanor, sensitive to Dianne's feelings, chatted on with pragmatic British style, hoping to smooth Dianne's angry edges. "Darling"—she patted Dianne's fist—"the press is simply curious, as always. If Rosalind's a smash, they can only help the production and if she's terrible, they'll stick out their ridiculous tongues and go away. Either way, it's no major tragedy."

"Eleanor, you know this is supposed to be an educational experience for her, not a circus."

"This is the preview, right?" Billy asked.

"Are we coming opening night too?" Timothy continued. "We'd like to, Mum."

Dianne did not answer as the lights dimmed, sending friends and relatives of the cast scurrying beside the critics to fill the house.

_ల_ _ల_ _ల_

From the moment Rosalind's Joan bobbed a curtsy to Robert de Baudricourt and demanded her horse and armor courtesy of heaven until she grabbed Poulengey's hand with a "Come, Polly" to lead him off to find the Dauphin, Scene One was hers.

The lights brightened and the curtain fell to give the stage-hands two minutes to convert the set to the throne room of Charles VII.

Billy grinned at Timothy. "She's terrific! Our sister is really terrific!"

Timothy turned to his mother. "Mum, she's really good. Really."

"Really wonderful," agreed Lady Eleanor. "And so strong. I had expected the sensitivity, of course, but . . . Dianne, she's absolutely marvelous. And this is far beyond my concept of a student performance. It's quite professional, really."

It was far beoynd Dianne's expectations, also. The smooth production, the slick scenery, the beautifully restored interior of the theater and the presence of critics from the major news-papers made Dianne realize she had grossly underestimated Rosalind's "Oscar" Wilde and his "little" theater. She felt a surge of anger at Kiki for not telling her how professional the group was, conveniently forgetting that her instructions had been to find out if it were bad, rather than how good.

Dianne found Rosalind's performance disconcerting. The bold young woman riveting the attention of nearly two hundred spectators as she played with emotions—both hers and theirs—was not her Rosie. But she was. And she was doing a remarkable job. In a quiet corner of her soul, Dianne acknowledged that Rosalind was better than Dianne ever had been; the most chal-lenging role she had played was a Noel Coward maid with seven lines. Intently, Dianne watched for Rosalind to bungle a line, overact, underact, anything.

In the last act when Saint Joan, on trial, refuses to sign the writ and deny her heavenly voices, Rosalind's intensity threat-ened to go out of control. Dianne held her breath expectantly, but Rosalind walked the fine line between passion and theatrical awareness with style. Rosalind's Joan surged through the role like a summer wave, impelled by natural rhythms, inevitably driven to the crashing climax.

Watching from the wings, Oscar questioned his own senses. The wooden creature he had seen the night before had broken loose from its casings. He felt like Geppetto, the day Pinocchio had come to life.

The rehearsed movements had become natural. The spark he feared had been snuffed out with the hurried applications of technique flamed. Rosalind's Joan was hell-bent on saving

France—and Oscar's dream—with an inspired performance. He reminded himself that any profits must be shared with St. Thomas Church. Not a man of deep faith, he nonetheless glanced up beyond the catwalk. He stood very still, breathing shallowly, not wanting to disturb his luck.

Rosalind ended the Epilogue with, "How long, O Lord, how long?"

The house went wild. Even the irascible *Times* critic rose to his feet, applauding.

"She was really good." Dianne overheard the remark from behind. "I thought she had been cast for her name, but she was wonderful."

Dianne stared at Rosalind smiling and bowing before her eyes. The publicity would be outrageous, possibly even dangerous. It would be so simple for someone wanting to get at the Connollys to buy a ticket and conceal a gun. Rosalind was only a young girl, not ready for all this, she thought, gathering her ammunition. Unless Dianne moved quickly, Rosalind would be headlined tomorrow.

"Bravo! Bravo!" The twins chorused as the cast finished the eleventh and final curtain call.

"Well!" Dianne forced a wide smile for her sons and Eleanor. "Let's hurry backstage and tell her how very, very wonderful she is!"

Agents in tow, the twins led the way backstage.

"Over there!" Timothy spotted Rosalind surrounded by an excited cast.

At the moment Dianne caught her daughter's eye and beamed her famous smile, Richard stepped between with a basket of pink miniature roses.

"Rosie!" Dianne called past him.

"Right on cue." Rich laughed and presented his offering to Rosalind. "And this is your reward for not even getting singed!" He led the others in applause.

Irritated by the backs in front of her, Dianne searched for an opening in the circle. Rosalind finally caught her eye. "Mummy!"

Suddenly aware of who was standing outside their circle, Rosalind's fellow players made a path, all eyes on Dianne to watch her—and her reaction.

Ignoring the others, Dianne moved in with Billy, Timothy and Lady Eleanor. She hugged Rosalind quickly, smile perfectly in place. "You were fantastic, darling. I can't believe you're mine."

"No, Mrs. Connolly," Rich interjected, "now she belongs to the world."

Rosalind giggled. Dianne frowned at Rich.

"You were great!" Timothy gave Rosalind a bear hug.

"Even if you are our sister." Billy added his own hug.

Rosalind laughed and rescued her pink blossoms from the embraces.

"Even Paul Silas of the *Times* was on his feet," Lady Eleanor added.

"Are you sure?" Rosalind's eyes sparkled. "Wait till Oscar hears that!"

"Where is your Mr. Wilde?" Dianne asked softly.

"With the box office people. There is some mix-up about seats for tomorrow night," Rosalind answered.

An attractive man in his mid-forties, wearing a soft blue suede jacket, approached Rosalind, hand extended. "Miss Connolly. Dave Driver. I had to tell you personally that you were terrific, smooth as custard. You made me want to disband NATO and fight the British."

"Uh . . . thank you." Her tongue tied and she tentatively shook his hand.

The man turned to Dianne. "Mrs. Marino. You must be very proud of her. Congratulations."

Dianne rewarded him with a frosty blue stare. Unintimidated, the man thrust out his well-formed hand a second time. Dianne ignored it and him, turning to Rosalind. "Come, darling, let's all go to your dressing room. The boys and I have a surprise for you."

Rosalind waved her roses at her colleagues. "See you at the party!"

Dave Driver, columnist for the *News*, stared after them, his mouth lifted in a half smile. An unforgiving lady, he thought. She couldn't take half a step toward civility. When he had written that she was a cold fish who had married Tony Marino for economic "better" alone and that she deserved Tony's cavorting with starlets coast to coast, he must have been right on the money. Yet, he seemed to sense something vulnerable behind the ice. He wondered what he would find if he cracked the shell. Idle question. They didn't play in the same ball park.

Enough musing about museum pieces. He had to find Oscar.

The production had looked good. Oscar deserved a lot of respect for struggling to maintain a subscription theater in the Village. The Rosalind Connolly publicity should help.

∽ ∽ ∽

Rosalind looked from the engraved gold charm, a miniature Rheims Cathedral, to Dianne. "It's perfect!"

Dianne beamed.

"I was really nervous for the first three lines," Rosalind answered Billy's earlier question. "But then I relaxed into it and it felt good."

"You really are a natural." Lady Eleanor spoke from her perch on Rosalind's dressing table.

"Why were there reviewers here tonight, for the preview?" Dianne asked softly without evident emotion. "I thought they only came opening night."

"The reporters who were here this afternoon said critics often come to both the preview and opening night to compare," Rosalind said.

"Reporters here? This afternoon?" Dianne paled.

"Yes." Rosalind spoke with a touch of Saint Joan's defiance. "Oscar and I were interviewed. It was only on the history of this theater and preparing for the . . ."

"Oh, Rosalind," Dianne interrupted dramatically. "It's what I feared. You—and your name, your father's name—you're being used. People are so selfish."

"Mother, it's not that way at all." Rosalind clenched her 18-karat cathedral.

Dianne sank down on the single chair in the room. "You are so young and vulnerable. You don't know. Perhaps it's my fault for overprotecting you and the boys. It is so hard for me to . . ." Her voice trailed off as she closed her eyes.

Rosalind recognized the look that said, "It hurts me to hurt you for your own good." She had seen it before: the day Dianne gave away Rosalind's beagle that was chewing furniture; the time she had told her she could no longer see a certain friend from Spence. The look. It sent a chill of fear through Rosalind.

"What's done is done," Rosalind spoke quickly. "We only have a day left before the opening. If I'm being exploited, I don't care, because I'm enjoying this."

"You're really good, too!" Billy sided with his sister.

"She is, Mum." Timothy added his support.

Lady Eleanor watched, keenly wondering what Dianne was planning to do.

"At least I can talk to your Mr. Wilde about the excess publicity," Dianne said mildly and rose. "You run along to your party and have a good time. If you want the car to pick you up later, call; otherwise, call a cab. But don't be too, too late."

"No, I won't." Rosalind's lips moved automatically as she watched the quartet suddenly uncrowd the room. Silently she changed into jeans for the party at Rich's loft, trying desperately not to think about what Dianne might do.

ـ‫ى‬ ـ‫ى‬ ـ‫ى‬

Dianne sent Billy and Timothy to the limousine and led Lady Eleanor to Oscar's back office. She wanted Lady Eleanor along for moral support. When they reached the office, Dianne saw through the glass panes that Oscar was still talking with Dave Driver. "Damn."

"What's wrong?" asked Lady Eleanor.

"He's still with that horrible man."

"Who is that 'horrible man'?"

"Dave Driver," clipped Dianne. "The so-called columnist. I cannot begin to tell you how he has offended both Tony and myself with his drivel."

Lady Eleanor shrugged. "I don't think I've read him."

"Neither should the rest of the world. God knows what he'll write in his column about this." Dianne shuddered.

"Shall I announce you?" offered Lady Eleanor.

"No. If the important Mr. Wilde won't come outside like a gentleman and explain his panderings, then I shall handle things in another way." She smiled at her friend.

"What are you going to do?"

Dianne eluded the question. "It's outrageous—turning Rosalind into a billboard. It makes my blood boil the way my poor children are abused. They can't do anything in a normal fashion. Oh, Eleanor, what if some insane assassin tries to kill her?"

Lady Eleanor gave Dianne a sharp look. The Secret Service had been conspicuously alert tonight.

"It's truly sad," Dianne continued. "I have to keep my antennas up twenty-eight hours a day." She led the way to the limousine and her impatient sons.

"Mummy," Billy spoke quickly. "Rosalind just invited us to the preview party."

"We'd love to go. May we?" finished Timothy.

"Not with the early morning tennis lessons you have tomorrow." Dianne did not want the boys involved with that group.

"We're not babies anymore," groused Timothy.

"And we don't need all that much sleep," added Billy.

"You both look tired to me." She brushed the hair back from Billy's forehead and patted Timothy's cheek. "Besides, you promised to walk Leda for Marie tonight."

They did not discuss the play as they drove Lady Eleanor home.

∽ ∽ ∽

Dave Driver sat on the edge of Oscar's antique oak desk and lit a cigarette. "Okay, Oscar. Did you cast Rosalind as Joan because she was good to begin with or because she was Rosalind? You know we'd never do a special column on the Eighth Street Theater without her, don't you?"

Oscar was disconcerted, uncertain how to answer. Dave's tone had a sardonic edge, but Oscar knew Dave attended his plays even when it had nothing to do with his column. Dave was a subscriber, an ally.

"You're going to get heavy publicity out of this, Oscar." Dave grinned.

"Dave," Oscar began slowly, wanting to share his relief and emotions with someone, but feeling reservations about spilling his guts to a reporter. "Okay, this is off the record. Nobody in that audience tonight was more surprised than I was that she was better than competent. Last night, she was technically proficient and absolutely inspiring. I never expected . . ."

Dave raised his eyebrows.

"Dave, I'm pushing forty. I've been chewing sawdust in loft theaters and worse for a long, long time. In this business, you have to make your own breaks."

"Hey, I have a lot of respect for what you're doing down here. And tonight's performance was as good as anything I've seen you stage. Rosalind was amazing. You've just gotten my vote for Director of the Year. I've seen her freeze at less intimidating rallies."

"I didn't know I was that good myself." Oscar grinned

nervously. "I just pray we can repeat the performance tomorrow night."

"You'll simply have to tempt fate and keep the faith." Dave stubbed out his cigarette. "Back on the record, for the column, was she easy to work with?"

"It's never easy to work with an inexperienced actress and blend her performance with a professional cast's, but I've never seen anyone work harder at anything in my life. I'd say she has a stubborn streak a mile wide."

"They say it runs in the family."

"Oh? Yes, I suppose Bill Connolly had one, too."

"I'm thinking more in the present tense. Her mama has a will of her own. Have you spoken with her?"

"No." Oscar realized that he had never even met her.

"I wonder what she thought about Rosalind's performance. I said hello and got a pretty cold shoulder. She isn't terribly fond of the columns I write." Dave lit another cigarette. "Would you like to go out for a drink and celebrate?"

"Thanks, but I have to keep tabs on my stars. We have a cast party."

ೲ ೲ ೲ

Back on her own turf, Dianne settled her glum sons by the TV with ice cream and chips. Then she shut herself in her study to plan the attack. Her first phone call was a breathy one to Kiki. "I need you right now. Drop everything and come over."

Kiki handed eight dinner guests over to her disgruntled husband and rushed twenty blocks north to the emergency war room.

ೲ ೲ ೲ

Rosalind walked the five blocks to Rich's loft. She needed the air. The agents trailed her as close as muggers. She didn't notice. Her mind was filled with elation and apprehension, like oil and water, an uncomfortable mix.

Rich's Village loft was a potpourri of style and invention. A massive red velvet couch was angled across one corner beneath a gilt chandelier he had discovered at a flea market. Old Oriental rugs mixed with oversized floor pillows covered the floor for thirty-five feet of decadence. Rosalind found it wonderfully whimsical—like Rich.

The cast and crew had chipped in for cheap New York

champagne and cheese and they dove into the cheese as though they had not eaten for weeks.

Rosalind basked in the free-flowing compliments and drank more champagne faster than she ever had in her life. But beneath the glow from the adulation and bubbly was an unspoken suspicion that Dianne would do something to destroy this new feeling of camaraderie and achievement. She had been a success. Her fears that she would freeze when confronted with a real audience had been dispelled. She knew for herself that she had been good. She grinned at Rich and poured herself another glass of champagne. At least she would enjoy tonight.

"Rich," she said as she sat down to look up into his sparkling eyes, "I really don't know what got into me tonight. Everything flowed. When I would feel myself stiffen, something in the back of my head reminded me to relax and go with Joan—like you told me backstage before the curtain went up. It was an incredible experience. I could literally feel the energy from the audience flowing into me. It was like a charge."

"*En theos.*" Rich nodded. "Meaning 'from the gods,' the root word of 'enthusiasm.' It's your own divine self reaching a higher level of communication. For the Greeks, actors were representations of the gods. In today's world, we prosaically say, 'inspired performance.'" He leaned over and kissed her nose.

Rosalind smiled and reached for the tiny ring suspended around her throat.

"I could not have done it without you—on or off stage. I mean that, Rich."

"I hope at least twenty percent of it is true." He raised his glass to hers, knowing that at least eighty percent was fact: "To opening night."

She was about to return Rich's toast when Oscar arrived and the room exploded in cheers for the director.

"Where's the champagne?" Oscar demanded. "I wish to toast my fabulous cast."

Rosalind joined the others in wild applause for Oscar and themselves. Later, when everyone had replayed the play and reviewed the audience, Rosalind perched on the arm of Oscar's chair and attempted to ask casually, "Did my mother talk to you tonight?"

Mellowed and artistically content, he patted her hand. "No,

114

and I am sorry I didn't get a chance to meet her. Lovely woman. It must be in the blood."

Rosalind brightened, kissed Oscar on the cheek and crossed the room to struggle with opening another bottle of champagne. The cork popped and everyone cheered. Here she could do no wrong.

At 3 A.M. Oscar insisted that the party break up. He didn't want a disabled cast for opening night. Realizing that she had no cash as usual, Rosalind borrowed five dollars from Oscar, called a cab and went home. If Colin and T had been on duty, she would have bummed a ride home with them, but she didn't want to share this evening with the strangers outside. She felt a moment of melancholy, thinking of Colin. She wondered how he would have liked the performance and her new friends. He might not understand Rich, but Oscar was of his generation. She turned aside the thought that Oscar and Colin had little in common besides herself.

Kiki was leaving the lobby as Rosalind hopped from the cab, back on a high. "Kiki!" She waved.

"Hold the cab," Kiki called to Rosalind.

"Kiki." Rosalind took her hand. "You missed my play tonight, but you can come another night . . . tomorrow or next week or the next. It was so . . . so wonderful—really you must see it."

Kiki gave her mistress's daughter a quizzical look. It was obvious Rosalind was far from sober. "You better get inside and get some sleep, honey." Kiki didn't know what else to say. She was too aware of the fate of those who opposed Dianne to discuss the play with Rosalind.

"Yes. That's what Oscar said," agreed Rosalind, past the point of realizing that 3 A.M. was an unusual hour for Kiki to be leaving the building alone.

"Well, good night, dear." Kiki disappeared into the cab.

The apartment was quiet. Only a dim hall light kept the vigil. Rosalind had hoped that Dianne or the twins would still be awake. Curled up under the hall table, Leda woke and looked at Rosalind for a moment before she sighed and closed her eyes again. Not even Leda, Rosalind lamented.

Rosalind wasn't ready to end this night. She staggered slightly into the kitchen and poured a glass of milk, giggling to herself as she pictured the milk churning the champagne into little bubbly bits of butter. She was getting silly, she scolded herself. Kiki was probably right. She should go to bed.

She dropped her clothes on the floor and crawled naked between the sheets. The linen felt cool—perhaps her body was burning up like Saint Joan's. She felt the bed slowly sway back and forth, then go into a spin. She reached for her face, covering her eyes. Everything was spinning. The curds were warring with the champagne. She tried to rise from the bed but she felt faint and flopped back down, letting her body sink into the spin. She willed herself to relax and stop fighting the vertigo. Then she let go and swam with it, allowing the black undertow to pull her into sleep.

∽ ∽ ∽

The next morning began in the afternoon for Rosalind. The clock read twelve forty-five. She fought to wake, remembering she had a two o'clock call at the theater.

As her feet hit the floor, she recognized a major headache. She stumbled into her bathroom as quickly as she could under the circumstances. Aspirin and a shower—first things first. She felt forty percent human by the time she reached the breakfast room in jeans and a soft green T-shirt.

"Good morning." Dianne smiled up from her coffee.

"Why didn't you wake me? I'm late!"

"I thought you needed your sleep, darling. And from the looks of your little red eyes this morning, I was right as rain."

"It's afternoon, but I do feel terrible," Rosalind conceded. She looked at the pile of newspapers beside Dianne. "Did anyone write anything about the preview?" She eased herself into a chair.

Dianne gently pushed the *Times* toward Rosalind. "I didn't want to upset your evening last night, but after I explain I'm sure you will understand that we must do this."

"What are you talking about?" Rosalind's stomach picked up the throbbing tempo of her head.

"The fact that you cannot continue in that place," Dianne spoke calmly. "Darling, I know it has been great fun for you, but it also exposes you to terrible publicity. Your Mr. Wilde was shamefully milking the situation. It simply wasn't fair to you." She paused and watched Rosalind read the *Times* article. "I must admit that he had the grace to refuse to take a dime when I offered to make the theater a financial settlement. He said—extremely unpleasantly, I might add—that he didn't want a thing from me. The play could go on with the understudy and his subscribers would support it just fine. It seems it won't be any great loss to him."

Rosalind stared numbly at the article. "Mrs. Anthony Marino announced today that her daughter, Rosalind Connolly, is leaving the Eighth Street Theater production of *Saint Joan* because of excessive publicity surrounding the production. Miss Connolly, daughter of the late President William J. Connolly, had been scheduled to play the part of Saint Joan."

"Everyone in the press was very considerate for a change," Dianne continued. "Everyone ran my release as written except the *News* and that dreadful man Dave Driver. He'll be sorry someday." She paused. Rosalind wasn't reacting but was staring fixedly at the paper. "I really hated having to do this, Rosie, but I simply had to protect you." Dianne had reached for the bell. "Would you like some breakfast? The boys left an hour ago, but they took Leda with them so Marie is still on call."

Rosalind shook her head and closed her eyes. How could Dianne sit there and ask about breakfast? She was a double-crossing witch. Fun and games—as long as the games were Dianne's. It made Rosalind sick. She felt her stomach tense; then it rumbled audibly. The insides of her cheeks trembled and her throat felt dry as the morning-after bile rejected both coffee and conversation. Rosalind crumpled the *Times* with her hand. "How could you?" she whispered, fighting back tears as she ran from the room into her pink bathroom and threw up.

White-faced, empty of everything but outrage, she returned to confront Dianne. "I won't even go into your possible motives." Rosalind remained standing, trying to face Dianne down. "But it's wrong of you. It was wrong for you to make the announcement at all, but to do it without consulting me is a complete insult. I am not some object for you to push around to suit your whims."

"Of course not! You're a young lady who needs some guidance from her mother." Dianne smiled gently. "And you still can get carried away. But I must share the blame for not having Mr. Wilde and the theater checked out more thoroughly. Fortunately I was able to move quickly enough to stop his game before you were drowned in excessive publicity."

"You are really crazy, paranoid and crazy. The play is fine, the theater is fine and there wasn't going to be excessive publicity."

"To publicize the fact that Bill Connolly's daughter is appearing nightly in a play is excessive. It makes you an open target for terrible things. You'd be like a clay pigeon waiting to be shot."

"Oh, Mother, no one wants to shoot me."

"Don't even talk about it." Dianne shuddered dramatically.

Rosalind searched for the key words to influence Dianne. "Mother, if you love me, you'll retract that announcement."

"Rosie, I can't do that. I have my responsibilities toward you. Besides, we would look like total fools to retract such a statement now. No." She stood, a slender vision of efficiency. "The decision is final—and correct. We can discuss it later, but I have a lunch date with your father's estate people." She reached toward Rosalind, but her daughter shrank back. "Chin up, old girl. It's not the end of the world. Someday, when you're a mother, you'll understand." She frowned at her own choice of words. She was using Jane's favorite phrases, phrases she had sworn never to use.

"Never!" Rosalind flung at her mother's azure back. Dianne did not look back.

Rosalind rifled through the papers, looking for the *News*. Between the pulses of her rage, she had heard Dianne say the *News* had written about the preview. There it was: "Dianne M Strikes Out Again," headlining A DRIVE THROUGH MANHATTAN, the column by Dave Driver. Her smile appeared for the first time that day as she read Dave's critique. He wrote that she had shown "inspired sensitivity" and "unexpected natural qualities. As a firefly blinks, Rosalind Connolly acts, sparking the stage." The review included a lament that Rosalind would not be continuing in the role, attributing that to Dianne's paranoia and concluding, "Mrs. Marino's whimsical treatment of the world around her—which appears to include her daughter, Rosalind—is getting tedious."

Amen, thought Rosalind, if he only knew.

She turned from the column into devastating reality, put her head down on her arms and unleashed the tearful furies.

After a few minutes, she sniffed hard and wiped her face. Tears wouldn't help but Oscar might. How could he have allowed this to happen? Should she call him or face him directly? She decided it was better to be brave. After all, she hadn't done anything underhanded to be ashamed of. Her performance had been good, too good to let Dianne dismiss it with an imperious wave.

⌇   ⌇   ⌇

The streets were already hot in the early afternoon. She could feel sweat beading like tiny tears on her upper lip. Oscar was an idealist, she thought. He wouldn't be cowed by Dianne that easily. At least Rosalind hoped he wouldn't as she ran down the steps of the Lexington Avenue subway entrance.

She walked blindly past the pretzel and T-shirt vendors at the underground platform on 14th Street where she had to change subway lines. She considered summoning Rich for reinforcement, but seeing Rich first would make it a double trauma in a way. It was better to go directly to Oscar.

⌇   ⌇   ⌇

The gilded ticket cage caught a ray of sun as she approached the marquee—an omen of hope. But the front door was locked: a premonition of doom. She hurried around back to the stage door. It was open. She walked past the dressing rooms, hesitating by the door with the carefully lettered sign Rich had tacked there: ROSALIND CONNOLLY, STAR. It hadn't been taken down.

She heard voices onstage. She recognized Rich's tenor and inched closer.

"I don't want a messenger; but can you tell me any secrets? Can you do any cures? Can you turn lead into gold, or anything of that sort?"

Rosalind's heart sank as she whispered along with the understudy, "I can turn thee into a king, in Rheims Cathedral, and that is a miracle that will take some doing, it seems."

She stepped closer, curious in spite of herself about how the understudy was interpreting the role.

Rich caught the peripheral movement and glanced toward the wings. "Rosie! You're back! I thought . . . "

"Keep working." Oscar cut him off. "I'll be back." Oscar crossed the stage to Rosalind, who was in the same spot from which she had watched the auditions less than a month before. "We can talk in my office." His face was a mask.

"Sit down." He waved at a chair as they entered the office.

He moved behind his desk, creating an instant barrier between them.

"Did Rich think I left willingly? Why did he seem so surprised—and happy—to see me?"

"That's my fault. I told him you and your mother had decided there was too much publicity connected with the production." He frowned at her. "That's the way it was handed down to me."

"I didn't know a thing about it until this morning when she handed me the paper with that horrible announcement in it. I had nothing to do with it. I'm over eighteen, Oscar. She can't legally do that."

Oscar sighed. "You are still your mother's daughter."

"What does that have to do with it?"

"Do you know what she could do? To my theater? To my life?"

"Not much, I would think."

"Half our subscriptions come from her uptown set. The wrong words from her could bring in a lot of cancellations. Then add some bad press and actors mysteriously getting better offers and good-bye Eighth Street Theater. Good-bye Oscar Arnold Wilde."

"I think you're getting as paranoid as she is."

"Am I? Ever hear of Arturo Bernini?"

Rosalind shook her head.

"Arturo Bernini was once a well-known clothing designer. Ten years ago he did a special line of lingerie for your mother. It turned out so well that he made modifications and had the line mass-produced—not carbon copies, but close. Your mother was furious. She felt her exclusives had been stolen. Although she lost the court case, she made certain that the major department stores and exclusive boutiques never bought another Bernini."

Rosalind was silent. She had not heard the story before, but it sounded credible.

"I don't have the ammunition to fight your mother, Rosalind. If I did, I would. I think you played Joan fantastically last night and I would love to see if you could repeat that level of performance."

"I could, Oscar. I know I could."

"Unfortunately, we're not going to have an opportunity to test that here. Since this is my theater and my livelihood, I'm

120

not going to take the chance of ending up like Bernini. I'm sorry, Rosalind."

"There must be some way you could fight back—if you wanted to," she pleaded.

"When an adversary is bigger and stronger than you are, the wise man retreats and waits for another day when he is stronger."

Tears misted Rosalind's view of Oscar. His features blurred and he lost form. It was totally unfair. Dianne thought she could control the whole world and it seemed that she really could control part of it—especially Rosalind's part. And the Oscars of the world sat there and took it. Hot, angry tears splashed on her cheeks as she stood. "You're a coward, a lousy coward. That's why you'll never be anything but an off-off-Broadway loser! You're afraid of your own shadow!"

Oscar watched his former star storm from the office and slam the door. Perhaps she was right, he thought.

Rosalind ran down the street, away from the theater and her outburst of rage. She stopped on 11th Street, gasping for breath. The headache returned in a throbbing reminder of her hangover. Too tired to fight anymore, she hailed a cab. There was nowhere to go but home.

∽ ∽ ∽

Late in the afternoon, Dianne breezed into the apartment with a large illustrated book on medieval armor. She knew her daughter well enough to be certain she was still sulking and hoped the book would divert Rosalind. "Rosie!" she called from the hall. "Rosie!"

Leda answered from the kitchen with a bark.

"Hi!" Billy emerged from the kitchen, apple core in hand, followed by Leda whose eye was on the core. Billy grinned at Dianne and flipped the core to Leda who caught it neatly. "She'd make a great shortstop."

Dianne ignored the statement. "Have you seen your sister?"

"For one terrible minute. She's in a real black-and-bleak. Why did you pull her out of the play, anyway? Tim and I thought she was good."

Dianne shook her head and tugged at his earlobe. "It would have been dangerous for her. You understand that, don't you?"

"Sort of, I guess." He looked uncertain.

"Not sort of. You know Mummy's always right about these things, right?"

"If you say so. I'm late. I have to go to Gary's. Tim's already there."

"Go ahead, but I want you both back by seven. Tony's coming for dinner."

"Oh." Billy spoke dryly. "Sensational. That's just what Roz needs to cheer her up tonight." He was gone before Dianne could respond to the sarcasm.

Dianne tried the door to Rosalind's room. It was unlocked. Rosalind was sitting at her desk, her back to the door. She didn't turn as she heard Dianne enter.

Dianne slid the book in front of Rosalind. "Isn't it glorious? Just wait until you see the illustrations."

"The last thing I want to look at today is armor."

"Oh, I am sorry. I hadn't thought of that. Well, forget the connection and simply look at it as a history book."

Rosalind made no comment.

Dianne glanced around, seeking a diversion. The wall behind Rosalind's bed was covered with photographs and sketches of Bill Connolly. It sparked an idea. "Rosie, there's another thing. When I saw your play, I realized how inappropriate it is for you, the daughter of Bill Connolly, to play a martyr."

Rosalind thought Dianne's statement was absurd. Her father had neither burned at the stake nor been made a saint. But he had been all for action: "Dare. Do." He had used the directives in his speeches, saying that risk was a necessary part of a rich, full, committed life.

She looked at Dianne with detachment, wondering if Dianne had put him through changes too, sneaking up on him from behind and making statements without conferring with him. Rosalind determined to go to the library and read all those books Dianne called trashy and dishonest.

Dianne rose. "Life is not always easy, but we all go on. Incidentally, Tony will be here for dinner this evening."

"Don't set a place for me. I'm not hungry, and Tony never improves my appetite."

"Oh, Rosie, he'll be so disappointed. You must join us. This will be the first real family dinner we've had in months and months." Dianne noticed Rosalind's hand clench around a pen. She knew she was making her even angrier, but Rosalind had to come to dinner. Tony was coming to help.

Rosalind wasn't worried about disappointing Tony, but she knew Dianne would cajole and pressure her for hours until she agreed. "All right." She sighed. "I'll be there."

Rosalind came to dinner as an observer. She wanted no part of this phony Marino family. To her surprise, Dianne and Tony acted like old friends, exchanging anecdotes and commenting on the weather at their favorite spots worldwide. Rosalind had been lulled off guard by the time Tony turned to her.

"Rosie," he boomed and lifted her chin with his stubby forefinger. "Why so down at the mouth? You can do another play someday. Life is long and you are young."

Rosalind bit her lower lip. How could he understand? He never had a mother who took his successes away from him. She turned her chin away and reached under the table to scratch Leda.

Tony's hand dropped on the table with a thud. He glanced at Dianne.

Dianne gave him an encouraging smile. Rosalind must not be allowed to play the martyr. It was unhealthy for her and distressing for them.

Tony had accepted the dinner invitation without protest. He had already cleared his calendar for Rosalind's opening night and in spite of Rosalind's long-standing hostility, he felt sympathy for her personal closing night. As a frequent victim of Dianne's imperial whims himself, he felt he could share Rosalind's frustration.

He swallowed his half-filled glass of wine in one long gulp and signaled for a refill. He winked at Billy. "Billy, you're getting to be a real man! That's your second glass of wine."

Billy raised his goblet without animosity. "Then you must be a man and a half, because I think that's about your fifth."

Timothy grinned and Tony laughed heartily. "You've got it, son. At least a man and a half."

Rosalind sneaked a glance at Tony. She wished he wouldn't use the term *son* with the twins, but she couldn't help admiring his contagious laugh; it really was wonderful—if you weren't in a restaurant full of people.

Tony turned back to Rosalind. "Rosie, life is meant to be as happy as possible. Otherwise, what's the use? Pffft! I agree that Dianne should not have yanked you out of your play. I read the one review that slipped through. Dave Driver said you were excellent. I personally am very upset that I shall not see you

123

play Saint Joan." He looked carefully at Rosalind, noting her strong chin and high cheekbones. "Yes, I can see you would make a good Joan. I know how stubborn you can be." He laughed again.

"She was great, Tony, really great." said Timothy.

"I couldn't believe it. I mean, our own sister." Billy grinned.

Dianne ignored the twins' remarks. Her indignant attention was riveted on Tony. How dare he side with Rosalind! How dare he turn her into the wicked witch!

"It is a shame your mother acted so rashly, Rosie. She doesn't like anyone stealing her limelight, you know. But there might have been other ways to calm her down. Tighter security, a few deals to keep down the publicity. But now the terrible deed is done. There is no point in crying over your spilt milk." He raised his goblet. "You must live."

Rosalind felt confused. He was saying what she wanted to hear, what she believed to be true, but she didn't want to hear it from him. And he had no right to criticize Dianne. She pushed away from the table, accidentally knocking her wineglass toward Tony as she ran from the room, away from them all.

The glass rolled across the red, wet stain, coming to rest empty beside Tony. "Well, I tried," he said as he looked up at Dianne for understanding, only to be rewarded with cold fury.

"Well, indeed. Bringing up that horrible incident with the theater was hardly an intelligent way to shake her out of her depression. And siding with her—accusing me of trying to steal her limelight. Honestly, Tony, you have the sensibility of a toad."

The lines in Tony's face deepened; his flesh fell into the jowls of age. Life was too short and it was intended to be enjoyed. "I only know that toads can hop away."

"Oh!" Dianne stared after him as he rose and left. "That son of a bitch!" Suddenly she realized that her sons were still there, quietly fascinated by the scene. They were rarely party to Dianne's rows. She was careful to shelter her children from her own outbursts whenever possible. Tonight, it had not been possible. She gave her boys a sad smile. "I'm sorry, sorry for what he said and sorry he went off half-cocked like that."

Billy and Timothy privately agreed that Dianne had been wrong to pull Rosalind out of the play, but they knew better than to say so.

"Don't worry, Mum; we'll think of something to cheer her up," said Timothy.

"She can't mope forever," added Billy.

"You're right, darlings. Nothing lasts forever." Dianne smiled mistily. "How would you two like to cheer up your old mother and play a couple of round robins of backgammon? I'll even let you boys have white."

"Sure. But we don't mind playing with black." Timothy looked at Billy.

"You can have your white, Mum," Billy nodded.

"You are both such darlings. I don't know what I would do without my own little men."

When Rosalind tiptoed past the den en route to the kitchen for a glass of milk, she heard their laughter. It's all nothing to them, she thought. As she passed the dining room, she noticed Leda sleeping under the table. "Come on, girl," she whispered. Leda didn't move. There was no living comfort.

She returned to her room, milk in hand, and stared at the Bill Connolly wall. Would he have allowed Dianne to stop her debut so arbitrarily? Never, she decided. If even Tony were supportive, her real father would have fought Dianne for her. But there was no one alive who could stop Dianne.

∽ ∽ ∽

For the next week, Rosalind remained sullen, taking long unexplained walks, monosyllabic at breakfast, silent at dinner. Billy tried to convince her to go to the Hamptons with them to visit the cousins and Grandma Bea. She wasn't interested. Dianne bought tickets for the Alvin Ailey dance concert Rosalind had talked about seeing and ended up selling them to Kiki. Rosalind kept to herself, quietly consoling herself that Colin would be back in a few weeks. He would understand and ease the hurt.

Following a four-person, three-voice dinner at the end of the week, Dianne went to Rosalind's room. Her daughter was sitting on the bed, leaning on a giant pillow.

"Rosalind?" Dianne began tentatively. "Rosalind . . . we can't go on like this."

Rosalind glanced up. Dianne looked so young and vulnerable when she was in a supplicating mood. "Like what?"

"Your silent treatment. I'm sending your brothers to Grandma Bea's tomorrow to get them away from the depressing atmosphere you've created. You can't keep up this withdrawal. You'll make yourself sick, and it's making me sick with worry."

Dianne was right. Rosalind was sick of the situation, too.

"I think it's time we pour out our souls, kid. Let's talk it out."

Rosalind was still light-years away from wanting to open her soul to Dianne. "I have an idea."

"What is it?" Dianne asked brightly, determined to be positive.

"The internship in Washington. It's only the third week in June . . . well, almost the fourth. I would still be able to help in July and August. Do you think O'Brian would still take me?"

"But this was to be our summer together," Dianne protested, realizing as the words slipped from her mouth that "together" was far from the reality. Perhaps Washington could divert Rosalind from the bad beginning of their summer. She and the twins could go to Europe themselves. Dianne knew she also needed some open time to work on shoring up her relationship with Tony. If Rosalind were in Washington, neatly tied up with Sean's internship, she could maneuver more easily. It certainly would remove the current strain.

Rosalind waited patiently for Dianne's mental wheels to turn at their own speed. She didn't want to push lest Dianne resist instinctively.

"That might work out very well." Dianne rose. "You need something positive to occupy your mind, darling, and helping Jim O'Brian might be just what the doctor ordered. I'll give him and Sean a call tonight."

Dianne avoided mentioning the play in her phone call to Sean. She explained the last-minute decision as a little "change of heart" on Rosalind's part.

Sean, who had already seen the clippings of the announcement, read between the lines and agreed immediately. If a Connolly niece needed him, he was there.

Rosalind felt too embarrassed to answer Rich's frequent calls. She remained "not in" to anyone connected with the incident. A summer with Uncle Sean had been her first choice, before she had ever heard of the Eighth Street Theater. Perhaps she could pretend it had never happened once she was in Washington.

Dianne packed her off on a Marino jet, promising to visit soon.

Rosalind sat in the first seat on the right, closest to the door, and leafed through a magazine. The steward couldn't interest his sole passenger in the well-stocked galley or bar. "Help yourself," muttered Rosalind.

The highly disciplined Marino crew ignored the offer and the VIP larder went untouched. Rosalind didn't feel much like a VIP.

Rosalind was met by Sean's assistant bearing apologies that Sean couldn't be there himself. He would see her at dinner in Great Falls; he was also bringing home Congressman O'Brian to brief her on the new job. She liked the sound of that.

As she entered the sprawling stone house set on twenty acres between the highway and the Potomac, she was greeted by an enthusiastic attack of cousins.

"Hey!" Thirteen-year-old Terry grinned. "Want to go for a swim?"

"When are the twins coming for a visit?" Sean, Jr., spoke a beat behind his sister.

"How's your tennis these days?" chimed in Kevin.

"Whoa!" She laughed.

"Things were getting boring with only these guys around." Terry grinned. "I'm glad you're here."

"I forgot how wonderful this place is!" Rosalind looked from the hallway into the living room as though she had never been there before. The colors were soft greens accented with golds, beige and earth tones. The floor-to-ceiling windows looked out across the pool toward woods on one side and a field that dropped off to the river on the other.

"Yeah!" agreed Sean, Jr., as he hurled a large pillow onto a roomy couch. "Like Dad says, it's livable for Indians."

"Wait until you see old Gruff-and-Grum," Terry presaged. "Is she something!"

"You wouldn't be talking about me, would you?" A tall, middle-aged woman, complete with apron and tight bun, appeared in the hall. The woman looked stern, almost Gothic, until a warm smile cracked her face into hundreds of merry wrinkles. Rosalind thought old Gruff-and-Grum looked fine.

"You must be Miss Rosalind. I'm Mrs. Railes, the housekeeper that wild pack calls Gruff-and-Grum. It appears to take quite a bit of gruffing and grumming to keep them in line."

The cousins giggled.

"Mr. Connolly called to say he and Congressman O'Brian would be home for dinner by eight tonight, in honor of your arrival," Mrs. Railes said to Rosalind with a smile.

"Yay!" the cousins cheered in chorus.

"Now," she spoke briskly. "Masters Kevin and Sean, Junior., use some of those tennis muscles to help get your cousin's things to her room."

"Which room?" asked Sean, Jr.

"Your mother's for the moment. She told me to put her there. It's the most cheerful bedroom in the house."

Rosalind agreed with that appraisal as they entered her aunt's room, gay with pastel wildflower spreads and drapes. Fresh daffodils and bluebells cheered the dressing table and a basket of pale pink roses graced the dresser. Rosalind read the note beside the roses:

Welcome to Washington, Rosie. Hope to see you later this summer. Don't let the cousins bully you. Much love, Aunt Laura.

Laura's note dispelled any feeling of intrusion. She had never given Laura much thought; she had always seemed a quiet extension of Uncle Sean. "How is your mother these days?" Rosalind asked.

"At Grandma's," Terry replied noncommittally.

"We're going up to visit later in the summer," added Sean, Jr.

Kevin, the most serious of Uncle Sean's brood, said, "She hasn't been very well lately, you know. Washington life is very hard for her."

"You're our cousin, so we shouldn't have to hide things," Sean, Jr., continued. "She has what the doctors call severe psychological depression. She's getting therapy full time these days." He spoke with a touch of pride. His school was filled with students whose parents were in and out of therapy.

Terry had her fill of the topic. "Are we going to stand around all day and talk, talk, talk? When are we going swimming?" She missed her mother more than the boys seemed to. It made her sad to think about her mother surrounded by doctors, not being well.

"Right now!" answered Rosalind. "I'll change right away and unpack later."

The pool was as refreshing as her summer home and cheerful companions. They played water polo and swam races until Mrs. Railes gave them the one-hour warning signal.

"See what I mean about old Gruff-and-Grum?" Kevin asked Rosalind. "Mom never called us in from the pool an hour before dinner."

"Yeah," laughed Sean, Jr., with sixteen-year-old wisdom. "She was always taking long, long naps all afternoon. And she'd sleep right through dinner and when Dad got home— the nights he did at all—he had to chase us in, still in our bathing suits."

"Half the time we could eat in our bathing suits if we wanted to. Mom never noticed." Kevin grinned. "That's why the dining room chairs are different. We drowned the old ones."

Rosalind did not comment as she got an insider's picture of how confused things had become for them all. She hoped Laura's therapy was helping.

∾ ∾ ∾

Sean and Jim O'Brian, his friend and congressman from New York, were delightful at dinner, letting the cousins chatter about sports and camp schedules. No one mentioned Rosalind's late start or her New York theatrical experience as O'Brian briefed her on the role of a congressional intern.

"I've made you a special campaign intern. You'll be compiling reports sent in by campaign offices across New York State and making hundreds of calls. A lot of it is grunt work, but it's very critical grunt work. The polls show we can't lose, but we can't get fat and sassy either or Congressman O'Brian won't evolve into the honorable Senator O'Brian.''

"What are we going to play tonight?" Kevin was tired of hearing about office routine.

"How about a challenging game of darts?" Sean stretched.

O'Brian excused himself from the challenge on the grounds of an early meeting the next day. He repeated his pleasure at having Rosalind on board the O'Brian campaign; he would look forward to seeing her in the morning.

The Connolly dart game turned out to be unexpectedly competitive. A few months before, Rosalind and Colin had discovered a Northampton bar with an English dart board. She had practiced and become quite skillful. Sean pretended to let her win the first game, frowned as she easily won the second and declared her the Connolly all-time champion as she won the third. He made a mental note to practice at his downtown club before their next match.

Rosalind laughed as Sean insisted they have one swimming race before calling it a night on the games. When Sean was declared winner of the Connolly swimming competition for the evening, she quipped, "Good thing you won, Uncle Sean, or we'd be playing new games until sunrise."

He snapped at her bottom with a damp towel. "I thought having three wise-ass kids in the house was enough, but I had to go get me a fourth." He stopped short. "Do you play bridge?"

"So-so," she said with a smile, not wanting to admit proficiency.

"Sure you're not a ringer at bridge, too?"

"You'll never know until we play, will you?"

૭   ૭   ૭

It was only ten o'clock, but Rosalind yawned as she entered the warm kitchen dressed in a soft terry robe where Sean was supervising milk and cake dispersal, scotch in hand.

Kevin stifled a yawn of his own as he finished his second piece of cake. Sean, Jr., blinked hard, fighting it, before he too yawned. Terry tried to conceal hers behind a large bite of cake.

Sean laughed. "You all are unusually full of vinegar at this hour, fighting to stay up another four hours, but tonight you look wasted."

Sean shook his head at them. "All I want to know, Rosie, is who wore out whom?"

Kevin raised a weary hand. "The verdict is mutual."

"Then the evening is adjourned," Sean announced. "I have to run back downtown for a late meeting anyway. Rosie, you can ride to work with me tomorrow morning. Then we'll see about getting you a car of your own, if you like."

"Oh, I'd like." She smiled. Her Washington remedy was turning out better than she had anticipated.

∽ ∽ ∽

The next morning Rosalind chatted happily with Sean as they left Great Falls and drove in the morning sun across Key Bridge toward the Hill. She dropped into silence as the white marble of the Capitol came into view. This was her father's Washington. She loved to picture him striding across the green lawns, stopping to shake hands and lobby for a bill during his years as senator. Part of him was still here for Rosalind.

"Where was my father's office?" she asked softly.

"O'Brian's office is in the Cannon Building on Independence Avenue. That's the street we're on now. It's the House side of the Capitol. On the other side of the Capitol are the Senate buildings. Bill's office was in the Russell Building, a fine old piece of architecture. You'll have to get over and see it. And if you do a first-rate job for O'Brian this summer, you'll help get him moved to the other side of these political tracts."

Rosalind laughed at that. "I'll do my best, but I suspect he can do perfectly well with just you."

"Every little bit helps." Sean patted her shoulder as he stopped the car to let her out. "And you're getting to be more than a little bit. Tell O'Brian I'll see him at lunch."

Rosalind admired the fine old marble and the winding stairs of the Cannon Building even though Jim O'Brian wanted to be on the other side of the Hill.

O'Brian welcomed her and guided her into the office, stopping at the reception desk for brief introductions and continuing down a short hallway into a spacious back room with rows of desks and files. With his shaggy dark hair and round glasses, he reminded Rosalind of an old schoolboy.

He motioned to a young man who looked like a younger version of himself, down to the tortoiseshell frames of the round glasses. "Byron, meet Rosalind Connolly. I want you to show her the campaign stuff we discussed."

Byron nodded cheerfully and stuck out a hand. "Welcome to O'Brian headquarters. We call this our war room."

Byron spent the next several hours explaining the ward and precinct organization of New York State. Each ward or precinct had a character of its own and each leader had his or her own personality. Rosalind's job was to call the leaders and get updates on how they stood on the O'Brian campaign. She was to introduce herself and say she and her uncle Sean Connolly were helping with Congressman O'Brian's campaign. Stressing the family relationship was important, because many of the old-timers had been fervent Bill Connolly supporters.

Welcome to politics, thought Rosalind, as Byron handed her another list of names and numbers. This was the first time she had been exposed to the mechanics of a campaign. She had not realized how detailed and personal a campaign could be.

Her first phone calls were made tentatively. One ward leader asked her to repeat her name three times before she stopped whispering. But soon she warmed to the voices of supporters. By dinnertime, she had weather and campaign reports from all corners of New York State.

After dinner, she joined her cousins for the traditional late-night swim. Rosalind had been too busy indoors to notice how muggy the afternoon had become until she slipped into the cool water. It felt wonderful. "Oooh!" Her head disappeared under the water as Kevin and Sean, Jr., played Duck-a-Cousin.

She was saved by the telephone bell. Mrs. Railes stuck her head out the back door and called for Rosalind. Kevin showed her where the pool phone was hidden—in a box that looked like a raised flagstone.

Perhaps it was Colin. He was due back soon.

"Hello?" her voice lilted. Her face fell quickly as she recognized Dianne's breathy "Hello, Rosie."

Rosalind dropped into a monotone for her terse replies. "It's fine. . . . Uncle Sean is fine. . . . They're fine, too. . . . Give Billy and Timothy my love." She tolerantly listened to Dianne gush about the upcoming trip to Ireland and Wales, politely declining to come along for the tenth time.

Dianne closed the one-sided conversation by saying she planned to be in Washington the next weekend. She wanted to see Rosalind before they left. Dianne breezed on, ignoring Rosalind's silence, sending her love to all before she rushed off to a dinner party.

Rosalind pushed the phone back into its camouflaged niche.

"What's happening?" Kevin asked.

"Not much. Dianne's coming down next weekend."

"Yeah?" Kevin's teenaged face lit up. "Do you think she'll take us all to dinner and let us get plastered like last time?" He raced for the pool and tucked into a bombshell.

Rosalind ignored the splash and walked into the house, dragging her towel.

∽ ∽ ∽

The next morning was overcast. The dark humid atmosphere tainted everyone's mood at breakfast. Sean leafed through piles of newspapers between bites, occasionally handing a page to Rosalind or Kevin without comment.

He tossed the *Post* aside. "Time to get to the office. Oh, Rosie, I forgot to tell you. Your keys are on the hall table, with a car to go with them in the drive."

"Hey, thanks!" she called after him, jumping up along with the cousins to take a look at it.

"Ask the guard in the Cannon Building garage for your space number," he instructed. "O'Brian has it all set for you."

Although she preferred Italian racers, the pale yellow Mustang gleaming at them suited her fine for the summer. Instantly, she named the car Yellowbird.

She glanced down the driveway to check for the agents' car parked by the entrance pillars. She noticed a dark head in the passenger seat. Her pulse quickened. It was Colin. The dark morning was beginning to shine.

There was so much to tell him, she thought as she slipped the little car into gear. She had missed him as much emotionally as physically.

She eased Yellowbird to a stop beside the dark Secret Service car, rolled down the window and grinned at Colin and T. Her two main men were back. "Hi!" she called, waiting for Colin to roll down the window. "Welcome back!"

Colin waved behind the glass.

Rosalind frowned, floored the accelerator and skidded out of the driveway.

"You never quite know how women will react, do you?" Colin spoke quietly, almost to himself.

"Not that one, anyway," added T. "Welcome back."

❧ ❧ ❧

Surrounded by relatives in Great Falls and aides in the office, it was difficult for Rosalind to arrange time to see Colin alone. And he wasn't helping. If anything, he seemed to be avoiding her.

After three days of frustrated attempts to talk to him privately, the opportunity came during a lunch break at Timberlake's, a popular pub near the office.

Rosalind had declined a lunch offer from Byron and walked the two blocks down Pennsylvania Avenue alone with her shadows. She liked the casual feeling of the restaurant. No one paid particular attention to anyone, including her. Occasionally a head would turn in her direction, but mixed in with Washington writers and political types who considered themselves celebrities in their own right, she had never been bothered. It was a comfortable spot.

The tables were crowded. Rosalind turned to Colin and T, waiting in line behind. "Let's eat together. We'll get a table faster."

"Good idea," T replied for himself and Colin.

Midway through their hamburgers, T's beeper went off. No one paid attention around them. There were enough beepers in the room to supply the staff of a hospital.

T pushed a button. "T Smith, call the signal board," insisted the small black box. "They could at least wait until after lunch," grumbled T, rising and going to the phone.

"Colin." Rosalind leaned forward intently. "When can I see you alone? Where are you staying?"

"I have a tiny townhouse in Alexandria. It's a postage stamp, but it's me own."

"I haven't heard about your trip or anything. And you haven't heard about Dianne's latest number with my theater job." She tried to laugh lightly. "You've been avoiding me since you got back."

"Perhaps." He looked down from her gaze and picked up his coffee.

She bit off her one-word question as T returned.

"Shit! I have to go see the commander right now." He took a farewell bite of his burger. "Cold already. It figures."

"What's going on over there?" Colin asked.

"The old man's got a flea in his ear about vacation schedules. It shouldn't take more than an hour." He turned to Rosalind. "You aren't planning any public speeches or mad dashes this afternoon, are you?"

"I could dream one up for you if you'd like."

T shook his head and made a fast exit. "Alone at last." Rosalind tried to keep it light.

"With only fifty people three feet away," added Colin.

"I know it's more difficult to get away here than it was at school, but I could meet you after bedtime . . . on your nights off. The fence by the road isn't wired. I could slip through any time I wanted to."

Colin shook his head. "It isn't the logistics that are the problem, Rosalind. It's the relationship. I think you're one of the most fantastic young ladies I've ever known. But you are you. You are not an ordinary girl. And I may seem like your Prince Charming right now, but I'm an ordinary man."

Rosalind felt her throat thicken. "Oh, Colin, you're . . ." She fought to not understand him. "Colin, I need you now, more than ever. You don't know . . ."

"I know I'm pushing forty and you're twenty. You need me because I'm here. And I don't want to need you too much." He looked away from her strained face.

"You can't just desert me like this. Period, end quote. Let's meet tonight and talk. Please."

"Rosie, you'll see it's the only right thing to do. You'll meet young men in your own circle and . . ."

"And that's bullshit. Tell me the truth. Did you meet some other girl in Ireland?"

He looked at her tenderly. "No. No, I didn't meet any other girl. You know that's not the issue."

"Then it doesn't make any sense to me." Her voice rose. "Why are you doing this to us?"

"Hey!" He glanced around. "No scenes, not for Rosalind Connolly!"

"It looks like everything worth doing or having is not for Rosalind Connolly!" She grabbed her purse and stormed out of the restaurant.

Colin followed because he had to. It was his job. But more than that, he wanted her to be safe. He hadn't told her how much he had missed her, dreamed about making love with her, wished hundreds of times she could have shared the castles and old stone inns with him. There was no point in telling her. He had realized during his vacation that the affair had to stop before he was in too deep. But he couldn't bring himself to the point of asking for a transfer. He rationalized that he had to be certain she was all right.

∽ ∽ ∽

The rest of the week Rosalind struggled. She accepted a lunch date with Byron and flirted outrageously, hoping to get a reaction out of Colin. She saw none. When Byron responded warmly and asked her out to dinner, she backed off abruptly. She wasn't even mildly attracted to Byron. She couldn't look at Colin and believe in her heart that she would never make love with him again. He couldn't really have changed so much. If he were completely sure, she thought, he never would have come back as her agent.

The busy pace of the campaign helped distract her thoughts, but inside, she was hurting.

By the time Rosalind met Dianne at the Hay-Adams Hotel on Friday night, she was almost glad to see her. Although Dianne was a double-crosser, she was not a deserter.

They agreed upon a casual evening and grabbed a cab for the Jockey Club. "It looks like a French inn off in the country," Rosalind observed in surprise; Dianne usually preferred elegant dining. But as the waiter in black tie guided them to their table with its checkered cloth, Rosalind realized that this country inn was not for farmers.

She pushed at the escargots without appetite, bobbing the creatures in and out of the garlic butter.

Dianne stopped midsentence, aware that Rosalind was not listening. She looked at her daughter carefully. "Rosalind, you look thin. Do you feel well?"

Forcing a smile, Rosalind said, "I'm fine. I've been working hard on O'Brian's campaign. He jokes that he's getting the *bugs* out of the Republican technique for his run at the presidency."

Dianne's humor was on a back burner. She smiled thinly.

"Rosie, why don't you drop Tony a note and tell him how nice it would be if he met the twins and me in England—or anywhere else abroad that's convenient?"

Rosalind stared at her mother. Did Dianne think a note from her could carry any weight with Tony? "Why? Why should I write to him? Doesn't he want to meet you?"

"I've asked him, but he has so many business commitments." Dianne sighed into her bouillon. Anything might help and a note from Rosalind would certainly surprise him.

"Mother . . . " Rosalind spoke slowly. "What do you think a woman should do if the man she wants to be with is backing away from her?"

Dianne refocused on her daughter. Was Rosalind reading the tacky articles in the *Enquirer* about Tony? But it was a good question, Dianne reflected. What should a woman do?

"I suppose she could find out why he is backing away or try to be as appealing as possible. Or she could back away herself and wait for him to come to his senses. Or she could simply walk away and keep looking. There are millions of people out there."

"But if she can't, because . . . because she doesn't want to?"

"It depends on the ties, darling. Both his and hers. Mutual need, marriage, whatever. But if the man doesn't need the woman anymore, it's very difficult. Then, if she wants him, she has somehow to make him want her."

"But if he doesn't respond and she really needs him?"

Dianne sighed again. "I don't know. She really should try not to show it and be brave, although sometimes I think showing it can be the most effective thing. When he feels she needs him—emotionally—it can make him feel strong. It can touch a tender corner of his soul."

Dianne spoke softly, thinking of the early days of Tony's courtship.

Rosalind chafed. The vague conversation wasn't helping her confusion about Colin one bit.

"It isn't easy, darling." Dianne smiled. "We simply must do the best we can with the men in our lives." Dianne felt warmed by Rosalind's concern for her trials with Tony. It was good to be back on Rosalind's bestest friend list.

As they said good-night at the hotel, Dianne ran down her Washington agenda. "Tomorrow I'm lunching with Russ Gilmore, the man who was secretary of defense for your daddy. Remember him? He visited us in New York several times."

Rosalind had a sudden image of a tall ascetic-looking man who seemed to worship Dianne. He resembled Dr. Sorokin at Smith.

"Tomorrow night I'll dine with you and the cousins in Great Falls. I promised Laura I would give her a first-hand account. Then, on Sunday, I'm having brunch with Iona Mitford, the art collector, and I'm flying back to New York about three. So we'll have lots of time to chat tomorrow at dinner. Sleep tight, darling."

∾ ∾ ∾

The next day Rosalind gulped down a five-inch-high corned beef sandwich carried in by Byron from a local deli while Dianne lunched with Russ Gilmore at Lion d'Or.

Russ had been in love with Dianne for twenty years. He found her vagueness ethereal and her *bons mots* refreshing. He was no less devoted to her as a lobbyist for the munitions industry than he had been as a member of Bill Connolly's cabinet. He thought she looked as lovely as ever in her sky-blue silk suit.

"Well. Here we are Russ, two old people who have survived—so far."

"You'll never be old, Dianne. You're like fine Bordeaux. You get smoother and smoother."

Dianne laughed spontaneously. Russ always had been able to lift her spirits. "You should talk about being smooth!"

"I have smoothed things for you across the years, haven't I?" He smiled, content to think of himself that way. "So tell me, my dearest Dianne, what needs smoothing or soothing today?"

They paused to order fillets of sole for Russ, a salad for Dianne and a vintage Meursault in honor of the reunion. When the wine arrived, Dianne began, "I don't know how to cope anymore, darling. Tony has become the satyr of the year. I cannot even pass by a newsstand without seeing his face, always with his nose half hidden behind some starlet's boobs. And that so-called actress . . ." She took a nervous gulp of wine.

"Nicole Turrell?"

"See? Even you know and you don't follow these seamy things."

Russ did follow them, because they concerned Dianne. Whenever Russ saw Tony featured in a magazine or newspaper, he bought it and carefully hid it in the folds of the *Times* until he could find a private moment to study it. "Well, I'm not sure what to say. As you yourself have said before, during another marriage, at another time long ago, men will act like men."

"It's different," she said impatiently. "Surely you can see how different. You know Bill was discreet. Yes, it was terribly painful, but it wasn't public. Those tacky, tasteless women were indiscreet later, after his death, but at least they didn't sully his image while he was alive. Tony would sling his filth on page one if he could arrange it."

"Have you spoken to Tony about it? Told him how deeply it offends you?"

"I might as well talk to this glass."

Russ refilled it. "Are things as bad as I fear? Are the rumors based on truth?"

"Probably worse," she whispered. "He began as my protector—so strong, so rich and powerful. He promised me everything, promised always, always to be there if I needed him." She shrugged. "Then I married him. . . ."

She stared at the white mushrooms on her salad and watched as the waiter delicately added a turn of freshly ground peppercorns.

"Mmm." Russ nodded sympathetically, waiting for the waiter to finish serving.

They concentrated on their lunches for a few minutes, exchanging trivial comments on their children.

Over the second bottle of wine, Dianne poured out her soul. "Oh, Russ, just thinking about Tony and those other women—filthy, loose women who would sleep with anything—has made me completely frigid. I can't bear for him to touch me. I can't even stand being physically close to him anymore." She illustrated her feelings with a long shudder.

Russ didn't like the thought of Tony touching Dianne either, although Russ had never made physical love to her. The image of Bill Connolly touching her had bothered him equally. Dianne seemed above those sweaty carnal pastimes to him.

"Men are all so self-centered—except you, darling." She reached out and touched his hand with hers. "You've always been there when I've needed you."

Russ's narrow face opened up into a wide smile and he

raised his goblet to the chaste image he cherished. "I'll always be there for you, Dianne. You know that."

"I think what bothers me . . ." Her words were beginning to sound slurred. "If I'm very, very honest with myself."

"Is that wise?" Russ asked lightly. "I try to avoid that whenever possible."

She continued as though uninterrupted, "I think what bothers me most is that he's out of control—out of my control, that is. It doesn't matter what I do or say, I'm beginning to believe he really doesn't give a damn anymore." Her eyes widened in surprise at her own statement. How terrible if it really is true, she thought.

"To tell you the truth, Miss Scarlett, honey, frankly, I jus' don't give a damn," misquoted Russ with a bad attempt at a southern accent. "And Miss Scarlett, you jus' shouldn't give a li'l ol' damn yourself. Tell him to stuff his corn pone right up one of his big ol' wells!"

Russ's attempt at comedy sent Dianne into uncontrollable giggles, bordering on hysterics. The pinstriped banker sitting next to them sent disapproving looks.

"I think we'd better go." Dianne hiccuped. "I have to go sober up for dinner." The thought sent her back into the giggles. "Sober up for dinner. That's funny. I sound like a lush."

"You are getting a little tipsy." Russ patted her hand. "But on you it looks marvelous." He waved for the check. When he glanced back at Dianne, tears were quietly rolling down her cheeks. "Hey, what is all this?"

She shook her head. If she tried to speak, she would only cry more. Gratefully, she accepted his handkerchief and tried to stem the flow.

"Poor darling." Russ gently touched her damp cheek. "It doesn't get easier, does it? Shall we take a walk? The air might help. It is a beautiful summer day out there."

She wasn't certain why she was crying. Frustration with Tony? All the problems with Rosalind this summer? Or did seeing Russ make her more aware of the empty feeling she was carrying around inside her? "I'm sorry, Russ. I'm too old to carry on this way."

"You're never too old to be a beautiful woman who is still very sensitive. Remember that. Now, I'll take you back to your hotel and you can get some rest."

Dianne rewarded him with a small wobbly smile and attempted to rise gracefully. "I hope you're steadier than I am," she whispered as Russ hurried to help her. It was so nice. Russ was so manageable.

Heads turned as he almost carried her out, but he didn't mind. He was delighted that she chose him to lean on again.

ℒ   ℒ   ℒ

By dinnertime, Dianne was still suffering. She struggled valiantly to hold up her end of the conversation, giving reports on Billy and Timothy and promising to send them to Great Falls after they returned from Europe.

Sean arrived late. The cousins were already frolicking in the pool again and Rosalind and Dianne were quietly drinking coffee, Dianne still wearing her sunglasses.

Aware of Dianne's resistance to conventional glasses, Sean waved hello and teased, "Why don't you get yourself some half-glasses for reading like I have? I think they're kind of sexy."

"Sean, you darling man, I don't need these to see. I need them to keep from seeing. Russ Gilmore took me to lunch and positively plied me with wine. I should have eaten aspirin for dinner."

Sean laughed. "That wily old fox. I always knew he had the hots for you." He grinned as Mrs. Railes appeared with a plate piled high with roast beef. "This is great, Mrs. Railes, really great."

"When's Laura getting back?" Dianne asked, getting even for the slur on Russ.

"I don't know," he replied between bites. "Three, four weeks. She's resting and helping her mother with some big community project."

"I talked to her last week."

Sean stopped chewing. "How did she seem to you?"

"It's hard for her, Sean."

Sean glanced at Rosalind. He didn't know how much the cousins had told her. "I know. I hope the doctors up there can do some good," he muttered. "I'd like to take her along when I join the O'Brian campaign trail for a week in September."

"Oh, God, I remember how I hated that scene," Dianne said. "It's brutal. Do you have to put her through that? It's not as though you were running yourself."

"Did she put you up to this conversation, Dianne? I hope

not, because that particular matter is something Laura and I have to work out privately. A *Marino* poll is simply not acceptable."

Dianne retreated back to her coffee. Rosalind wished she could applaud her uncle without Dianne knowing. Dianne, who railed about others prying into her business, was the worst in the family for poking into others' affairs.

Dianne politely waited for Sean to finish dinner and the conversation remained nonspecific. Sean had forgiven her and was back to his normal good humor as Dianne kissed all goodbye and handed Rosalind a photocopied itinerary.

Rosalind was relieved to see her mother go. She walked outside toward the pool, looking for Terry. They could casually walk over to the Secret Service car and talk with Colin. He couldn't maintain the wall forever.

Colin wasn't on duty so she dropped that mission and walked with Terry along the lighted garden paths, stopping beside a raspberry patch. "When will they be ripe?" she asked Terry.

Terry inspected the hard green berries. "I don't remember what the gardener said. Sometime this summer, before we go back to school, I'm sure."

"The precise information I get from my family could fill a thimble." Rosalind laughed. She could feel her stomach muscles relax.

Terry echoed the laugh. "Maybe the boys can start a pool for when they ripen."

"Raspberries are about the only thing I can think of that sound like a good bet."

   ◈ ◈ ◈

The following Monday, the cousins flew to Rye to visit their mother and grandmother. Rosalind found herself tiptoeing in the carpeted halls. The Great Falls house seemed like a shell, lonely for the rowdies. Suddenly she had the space to miss the Eighth Street Theater crowd, especially Rich, and the dull ache gave way to silent rage at Dianne's high-handed actions. She was a prisoner of Dianne's images and of her name. That's what bothered Colin. Her name. What's in a name? A Rosalind by any other name would be freer, she thought.

That night, she lay in bed rigid, willing her toes to relax, then her calves, moving up to her forehead. But by the time she reached her hairline, the tension had returned to her feet. She rehashed remembered conversations with Colin. Had she done something specific that had turned him off? The protestations about age and status might only be polite covers for an emotional brush-off. Without him, she thought, there was no one—not one person in the world she could truly trust and confide in.

The three-year-old that all twenty-year-olds carry up their sleeves wanted to go hide her head in her mother's lap and spill out the frustrations. But she had the witch with the soft smile and cruel rationalizations for a mother. During Dianne's so-called visit, they had been together, but they had played their scenes beside each other in different rooms. The rooms had windows, but the windows didn't allow people through to touch or really talk.

ᴗ ᴗ ᴗ

In his cozy Alexandria townhouse, third nightcap in hand, Colin struggled with his own demons, torn between certainty that the affair with Rosalind had to end and his sympathy for Rosalind's summer traumas. He was acutely aware of her pain. He knew he could help. But how much pain would it ultimately cost her—and him?

ᴗ ᴗ ᴗ

It wasn't getting easier for Rosalind. She asked her uncle first and then Congressman O'Brian if she could take a few days off the end of the week to visit Grandma Bea in the Hamptons. Then she settled into a routine of O'Brian campaign lists by day and intrigue novels by night. Since Sean's hours were irregular and he was rarely home for dinner, Mrs. Railes allowed Rosalind to eat with her in the kitchen.

Despite her warmth, Mrs. Railes with her brisk efficiency didn't seem the right bosom for Rosalind to unload upon, although for one weak moment Rosalind thought she might break down and let it flow.

Mrs. Railes had poured coffee for them and asked gently, "Are you feeling a little glum over something particular, honey?"

"Oh, no, ma'am. We're just so busy with the campaign. I'm pretty tired."

"Maybe you should get out more. I like having you here,

but a pretty young lady shouldn't spend all her nights in. There must be some nice young men down there, working with the congressmen."

But I don't want any of them, Rosalind almost replied. Audibly, she let slip a little sigh. What advice could Mrs. Railes possibly give her on Colin? How could she understand a Rosalind Connolly dilemma?

"Maybe your Uncle Sean or his friend Congressman O'Brian could come up with some good prospects for you. Shall I put a little bee in his bonnet?" A mischievous smile broke the serious lines of Mrs. Railes' face.

"That's all right." She smiled at the older woman. "If I get too bored, I'll holler at him myself."

"Well, if you need a little help hollering, honey, you let me know."

"First thing."

Warmed by the communication, Rosalind fell asleep quickly. She awoke with the sun streaming in her window, but she felt better than she had in weeks.

In the afternoon she scored a convert to the O'Brian cause and announced proudly to Byron that a Queens leader on the "iffy" list was now solidly with them. She agreed to have lunch with him the next day to celebrate—"on one condition," she added.

"Anything other than registering Democratic."

"Don't wear a regimental-striped tie, just this once."

"They're all I have," he protested.

"Then celebrate in a turtleneck."

At that moment, O'Brian entered the room. "What are you celebrating?" He adjusted his horn-rimmed glasses and gave her an owlish frown.

Rosalind briefed him. He was properly impressed. "The more we have for this race, Rosalind, the more we have for the big one in two years."

"Isn't there some law against campaigning early?" she teased.

"Wise ass." His dark eyes twinkled. "You're a younger version of your father."

Rosalind looked at the book he was holding in his hand. "*Last Lady* by P. Lengstrom," she read. "What's that about?"

He frowned, having forgotten he was carrying it. "Some new book. I was sent a publisher's copy."

"About my father?"

"It's probably another one of those exaggerated jobs where some broad takes a few meetings and blows it up."

"May I read it?"

"Sure. But my guess is that it's not worth reading." He patted the slender volume. "Uh . . . just don't tell your mother I am loaning it to you. I don't want to lose her vote."

"She probably won't be in the country in November, anyway." Rosalind laughed.

"Well, remind her to get an absentee ballot." O'Brian grinned.

Rosalind's phone rang. It was a committee woman from Albany returning a call. O'Brian called "Congratulations, again," and returned to his office, taking the book with him.

The game of converting "maybe" to "committed" had its own challenge. She had learned to field questions about Laura sweetly, to pull the heartstrings when discussing her father and to listen. There was nothing minor politicians liked better than to tell her things about their local efforts. She was making progress with her lists and decided to keep plugging and delay going to the Hamptons until the weekend. She didn't tell Mrs. Railes, who was leaving that afternoon to visit her daughter. Sean was off at a meeting and there was no one else to tell.

Thursday morning she was awakened by the sound of a car door slamming. She heard Sean call to his driver, "Wait five minutes. I forgot something."

Rosalind looked at her alarm. Barely seven forty-five. He must have an early meeting. Awake, she decided to get up and go in early herself. She showered and dressed quickly, then made the bed, remembering that no magic fingers would have it back in order by evening for her—or for Uncle Sean. She decided to surprise him with an organized bedroom. He never would have stopped to make the bed.

Humming cheerfully, she entered the room, walked toward the bed and froze at the foot of it. There, on Sean's pillow, was a blond head and a bare shoulder. Rosalind surveyed the rumpled bedclothes and the discarded cocktail dress on the floor.

The head turned and a hand emerged, revealing long red nails.

She's so young, thought Rosalind, noticing dark at the roots of the long hair.

The girl frowned and opened her large brown eyes.

146

"What . . . ?"she sat up, startled, exposing a slender body and small breasts. She grabbed at the bedsheet to cover herself and stared blankly at Rosalind. "Who are you?" The girl looked terrified.

"I'm just the day maid. I'll come back later." Rosalind almost ran from the room, out the door and into the car, breathing hard. Her reactions were mixed. She knew her uncle had a roving eye. She had seen him in action in Aspen. But in his own home? She felt a sense of outrage on Laura's behalf. The bleached blond looked like a call girl. Why should that make it better or worse? What was the difference between Sean sleeping with a call girl or a . . . regular girl? But to bring her into the house—Laura's home, too—was terrible form. She drove blindly across the Potomac and down Independence Avenue into the Cannon garage.

Rosalind wished she had kept to her original schedule and left the previous night. Had the girl believed she was a maid? Would she mention the incident to Sean? Suspicions of her uncle's wanderings were one thing, but proof in hand—or in bed—was another. Would he be upset? Feel guilty?

Rosalind looked at the Buffalo ward leader list and reached for the phone. She concentrated on O'Brian's campaign for the rest of the day.

As Rosalind pulled Yellowbird out of the Cannon garage, she debated between going to Great Falls and acting as though nothing unusual had happened, and going directly to the beach. She had lots of summer clothes at the beach house and didn't need to pack anything. She pulled over to the curb and rested her head on the steering wheel, trying to decide.

T eased the Secret Service escort car behind her and turned to Colin. "You better see what's wrong."

"Why me? You're the senior officer."

"I'm driving, that's why. Go check her out."

Colin walked to the passenger side of the bright car and tapped on the glass. Rosalind raised her head and stared at him blindly. He tried the door; it was open and he slid in. "Are you feeling sick?"

He looked at her pinched face. She looked thin and in critical need of a good hug. "Want to talk about it?"

"Are we back to talking suddenly?" she asked defensively.

"If you like."

She expelled the breath she had been holding and nodded. "How would you like me to drive you home? You look beat."

"I can't . . . I mean I'm not sure I should go there. It could be embarrassing for . . . me and Uncle Sean." The late afternoon sun caught the green flecks in her troubled eyes. "I found some bleached blond in his bed this morning. Colin, I don't know what to do. Will you drive me to the Hamptons?"

"If that's where you're heading, we have to follow anyway, but it's a long drive from here."

"Not to National." She grinned.

"You're not getting me on one of those little puddle jumpers out to the Island. No way."

"If I go, you have to go."

"Don't be unreasonable."

"You've been unreasonable for weeks." She paused and dropped her bravado. "Colin, how can you not want me anymore? Just like that?"

"Rosie, you know it isn't 'just like that.' I'm trying to stay away for both our sakes, but . . ." He stopped, watching the tears begin to well in her eyes. "Oh, I do want you."

"Then don't fight me," she choked. "Don't stay away when I need you more than anything in the world. It doesn't have to be forever if that scares you."

"That could make it worse."

"Colin." Her hand gripped his thigh. "Please."

He tried to lighten the mood. "Since you're being polite about it and you promise our pilot isn't a kamikaze, let's go to the beach."

"And not as strangers," she insisted.

"As more than strangers."

She searched his blue eyes for the absence of barriers. She sat back, satisfied.

Gently, he took her hand. "Still on the pill?"

"I knew you couldn't stay away forever."

"Anyone ever tell you that you're a wise ass?"

"Never."

"Then let me be the first."

Their laughter was interrupted by Smith's beep. Colin took over the driver's seat while Rosalind ran back to tell T the change in plans. She refused to let them go home and pack. There was plenty of stuff at the beach house.

148

The Connolly beachfront compound had private guards so T called headquarters and canceled the backup crew. East Hampton was completely booked for the summer weekend. The only place with space was the Bill Connolly house. Rosalind insisted that they all stay there rather than with Grandma Bea, even though Dianne's twelve-bedroom house, still known as the Bill Connolly place, was staffed only by one aging house-keeper, Molly, and her gardener husband, Tom. With a tightly scheduled weekend of garden parties and dinners, Bea did not object. So far, Rosalind remained in charge.

Rosalind assigned T and Colin to bedrooms on opposite sides of the house, insisting she would feel better protected that way. She didn't give Colin the opportunity to struggle with his conscience that night. Rosalind joined him in his large airy room with a beach view. They made the fast love of the needy, followed by the long, lingering love of desire. Cuddled close to Colin, Rosalind fell into a sound sleep, soothed by the rhythms of the surf and Colin's deep breathing.

The weekend was good for all of them, although T felt self-conscious about wearing bathing suits and shirts that had be-longed to Bill Connolly. "It's like wearing a goddamn flag," he protested to Colin. "Almost sacrilegious." But Colin liked the fact that his hero had walked these same beaches in this very clothing.

Accustomed to seeing the sands filled with volleyball nets, sailboats and cousins, Rosalind thought the beach seemed asleep. They filled the void themselves, swimming, playing badminton and dragging Rosalind's catamaran out of the garage. To housekeeper Molly's initial terror, Rosalind insisted on making lasagna for them all. Colin made the salad and fixed the garlic bread while T went out for strawberries and cheesecake.

"This is great." T paused between mouthfuls. "If all else fails, you can turn this house into a restaurant."

Rosalind laughed and shook her head. "Zoning problems."

"It's delicious, Miss Rosalind," said the old gardener, Tom. He and his wife, Molly, had protested against dining with them. Only when the trio set the kitchen table, did they relax. It was dinner on their ground.

Initially Molly had been taken aback by the "goings-on." "What with the one man black and the other white, who knows what to think?" she had said to Tom earlier. Now, Molly finished a second piece of cheesecake and smiled. "You did yourself proud, Miss Rosalind. I can't remember having this much fun in my kitchen since your daddy had his crazy gang running in and out. It was a regular circus, but it was nice."

Rosalind wished T would vanish so she could give Colin a hug of triumph. Old Molly would never notice; she wasn't really aware of what T and Colin's roles were. Instead, Rosalind turned to Molly and kissed her cheek. "Thank you, Molly."

Eyes watery with age and sentiment, Molly patted Rosalind's cheek. "You always were a good young'n, Miss. You always with a book and your naughty brothers with their horns and little drums. They were much noisier than you ever were, Miss." She smiled. "You was the apple of your daddy's eye. He'd be happy to know you growed up to be such a good cook."

"Do you really think so?"

"He loved eating, he did. Half the time he'd be too busy to wait for dinner, but he'd always come to me. He could charm the stew right out of my pot, he could. And he did, many a time. Since the time he was a little boy himself."

Rosalind loved hearing Molly talk about the old days with her father, but it was also a beautiful night for a walk on the moonlit beach. Soon they would be back in Washington, with only the Potomac to fill the need for surf. She rose and looked at Colin. "It is now time for the traditional evening stroll on the sands of the Bea hive."

Colin and T picked up their plates and headed for the sink. "Don't mind the dishes. I'll get them." Molly waved them out of her kitchen.

Molly and Tom seemed content to share the cleanup detail as Rosalind and her agents followed the moonlit sand to the ocean's edge.

Colin's eyes narrowed, focusing toward the limitless east. "That's a coast guard cutter out there."

"How can you tell?" T demanded.

"By the size and the lights, sir. They're easy to spot, so easy it's amazing that they ever move in on smugglers. You can see them for miles. That one's more than a mile out."

The breeze was smooth and warm. The full moon was surrounded by stars that seemed only an arm's length away. Rosalind felt a magic in the air while Colin was discussing boats.

"T." She gently placed a hand on his arm. "I forgot my sweater. Could you run back for it, please?"

"It must be eighty degrees out here!" he protested.

"There's a wind." She gave a mock shiver.

"If you insist," agreed T, "but only because you're a great cook and I want to change for a swim. Just don't leave the compound so I can find you." He jogged back toward the house.

Colin chuckled. "You do love to manipulate, don't you?"

"I just wanted to be alone with you."

Although the sky was clear, an offshore storm was kicking up breakers, sending phosphorescent sparks into the foam. Rosalind gripped Colin's hand; the surge of the waves in the endless ocean made her feel very small.

"When I was a little girl, Dianne would bring the boys and me out here for night walks. We loved it, especially when it was after bedtime. She never talked during those walks. She concentrated on what she called 'letting the wind blow out my mind.' I think I'm finally beginning to understand what she meant by that."

"Did you have good times here—generally?" Colin stared out at the waves, pulling the sound into his mind to bring back to Washington. He loved the beach, which had had no part in his midwestern upbringing.

"Yes and no. I remember lots of good times with the cousins, but it seems to me that Dianne was either very merry or off limits in those days. We played poem games. Billy and Timothy and I had to write poems about her and she would write them about us. Sometimes we wrote them about Grandma Bea or cousins—even visitors sometimes. Once I wrote one about Tony, before they were married. I remember it ended with, 'If you want good garlic with your baloney, make sure you dine with Tony Macaroni.' That ended our poetry game for that summer. I couldn't have been more than nine or ten."

"A confirmed wise ass." Colin gave her a pat to emphasize the location.

T's shirt appeared, a pale apparition against the dark sand.

Colin dropped Rosalind's hand. "Why didn't you smile, man, so we could see you."

"And break my cover?" T laughed. "No way. I'm best at night."

"Me too," whispered Colin as T dove into the surf.

Later, when the house was quiet and they were salty with lovemaking, they tiptoed outside, carrying only towels, and let the ocean refresh them. Even in the dark, Colin was uncomfortable naked, as though part of him was waiting for a searchlight to catch them on the beach.

Confident as a water nymph, Rosalind dismissed his fears. "We've done it for years. The guards patrol outside the compound and there are fewer tourists every year. Mummy says the first few years after my father died it was terrible. People lined up in the streets outside." She giggled. "One year Billy and Timmy were going to sell the tourists pictures of us all, snapshots Mummy had taken herself. She almost had a heart attack. I can remember pleading with her that Billy and Timmy were only little boys, that they didn't mean anything bad by it, but she punished them anyway. Hmm . . . I don't even remember what the punishment was."

"You and Dianne have been at it for a long time." Colin lit a cigarette and was disconcerted by the revealing flare of sulfur.

"Only a couple of decades. Oh, Colin. . . ." She leaned against a sand dune. "This summer has been like a war. I don't want it to be that way. I try to make peace, but every time things seem better, she throws me another curve."

"She probably believes she's protecting you."

Rosalind shivered and grabbed a beach towel. "Bullshit. When I need her to be supportive, she's lost in her own clouds."

She inhaled a deep breath of sea air. "But no matter how much I hate her sometimes, I love her. She is my mother. And she's the only parent I have."

The plaintive tone drew Colin closer and he added his arms to the towel swaddling her. He nuzzled her shoulder. "Come on, little girl, let's go back inside to cuddle." Suddenly, he jerked back. "Ow! That hurt." She had bitten his ear.

"To you, I'm no longer a little girl. Come inside and I'll prove it."

"Little girls bite," he retorted, feeling more comfortable on the return trip with his towel firmly wrapped around his waist. Rosalind danced ahead of him, unconcerned, with her soggy towel half draped over her shoulder. With Colin back, she felt free and secure.

ᗧ ᗧ ᗧ

They flew back Monday morning and Rosalind went directly to O'Brian's office, not wanting to stop in Great Falls lest she run into any extraneous bodies. She held her breath as she dialed her uncle's office to make certain he knew she was back.

Sean seemed relaxed and happy to see her, she noted with relief. He asked about Grandma Bea first and then told her Dianne was waiting for her to call. She and the twins had just arrived back in New York.

Rosalind wondered what mood her mother the manipulator was in. But duty called and so did she.

Dianne was exploding with breathless excitement. She interrupted Rosalind's report on the campaign to announce she had arranged for Rosalind to attend the Royal Academy of Dramatic Arts in London, starting in September. "It'll be so exciting for you—the theater center of the world!"

"But I'm all set to go back to Smith!"

"I'm not interrupting your education, darling, merely broadening it. You'll stay with Lord and Lady Boulder, cousins of Lady Eleanor's. Their own children are grown and they are absolutely delighted with the prospect of having a teenager around again."

"But what will I do?" persisted Rosalind, ignoring the "teenager" reference.

"You'll be studying directing and stage management. Lord Henry is arranging it now."

"I'll have to think about it."

153

"Everything's all set. I knew you would just love the idea."

"I said I'll think about it. I'll call you tonight."

"Oh, dear, Harvey Fineman is throwing a welcome-back thing for me tonight. Just a casual affair, but it could run late. Buzz me tomorrow."

Rosalind asked to speak to her brothers. They both sounded glad to hear from her. Billy reported that the Boulders were "a bit of all right." Timmy said they wouldn't mind spending a year with the Boulders themselves, but Dianne said they had to finish Andover first.

Dianne, who had obviously been eavesdropping on the extension, broke into the conversation. She told Rosalind she was sending Billy and Timothy to Great Falls for the last ten days of August. It had been cleared with Laura already. Then she blithely signed off before Rosalind could ask anything else.

It was already the first week of August. The cousins were due back the end of the week. Then add her brothers. How could she spend more time with Colin when brothers and cousins would be snooping around twenty-four hours a day? But that irritation seemed minor compared to Dianne's latest scheme—London. What courses were being arranged? Would Smith accept credits that weren't part of their official junior-year-abroad program? Why couldn't Dianne ever do things through normal channels?

Rosalind had no strong aversion to spending a year studying in London. She had never considered it, but she hated Dianne throwing things at her out of the blue.

The precinct lists could not hold her attention. She was grateful for the interruption when Byron stopped by her desk to compliment her on her tan. "Actually, I feel a bit feverish. I think it's more of a burn."

He stared at the red tip of her nose. "You should have built a base earlier in the summer."

"If, if, if . . . 'if ifs and ands were pots and pans there'd be no need of tinkers,' " she quoted from Saint Joan. At least she had gotten something out of the Saint Joan fiasco, if only a few obscure quotes.

"Why don't you take the day off and go buy some sun cream? Things are slow. Half the people we're trying to reach are on vacation."

"Thanks, Byron. I could use some air." It was difficult to

think clearly in a room full of pounding typewriters and ringing phones.

She turned from the marble stairs on the Independence Avenue side of the Cannon Building toward the Library of Congress. Peripherally, she noticed the agents moving into position. Colin and T were off duty because they had worked the weekend. Colin had promised to meet her later; she would finally get to see his house in Alexandria—or was it Arlington?

Arlington. A bell rang in her mind and she knew where she wanted to go. She stepped out from the curb and flagged a cab. It was sheer luck; cabs were rare during midsummer tourist season.

She watched the agents frantically searching for a second cab. Quickly she instructed her driver to cross the bridge and head for Arlington National Cemetery. She wanted to think by her father's grave.

The summer sky was lending an artificial blue to the Potomac and the humidity was high enough to make the air feel thick. The driver turned up his rock radio music and said with a Middle Eastern accent, "We have some summer music, yes?"

The music created a momentary barrier between Rosalind and her thoughts. "God, it's hot," she spoke aloud.

"What you say?" shouted the cabbie.

"I said it's hot!" Rosalind screamed over the music.

"Okay, I give you breeze," he countered with a gold-toothed smile as he pressed his foot on the accelerator. They swerved forward, around traffic, tires screeching on the hot pavement.

"Hey, I want to go to the cemetery, not get into it," she protested.

"Is better, yes?" The driver stuck his hand out the window to show her how the air was blowing in. One-handed driving didn't help the ride. The cab jerked through the Arlington gates and jolted to a stop.

"Would you wait for me a few minutes? It's terribly important." She wondered how to guarantee that he would wait. Should she pay him up front or promise a large tip?

"No. Muzafar wait, Muzafar lose money."

Rosalind took a deep breath. "I'll give you an extra twenty dollars to wait."

"Give it to me now and I wait," Muzafar agreed.

What should she do? Suddenly she remembered a scene

from an old mobster movie. She dug into her wallet for a twenty-dollar bill and tore it in half.

"What you do!" Muzafar was aghast.

"Half now and half when I return, plus the fare," she announced. "That way you'll be certain to wait."

"Muzafar is honest!" he raged. "I wait with whole money."

"I'll be back soon," she promised, feeling proud of herself. Dianne and the twins would love the story.

She turned up the narrow path climbing the hill to the foot of the obelisk. Neat white markers spread out on both sides of the path, standing at quiet attention. The place seemed deserted. She saw no other life except a grounds keeper in the distance with a basket and a rake. She guessed it was too early on a Monday morning for the tourist buses.

She sat on one of the small stone benches set on the edge of the marble plaza surrounding the monument and stared at the inscription that she knew by heart:

If we are to improve the race, if we are to win our great battles, we must place our nation first and our lives second.

᧞   ᧞   ᧞

It was a nice philosophy for governing a country or fighting a war, but it didn't tell her much about dealing with Dianne, unless she interpreted it to mean Dianne was wrong to keep the press at bay.

She rubbed her sweaty forehead and wondered if Bill Connolly would like the way she was growing up. Would the affairs of state have kept him away from her emotionally, if not physically? It hit her that he would have been relatively young when his second term finished—not even fifty. Would there have been time for travel and sharing things? Would he have liked Billy and Timothy and her? He might have been proud of her performance as Saint Joan and let her finish the run. London. Dianne. Her thoughts regressed beyond present concerns. Would he have let Dianne constantly plague her about cutting her hair? She felt her throat thicken and she swallowed back tears. She wanted to hug the base of the obelisk and ask, "Do you think my hair is too long, Daddy?" Instead, she clenched her fists across her solar plexus and closed her eyes, wishing she had brought flowers to place in the marble vase at the foot of the obelisk.

The sound of high heels clattered on the marble. She straightened her back and opened her eyes to see a slender woman dressed in a soft floral print approach the vase. The woman's fine blond hair swirled about her face as she leaned down and removed the dying roses and replaced them with a huge bouquet of lavender anemones. Rosalind didn't recognize the woman. Why would she bring flowers? The woman turned around to meet Rosalind's stare. Smiling gently, she wiped away a tear. Her step faltered, but she looked steadily at Rosalind with a question in her eyes.

"Some sadnesses never quite disappear, do they?" The voice was clear, with a trace of Scandinavian accent.

"Who are you?" The words escaped from Rosalind's mind. "Why did you . . . bring flowers?"

"Do you mind?" The woman perched on the edge of Rosalind's bench. "My name is Pia Lengstrom and I worked for Bill Connolly when he was a senator . . . and knew him a long, long time."

"What was he like?" Somehow this woman seemed familiar. Her voice, perhaps, her name—something was ringing a quiet little bell in Rosalind's mind.

Pia raised her eyebrows. "You're asking?"

Rosalind nodded.

"To me, he was grace and wit and humor. He had a strength and warmth I've never known before or since." Pia's pale blue eyes became dreamy and the corners of her finely chiseled lips turned up. She stopped speaking and settled into private memories.

"How long did you work for him?" Rosalind broke the silence.

"Only about two years, just before he ran for president. How old are you now . . . Rosalind?"

"You know me!" Rosalind was startled. "Have we met? I'm sorry if I . . . ."

"No, dear." A delightful dimple appeared at the corner of Pia's mouth. "You couldn't possibly remember me. You were only four or five when we met and you had your mind completely on where your Scottish nursemaid had put your brothers' 'tookies.' "

That sent Rosalind into a shared laugh. "Yes, I remember how Miss B would forget where she put the bedtime cookies and Billy and Timothy would scream for them while I played

157

detective. I didn't dare tell Mummy or she would have had a fit and yelled at Miss B." Rosalind bit her lip as if she had said too much, but Pia seemed so warm and open that Rosalind instinctively was drawn to her.

Pia continued cheerfully. "You were completely charming, determined to be polite, but also determined not to be swayed from your mission. I told your father that you definitely took after him."

"I wonder." Rosalind sighed. "I wonder if I'll ever be anything like him. I feel so . . . so unformed."

Pia laughed. "Neither Rome nor Rosalinds are built in a day. I doubt if Bill Connolly was formed at eighteen."

"Twenty!" corrected Rosalind.

"Twenty." The word seemed to deflate Pia. "I almost had a child who would have been your age. She might have been beautiful like you."

Rosalind felt a blush rising from her feet. She hated to blush. It made all her freckles stand out.

"You are beautiful and strong, Rosalind. I can see it and feel it. If you have the tiniest bit of doubt about it, remember that you are Bill Connolly's daughter and that he was the strongest and best man in the world." She finished in a burst of emotion. "There was nothing I would ever have done to hurt him while he was alive."

Rosalind was puzzled by Pia's last phrase.

"But we all must survive—as long as we're alive."

Rosalind perceived that Pia was speaking to herself in a way. She thought Pia was fascinating. It was difficult to guess her age, but if she had worked for Bill Connolly before he was president, she must be over forty. Pia had pale, translucent skin and high cheekbones, but she wasn't big-boned like Liv Ullman. Her frame was slight, almost frail. Suddenly, Rosalind remembered the waiting Muzafar. "Oh dear, it's been wonderful talking to you, but I have a cab waiting with half of my twenty-dollar bill."

Pia slowed her down long enough for Rosalind to explain. She found the story highly amusing.

"Please, come back downtown with me and have lunch," Rosalind suggested.

A look of panic flashed across Pia's face. "I'm afraid I can't. I have my car here and I have a meeting soon." She smiled an apology and extended her hand. "It has been lovely meeting you. I mean that sincerely."

Rosalind took her hand, wishing there were some way to arrange for them to be together longer. Pia seemed so—Rosalind groped for a word in her mind—magical.

Rosalind watched Pia disappear around the side of the obelisk, almost as though she were running away. Why? The question remained unanswered as Rosalind scurried down the hill toward her swarthy cabdriver who she hoped was still there.

Muzafar was scowling as she reached the cab. "What do I tell you? I always lose money when I must wait. You were there almost half of the hour. You know how many fares I can get in that time? You have the other half of my money?"

"Right here." Rosalind smiled sweetly and handed over the other half.

"Now I need tape for it," he complained. "You know how hard it is to put things together?"

She nodded.

On the ride back, she probed her mind. If Pia had worked in the Senate for her father before he was elected, then she hadn't worked for him in the White House. Yet the missing cookies they had laughed about were part of Rosalind's White House memories, memories of the family quarters. Pia must have been visiting the family—or her father.

As they turned onto Independence Avenue and she saw the marble Cannon Building, she made the connection. *Last Lady*, the book O'Brian had promised to let her read. Rosalind was certain the author had been P. Lengstrom. Where was the book now? Had O'Brian taken it home or was it still in the office? She stared at the building. It occurred to her that she should feel outrage swell as it had when she stumbled across the girl in Sean's bed. As she hurried past the security guards who nodded her past without checking her purse, she had a second thought. Perhaps outrage is often based on *who* as much as on *what*.

～ ～ ～

Dianne reread the memo she had handwritten moments before. The rounded Miss Potter's italic swirled across the page, interrupted by dashes and exclamation marks.

Tony! I cannot tell you how totally—and I do mean totally—humiliated I am by your persistent public indiscretions. I cannot even attend a simple dinner party these days without some fool insisting on mentioning that woman's name—just to see how I will react, I am certain. If this is a cross which you insist must be mine, I can bear it, but I cannot tolerate the humiliation— absolute disgrace—poured upon the heads of my children. Yesterday, Billy actually asked me about you and Nicole Turrell! I told him it was a question for you to answer for him, but it's a question for all of us! Tony, Tony—you must stop doing this to me and to us all. We are still married, in case you had forgotten.

She stared at it. Tony would only throw it in the wastebasket.

Angus said her memos were a device to avoid confrontation and direct communication. But she didn't want to go through the pain of arguing with Tony. She simply wanted him to become reasonable, to keep his philanderings private and his coffers open. It was no longer possible for her to accept him as the friend and lover she had married. But there had to be some way to make him be more discreet.

She let the memo flutter toward the floor and reached for a sweater. It was nearly time for her appointment with Angus. He was probably at Eleanor's already.

Last year, when she had decided to go back into therapy, she could not face going to his office or the possibility that the press might get wind of her psychiatric visits. Tony gave them enough tacky headlines.

She was equally vulnerable if Angus came to her apartment. Some bright young reporter might question who the man was that appeared on her doorstep every Friday morning. What if they probed back twenty years and discovered her private nightmare, the weeks of shock treatments in the very private Connecticut sanatorium? She had recovered from the grinding depression that had sent her there and she had stayed well enough to cope. But that skeleton had to be kept deep in the closet. No precaution was too extreme.

Angus treated the decades-old fear lightly, telling her she was being paranoid.

"Then you can treat me for the paranoia." She had been adamant. Angus had to disguise himself as a delivery man and enter Eleanor's apartment by the service entrance.

He succumbed to her demands, but stopped short of the grocer's jacket; slinking in the service entrance was more than enough. He would not have gone that far for any of his other patients, but he found Dianne's struggles within her golden fishbowl fascinating. And so he humored her as he charged her for double sessions plus travel time.

Dianne carefully applied pale blue eye shadow and redid her mascara, blinking hard at the result. She had a lash in an eye. She grabbed a tissue to repair the damage and started again. Perhaps it was her imagination, but Angus seemed to go easier on her when she was physically together with hair, clothes and makeup in order, as though he subconsciously recognized and accepted soical barriers.

Analyze thy analyst, she thought, satisfied with her repairs. The way of my world.

♫ ♫ ♫

Angus relaxed in Lady Babcock's den, well cared for with scotch, a narrow cheroot and *The New Yorker* magazine. If Dianne wanted to be late again, he thought, it was on her time.

She breezed in with her normal apologies for the "exceptional things" that invariably made her late. Today, the phone took the blame.

Brushing back the golden hair she had worn loose for a change, she did not wait to sit down before launching into a running report of her trip with her sons. It had been a rewarding and delightful experience for all three of them. They had communicated beautifully. It made her painfully aware that relations with Rosalind had completely bottomed out that summer.

Angus nodded. Before Dianne left for Europe, he had been unable to make her see that Rosalind's distress over the Eighth Street Theater incident had great validity for Rosalind, a validity that Dianne should recognize and take some responsibility for.

"So," she rolled on, "I worked out this marvelous program for Rosalind to spend the next school term in London with Lord and Lady Boulder. It includes theater and it comes from me to

her, with my obvious approval of her interest in the theater—
in the proper place. I'm hoping this will bring us closer even-
tually."

"You're certain that you're not sending her away from you
so you don't have to resolve things directly?"

"Of course not."

Angus surveyed her for a long moment, puffing on his
cheroot. "What does she think of these new plans?"

"She loves them," Dianne said too firmly.

"I see." Another puff. "You don't think this smacks of our
favorite word? *Manipulation?*"

"It's a wonderful opportunity for her. And she needs a
change of scene—and mood." Without taking a breath, Dianne
then plunged into her own immediate state of mind, neatly
changing the subject from Rosalind to Tony. She told Angus
about the memo she had almost sent that morning, admitting
it was too similar to the dozens of other ineffective notes she
had sent. This time she waited for Angus to respond.

"When you were a little girl, Dianne, and you wanted something unpleasant to disappear, you ignored it. And most of the
time it would go away. Now you're trying to do the same thing
with Tony—ignore him, lead your own life and hope he'll disappear. But it doesn't work that way in the grown-up world,
especially your world. You are both public figures, incapable
of disappearing. So far you've resisted my advice to talk to him,
preferring your quiet circumlocutions with notes and messages
to secretaries." He leaned forward. "How's it working?"

"Don't be nasty."

"I'm not. I only want you to take a square look at what you
are doing. I want you to ask yourself if it's helping you or
hurting you."

"So what else can I do?"

"There are several grown-up choices available. First, you
could divorce him."

"Never! You know I'm Catholic."

"You could try to move closer to a real marriage, work to
resolve the emotional differences."

Indignation sparked in her eyes. "You know what he's done
to me! How can you of all people think that's possible?"

"Okay, that's how you perceive it now. That could change.
In the meantime, you could talk things out a bit and attempt

to get him to modify his public behavior. Or . . ." He took another puff of his narrow cigar. "You could leave things the way they are and go up a tree every time you get a new report or see a new article."

"It's too horrible, all of it. He's such a fucking boor."

Angus smiled and scratched at his salt-and-pepper beard. "You could also work at not letting the gossip bother you. If you could become emotionally flat in relation to him, he couldn't upset you."

"How can I not get upset when it's my name and my reputation that's dragged through the mud along with him?"

"Of course you could poison him like a Medici. Right now you're poisoning each other emotionally. It might be more honest to do the real thing."

She glared at Angus. "He's the poisonous one."

Angus's watch alarm signaled the end of the session. "That's it for today, Dianne."

"But I haven't decided what I'm going to do."

"I wasn't the one who was late," Angus said dryly. "Think about it for a bit. I'll see you next week? You'll be in town?"

She nodded to both questions. "I don't seem to be going anywhere at the moment."

∽ ∽ ∽

The farewell barbecue for the interns was staged around Sean's Great Falls pool. In addition to the steaks and ribs, there were mounds of homemade salads and fresh rolls, fruit pies and decorated cakes.

Rosalind insisted that Colin and T join the festivities, protesting that it would be cruel and inhumane to make them sit at the end of the drive, smelling charcoaled sirloins.

A feeling of melancholy tinged the merriment; it was a sad parting for many of them. For Rosalind, many of these former strangers had become friends, if not confidantes. She watched Colin mix, drawing out other young interns. He seemed at ease asking them about their schools and ambitions. Remembering his son, Ian, she decided he was feeling fatherly.

"Rosie!" Sean called across the lawn which was quickly losing its manicured sheen under the dancing feet. "Come dance!"

"I'm game if you are."

163

"I think this is a cross between a frug, twist, shimmy, grind and shake," he grunted.

Rosalind attempted to follow, moving closer to him. She felt his warmth, the animal magnetism, and recognized his sex appeal with a touch of surprise.

Sean's eyes brightened when a buxom aide approached.

"Hope you don't mind my cutting in"—the girl smiled at Rosalind—"but I can't miss the opportunity of dancing with the boss."

Rosalind smiled mischievously at her uncle. "I was ready for another drink anyway." It was summer's end. Laura was not expected back for another week.

๏ ๏ ๏

Colin noticed her watching him and rose to meet her as she crossed the lawn.

Her tan had deepened in the last month of the summer and her dark curls looked clean and soft. Shadows from the pool lanterns created gentle hollows under her cheekbones. Colin's body responded to the lovely portrait of his private nymph.

"Hi," she said. "This party could go on all night. You know we leave for New York tomorrow." She wanted to be alone with him. Who knew when they could make love again as easily? Why couldn't he suggest it? Why did she always have to take the initiative, until they were alone? "Colin, let's say good-bye to Alexandria."

"Good-bye, Alexandria."

"You know what I mean! Tell T you're leaving. I'll officially go to bed and slip out the window to meet you."

"Yes, General." He saluted.

"That was a suggestion, not an order."

He smiled. He was as ready for some time alone as she was.

With the others caught up in their own pleasures, Rosalind and Colin went their separate ways to meet one hundred yards away.

๏ ๏ ๏

Rosalind's mild melancholy returned as they entered the narrow brick townhouse in old Alexandria. It had become her secret home since Colin had shared it with her—a place away from games. Her thoughts touched on the zany activities of

164

Great Falls. She would miss all of it. The combination of Colin and family had given the end of her summer a sense of stability she now felt slipping away.

"I wish the summer could go on like this for at least a year."

"Not looking forward to England? I am. I'll be closer to Ian. With all the Irish he has in him, he could use more monitoring." Colin chuckled.

Rosalind resented the talk about Colin's son. It divided his attention and reminded him that she was young enough to be his daughter. It inspired him to act paternal. She changed the subject. "I put a 'Do Not Disturb' sign on my door before I left. We can sleep until noon, right here."

"Since when do the cousins or the twins respect signs?"

"Since I locked the door from the inside."

He lifted her hair and pretended to study behind her ear. "Maybe it's not all wet back there." Then he whispered against her cheek. "Rosie, whatever happens, you are important to me."

He silenced her questions with kisses. Normally he began their lovemaking with gentle teasing that steadily built sensations until she begged for him to be inside her. This night he began deep inside her, as though he could not get close enough quickly enough. They moved in their particular rhythms that they knew by heart. He tried to hold back, to last longer and etch the feel of her in his mind, but he came quickly, too quickly.

She brushed aside his apologies and lay back, giving him time to recover while she enjoyed the air conditioner's breeze cooling her sweaty body.

∽ ∽ ∽

The Marino plane was waiting as Rosalind and her brothers reached the airport. Reluctantly, Rosalind handed Sean the keys for Yellowbird and gave him a big hug. "I'm afraid I won't be able to do much for O'Brian's campaign in London."

"As long as you're all here in full force for the big one, we'll do fine."

She had watched O'Brian dash from a meeting to a speech to a subcommittee and back to the floor before rushing off to attend three receptions and two dinners on an average day. Why did he do it? Some issues seemed important, but there had to be a more efficient and enjoyable way to run the country.

They all mouthed that they were looking for better ways to do things, but they all complicated everything, piling committees on top of committees, task forces on top of special studies, and subhearings for their hearings. Of one thing she was certain: she was not going into politics other than to help a Connolly-backed candidate occasionally.

Onboard, she watched Billy and Timothy slurp their ways to the bottom of their chocolate milkshakes. Did either of them find politics interesting? Neither had ever run for school offices, as far as she knew. As close as she felt to her brothers in many ways, she had no idea what interested them in the outside world.

"What are you guys taking in school next year?" she asked.

Billy reached the bottom of the glass with a final slurp.

"The usual. English, history, math, science—and band. And I'm taking piano and guitar too."

"He's the Music Man," Timothy grinned. "We can't really be identical twins, Roz, because I'm tone deaf like you. And Billy runs like a platypus."

"And Tim is on the track team," Billy explained. "But that's good. It's important to have something that's all yours now and then."

Rosalind understood.

"Roz," Billy turned serious. "Tim and I have been wondering what is really going on with Mum and Tony. Did you know she made us call him from London and ask him to come visit us there?"

"He didn't, of course," added Timothy.

"I can't believe that she made you call." But Rosalind could believe it, only too well. "I think Tony has gotten out of her control."

"Ha." Timothy shook his blond head.

"That must drive her crazy," added Billy.

"I'm sure they're having trouble, but she doesn't talk with me about it," Rosalind said with a little frown.

"Or us." Billy glanced at Timothy for confirmation. "She always says 'Everything's fine' with that blank look on her face."

"Or she says 'Tony sends his love,' but we haven't seen him since that dinner earlier in the summer." Timothy leaned back against the seat.

166

"Oh, well." Billy wiped chocolate from the corner of his mouth. "If we really want to know what's happening we can always read about it in the *National Enquirer*."

"Very funny," Rosalind said.

"Yeah. Funny peculiar." Timothy grimaced.

᪉   ᪉   ᪉

Kiki was waiting for them at La Guardia with Dianne's love and apologies. Tony had summoned Dianne to Mexico the night before.

"Shit!" Rosalind spoke under her breath. Just when she was willing to make peace and spend some time with Dianne, her mother was heading south to hold hands with the Italian boor.

"Everything's organized," Kiki continued. "I'll take you and your brothers shopping for school things. Your mother and I have made lists of what you'll need." She gave them a bright smile, trying to compensate for the missing parent. "And tonight George and I will take you to dinner and a movie."

Billy shrugged and looked from Timothy to Rosalind. "So what else is new?" he muttered.

"When will she be back?" Rosalind asked.

"At least a day before you leave for London, she promised. You know she wouldn't want you to leave without her being here."

"If it's convenient," agreed Rosalind.

The next several days were spent organizing and shopping. The expeditions were peaceful with Kiki making gentle suggestions and checking things off lists. Rosalind admitted to herself that she was glad her mother wasn't there. She could live without the "Oohs" and "Aahs."

She enjoyed helping outfit Billy and Timothy. As adviser to Colin on wardrobe matters, she had taken a greater interest in men's clothes. Consulting on tweed jackets and ties for her big "little brothers" made them all feel mature. And they were discovering they liked one another as adults.

Dianne called midweek to say she was devastated, but she couldn't get back to New York that week. She swore on her sacred honor that she would come to London within the month.

"But there's so much you haven't told me. The Boulders know when I'm arriving, don't they?"

"Of course, darling. Kiki has all that information for you.

Now, put my little pals on, will you? Lots of love. I hear you have a marvelous tan."

Rosalind handed the phone in turn to Billy, then Timothy. None of them asked about Tony.

Dianne removed her sunglasses long enough to smear more tanning lotion on her face. She felt as though she were turning into an *objet d'art* by the pool. The luxurious rented villa was on the outskirts of Mexico City. The view above the high courtyard walls was breathtaking. It all felt unreal to Dianne. Watching herself sunning beside the great circular pool with the bottom carved to replicate the Aztec sacrificial stone, she felt detached, emotionally spent. Her marriage had already been sacrificed.

With her Spanish as minimal as the servants' English, she waited in silence. The serenity of the scene as she lounged and the servants who served her with voiceless smiles belied the fury churning in her gut. Tony had summoned her four days ago. "It's important, Dianne, so important that if you do not come, your checks will not arrive on schedule this month. I cannnot leave right now or I would come to New York. Besides, Mexico is beautiful. The change will be good for you."

He had called each evening from some unpronounceable town to apologize for the further delays. "Enjoy the villa. Relax. I shall be there as soon as I can."

"Bullshit." That was her only comment this morning. He promised he would be there the next day, no matter what.

The sun was becoming unbearable. There was no reason to worry about her hair today so she would brave the pool. After testing the water with a delicate toe—warm—she poised and made a shallow dive toward the center of the design.

Behind the lead-glass doors leading to the pool, Tony watched. She was still so slender, almost frail. The trace of his former protective feeling for her lingered briefly. Frail like a piranha, he thought.

"Oh!" Her hand clutched at her wet hair and she treaded water as he walked across the tiles toward her. "I thought you weren't coming until tomorrow."

"My plans change from minute to minute. You know that. But don't let me interrupt your swim." He reached into the inside pocket of his crumpled Brioni blazer for a cigarette.

"Me too." She paddled to the side of the pool and reached for the cigarette. She frowned at the long, slender Turkish one he offered and climbed out of the pool for a towel and her brand.

"My kind too strong for you?"

"When did you start smoking those nasty things?"

"Twenty years ago—on and off."

"You never smoked them around me!"

"You just didn't notice. You don't notice a lot of things."

She ignored the slur. "This place is magnificent! If I had known how lovely it is, I'd have come sooner. Why don't we buy it? It would be marvelous just to know this place was always here in case I needed it, like Walnut Hill." She gave him a dazzling smile. "The boys would love it. They could go on digs in the hills."

"Why don't *we* buy it?" His eyes narrowed and disappeared in the pouches. His trader's smile, with one raised corner of the mouth, accompanied the next question. "We shall become partners for a change? I pay half, you pay half?"

"Don't be silly, darling. You know I can't afford to buy the Spanish tiles. I meant, why don't you buy it for us?"

He tensed visibly as she put her hand on his arm. "What *us*? The only partnership, the only *us* I know about is where I buy, I give and you take. There's a you and a me—no us."

"That's unfair!"

"I could not agree more, Dianne. It is not fair."

She pulled the towel protectively around her shoulders. "Tony, things have become difficult between us because you

170

have lost your sense of values, social values. You seem determined to get written up in every trashy magazine and paper
in the world. The great bon vivant! The new Valentino. And
if I hear one more word about you and that tramp Nicole
Tur . . ."

"Leave her out of this," he barked.

"You're the one who keeps bringing her into things—and
in public. I'm not the one who decks her in diamonds while
my wife doesn't have enough to live on."

"Cut the crap, Dianne." Lines of fatigue accented his jowls.
Bone weary, his temper was held by a desire to handle this
confrontation quickly and as painlessly as possible—for him.
He went inside to refill his drink and unkindle his irritation.

Dianne followed, trailing her towel. "Tony, it's not crap.
There are a lot of things we have to work out. More than just
money. Our marriage is falling apart and we have to do something
about it. I did not call a single friend in Mexico City. I didn't
have the nerve to hedge about when you were coming—or if.
I'm tired of making up excuses."

"Get dressed. We'll discuss it over drinks."

෴ ෴ ෴

Safe in her bedroom, she slipped into a soft Missoni summer
knit in blue and gold, tying her hair back with a coordinated
scarf. There was no time for dryers or curlers. It was time to
have it out with Tony. Quickly, she added blue shadow and
mascara and thanked the Mexican gods for her tan. She was
ready.

Tony had not changed. She wondered how many bourbons
he had consumed while waiting. More than four always wound
him up into a party mood. Tonight she was determined to have
a serious conversation if she had to tie him to a chair.

"Well?" She looked at him.

"Well, what would you like to drink?"

"Wine is fine."

"Wine is fine," he mimicked. "Watered? Iced?" Immediately,
he regretted his attitude. He didn't want to bait her. It was a
bad habit.

She sat quietly on the white couch, deciding to be a portrait
of calm reason. Besides, the white was an ideal background for
the blues and golds of her dress.

"I have been thinking, ever since the time you came to me

with your financial difficulties and your distress about my style of life," he said as he uncorked the wine.

"I am distressed about our not having a life together."

"You were the one who backed away from me, as I recall. I remember it rather vividly." He handed her a goblet.

"I backed off to give you a gentle message that I could not tolerate your crass behavior. I was hoping you would come back and ask my . . ."

"You treat marriage and life the way a little girl would," Tony interrupted harshly. "You go away and sulk, wait for a present, wait until Daddy says he's sorry. It got too old too quickly. You sing one boring tune—me, me, me, me, me. It's crap, Dianne."

"You twist every damn thing I do or say. You are the crudest, most offensive . . ."

"Then I don't understand why you want us to have a life together if I am such an ogre."

"We're married, remember?" Her blue eyes welled with frustration and hurt. "You can't snap your fingers and say you never begged me to marry you or that I didn't accept in good faith."

"Life is filled with mistakes." Tony's voice was cold. "Fools accept them. Wise men seek remedies."

"What are you saying?"

"What was done can be undone. Everything has a price, including you—especially you."

"After everything I gave up, everything I have put up with— the horrendous publicity, the friends begging me not to marry you, the angry letters, the difficulties with the children—you're suggesting . . ." She couldn't finish.

"Divorce is the only sane way out for both of us."

"No. No way. I will not face the ridicule of friends and the press. I will not subject my children to the trauma of a divorce. Tony, Sean tells me we are only weeks away from getting papal blessing for our marriage. It's taken thousands of dollars and all these years. No. I am still Catholic in my own way."

He studied the ice in his glass, then looked up through his craggy brows. "I could have a contract taken out on you."

"Tony, you're not being serious."

He averted his eyes. "Maybe and maybe not." Then he reached for his briefcase and pulled out a sheaf of papers which he handed to her without comment.

She put on her glasses and skimmed them quickly, taking more time over the pages with the financial arrangements. Then, without looking at him, she tore each page in half and dropped it on the floor at his feet. "No."

"Twenty million isn't enough? You could buy this villa forty times over."

"Two hundred million isn't enough. I am your wife and you are my husband according to the law and to God. Period. Now if you would like to discuss anything else, I would be delighted." She leaned back against the white couch, drained. "Oh, Tony, you used to give me surprises that I loved so much. Remember?"

"I remember a lot of things."

She stared past him. "Yes."

"We have nothing else worth discussing anymore."

The next sound was that of the door slamming behind Tony. She swirled around. "Tony! Tony!" She cursed softly at the sound of the car pulling away from the entrance. There was nothing she could do. If she sued him for divorce and put his adulterous affairs on public display, it wouldn't bother him one iota. He already displayed them. The only way to punish him was to do nothing, especially not give him a divorce.

She still had his planes and cars and charge accounts to use. If he wouldn't increase her allowance, she could juggle things. He wouldn't have the nerve to cut it off. What did $45,000 a month mean to him? It was a speck on the nose of a fly. She picked up his empty glass, suddenly remembering the pleasures of their wedding night a thousand tears ago. He had been strong, yet gentle and adoring. She hurled the glass against the brick wall. So much for romance.

 ⁓ ⁓ ⁓

"Colin! You can't be serious!"

"That's the whole point, Rosie. I can't. And every day you burrow a little farther inside me."

She watched her agent, friend and lover slip into his clothes. "It's absurd for you to stay behind for six weeks."

"If I'm ever going to reach T's rank or better, I have to take advantage of this special training course now."

"Bullshit. You're only taking it to avoid me."

"The timing is coincidental, but possibly providential." He handed her her jeans and T-shirt. "You know we can't go on forever. You've got to start going out with men of your own age and social position. Yes, that, too. London will be a change of mood. It's better if I'm not there for a while." He was working hard to convince them both.

"At least wait until you get to London before making it so final. Let's wait and see." She punctuated her plea with a sniff.

Colin looked out the window that overlooked other windows. It had been better when he could take her to his room at the Northampton Inn or his house in Alexandria. Sneaking her into the Waldorf had felt sleazy.

"Colin?" She stared at the strong back, missing him before he had gone. "Colin," she sobbed.

There had been too many painful good-byes for them. He knew it was his fault for falling back into the affair continually. But somewhere deep inside of him she had a hold that he couldn't break. He was always half a breath away from wanting her. Perhaps that would never change, but he had to step back. His $30,000 a year was no match for her multimillion-dollar trust funds. She wasn't even aware of that yet. She was an innocent. Steeling himself against himself, still facing the window, he said, "It's three A.M., time to get dressed."

She sobbed harder.

Colin knew it had been a traumatic summer for her. She didn't deserve this last disappointment, but since he had been offered the course and promotion, it seemed the perfect time to break things off. His resolve to stay cool melted and he crossed the room to fold her into a warm hug. "It'll be okay, Rosie. You'll see."

"It's only okay when you're around." She snuggled closer. "Colin, I love you."

"I love you too, baby, and that's why it has to be this way, *because* I love you."

"If you *really* loved me, you wouldn't want *us* to end. It doesn't make sense."

"Who ever said life makes sense?"

He disappeared into the bathroom, calling, "You have five minutes."

She heard the toilet flush. Down the drain. "No!" she screamed at the closed door. "I won't have it!"

"You want the hotel detectives storming in here?" Colin emerged, sober and irritated. "You are too tall for tantrums. Even my crazy son Ian doesn't throw tantrums anymore."

174

She sat down, woebegone. "I'm sorry, Colin."

It was an emotional trampoline. He was sorry, too, sorry she wasn't ten years older and a distant Connolly cousin.

∽ ∽ ∽

To Rosalind's surprise, Dianne was waiting at the breakfast table the next morning, filled with nervous energy, shuffling papers and taking quick little sips of coffee.

"When did you get back?" Rosalind greeted her.

"Four this morning."

"You have two cigarettes going—burning the candle at both ends again?"

Dianne gave her daughter too bright a smile. Her hair was tied back, accentuating the purple smudges under her eyes. Tan notwithstanding, she did not look like a lady just back from vacation. She skimmed past the questions about Mexico. It had been marvelous and beautiful; Tony sent his love. She rattled on through her lists while Rosalind poured herself a cup of coffee. "We have a lot to organize in two days—a lot to buy."

The scene with Colin the night before had left Rosalind shattered, still searching for the shards to glue herself back together. Obviously, Dianne was gearing up for a marathon shopping session. Even the thought of it was exhausting. "It's all done, Mother. Kiki and I have everything organized."

"The lists are sadly incomplete. You'll need warmer clothes and more of them. You can't wear the casual, ratty things you got away with in Northampton. Only a mother can help you with this."

There was no way out. Dianne intended to shop.

Aware from a casual remark from Dianne that Tony had refused to raise her mother's allowance, Rosalind said she really didn't need so many expensive things. "Won't Tony be upset?"

Dianne laughed merrily and explained that the bills went directly to Tony's office and had nothing to do with the normal household allowance. Dianne loved no-cost shopping. She felt like a child whose father owns a candy store.

Dianne's euphoria did not lend itself to confidences. There were no leisurely lunches. Although the frenetic pace diverted Rosalind from her emotional upheaval, she tossed in her bed at night, fluctuating between self-pity that she had to be Rosalind Connolly and indignation that Colin couldn't accept her, whatever her circumstances. And crying didn't help.

If he really thought their affair had to end, why was he coming to London at all? It was illogical, just as it had been at the beginning of his Washington return. She was tired of cajoling him and pushing him, but she wanted him. There was so much she hadn't thought to ask him or tell him at the Waldorf but filled her mind now, when it was too late. Maybe if she had made him talk it out, she could have changed his mind. Maybe. She didn't know.

And what was waiting for her in London? A dusty old lord and lady and God knew what else. Maybe if she looked for the wildest crowd she could find and turned into a kinky swinger, Colin would be sorry he deserted her. That was a good answer for a three-year-old. Wait and see. She thought about Colin's good-bye kiss, long and sweet and sad, and burst into tears—again.

~ ~ ~

Another stranger to sleep lay a bedroom away. Dianne put down her book and smiled as she heard Rosalind's toilet flush. She was glad she had made it back for these last two days. Rosalind must be excited about going to London. The children were growing up. Now was the time to share things with them.

She felt her face. The night cream was totally absorbed. Suntan is marvelous but drying, she thought; the bedside mirror confirmed it was fading as well. Just like me, she told her image. Pushing fifty and fading—with a husband fading out of the picture. It was a classic middle-age story. But Nicole Turrell was older than she was, almost as old as Tony. She wasn't young and fresh like a twenty-year-old secretary, just brassy and tacky like Tony. They were a well-matched pair who would never become a couple if she could help it. The meeting with her attorneys to determine if they could prevent Tony from publicly suing for divorce was scheduled for the next day. Distasteful as she found discussing his latest threat, she had to have her ammuniton ready in case he opened fire.

She was filled with self-pity for being victimized by her faith and trust in a louse. She turned out the light and adjusted her sleeping mask. With the children away, there would be more time and space to maneuver again. She would give Tony something to get jealous about. She could be splashier and more glamorous than his overblown trollop—and with better taste.

Shit, she thought. It was too late for those games, which had already been tried and found useless. Trying to stop her thoughts, she lay on her side, then on her back, searching for a comfortable position.

13

The great granite house of the Boulders was firmly planted beside the Indonesian Embassy, facing the statue of Franklin Roosevelt in Grosvenor Square. Contrasted with the modern United States Embassy across the square, Boulderdash, as Sir Henry had titled the ancestral manse, was a London anachronism, harking back to an era when double wings, twenty bedrooms and acres of formal gardens were the norm for fashionable townhouses.

Sir Henry's father had been born an individualist. Rather than disdain commerce as did many of his peers, the fifth Lord Henry Boulder disdained Parliament and the House of Lords. He spent a long and productive lifetime in the pursuit of diamond shares, South African gold, real estate and oil, assuring the finanicial future of his children and grandchildren, all of which left the present lord with a sense of security enabling him to pun at will, vote as he damn well pleased in the House of Lords and tolerate Lady Gillian's flutterings with good humor and the help of the Irish mistress he kept nicely in a charming row house in Mayfair.

Not a celebrity seeker, Sir Henry had suggested that Rosalind stay with them because he deeply missed his daughter Katherine, newly married to a minor earl in Chichester. Although Lady Gillian had echoed her husband's invitation, she worried that she wouldn't have time to properly supervise a young lady. She was busy with her charity work, gardens, houses, horses and visits to her children. But Lord Henry had waxed so enthusiastic she didn't have the heart to demur.

Dubbed "Tulip" by her family, Lady Gillian was usually more attuned to foxgloves and hydrangeas than to Lord Henry. Rosalind found her pleasantly vague. Dianne seemed down to earth and direct in comparision. But in many ways, Tulip was an ideal hostess for a twenty-year-old with an urge to explore. "Let Cook know if you're going out to dinner" was much less constraining than "Let us know what time you'll be in."

Lady Gillian was not totally vague, however. She was well aware that Rosalind was guarded by the Secret Service; her secretary had helped find flats for the agents. Futhermore, the London press was paying scant attention to its Connolly visitor. Rosalind would be perfectly safe testing her wings here. With that rationalization, Lady Gillian awarded Rosalind equal concern with Sir Henry. If they were around, fine. If not, Tulip assumed they were visiting.

On the other hand, Lord Henry insisted on becoming a one-man British tourist board, taking half days off from Parliament to show Rosalind around. They sailed on the Thames, visited Parliament from the inside out, played Henry and Anne Boleyn at the Tower of London and made a merry list of the paintings at the Tate worth stealing. Rosalind enjoyed his dry humor and running commentaries on every subject from social systems to horses. Lady Gillian excused herself from the expeditions, especially the ones to discos and gambling clubs.

It struck Rosalind as peculiar that Lady Gillian didn't seem upset when Rosalind usurped Sir Henry's time and attention. Rosalind's affections for the middle-aged lord were those of a niece, but she knew that in a similar situation, Dianne would never have allowed her to monopolize an adult male. Perhaps Lady Gillian's laissez-faire attitude was part of the reason the marriage had lasted more than thirty-five years.

For the first fortnight, as Rosalind termed it with her new tinge of a British accent, she was too busy with Lord Henry's tours to miss Northampton or Colin. And by the third week, there was Lydia. The first moment Rosalind had walked under the gilded wrought-iron decor in the Royal Academy's offices, she had seen Lydia waiting restlessly in line. Lydia's clear blue eyes held a deep Irish twinkle that reminded her of Colin, as though a secret joke were waiting to be shared. Small and slight, Lydia's full, rounded breasts belied Dianne's assertion that small people should be small breasted or they looked out of proportion.

Dressed in an ankle-length rose skirt and a lacy ecru blouse, Lydia looked like a Whistler portrait. Rosalind was charmed at first sight. Isolated among the norms of her select schools, she had never experienced a schoolgirl crush on a special classmate before.

Lydia could do no wrong. When Lydia slipped into rough street talk to swear at bobbies or shopkeepers, Rosalind applauded her freedom of expression. When she flirted openly to charm a free lunch at a local pub, Rosalind admired her ability to influence people. She envied Lydia's "raging childhood" in the streets of Liverpool, learning to pick pockets at the age of four and rising above the limitations of a poor ten-person household to study drama at the Royal Academy, independently. Lydia averred that she had been acting all her life. She only needed the Academy to acquire the right contacts.

At first, as Lydia dragged her in and out of classes, pubs and friends' flats, Rosalind felt too awkward to join in freely. Lydia was amused to think that Rosalind with her cosmopolitan background, acquaintance of the rulers of the world, felt shy among the free spirits of London. She said as much and promised to tutor Rosalind in the "art of other people."

Rosalind soon became aware that Lydia's independence included a mysterious backer who arrived at strange hours to turn Lydia's comfortable flat close to the Academy into a scene of all-night revels. But she still admired Lydia's self-reliance and spunk.

Although her admiration for Lydia was unaffected, Rosalind instinctively mistrusted Lydia's friend Dickie, a rakish man in his mid-thirties whom Lydia called a "Clark Gable type." She excused herself from the parties, saying the Boulders didn't allow her to stay out late, knowing full well they would never notice.

Lydia mysteriously mentioned big deals, tax problems and quests for unnamed materials that sent Rosalind's thoughts to rum and gunrunning. When she discovered that Dickie's deals included manufacturing phony war medals for selling at flea markets and forging sterling markings on silver plate, Rosalind was disappointed. She believed that Lydia deserved someone far better than Dickie.

During September and early October, Rosalind invited Lydia to tea and dinner at the Boulders. Lady Gillian paid little attention to Lydia—or Rosalind for that matter—during the tea. She was excited about a new breed of aphids she had discovered in her gardens and her plan to have the horticultural association codify them as the "Boulder aphid." "Pity it's not a beetle," she rattled. "The Boulder beetle has such a nice ring to it, don't you think?"

Lydia's review of Tulip was "choice, a proper aristocratic pink and beige air-head."

Lord Henry was home the night Lydia came for dinner. Lydia did her best to make a good impression; she considered herself an expert with older men. But an uncharmed Lord Henry directed his best sallies at Rosalind and Tulip. When Lydia attempted to enter the conversation, Lord Henry raised his eyebrows and asked, "Liverpool? You say you grew up in Liverpool? I say, do you know the Anthony Mountbattens? Hmmm?" Lydia mumbled "No" and became quiet.

If Rosalind missed the snub, Lydia did not. She no longer pushed to have tea or dinner at Boulderdash. Instead, she became intent on drawing Rosalind away from the Boulders, offering a constant stream of sympathy and encouraging her friend to stay late at her flat.

"It must be terrible for you in America, with everyone dreadfully aware of who you are—who your father was, really. Everyone gawking all the time."

"It's not so bad. Once they've said, 'I've seen Rosalind Connolly,' they get over it and leave me alone." Rosalind gave Lydia a resigned smile. "The thing I still find strange, and I know it's silly, is seeing my father's face on matchbook covers all over America."

"Matchbooks?"

"Yes, matchbooks. The covers promote stamps for collectors. Roosevelt, Truman, Kennedy—all the presidents are on stamps. Why they picked my father's stamp to display on cheap matches is beyond me. At first I resented it. It seemed so tacky. Now, I try to take it as a fast hello to him."

"So you don't mind being famous?"

181

"Only a little, sometimes."

"Someday I plan to be very, very famous, like Vanessa Redgrave or Julie Andrews, but I shall never, never let them put my face on a matchbook cover."

"Are we going shopping before rehearsal?" Rosalind changed the subject.

"Yes!" Lydia threw on her pink raincoat. "I've found us the most divine little everything shop!"

En route to the underground, Lydia explained that the Blue Goose was a shop in the Portobello Road. "Even though they have mostly lamps and shades, in the back of the shop they have the most incredible clothes. Wait till you see them!"

Rosalind loved the old wooden banisters of the underground escalators. Unlike New York subways, London's were clean, but when Rosalind commented on this, Lydia protested, "Oh, but New York has so much more of everything!" No matter what Rosalind admired about London, Lydia would reply with her American dreams. Her sights were set on Broadway rather than the West End.

They walked through heavy mist, Lydia grimly promising that winter would be more of the same, only colder. "There!" She pointed a crimson-tipped finger at a shop across the street.

Rosalind could see goose-neck lamps with fluted shades filling the window. Inside, the portly owner, a man in his early sixties, eyed them, trying to determine if they were browsers or shoppers. He went back to his newspaper; if they wanted something, they could ask.

Lydia poked quickly through the racks of old dresses, past yellowed laces and spotted voiles. She stopped as she found a long velvet gown of muted pastels, blues merging with roses and golds. Holding it up, she called, "It's perfect for you and much too long for me!"

Rosalind examined the dress. It was wonderfully theatrical. "But where would I wear it?"

"Anywhere, everywhere. Put it on. I want to see!"

Rosalind slid the silky garment over her jeans and T-shirt. A little tight. She took off her jeans and shirt and tried again. Perfect. Cut low, it practically gave her cleavage.

"Smashing! Absolutely smashing! I'm green with envy!" Lydia chortled. "How much is it?"

Rosalind checked the smudged crayon mark on the tag.

"Twenty pounds. I can't afford that!" Her $150 a month translated into about £65.

"Then we won't pay that much." Lydia called to the owner. "See here, you have this dress marked incorrectly."

"How's that?" He frowned up from his newspaper.

"Twenty pounds is far too much for this. Somebody bled the colors."

"That's the way it's supposed to be!"

"I doubt it, and besides, it's missing a button!"

Rosalind felt a jerk at her back as Lydia surreptitiously plucked off a button.

"I don't believe it. All our garments are thoroughly checked and cleaned. Show me!"

Lydia turned Rosalind around and displayed the site of the missing button. "See? We won't pay a penny over seven pounds."

"I paid eight pounds for it myself!" he protested.

"All right, ten pounds. That's our final offer." She looked at Rosalind. "Is that all right?"

Rosalind nodded numbly.

The shopkeeper agreed reluctantly, but Lydia wasn't finished with him. She returned to the rack and pulled out a beaded dress at least fifty years old. The price was marked £25, but he let her have it for £10 just to be rid of her.

"You must never, never pay the first price asked at any of these shops. They expect you to bargain."

"You're a wonder at it, but I couldn't haggle like that."

"Sure you could. It simply takes practice."

"My mother loves to bargain for things."

Lydia smiled contentedly. "It can get in your blood. Even when I have millions as a star, I'll still enjoy a good battle over price."

"Don't you feel a bit strange dressed like this in the middle of the day?" Rosalind felt uncomfortable with the stares of the lunch crowd.

"I feel wonderfully free. We're showing the world that we can do as we please!"

"Mmmm." Rosalind still felt as though they were headed for a masquerade rather than the Academy.

The sun had burned through the mist, giving shadows if not beauty to the old granite row houses on Gower Street. Lydia glanced at one of the "Bed and Breakfast" signs in a window and shuddered, "Thank goodness we don't have to live in one of those places."

As if to punctuate her words, a door flung open and a man rushed out in front of them with a camera and started snapping. They posed in surprise. Then he continued down the street, turning to take more pictures.

"Now what do you suppose that is all about?"

Rosalind shrugged. Nothing, she hoped. She glanced back to see her agents about forty feet behind them. They seemed unconcerned with the strange photographer.

∽ ∽ ∽

Rosalind didn't give the incident another thought until the next week when Dianne called in a twit. A picture of Rosalind "decked out in hippie-looking clothing with another girl in beads like a flapper" was on page one of the *National Enquirer*, Dianne raged. The headline read "Rosalind Goes Wild for London."

Rosalind explained it was all a mistake. They weren't leading a wild life; it had simply been a whimsical afternoon.

Dianne refused to be soothed. Sir Henry had told her that Lydia was a "pushy little thing." She was undoubtedly a terrible influence. "She is probably only using you for your name. I think you should stop seeing her."

"Mother, she's the nicest, friendliest person I've met!"

"The Boulders have been charming to you. Your statement is an insult to them."

"Mother, I love them and Sir Henry is wonderful, but I can't spend all my time with them. I'm twenty years old."

"And you're acting like a four-year-old." Dianne's sigh could be heard clearly across all 3,452 miles. "Rosalind, you know you have to be more selective than ordinary people about your friends and public behavior. Do you want me to look like a bad mother? Is that it?"

"Of course not. That's ridiculous."

"So was your costume and your behavior. I suggest you tighten up your act, young lady."

"All right. It was a mistake to wear the kinky stuff on the streets, I'll admit that."

"And the girl?"

"We're in the same school and she hasn't done anything

wrong. I don't see that she is an issue."

"Rosalind, from the sound of things, I think you should be very wary of the whole theatrical crowd there. I don't want to see you hurt."

Or really happy, Rosalind added to herself as Dianne's words echoed back to the theatrical fiasco of the summer.

"Can you understand that, my darling?"

"Mmm." She understood that Dianne was making a tremendous fuss over nothing. She couldn't help wondering if the photograph had been good, but she knew better than to ask.

Her curiosity was rewarded the next day when the *Evening Standard* ran the same picture. Lydia thought the picture of them was "wonderfully flattering" of Rosalind and "dreadfully dreary" of herself. Rosalind conceded that the slinky velvet did flatter her own lean figure, but she insisted that Lydia looked like the star of *The Boy Friend* or another twenties musical.

Lydia was amazed when Rosalind recounted the lecture from Dianne that the photo had elicited. "I'd think your mum would be used to it by now, lovie." Lydia's carefully arched brows lifted. "After all, she's been pursued for decades, really. Maybe she's getting jealous that you're getting the attention and not her."

When Lydia pressed for more details of the conversation, Rosalind admitted that Dianne had expressly requested that she stay away from Lydia. "She's completely paranoid, sometimes. Just because you were in the picture with me, she's decided it was all your fault."

"Leading you astray, lamb?" Lydia laughed merrily. "I can't even get you down here for our best revels. But you're here, aren't you? Mummy mustn't carry too much weight with you these days. Don't feel glum about it. I haven't listened to my own in years—haven't even seen her in three or four. She think's Dickie is the devil incarnate, bless her Catholic soul."

Dickie entered the flat in time to hear his name mentioned. "Who thinks Dickie Lorryman is the devil incarnate? Can I buy a soul or two here?" His laugh was rough and heavy.

"Ah, it's me devil himself. We're in the kitchen having a bit of tea," Lydia called to him. "Got hot buns and everything!"

Rosalind used the interruption to excuse herself, saying she had to be back at Boulderdash early, her British boat had been rocked enough for one week.

Dickie stared after Rosalind. "What was all that about rocking boats and in early? Is the poor little rich girl being punished?" Lydia showed him the photo and the brief article. "Doesn't even give your name," he grumbled. "You can bet if you were Lady Mud-in-Me-Eye or something posh it would be bloody mentioned."

"I'll be famous in my own right, one of these days," she answered mildly. "And it's an awful picture of me at that."

"Her mum's really buggy about her getting publicity?"

"Seems dotty about it," agreed Lydia.

"That's a bit of all right."

"How's that?"

"I'm thinking, my little canary, so be quiet a minute. When opportunity raises its pretty little head, Dickie Lorryman likes to take advantage." He reached for a hot bun with one hand and tweaked one of her breasts with the other. "Strike when it's ripe, that's what I say."

"Dickie, I don't know what you're talking about."

"The world's most famous mum doesn't like publicity, right? I would imagine she would pay a pretty penny to stop some that was a bit nasty. Then again, if these blokes are such hot news stuff, how much would the *Standard* pay for a story, a good story?"

"And what kind of story do you have?" She scoffed. "Rosalind Connolly likes to drink English ale?"

"I'll get it together. Give me a day or two to work out the angles."

෴ ෴ ෴

Dianne's warnings about Lydia only made Rosalind more determined to spend time with her friend. When she learned that Lord Henry was planning a country trip to check on his estates, she told Lydia that she had a free weekend. Lady Gillian would never notice if she were there or not.

Lydia instantly set to planning a Friday all-night bash. "You'll love it! Everyone stays right through the night and we end up having rashers of bacon and mounds of eggs. And Bloody Marys, of course, which we take to the Tower of London to toast the original!"

෴ ෴ ෴

The week passed calmly. Rosalind spent most of her waking hours as assistant stage manager for *Twelfth Night* rehearsals. Lydia was playing Viola who masquerades as a page and is revealed to be a lady. Rosalind tried to bury her jealousy. She would have preferred being onstage to checking lighting cues.

Friday arrived. In psychological defiance, Rosalind donned the controversial velvet and told the cook she wouldn't be there for a meal until Saturday evening. In a whimsical mood, she hailed a cab on the square. She immediately asked the driver if he had the regulation bucket of water and bale of hay in his cab, a law still on the books from the days when all hansom cabs were pulled by horses.

Evidently he had missed the *Times* article about the obsolete law. He gave her a blank look and said the only thing he knew about English law was that it was always bad for the Irish. Before she could ask, he told her, "My home is Ulster where the IRA are winning and shall continue to win until all the damn British are driven into the sea."

"But after all these generations, aren't many of the Irish part English? And don't the English over there consider themselves Irish? I'm part Irish myself, but I consider myself American because I live there."

"You've answered your own question. It's the soil that counts. And the Irish should rule their own land, not be ruled by the Protestant English!"

"What about the Protestant Irish?"

"They'll fall in line once the British are gone," he promised. He pulled up in front of Lydia's building and simplistically ended the discussion. "The IRA will have their day, miss. You can be sure of that."

Not certain she wanted to support Irish bloodbaths, Rosalind gave him a minimal tip.

Dickie met her at the door to the flat, attired in a bright tweed jacket and a bow tie. "So you have escaped your gilded cage?"

Rosalind looked around. She didn't recognize any of the faces from school. "Who all is here?"

"Friends of ours. You must meet them. Here's Randy the former leper." He gestured toward a small, dark man mixing a drink. "And over there is Juliette of the Streets." He pointed at a redhead wearing wisps of silk. "You must meet them all."

He waved at the group. "Hey-ho!" he called above the blaring disco music. "Meet Rosalind the Oh-So-Straight!"

"Where's Lydia?" Rosalind panicked and looked about the room. She didn't relish being alone with Dickie and his strange friends.

On cue, Lydia entered from the bedroom wearing a transparent coral blouse and a black silk skirt.

"That is a wild outfit," Rosalind gasped.

"Don't you approve?" Lydia asked with a half smile. "Well, Dickie has promised that this will be a wild party. Mix us drinks, Dickie."

"Lord Henry left on schedule and Lady Tulip was last seen burrowing under her glads," Rosalind reported.

Lydia chuckled nervously and patted Rosalind's arm. "Good, good. I'm so glad you're here."

"You're really wound up tonight. Is everything okay?"

"Super, really super, love. But I would like a drink."

Dickie reached around from behind Lydia to cup her breasts. "Your wish is our command. Your drinks, ladies."

Carrying a small silver tray of scotch and sodas, Randy nodded and silently offered the drinks.

Rosalind felt uncomfortable with Lydia standing there in Dickie's double-breasted grasp. She accepted a drink and took a deep swallow. It could be a long party.

The liquor soon elevated her spirits—or suppressed her misgivings, more accurately. Like a dark wraith, Randy appeared whenever her glass threatened to become empty. She had no idea how much she was drinking, but it was becoming increasingly difficult to find the beat of the music.

"Over here, ducks!" Lydia called from the bedroom doorway before she disappeared in a streak of shimmering silk.

Dizzily, Rosalind followed the fleeting image. Softer music played in the dim bedroom and candles in red glasses gave a satanic glow.

"Oh." Rosalind blinked. "Who all is here?"

"Just a few of us with some very special stuff," Lydia said huskily. The candlelight from below made her eyes look like dark pools. She ran her tongue along the wet red track of her lower lip.

Randy slipped in and closed the door behind him. "Did you save some for me?" He had another drink in his hand for Rosalind, laced with angel dust and barbiturates just like the last two he had given her, only stronger.

Rosalind took a deep swallow of the new drink and fought to get her bearings.

Lydia patted the bed beside her. "Sit down and try some of this." She lighted a joint, inhaled deeply and passed it to her friend.

Rosalind had no idea of how to inhale properly. She had watched others at New England parties, but she had never had the desire to try it for herself. Maybe she deserved the title of Oh-So-Straight. She was determined to be devil-may-care to show Lydia that she was her friend no matter what Dianne said. She tried to inhale and let out a racking cough as the acrid smoke hit her throat.

Lydia laughed and gently showed her how to suck in the smoke slowly and hold it until her head swam and her eyes watered. Then they moved on to the *pièce de résistance*, Dickie's cocaine. Lydia carefully held one of Rosalind's nostrils shut so Rosalind could sniff with the other. Lydia's hand on her nose felt far away, but at the same time Rosalind's skin felt sensitized by newly discovered nerves. It tickled and she pulled back, laughing.

"Good? Nice? More?" Lydia asked.

Rosalind took a large gulp of scotch and shook her head. She felt strange. The music that was so soft seemed to be blaring louder and louder.

There was something important she had to tell Lydia, something about her father, Bill Connolly. She suddenly knew for certain that he wasn't dead, only desperately wounded with a heart riddled with holes. They had spirited him away because the country couldn't have a president with holes in his heart. He was hidden on Tony's island where doctors were trying to replace his heart, but none of the hearts they had tried worked.

Dianne and Tony weren't really married. It was all a front so the doctors could work in secret, looking for a heart for Bill Connolly. Rosalind had to go to them and talk to them because only Rosalind, the real daughter, knew the secret, knew how it could work. He had to be given a blood heart, her own heart, and then they could take him out of the refrigerator and off the machines. And she would get another heart from somewhere and if not, if she had to die, it didn't matter. The fallen king could only rise with the help of a blood heart and it was important for the Aquarian Age that he return.

"Lydia," she gasped, trying to loosen her tongue enough to tell her friend what had to be done. She saw Lydia's eyes close to her own and felt Lydia's tongue slide across her lower lip. I'm turning into Lydia, she thought, panicked. I can't. It can't happen or there will be no blood heart for my father.

Something tickled. She laughed harder and harder as she felt her dress being pulled from her body, then her panties. Nothing left, she thought. That's hilarious. Someone was rubbing the insides of her thighs and it didn't matter. There was nothing left.

Rosalind looked up to see Dickie's rough hands reaching down to grab her breasts. "A comparison study." She heard him laugh. Then he disappeared and Lydia's white body, smooth and bare, lay next to hers. Maybe it was time for the operation. Maybe they would cut her heart out and send it to the island and give her Lydia's heart. And who would give Lydia a heart then? It didn't matter. She had to be brave. "If that's what you want, *my* father," she whispered to her drug-addled mind. "Take my heart."

Lydia's lips pressed against hers. She felt Lydia's small hand move to her breast a thousand miles away. Then she felt a nibbling on her inner thighs. The sensation was strange and acute, but she had no voice left that could form words to protest.

Lights were flashing. Lightning, Rosalind thought, waiting for the rain.

Somewhere in the sky she heard Dickie call, "Got it!"

She felt a weight roll away from her. "Thank God," Lydia's voice said.

Rosalind couldn't move. Had they taken her heart yet? She couldn't speak. Her jaw was frozen. Maybe they had frozen her like her father, maybe she was waiting for a new heart. She was drifting farther and farther away from her body. She tried to pull her consciousness back. She had to find her father, had to find him and give him the heart before it died.

"Rosalind!" Lydia seemed to be calling from the TV set in the next room, distant, electronic. It didn't matter. She didn't need Lydia to find her father—as soon as she could move again, she would find him herself. This was all part of a test, a test to see if she was worthy. She had to be worthy in order to save him.

"Damn it, Dickie, if you gave her too much stuff and you fucking kill her, we're all done for."

Rosalind was drifting. Somewhere nearby in the operating room they were waiting for her heart.

"She's all right," Randy reported, back to his self-appointed task of rubbing Rosalind's inner thighs.

"What are you doing?" demanded Lydia.

Randy licked his lips. "I'd like to fuck her, Dickie."

Dickie shrugged as he carefully removed the exposed film from the camera. "I don't care."

"Get your filthy paws off her. Enough is enough." Lydia glared at Randy.

But Rosalind didn't see Lydia push Randy away. She was out cold, her breathing as shallow as her friends.

ও ও ও

The next morning she awoke on Lydia's couch dressed in the velvet gown. She didn't know which felt worse, her stomach or her head.

"Sleep well?" Lydia bounced into the room, stopped beside Rosalind and stared at her curiously.

"I feel like death. What was in that joint we were smoking? How can you look so perky?"

"We didn't smoke that much, really. It must have been the booze. You were drinking it like water, ducks."

Rosalind frowned, trying to clear her head. She couldn't remember anything after the time Lydia had handed her a joint in the bedroom.

"How about a good strong cup of coffee before you head back to the posh world of the Boulders?" Lydia gave her a dazzling smile, the one she had told Rosalind was her "phony for the phonies."

Why was Lydia being so strange? "Hey, I thought we were going to spend the weekend together, remember?"

"I know we were and I'm really upset that we can't, but Dickie insists that I go along to Cornwall with him on business. It will be dreary and dreadful, but he does pay for my flat and my fluffies."

Rosalind wasn't ready to cope with the change of plans. The last thing she wanted was to crawl back to Grosvenor Square in her strange velvet dress and encounter Tulip trotting in from the garden.

"How about if I sleep for a few more hours, borrow some jeans or something from you and go home later myself?" The coffee Lydia was pouring looked thick as blood. Saliva flooded her mouth as her stomach turned.

"Impossible. We don't have an extra set of keys. Dickie is dying for you to see his new Princess, anyway. That's a kind of car, you know. I didn't know there was a car called a Princess until he went and bought one. We'll drop you off on our way."

Rosalind's head pounded harder as Lydia rambled on.

"Look, if the velvet thing is really bothering you, I'll lend you jeans. Oops, you're ever so much larger than I am. I know, I'll give you a skirt."

Lydia scurried off to find something suitable. Rosalind picked up the cup and took a tentative sip of coffee. It was the worst stuff she'd ever tasted; shoe leather would have compared favorably.

Rosalind slowly buttoned the skirt Lydia provided, pleased the waist wasn't too tight, even though she was five inches taller than her friend. "Fits fine. See?"

Lydia barely glanced at her. "Good. Then let's be off." She set a pace toward the elevator much faster than Rosalind's wobbly legs could keep up with.

Lydia chattered nonstop across town. As she stumbled inside, Rosalind was grateful for the solid peace of Boulderdash.

A shower and a two-hour nap helped, but it still hurt to move quickly. Rosalind rested in the greenhouse, garnering strength from the cool, green plants, and wrote a long letter to Cynthia, dear, sane Cynthia. She gave a glowing account of life in London and her new "delightful and daffy" friends. Rereading it, she realized she was protesting too much, but she mailed it anyway.

Lord Henry returned early Sunday evening in time to take Tulip and Rosalind to a concert. He was delightfully irreverent, whispering in Rosalind's ear, "Watch the violinist's coat button. It's going to pop any second," and "Do you suppose the pianist has worms? He can't sit still a second." Tulip whispered, "Oh, hush, Henry, hush," which only made Rosalind giggle harder.

They supped at Lord Henry's club, a well-oiled leather and wood establishment with an equally well-oiled clientele. It was all so clean and straightforward, thought Rosalind.

"Well, my ladies, what did you do without me?"

Tulip fluttered a hand. "Same as ever, my dear. I caught up on our correspondence and tended the blossoms."

"And our visiting Rosebud?"

The nickname sounded fine on Sir Henry's British lips. "Wrote some letters and went to a beastly party." The British favorite "beastly" was more apt than she was willing to describe. "This is so much nicer with you back."

Sir Henry basked in the compliment and ordered more wine, adding "Now, no 'Oh, hush Henry, hush'es," before the thought could enter Lady Gillian's mind. Rosalind went easy on the wine, letting Lady Gillian's complexion get pinker and Lord Henry's jokes grow sillier as they finished the second bottle. Rosalind's stomach was still feeling too rocky for her to do better than nibble at the roast beef and feel warm and safe.

🖎 🖎 🖎

The next morning, Lord Henry drove Rosalind to the Academy. A bit reluctant to enter and encounter Lydia, Rosalind chatted with her host for a few minutes by the curb. He looked over Rosalind's shoulder and blinked. "Isn't that your friend Lydia Something-or-Other?"

Rosalind turned in time to see Lydia's back disappear into the building. It was impossible to believe Lydia would walk past a silver Rolls-Royce without a glance. It was only ten minutes before nine; they weren't late.

"Rosie. Rosie!" Lord Henry broke into her thoughts. "Wake up and get moving, my dear. It's going to be a fine day. There's not a drop of rain in our October sky. We must enjoy it while we can!"

Rosalind echoed his grin and thanked him for the ride, wondering if he had patterned his mustache after David Niven or if David Niven had copied Lord Henry's.

Inside, Rosalind greeted Lydia with a cheery wave and an apology for forgetting the skirt. Lydia was as terse this morning as she had been garrulous on Saturday.

"Not important. Another day will do."

Rosalind asked about the drive to Cornwall.

"Fine," Lydia replied.

Rosalind began to wonder what she had done at the party to offend Lydia, but her memory remained shrouded.

At lunch, Lydia was nowhere to be seen. Rosalind determined to be cheerful and went to the Arts Café down the street with Alan Heightsbury, who reminded her of Rich from the Eighth Street Theater. Short and dark, Alan was proud of his mixed Welsh and English heritage and open about being homosexual. "It takes all kinds, my darling," he had told Rosalind. "And we can be delicious friends."

As they turned right on Store Street, Rosalind saw Lydia and Dickie on the corner of Ridgemount and Store. Deep in argument, they didn't see Alan and Rosalind approach.

"It's risky and it's lousy. It feels scummy," Lydia's clear voice protested.

"She'll never know, ducks, and if you avoid her it'll point the finger right at you."

"You're a lousy con man and it's a lousy story no one will buy!" Lydia shouted at him.

"And you're in it up to your sweet ass, so play it my way or take a fucking walk out of my life!"

Lydia swung around to leave Dickie and stopped short five feet from Rosalind and Alan. She smiled weakly.

"What was that all about?" Rosalind asked.

Lydia let out a breath and glanced behind her. Dickie was striding down Ridgemount toward the flat. "One of Dickie's stupid schemes. Going to lunch?"

Alan spoke for them. "Nothing fancy. Just some leek soup at the café."

"Fine with me." Lydia fell in step, brightly chattering about *Twelfth Night* and her costumes.

Rosalind's mind swam with the snatches of conversation they had overheard. Who would never know and who was Lydia not supposed to avoid? Were they talking about her? She was getting as paranoid as Dianne, she told herself.

For the next several days, Lydia stuck to Rosalind like a shadow, full of bright witticisms and forced cheer. Gone were the quiet confidences, the shared thoughts and feelings. Lydia was one long anecdote. Rosalind watched her flounce away one Wednesday afternoon and followed. Lydia's step slowed as she turned the corner; her shoulders drooped as though someone had stuck a pin in her. Why was she putting on an act for Rosalind?

∽ ∽ ∽

Friday morning, the editor of the *Evening Standard* was staring at the photographs the strange young man had brought in, giving him twenty-four hours to pay £5,000 for them before he would take them—and the story—to another paper.

Roger Davis's first instinct was to throw the young man and his foul photos out of the office; the *Standard* was above printing smut. But if the pictures were genuine and the girl involved really Rosalind Connolly, the paper might be able to put them to better use.

Whom did he know in the American press who might help? He needed someone reliable. He mentally checked his list. There was Bob Greene, the two-time Pulitzer winner on that paper on Long Island. Greene was great, but he didn't owe Roger any favors. It would take his New York stringer for the *Standard* a week to get through to Dianne Marino and an unknown would probably need one of the photos for proof. Roger couldn't risk wiring one of these photos.

Who else could help? Dave Driver came to his mind. The man was a self-proclaimed expert on Tony Marino. He should know how to get to Dianne. Besides, Roger had personally bailed Dave out of jail after a brawl at the Sherlock Holmes pub in 1971. Dave was the man.

∽ ∽ ∽

When Dave Driver called for an emergency appointment, Kiki was cool. She doubted if Mrs. Marino would be in for Mr. Driver at any time. Dave was insistent. After Roger had given him the full details, he had promised to get through somehow.

Kiki ignored Dave's pressure. Mrs. Marino was a busy woman who did not see newsmen personally. Finally, Dave snapped that he had information on a London blackmail situation involving Rosalind. He would only give details to Dianne in person. Kiki put him on hold and was back on the line in two minutes. Mrs. Marino would see him at four o'clock that afternoon; she trusted it would warrant the inconvenience.

Dave pulled on a navy blazer. It would have to do. He hadn't brought a tie to the office.

Dianne was wearing pale blue slacks and a white shirt open at the neck. She hadn't bothered to dress for Dave. She led him into the den without offering him anything, regardless of the cup of coffee she carried in her hand. A large husky dog came out from under the desk to lick Dave's hand and sniff his shoes in greeting.

Dave noted the absence of hospitality and sat without waiting to be asked.

"Well. What is this about, Mr. Driver?" Dianne rested her slender hips on the edge of the desk. "You're involved in blackmail now? Am I supposed to be surprised?"

"Look, I know I'm not at the top of your favorite persons list, so let's not play games, Mrs. M. I don't like this any better than you. It's nasty. I'm here as a favor to an old friend, a very straight, reliable guy named Roger Davis, city editor of the London *Evening Standard*."

"Go on."

"This morning a young man came to Roger with photos of Rosalind stark naked in some extremely compromising poses with another young woman, also jaybird naked. The young man also brought a signed statement from the girl involved, a Lydia Blume, swearing that she and Rosalind are lesbians."

"I don't believe it! Rosalind has been in London less than two months. And she is not a lesbian!"

"I don't know anything about that. Roger is checking out the statement and story as far as he can without bringing in Scotland Yard. So far, the young man has done nothing illegal. He has only offered the *Standard* some photos and a story for sale."

"Photographs can be doctored." Dianne sat on a chair facing Dave. "Real heads on phony bodies."

"Roger says they look clean, unretouched."

Dianne's mind swam. On Monday she had talked with Rosalind. Everything had sounded fine, but she would hardly chat about a lesbian affair. Lydia was the name of the girl in the picture with the bizarre clothing. She had warned Rosalind about that girl. But a lesbian!

"Mrs. Marino, there's more."

She started. She had forgotten Dave was still there.

"The young man is asking the *Standard* for five thousand pounds."

"Absurd! They surely aren't thinking of publishing it, are they?" Panic elevated the pitch of her soft voice.

"If they don't pay, the man will take it to another paper— so he says."

Dianne gasped. "Then that is blackmail! It is illegal."

"It depends on how you look at it. It's standard for freelancers to peddle stories."

"But not my daughter's reputation!"

"Roger has an idea that might bail everyone out of this mess. He can't justify the *Standard* paying that kind of money for a story it wouldn't run. As Roger says, the *Standard* is sensational, not sleazy."

"I'll put up the money, as long as we get the negatives and put an end to it."

"Roger wants something else, something he thinks would justify the *Standard* spending five thousand pounds. He wants an exclusive interview with you. The usual stuff—your likes and dislikes, fears, ambitions. . ."

"Christ!" Her coffee cup banged on the table; the dog barked in protest at the noise. "Quiet, Leda. I have not given an interview for fifteen years, not since the White House, and I don't intend to now! I'll pay the five thousand pounds or twice that first. That deal is blackmail, too!"

Dave had never seen Dianne lose control. The blue fire in her eyes fascinated him. "God, you're gorgeous when you're angry. I retract it all, the bit about ice in your blood."

She stared at him, digesting the apparent non sequitur, then burst out laughing. "How can you think about that at a time like this?" She shook her head ruefully, but the laughter had helped bring her down to earth. "Do you think your friend Roger would let me pay those people off and forget it?"

"Roger is a straight guy, but I think he'll hold firm for the interview. You could try hiring private detectives over there, but by the time they track everything down, some other scandal sheet might pick it up."

Dianne widened her eyes. "But Dave . . ." She unconsciously used his first name. "It is blackmail."

"On all sides," he agreed.

"Would you like some coffee or a drink?"

"I thought you would never ask," he replied quite seriously. As she rang for Ardyth, she noticed that Dave's soft brown eyes matched his wavy hair. He looked so sexy and kind. How could he have called her all those terrible things in his columns? "What do I tell Roger? Do I say, 'Under the circumstances Mrs. Marino would be delighted to give your New York correspondent an exclusive interview'?"

"You can tell him that since he has me in such a goddamn vise, I'll do his fucking interview—but just watch my powder puff answers!"

This time Dave burst out laughing.

Kiki arrived with the fresh coffee personally. She was surprised to find the atmosphere friendly, having half expected to mop up blood.

"Oh, Kiki, it's worse than I feared!" Dianne cried, shattering the friendly atmosphere. "Book me immediately on the first Concorde to London. I'll give you the gruesome details later."

Kiki hurried back to the office at the rear of the apartment.

Leda had risen at Kiki's entrance and settled her eighty pounds on Dave's feet. He absentmindedly scratched her thick ruff. "You're a big broad, aren't you?"

Dianne smiled at the interchange before turning serious again. "Dave, tell Roger to get the negatives. I want personally to watch them burn. I also want to get to the bottom of this . . . this farce. There's no point in my calling her. I'll have to do it face to face."

Although Dave had no children of his own, with one short marriage long over, he liked young people and sympathized with Rosalind's plight, whatever the facts.

"Dave . . ."

"Mrs. Marino . . ."

They spoke simultaneously. Dianne laughed softly. "That's not fair. You'd better call me Dianne. You've called me everything else in the book until now."

"Ouch, lady. You know how to throw a knife."

"You've been throwing them at me for years."

"I've got a column to sell, you know."

"But to do it at my expense hardly seems fair."

"We'll have to discuss the facts sometime."

"I didn't know you had any interest in facts."

"Try me." He laughed.

"Only if you give me your solemn promise that you won't print a thing about anything I say."

"Damn, what is happening to my life? Everyone is demanding promises that I won't write the facts. Where's my poor column supposed to come from?" He pulled his feet out from under Leda; she was feeling heavy.

"Do you mean to tell me Roger made you promise not to print a word about this?"

Dave nodded sadly. "Not a comma."

Dianne smiled. "That's unbelievable. You're not getting one teeny, tiny thing out of this?"

"Only the pleasure of meeting you," he said, flashing a grin, "and the exclusive U.S. rights to your interview."

"Damn you! I knew you weren't all that noble!"

"My secret is out."

"Well, since you have the U.S. rights, you might as well come with me to find out the truth."

Dave had not anticipated this turn of events. He had been doubtful he could get this close to Dianne, having thought it more likely she would turn him over to her attorneys.

"I don't know. The possibility hadn't occurred to me. Besides, think of the new rumors that would fly if I went with you. I could even print a few myself."

"No. You promised not to print anything I say."

"Maybe I'm a liar." He shrugged.

"I hope not." She spoke more earnestly than she had intended to. She vacillated between wanting him to come with her, to test the physical attraction she felt, and wanting to keep him at a safe distance. "Well . . ." She considered. "If I agree to do a very brief exclusive interview for the *News* on something like my views on living in New York City, would your paper send you along?"

"I doubt it. We could do that interview here."

"Tell them I'm giving interviews only in London."

"It might work, but don't expect me on the Concorde. With our budget, I'll fly with the peasants." He chuckled and hugged himself, illustrating the budget-airline squeeze.

"Dave, I'd be happy to pay the difference."

"Look, lady, I may write a bullshit column in your opinion,

but I'm not for sale. If I can be there, I'll be there, because I'd like to help—and because I like a good story. Period."

"I didn't mean that. I only meant if there was a problem with . . . " She trailed off lamely. "Are you going to call Roger or should I?"

"I'll call him and get back to you. Where will you stay in London?"

"I . . . I'm not sure. Where will you stay if you come?"

"Probably the Curzon by the Park. View's good and it's not too outrageous."

She nodded. Kiki would have automatically booked her into Claridge's, although Lord Henry would press her to stay at Boulderdash. But this time it would be better to have neutral turf on which to deal with Rosalind. She always felt more in control on her own territory, if only rented by the night.

She looked at Dave; he was still waiting for a reply. "Claridge's, I suppose."

"It figures." He gave Leda a last pat and rose. "I'll call you back within the hour."

"Thanks, Dave. And do try to come."

∽ ∽ ∽

After Dave left, Dianne let her irritation boil into angry frustration. What was happening over there? Should she call Rosalind immediately? Too much was unclear. She would wait until she saw the photos, proof positive. There was no point in reading Rosalind the riot act until she was certain.

Dave called back to say Roger would be waiting with the negatives and prints on Monday morning; the young man would be there, too. So far, all the tests showed the photos to be unretouched. Then, before she could ask, Dave added that he wouldn't be going along. The U.S. rights for the *Standard*'s interview were enough for his editors.

"Oh," Dianne whispered. Her defenses were too low for her to summon outrage. "I guess I'll have to go it alone."

Dave bit his tongue before suggesting that she call Tony. If anyone had thugs on his payroll who could handle this, it was Tony. But the suggestion might be cruel, because if Tony were on tap to help, Dianne would have already summoned him. Obviously, his column on the estrangement had been accurate. In a way, he was sorry for he knew she needed some strong support. He signed off, promising he would call her in London.

As long as she believed she had someone to rely on—Dave—Dianne's upset had been contained. Now she became a caged animal, wanting immediate action. She dialed the number Dave had given her for Roger at the *Standard*. She had to hear the story firsthand.

Working late, Roger answered the phone himself, surprised to hear directly from Dianne. He confirmed everything Dave had told her. The photos were unretouched and certainly looked like Rosalind. And there was a new problem. Lorryman, the strange young man, had upped his price to £15,000. The *Standard's* budget couldn't handle more than £10,000. What did Mrs. Marino suggest?

Dianne gritted her teeth for a moment before agreeing to contribute £5,000. "Not a penny more. And I must say that blackmailing me into an interview is a tacky way to handle this!"

"I think when you see the photographs, you'll agree that the entire situation is tatty and tacky. The interview is really the sanest and kindest solution for you."

∽ ∽ ∽

Dianne stared at the pictures in horror. Rosalind lay spread-eagled, her head thrown back in what looked like ecstasy, while Lydia's dark curls fell across Rosalind's inner thighs. Her head seemed buried in Rosalind's crotch. Other poses showed Lydia French-kissing Rosalind with Rosalind's hands grasping Lydia's breasts.

"How and where were these taken?" Dianne demanded.

"I don't know. Maybe with hidden cameras."

Roger Davis was waiting with Dianne for the delivery of the negatives. Dianne had a pile of hundred-pound notes beside her.

The intercom buzzed. "Mr. Lorryman to see you, sir."

Dianne sat stiffly, hands folded in her lap.

Lorryman entered wearing a loud striped suit with a garish yellow tie. A dark, greasy curl fell across his forehead to complete his rakish, seedy look. His eyes fastened on the stack of hundred-pound notes. "Ah, I see you're ready for me."

"First, a couple of questions." Roger laid his hand on top of the notes. "How and where were these photographs taken?"

Dickie shrugged and lit a cigarette. "Just at a party. I saw the girls disappear into a bedroom and thought it all looked interesting. And it was." He met Dianne's gaze defiantly. "When opportunity strikes, one takes advantage, you know? It's a cold world out there when you ain't one of the rich and privileged."

Dianne did not respond; she felt too disgusted with Lorryman and the whole sordid situation.

"Just how did you happen to have your camera all ready?" Roger probed. "More than circumstantial, I'd say."

"It was a party, like I said. Blokes like to see themselves. I always take pictures at parties."

Dianne cleared her throat. "About this girl . . . this Lydia. You have a signed statement that she and . . . and Rosalind . . ." Dianne choked on her daughter's name. "She swears they are lesbians. Do you know that for a fact?"

He shrugged. "I only know what I saw." He thrust a dirty fingernail at the pictures. "See for yourself. There isn't much doubt about it, I'd say."

Dianne closed her eyes. She couldn't stand the sight of him.

"Is there anything else you would like to ask?" Roger looked at Dianne.

Without opening her eyes, she gave a negative shake of her head. There was no question in her mind that the pictures were of Rosalind. It made her sick.

Dickie eagerly reached for the money.

"Not so fast." Roger's hand slapped down on the final £5,000. "First, the negatives."

Dickie produced a long white envelope. "You got to give me the money at the same time as I give you the negatives."

"Fine. And I know you'll be happy to accompany our photo lab technician while he makes certain that you haven't duplicated the negatives." Roger picked up the intercom. "Send Garrod in." He looked at Dianne. "Just a final precaution. We have ways to check if a negative is a copy."

"There ain't copies. I'm honest."

"Nothing like an honest con man." Roger shook his head as Garrod led Dickie off to the lab.

Dianne's mind was whirling. Now she had to confront Rosalind. She had left a message for her to come directly to Claridge's from class. The receptionist had said Rosalind's class would be over at four-thirty. She glanced at the clock: 3 P.M.

"I know this is very difficult for you, Mrs. Marino. If you would rather, you can return to your hotel and rest. I promise to burn the negatives as soon as they're checked."

"No. I want to see them burn myself. I want to see this thing finished." She knew, however, that it would be far from finished until she had things straightened out with Rosalind.

Dianne had decided not to involve Lord Henry and Lady Gillian. The fewer people who knew anything about the affair, the better. She had not even called her attorneys, or Sean, Tony or her mother. God forbid anyone should slip and talk about it—ever. If Rosalind were turning into a lesbian, she needed psychiatric help, and it would be easier to deal with that discreetly here in London than back home. Dianne glanced back at the pictures and shuddered. It all seemed impossible, but the proof was in front of her eyes.

The negatives checked out and Dickie signed a sworn statement that all prints and negatives had been turned over. Then Roger ushered him out and returned to Dianne. "If there were ever a moment when I wished I had hobnailed boots to kick someone out with, this was it."

Dianne gave him a faint smile.

Roger reached for a large round ceramic ashtray that had "Daddy" scrawled across the center in green paint. "My daughter made this for me when she was four."

Dianne thought wistfully of the time when Rosalind was four and wished for a moment that Bill Connolly were here now to help.

Roger covered the childish letters with the small pile of negatives and lit a match. They hissed and melted as they flamed, emitting dark, pungent smoke. "Silver nitrate smells dreadful," Roger commented.

"The whole thing does," Dianne murmured. "They are melting into fossils. I expected them to disappear into ash like paper."

"Don't worry. The images are destroyed forever."

Yes, she thought, but the facts, as ugly as the charred images, remained.

"Now, shall I shred the prints?"

"I'm afraid I do need one complete set."

Roger silently handed her a set and dropped the rest in the paper shredder. He had not inquired about how Dianne planned to deal with Rosalind who, as far as Roger knew, was unaware of the matter to date. That was between mother and daughter as far as he was concerned. The prospect of publicity was his domain; once that had gone up in smoke, he believed that even public figures deserved their privacies.

◌ ◌ ◌

Rosalind had received Dianne's message before lunch. A surprise visit. Whoopee.

"You want to meet her, right? Now's your chance, Lydia. Come along and we'll have tea with her. Claridge's has a wonderful tea with delicious pastry and strawberries dipped in pink icing."

"I know, I know. I made Dickie take me there once." Lydia fumbled with her purse nervously. "I think I'd better pass on it today. I forgot a book. I have to dash back to the flat for it."

"I've been sitting all morning and I could use some exercise. I'll come with you."

"No!" Lydia screeched. "No," she repeated more calmly. "Go on to the café and save me a seat." With that, she turned and ran down the street.

Rosalind found a spot beside Alan at one of the tables covered with bright yellow oilcloth. She didn't hold a chair for Lydia; she had a premonition that Lydia wouldn't catch up. In fact, Lydia did not reappear at all that afternoon, despite an important rehearsal.

As Rosalind rode across London in a cab, heading for Claridge's, her mind focused more on Lydia's strange behavior than on Dianne's unexpected visit.

Dianne was obviously on edge as she greeted Rosalind with a hug and kiss. She fluffed Rosalind's short curls and tried to blot out the image of her daughter naked in those terrible poses. "Well, shall we have tea?" she asked brightly.

"Pink and perfect," Rosalind commented on the soft Art Deco surroundings of the dining room. "Lord Henry has brought me here a few times. It's one of my favorite places."

"Rosie," Dianne spoke slowly, trying to form her thoughts. "I know that . . . many times . . . when young girls, young women, really, are growing up they can develop strong attractions for one another."

"Mmmm." Rosalind spooned sugar into her tea.

"Not so much. It's bad for the complexion."

"Huh? Oh, the sugar. My complexion's fine." Rosalind patted

204

her smooth cheek. "A bump or two during periods, but that's about it."

Periods and sex, Dianne thought. There was no way she could avoid the difficult conversation she had to have with her daughter. "Well, as I was saying, during puberty, these feelings can be very strong."

"I know." Rosalind nodded. "We read about that in psychology. I never really had close girlfriends at that age. Somehow, I must have missed that stage. Maybe it was going to Spence and living at home. Anyway, I don't think I ever had a close female friend before Cynthia."

"I see." Dianne took a nervous sip of tea. "Sometimes it isn't healthy to be too close to other girls. It can stunt your normal development and make you seek physical affection from the . . . the wrong sex."

"You mean like lesbians. You know, there were two girls down the hall from Cindy and me in Martha Wilson House who were always in their room with the door closed, holding hands and taking showers together. It was disgusting. Yuk." Rosalind popped an iced strawberry in her mouth to change the taste. "Why are we on this subject, anyway? Did you run into some lesbians?"

Dianne was beginning to get agitated. How could Rosalind just sit there and play the innocent? Here she was, trying to be understanding and look at things from a psychological point of view, and Rosalind was deliberately playing dumb, trying to cause her greater anguish. "Did I run into some lesbians?" She emphasized each word. "Can you really be so dense?"

Rosalind frowned at Dianne. Her mother's face had turned ashen. She was on the verge of tears. "Well, it's not such a big deal. We know they exist."

"Rosalind, I really don't know what to say next. I think I had better show you something I have in my room."

"What's gotten into you? I don't understand."

"Suffice it to say that I was dragged to London and put through a humiliating ordeal thanks to you and your indiscretions."

"What are you talking about?"

"Your friend Lydia. Is she naïve also when it comes to lesbian relationships?"

"Mummy, that's absurd. She lives with a man—Dickie Lorryman, if you'd like to meet him."

Dianne's stomach churned. "I have already met him and I don't care to meet him again as long as I live. And he has already assured me that Lydia is a lesbian. She has even signed a statement to that effect."

Rosalind's mind was whirling. Why had Dianne met Dickie? Why would Lydia sign a statement saying she was a lesbian? Why was Dianne's trip to London her fault? The argument she had overheard between Lydia and Dickie flashed in her mind. "Lousy con man, lousy story. . . ." Lydia had been an emotional ping-pong ball all week. What was going on? "Mother, you have to explain."

Dianne waved for the check. "No, Rosalind, you have to do the explaining upstairs."

Dianne did not say another word until she had handed the pictures and Lydia's statement to Rosalind. "Explain these, please," she said tersely.

Rosalind stared at the photos for several minutes before looking back at Dianne, obviously shaken.

"Well?" Dianne remained stony.

"They have to be fakes. I mean, it is my face. . . . It looks like us . . . it's Lydia's body, I know. . . ." She stopped, aware that knowledge of Lydia's body sounded incriminating. "But we never—believe me—never did these things."

"Rosalind, I hate to call you a bald-faced liar, but the pictures are quite genuine. There has been no tampering with faces or bodies or anything. I am beginning to think you are a very sick young lady and that the only answer is to find help for you— a good doctor, perhaps a hospital for a while."

"Mummy, there has to be some reasonable explanation." Tears caught in Rosalind's throat. "So help me, I'm telling you the truth. I never had an affair with Lydia. Let me call her and put her on the phone."

"I don't want to talk to the slut. Speaking to her so-called boyfriend was quite enough for me." Dianne lit a cigarette.

"You haven't even read her statement."

Rosalind dropped the photos and picked up the single typed page of Lydia's statement. "Lydia can't type!" Rosalind protested. "It couldn't be her statement."

"Read it," ordered Dianne.

Rosalind did not protest further. The signature was unmistakably Lydia's. The statement said that she and Rosalind had been having a lesbian relationship for more than a month.

"Make her take a lie-detector test! Dickie coerced her into signing this. It isn't true!" She looked up at Dianne for a reaction, but her mother's head was buried in her hands.

"What about the pictures? Can you explain them as easily?" Dianne's questions were muffled, but clear.

"I don't know about the pictures! I don't understand them any better than you do! I only know I am not having an affair with Lydia."

"Rosalind, how can I believe you? You may be so sick that you don't even realize it. I always thought you were the level-headed one in our family, the one who could bounce through every storm, storming a little yourself perhaps, but making it through in one piece, aware of what you were doing. I suppose they drugged you and then took the pictures."

Rosalind's eyes widened at Dianne's last sentence. "That's it! That's it, Mother. That's exactly what they did. At that party last weekend. Randy, this little toadlike creature, kept giving me drinks and I kept getting dizzier and dizzier. I can't remember a thing that happened from—oh, about nine o'clock on that night. And I know it was all Dickie's idea. I even heard them fighting about it. Lydia was trying to stop him. I didn't know what they were talking about, but now it makes sense!"

Rosalind's face cleared as she pieced together Dickie's plot and explained it to Dianne. "There was a party at Lydia and Dickie's flat near the Academy a week ago Saturday. There was lots of booze, grass, coke, all kinds of stuff."

"Rosalind, how could you get mixed up with that kind of people?"

"I wasn't mixed up with them. I'd never met any of them before except Lydia. I've always tried to avoid Dickie; I don't like his looks."

"I should hope not."

"Anyway, I was drinking more than I should have because the strange types in the place made me nervous. Then Lydia called me into the bedroom to try some grass. I'd never tried it before and I know I shouldn't have, but I was so bombed by that point it didn't seem to make any difference. I remember getting very dizzy. The next thing I knew I woke up on Lydia's couch, feeling like death. When I asked Lydia what had happened the rest of the night, the part I don't remember, she only said, 'Nothing much,' in a strange tone of voice. And she has been strange ever since. That's why she looked so scared when I suggested she come along for tea today and meet you. Mother, you've got to believe me. I didn't do anything wrong!"

"You certainly did do something very wrong. You put yourself in a vulnerable position, something Rosalind Connolly must never, never do. The Rosalind Connollys of the world are more vulnerable than other people. Friends can deceive you, use you, and in your case, sell you—and your reputation."

"Dickie made her do it. I know it."

"If she let him push her into helping, it's the same thing. You get destroyed either way. Rosalind, you persist in trusting people you have no way of knowing anything about. One of these days it could get you killed. This time it has cost me great mental anguish, thousands of dollars and a promise to do an interview that is the last thing on earth I want to do. All because you are pigheaded and totally irresponsible."

"But you don't really believe I'm a lesbian." She crossed the room and took Dianne's nail-bitten hand into her own. "Do you, Mummy?"

"Just look at my nails," she accused Rosalind. "Bitten bloody. When are you going to learn discrimination? First those wretched, pushy people at that tacky Village theater and now the dregs of London's gutters!"

Now that Dianne was convinced Rosalind had done nothing wrong intentionally, she felt justified in venting her anger and frustration on their source. "I won't have it, do you hear me? It hurts me too much. And you. It hurts you, too. Do you know what this could have done to your reputation—and your brothers', too, for that matter? Or your father's memory which is sullied enough these days?" Dianne sighed. "I hope this isn't the way it's going to be with you. God help me if you grow up to be another famous person's wild daughter with problem after problem. And there's always money involved—my money."

The drinks and dinner that Dianne had ordered earlier arrived at that moment, saving Rosalind from having to respond.

They both pushed the food around the Wedgwood plates without appetite. Rosalind declined any wine, but Dianne drank enough for both of them.

"I'm debating what to do with you," Dianne slurred. "I

don't think I should bring you back to New York to loll around until the next term at Smith. No, I think you need the discipline of finishing your courses here. And if I could think of some way for you to pay the piper for your stupidity, I would make you do that also. I can only hope that by staying here and rising above this sordid business you will learn from it. I intend to speak to Lord Boulder about setting some very firm guidelines regarding hours and the like. Incidentally, I have told the Boulders nothing about this incident and I expect you to do the same."

"Mummy, why on earth would I tell anyone?"

"At this point, with your passion for indiscretion, I'm not sure what you would do. You act without thinking. For all I know, you could drink too much wine at dinner and blurt out the whole story in graphic detail. Who knows, you might not even remember what you said unless someone taped it all to jar your poor addled little memory."

Dianne watched Rosalind cringe. She knew she was being cruel, but she wanted Rosalind to suffer for being so stupid and naïve—if that was really all it had been.

"Excuse me, Mother, but I want to give Lydia a call. I have to know how deeply she was involved in this."

"I rather doubt if she had to be druggd too in order to take part in that revolting photo session."

"I want to hear her side of it."

"Well, just don't say hello to your lesbian friend for me," snapped Dianne.

"She is not a lesbian—any more than I am," Rosalind retorted with malice brought on by Dianne's bitchy attitude. She went into the bedroom to place the call.

Dianne poured herself another glass of wine and quietly picked up the parlor extension to listen. She assumed that the high, brittle British voice was Lydia's. Dianne held her breath while Lydia poured out her tale of woe to Rosalind. Dickie had taken off for Liverpool to set himself up in a business. He had wanted Lydia to come with him, but she was never going back to Liverpool. She had to finish at the Academy. Getting into the Academy was the only honest thing she had ever done; she had gotten in through talent alone. She hadn't wanted to set Rosalind up, but Dickie forced her to do it, she insisted. Dickie said it was their big chance. He had promised to produce a play for her with the money, but he had lied. He had packed up, taken the Princess, and left her £200.

Rosalind was sympathetic. "Oh, Lydia, I always knew he was a rotter. Didn't I warn you?"

Dianne slammed down the phone. How dare Rosalind be sympathetic after what that girl had done to her? She poured more wine.

"Well, Mother, did you hear enough to convince you?" Rosalind spoke, framed in the bedroom doorway.

"I heard enough to be convinced that you are more of a fool than I had thought possible." Dianne returned Rosalind's stare, icicle for icicle. "If he's left her, she deserves it—and more. Remember, without her cooperation and participation I wouldn't be minus over eleven thousand dollars with a repulsive interview scheduled for tomorrow. Your sympathies seem ill placed."

Rosalind hated conversations with Dianne when she was drinking. Alcohol turned her tongue to vinegar.

"Unless you start looking out for yourself a lot better than you have been doing, you are going to be worse than sorry. We all will. I simply can't spend my entire life watching you every second to catch things before they become public. And you can be certain that the Secret Service is going to tighten their act—and yours."

"You're not going to tell them about it? You can't!"

"I don't have to give them the graphic details, just enough. I may even lobby to have your protection extended until you're thirty. If I ask doctors to verify that you are permanently unstable, I might be able to extend it for your entire life."

"Mother." Rosalind shook her hair away from her face and crossed the room. "You know that's unfair."

Dianne seemed to deflate. She sat down, gripping the stem of her wineglass, seeking support. She blinked and focused on Rosalind. "I have spent twenty years trying to keep publicity away from you and your brothers, trying to prevent you both from being hurt. I knew it can be awful living in a fishbowl. I have done it. There is no pleasure in life when you are walled in by photographers everywhere you go, when slimy reporters act as though they know more about your private life than you do. If you want to be normal, as you keep insisting you do, then you cannot do things that are going to excite the press. Because once they start on you, they never stop."

"Then why did you marry a man who wanted to be president? You knew it when you married him. You told me so."

Dianne finished her wine and stared down into the empty goblet. "Because I didn't realize what it all meant, really. If it hadn't been for you . . ."

"What do you mean by that? What do you mean, if it hadn't been for me?"

"I wanted to leave your father when you were ten months old." Dianne's voice was harsh. "Before your brothers were even conceived. My lawyers spoke to his lawyers about a settlement, but your grandfather Connolly intervened."

She continued bitterly. "He let me know in no uncertain terms that if I left, we would get nothing but token support tied up in trusts. If I stayed and played the role of wife and mother, you and I would each receive a million-dollar trust fund. What could I do? I couldn't have taken care of us in the style we were accustomed to. And I couldn't go crawling home to Mother and Uncle Herbie. I didn't really want a divorce, anyway. I only wanted to shock and hurt your father as much as he had hurt me, over and over again. But the devil's deal with your grandfather destroyed my bargaining position."

Dianne raised her eyes from the empty glass to look at Rosalind. Her glazed eyes held a strange kind of triumphant quality as she relentlessly shattered the illusions she had tended so carefully for two decades. "Do you know where your father was when you were born?"

Rosalind shook her head numbly.

"He was with one of his goddamn women. Oh, he arrived at the hospital the next day all sweetness and light to pose for pictures. It's a wonderful picture of the handsome young senator and his beautiful wife with the perfect little baby. You've probably seen it.

"But it got worse. When Billy and Timothy were born, he wasn't even in the country. He was vacationing in Paris with another sweet young thing. It was a disease with him. He couldn't stop screwing anything that came within ten feet of him, even when we were in the White House. Nothing was sacred.

"Why do you think he encouraged me to make so many official state visits? When I was away, he could turn the historic White House into a playboy circus!"

Dianne paused. The goblet dropped, rolling a few inches on the thick wool pile before it came to a halt. Dianne's mind swam with wine and anger. Maybe her daughter took after her father—oversexed like a common rabbit. Like a bunny. She had affectionately called Bill "Bunny" when they were first married. She had discovered all too soon why his best man, Senator Jasper Perkins, had snickered the first time he heard her use the nickname.

Rosalind's protests broke into her pained reverie.

"What is truth to you, Mother? Whose truth matters? You told me again and again that you loved him and that he loved you. You said the stories were all blown out of proportion. Which was the lie?" In spite of Pia's book and the dozens of other books and articles Rosalind had read, she wasn't ready to hear the bitter truth from Dianne's lips. Deep within she needed the idyllic version of their past held sacred.

"What does it matter after all these years?"

"But my father loved me and he loved the twins, didn't he? Everyone who knew us says so." Rosalind's voice quavered. She suddenly felt very young.

Dianne fought to compose herself. "Of course he did. You made him laugh when no one else could. And I think you, Timothy and Billy were the only people on earth who could make him take the time to feel love and warmth for more than a brief moment—especially you. You were older and he could talk and joke with you. You were free. Your heart was free to love him. By then, I had built up too much scar tissue to feel free. Too many things and phrases triggered reminders of bad times. At first I loved him for what I thought he was; then, for what I hoped he could become and finally, for what we might have had. It was a sad way to love. In the six months before he died, I thought we might have a chance at a relationship, a small one, but a chance. He was mellowing and the other women seemed to be becoming less important. I don't know what would have happened and it's been too late for a long, long time to bother wondering.

"But the one thing I know deep inside, Rosalind, is that he never could have completely controlled his lusts any more than Tony can. Men who lust for power are often womanizers. I think it's all part of an incredible ego need. And unless you want to be the rug under their feet, don't lie to yourself in the beginning as I did. Please, please don't try to paint rainbows on top of people, unless it's only on canvas. From what I know, as far back as your Van Druten and Connolly grandfathers, you

212

come from a long line of women who made wonderful victims for womanizing husbands."

Dianne's tirade, initially intended to hurt Rosalind, was turning into a personal purge. She was sharing more with her daughter in this uncontrolled conversation than she had in all the twenty years before.

Rosalind sat down gently beside Dianne. "If all that's true, how did Grandma Bea survive?"

"By having the strength to do what I never could. By closing her eyes very tightly and, I suspect, praying the whole time they were closed."

"What about Grandma Jane? She divorced your father. If it was too awful, you should have left, not sold out. It couldn't have been that bad." Rosalind fought against feeling sympathetic. "If my father played around, it was only because you were mean and cold to him."

"No. No, nothing I did or didn't do could change anything. It was his style, Rosie. It didn't make him an evil person in every way or affect his being a fine president. But it did make life hell for someone not prepared to accept his standards, someone like me who died a little every time I learned about a new mistress or escapade."

Dianne blinked back tears. She knew Rosalind hated to see her cry. "Oh, Rosie, I only want something better for you."

"Why did you ever marry Tony then? Everyone knows he's the world's worst skirt chaser, especially Nicole Turrell's." Rosalind mentioned Nicole with malice aforethought; she knew Dianne hated to hear the name.

"I thought Tony could offer me comfort, some joy and absolute security for all of us. I walked in with my eyes shut very, very tight to anything except what he could give to us. I didn't realize until it was too late that it was equally important for me to learn what I could give him in long-term satisfaction. He used me for my status and fame until he didn't need them anymore. Then he reverted to form. I hadn't really probed his past because I needed him so much then. In my own time, Rosalind, I have been as blind and trusting and stupid as you are. I don't want you to have to go through the years of hurt and tears that I have. Can't you understand that?" Tears racked her slender shoulders. "You and the twins are the most important things in the world to me. I only want us all to be happy." She

213

sobbed quietly.

Rosalind had exacted enough vengeance. She felt ashamed that she had pushed her mother as far as she had. She didn't want Dianne to hurt, not anymore. She put an arm around her shoulder. "Oh, Mummy, it will be okay. I'll learn to be careful, I promise. I love you. I'll always love you, no matter what." She patted her soothingly. "What you need is a good night's sleep."

While Dianne's sobs subsided, Rosalind poked through suitcases until she found a soft nightgown. Then she helped Dianne change for bed and tucked her in.

As she climbed into a cab to return to Boulderdash, Rosalind wondered if Dianne would remember her drunken effusion in the morning.

Rosalind questioned her own reactions to Dianne's emotional outpouring. Why had she reacted so strongly to Dianne's admitting that Bill Connolly was unfaithful? She had realized at the time that Dianne was trying to shock and hurt her, but that wasn't what bothered her. Perhaps she was startled that underneath the idealized version of Bill Connolly that Dianne had painted for her children, Dianne saw the original intaglio for what it was. Rosalind had to give her mother unexpected credit.

Lydia's plight flitted through her thoughts. She didn't believe that Lydia was venal but saw her as weak, as much a victim in her own way as Rosalind, but Rosalind's compassion had limits. She would gladly have lit the kindling under Dickie Lorryman's feet.

∽ ∽ ∽

The next morning Dianne throbbed everywhere, but she had total recall of the previous night's conversation. It had been a grave error in judgment to lose control and display weakness when she needed to get Rosalind back in line. It would be very difficult now to confront Rosalind and elicit a meaningful promise to avoid the Lydia creature.

Two cups of coffee and four cigarettes later, she called Dave Driver, feeling a need to discuss the most recent developments. Dave was already privy to the seamy details and would make a safe sounding board, she hoped.

Dave accepted Rosalind's explanation of events as Dianne related them. It all made sense, right down to Lydia's confirming conversation. "Don't be too tough. Kids are bound to experiment."

"You sound as if you really think she was giving lesbianism a try!"

"Hey, I didn't mean to suggest that, but it wouldn't be the worst thing in the world."

"You are being dreadful!"

"I see. We've come full circle and we're right back to the horrible Dave Driver."

Dianne laughed in spite of herself.

"What I'm saying is that Rosalind didn't do anything intrinsically evil. She simply has to learn to be more careful in picking friends and going to strange parties. And it's not just because she's *the* Rosalind Connolly, either, although that can make it a more expensive problem. I'd give the same advice to any twenty-year-old. Mess with people who are into drugs and weird things and you'll get hurt. And that means you too, lady."

"What?"

"I've read those articles about your friendships with the stars who carry coke around in their handbags."

"You really are incorrigible!"

Dianne felt better after her conversation with Dave, but she was still concerned about Lydia's future influence on Rosalind. Rosalind was capable of trying to prove what a wonderful friend Lydia could become. Dianne was determined to make that impossible.

She had not spoken to Tony since the impasse in Mexico. So far things had been quiet and the household money was arriving in her bank as always. Perhaps he had reconsidered. At any rate, he was still her husband and Rosalind's legal guardian.

Her call caught Tony in his New York office.

"Dianne." He spoke flatly. "I noticed in a column that you're in London these days. How long do you—and my jumbo jet—plan to stay?"

"I didn't take your big, fat jet. I took the Concorde. It's faster."

He laughed. "You caught me. I jumped to that conclusion. But you must admit it is a logical one."

"Tony," she said sweetly. "There's a little problem that's

215

come up here that only you can solve . . . for Rosalind. There's this tawdry little British girl at the Academy who has Rosalind bewitched, even though this Lydia is a lying, blackmailing bitch."

"You know that for a fact?"

"Yes," Dianne said dryly. "Five thousand pounds' worth of fact.

Tony detested blackmailers with all his heart, but in Dianne's case he was more interested in leverage than justice. "What do you want me to do? Have the girl rubbed out?"

"Don't make nasty jokes."

"I wasn't. So what do you want me to do?"

"I want you to get this girl an acting contract in Hollywood. Nothing great, just bit parts, lots and lots of bit parts until she chokes on them. The money has to be good enough to lure her out of London. Tony, you have to do it for me. You're the only person I know who can do it by the end of the week."

"And what will you do for me if I do this for you? Will you stop tearing my expensive legal papers in half?"

"I don't know what you mean. Things are fine aside from this little problem with Rosalind."

"We haven't seen each other in months, that's what you mean." His laugh made the Claridge's pastel phone quiver.

"That's your choice, not mine. You've known where to find me. Will you do it?"

"On one condition. You must go to your attorneys and work out a proposal for divorce that is satisfactory to you. Then we shall have something to bargain with."

Damn, she thought. She should have expected this. There were no more favors with Tony, only bargains. "All right. But I'll only do an agreement for a tacit separation, not a publicly filed separation and not a divorce."

"Ah well, the favor you ask is not so difficult for me. I suppose it is a fair trade. A step at a time. Now, give me the details for this thing."

ॐ ॐ ॐ

When Dianne returned from her long interview with the *Standard* the next afternoon, she found an irate daughter waiting for her in her suite.

"Who do you think you are, God?"

Dianne blinked. Her thoughts were still on her contrived,

elusive answers to some of the more difficult questions. She had been looking forward to calling Dave with a report. "Rosalind, calm down and brush your hair. You look like a demented rock star."

Rosalind ran a hand through the tangled curls and held her ground.

"Rosalind, I have just gone through a very difficult interview which I only did to save your sweet little bottom. I don't need any grief from you on top of it. If you want to stay and visit, sit down and be pleasant while I take a shower."

"Lydia's going to Hollywood," Rosalind announced accusingly.

"How nice for her." Dianne tensed.

"There have been no American talent scouts snooping around the Academy. It came right out of the blue, except I happen to know Mrs. Blue."

"Don't be silly. I couldn't arrange something like that."

"But Tony or a dozen other of your arty friends could if poor little Dianne wagged a finger for help. It's obvious. You want me to stay away from Lydia so Magic Mummy waved her wand to make Lydia disappear. I want you to know I am aware of your manipulations and that I shall continue to select my friends where and when I choose."

Dianne stared at her feet, upset that the scheme had been so transparent to Rosalind. The news had come as a surprise; she had no idea Tony could work things that quickly. Without a word, she left the room.

Rosalind heard her mother start the shower. The compassion she had felt for Dianne the night before had evaporated with this new maneuver. Manipulation—Dianne was addicted to it.

When the telegram from Hollywood arrived at the Academy, Lydia had been unquestioning. Someone had finally recognized her great talent. Rosalind said nothing, but she knew better.

Another emotion surfaced when Lydia announced she was leaving for California immediately: relief. Rosalind knew she could no longer feel free and open with Lydia. Like a shattered vase, blind trust once broken can be pieced back to form an outline of its former shape, but it can never be whole and unblemished again.

Despite the sense of relief, Rosalind's predominant feeling was the outrage that drove her across the city to confirm her suspicions that once again Dianne was playing *dea ex machina* from the wings. And she had done so. Caught unaware, Dianne had reacted defensively. Rosalind was satisfied that Dianne knew she knew. She felt in control of the situation.

But the battle was neither over nor won. Dianne emerged perfumed and composed in a pale lavender wool suit with matching shoes and purse. "You are expected at Boulderdash for dinner?"

"Yes," Rosalind answered calmly. "But all I have to do is call the cook and say I'm dining out whenever I want to."

"That won't be necessary since I'm dining there, too. I want to speak to them about keeping closer tabs on you. And you can expect a new team of agents by the end of the week." Dianne smiled softly. "You need better protection than you have been getting."

Rosalind reached for the chain holding her father's baby ring which she had worn around her neck since the Eighth Street Theater incident. She didn't care about the agents currently watching her, but the thought of Colin made her blink back tears. The whole mess was half his fault. If he had been there, none of it would have happened.

"Everything's under control now, wouldn't you say?" Dianne dropped the key to her suite in her silk purse and snapped it closed. The click echoed loudly in the silence. "I'll spend tomorrow shopping. I would kill myself if I came to London and didn't stock up on shoes and bags. And I promised your brothers new riding boots. Their feet never seem to stop growing. If you wish to take a day off from classes and come along, you may, but I don't think you deserve any special presents right now, do you?"

"I can't cut classes tomorrow, anyway." A major rehearsal had been called for *Twelfth Night* because Lydia was dropping out of the student production scheduled to open that weekend. She could have waited to leave until the short run—only a week—was over. But Rosalind knew that Lydia put herself first, whatever the occasion; however, she did not share that observation with Dianne as they drove through the misty chill to Boulderdash.

ᔕ ᔕ ᔕ

Sipping sherry and paying polite compliments to Tulip's

218

shrubs, Dianne played the charming and elegant matron. She sighed and wished aloud that her own gardens in the Hamptons and at Walnut Hill did half as well.

Rosalind restrained a giggle. Dianne never paid any attention to the gardens. They would have to be bombed out before Dianne would notice. And the truth was that old Tom took great pride in the flowers he coaxed from the sandy soil. His roses were the best in the Hamptons. It seemed unfair for Dianne to disparage his fine efforts for the sake of idle social chitchat.

To make matters worse, Dianne directed the dinner conversation to a discussion of Rosalind, speaking of her in the third person as though she were not present. "I really believe our Rosalind needs a little bit more watching. I had to straighten out a rather difficult situation with another student at the Academy."

"I'd wager it was that Blume girl." Lord Henry nodded sagely. "I knew you might find those photos upsetting if they made it over to American newspapers. I tried to discourage our Rosebud from seeing too much of her. She rang wrong, you know."

"You saw the pictures in the papers?" Dianne gasped.

"Rather a good likeness of Rosie, if I must say so." Lord Henry winked at Rosalind. "But the costumes were a bit much for the middle of the day."

Dianne relaxed. She had forgotten about that earlier incident.

"It was an afternoon lark." Rosalind made a moue.

"I never saw the pictures you're talking about, Henry," complained Lady Gillian.

"You read the wrong papers, my dear." He chuckled.

"I don't read the papers at all. They're entirely too depressing."

Dianne felt the conversation was getting sidetracked. "What I'm asking, dear Lord and Lady Boulder, is that you help monitor the people Rosalind spends time with. Perhaps it was a mistake to allow her to enroll at the Academy at all."

Rosalind poured gravy on the Yorkshire pudding, watching the thick, dark liquid fill the air pockets of the giant popover, determined not to look at Dianne.

"For theatrical studies, it is the best in the world, if I must say so," Lord Henry countered. "I say, if this Blume girl is causing difficulties, I could arrange to have her sent off to a provincial theater for a while—get her out of the picture, as it were."

"No, no," murmured Dianne, wishing she had known of Sir Henry's powers the day before. It would have saved her the humiliation and anguish of bargaining with Tony. "The unfortunate girl is leaving the Academy of her own volition. I do wish Rosalind's taste in people were half as good as her taste in art. She has always had a remarkable eye for good art, even as a little girl." Dianne laughed lightly.

"I myself have seen your daughter's eye for art in action. We've been getting around to the galleries, having a rather marvelous time of it."

"It's so good of both of you to take an interest in Rosalind. I don't know what to do sometimes. Perhaps if her father were still alive, things would be different and I would have someone to share the responsibility." Dianne glanced at him pathetically.

Rosalind suddenly felt orphaned. Should she laugh or cry?

"Just remember, you do have a backup team right here, solid as a boulder." Lord Henry puffed out his chest and thumped it with his fist.

Rosalind chuckled. He looked like a mustachioed rooster in that pose.

He rewarded her with a fatherly pat on the hand. "And it's not so bad, is it? Just a few growing pains. I still have them myself, sometimes. Mostly during the week, listening to the poppycock in Lords."

Dianne jealously watched Lord Henry and Rosalind together. There seemed to be a genuine warmth between them. She was half tempted to lay out all the sordid details and see if he would still say, "It's not so bad." But there was no point in doing that if she wanted Rosalind to stay through the school year.

"Then you will find some proper young people for Rosalind to meet? It would ease my mind so much."

"Proper young people? I can't guarantee the propriety of all of them, but it seems to me there are more young lords, earls, dukes and minor noblemen in London than anywhere else in the world."

"I don't need titles," protested Rosalind.

"I suppose you're right." Lord Henry winked at Rosalind again. "Connolly is title enough to deal with."

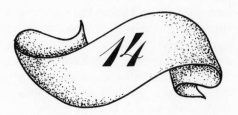

Colin was pleased with his flat at Windsmoor, a private building in the center of Mayfair, several blocks from Grosvenor Square. He had been duly impressed by the doorman in the neat glass cage inside the marble lobby, and the flat itself was more than comfortable; it was gracious.

He and T had been pulled off leave forty-eight hours earlier and told to report to London at once. Colin hadn't been given details, but the implication was that the agents they were replacing had screwed up.

His attempts to refuse Connolly duty had fallen on the commander's deaf ear. Colin and T were the most experienced and best qualified to handle Rosalind Connolly. There were never any complaints from Dianne Marino when they were on duty and that's what the commander wanted, an absence of calls from Dianne.

The officer's training course had been demanding. He had had little time to question or understand his feelings about Rosalind, but he hated wishy-washy relationships and he had sworn to himself that the farewell scene should stand. At the same time, he couldn't deal with the prospect of Rosalind's getting involved with some young man. He didn't think he could handle watching her hold hands or stroll arm in arm with another man while he stood guard, wondering what they did inside doors he couldn't enter. Those images had driven him to request the transfer which had been summarily rejected.

He was a professional, he lectured himself as he unpacked the fine wool suits he had ordered custom-made in Dublin the summer before. He couldn't help wondering if Rosalind would approve of the well-tailored gray herringbone and the blue-toned tweed. He had to stop thinking of her as a lover. It was over. He was only here because of a direct order.

Colin dreaded the prospective encounter. If she appealed to him the way she had in Washington, all the reasoned resistance could melt in the face of desire. He would be lost—he had never felt a stronger physical attraction for anyone.

He carefully arranged the tartan ties he had bought to complement the suits. He had not been able to resist buying a Connolly tartan along with the McReady one. Now it hung before him like an admission that she was still next to his heart.

He glanced at his watch. In five minutes, T would be downstairs waiting to lead them to the local pub.

ఌ   ఌ   ఌ

Rosalind belted her raincoat and grabbed her stage notes. Sir Henry had already left for an early meeting so she was on her own. She could dash for the underground, but the day looked gray and dismal. She asked Ronald, the butler, to call a cab. Her good spirits would be sustained better in the comfort of a warm cab.

Ronald nodded in the doorway of the breakfast room. "Your cab is waiting, Miss Rosalind."

"Thanks." She hurried out the door, adding a little skip as she crossed the sill. She stopped short and stared at Colin and T, standing in the drive beside the Secret Service sedan. The morning mists seemed to thicken as Rosalind tried to look into Colin's eyes and heart from forty feet away.

"Hey!" T grinned at her. "I thought you'd be glad to see your main men back!"

A shaky grin widened her face. "I am! I'm just surprised."

"Miss, are you the one that called for a cab?" The elderly driver sounded impatient.

"I'll talk to you later—how about lunch?" she shouted as she scrambled into the cab.

The peaceful drive across town was not to be. She tried to remember all the plans she had devised for Colin's return. She was going to make him jealous if he acted distant. But with whom? Lord Henry—or Alan? She laughed at the thought. But she was jumping ahead. She didn't know what was in his mind yet. She only knew what was in hers—no pleading or begging.

Still, just knowing he was in the car cautiously following her made her pulse quicken. I will not think about making love with him, she told herself.

She stepped out on Gower Street across from the Academy doorway with the carved images of Comedy and Tragedy above it. Should she dash inside before T or Colin could catch up? The question became moot as T approached.

"So this is it. The very Royal Academy of Dramatic Arts. Have you acquired a proper British accent yet?"

"Rah-thuh!" Rosalind laughed, but the sound caught in her throat as Colin joined them.

"Good morning." He smiled coolly, avoiding her eyes. "Is this our typical weather these days?"

"Cool and drizzly or drizzly and cool. That's about it," she said, wondering if that was to be the forecast for their relationship as well.

"How long before you come outside again?" asked T.

"Not before our lunch break, around twelve-thirty."

"Excellent. We haven't had breakfast yet. I say, old boy, a spot of tea would go down the hatch rather well, wouldn't you say?" T's vowels wavered between an American accent and a ludicrous British one.

"Try the Arts Café on Chenies Street. It's a dive, but not a bad dive—and it's open all the time. The Yorkshire Grey is a dynamite pub with great everything, but it's not open until lunch. Scout around. You're the agents."

Colin noticed the moisture beading on her raincoat. "You better get inside. This mist is turning into a downright rain." The habit of concern was hard to break. The mist was collecting like dew on the tips of her long lashes, reminding him of the night in Northampton when she had run to him for comfort, a comfort which had turned too easily to love. He watched her bound across the street, gracefully taking the steps in one fast hop. God, how he wanted to hold her again, taste the salt of her. He had known he would have to steel himself against his own emotions, but he had forgotten how strong the chemistry was. He silently cursed the commander for making him come back. He might have been able to let sleeping Rosalinds lie— but perhaps he was only lying to himself. "Let's get going," he urged.

"Why couldn't she have gone to school in sunny Spain? We're going to die of terminal shivers here," T grumbled.

Or horniness, Colin added to himself. "Come on, T, you're the toughest, meanest agent in the world, remember?"

"Only on sunny days." T lengthened his strides as he sighted the café's crude sign.

Colin's pace kept up, but his mind was busy searching for ways to remain detached about Rosalind. Maybe he should look for a hooker and get fast, if temporary, relief. It would help the body, if not the soul. The attraction was too strong for him to stay away from Rosalind for long.

♪ ♪ ♪

By the end of the week, both Rosalind and Colin were in miserable moods. Even Lord Henry noticed her gloominess and tried to help. He took her to a rugby match late Thursday afternoon and then on to a quiet dinner at his club.

She tried to be cheerful, but it was an obvious effort. Lord Henry felt at a loss, a sensation that was both disquieting and rare. Perhaps she was having a bad menstrual period. There were times that Ellie, his mistress, fell into a "blue funk" for no more reason than that. She always told him not to worry; it was all part of the female nature. He decided to give Rosalind a week before he worried in earnest.

On duty outside the club, Colin chided himself for feeling jealous of the middle-aged lord having dinner alone with Rosalind. But where was Lady Gillian? Did the old geezer have a penchant for young girls? His replies to T's good-humored remarks became curt and ill-tempered.

T pulled out *Sports Illustrated* and switched on the car reading light. It was better company than Colin.

♪ ♪ ♪

Friday night Rosalind was scheduled for a private party at the Savoy. Lord Henry had arranged it personally.

"All nice young people from good families, Rosebud, just like I promised your mother. A certain young Lord Clayburne is coming to call for you. He's considered the catch of London. He's got a full seat in Lords at the age of thirty-three and several estates to back it all up nicely—all thanks to his late father's weak heart." Lord Henry chuckled. "Though, personally, I sometimes think that young Clayburne has a will to match—weak."

Lady Gillian "Oohed" and "Aahed" properly at the soft rose crepe gown with floating panels and a gently scooped neckline that revealed the soft swell of Rosalind's breasts.

"Very romantic, my dear. I am green with envy of young Clayburne," Lord Henry joked. "Don't let him steal you away."

Sir Henry had no need to worry. Prematurely gray, with a hawkish nose dominating small brown eyes, Lord Clayburne's clothes and manners were carefully tailored. And both were a bit too precise for Rosalind.

Rosalind admired the Art Deco lines of the spacious Savoy lobby as they swept across the marble floors and up lush red-carpeted stairs toward the private rooms.

"It's a bit tacky for my taste, but the place has a certain amount of tradition," young Clayburne said in his stuffy manner.

She didn't reply as she pictured herself sticking a huge pin in his rounded rear to see how far he would deflate.

The party was in progress in the Princess Ida room, a pleasant private dining room with windows that suggested portholes looking out on the Thames. The view of the river's bridges was magical, with lights draped like sparkling tinsel above the dark water.

A seven-piece string orchestra played in the far corner and ivory candles in silver sconces on the wall cast soft light on the elegant partygoers. Draped across firm young bodies in well-designed splendor, the women's gowns created a pastel rainbow among the black tails of their escorts. Round tables were grouped to the side, sparkling with crystal and silver baskets of rosebuds on fine old damask. Rosalind noticed placecards in small silver holders at the tables. Please God, she thought, let me have one interesting person at our table.

Waiters circulated discreetly, bearing precious goblets of champagne and tiny puff pastries filled with pâté and crab.

"I promised Lord Henry that I would have you meet some people, and so I shall," Rosalind's escort announced.

She was more than willing to ignore him, but he was determined to play the proper cicerone. He immediately led her toward their host and hostess for the affair, introducing her as "Miss Connolly, daughter of the late American president," as though she were an institution.

Rosalind estimated there were forty guests in the room and it took Lord Clayburne more than forty-five minutes to introduce her to the first ten. Once he had made an introduction, he would launch into a boring account of some incident in Parliament. Finally, she was rescued by another stuffy young lord who asked Clayburne if he could speak to him privately on a "most important matter." Graciously, Rosalind assured him she would be fine left unattended for a few minutes.

The high heels Dianne had bought her to match the rose silk were beginning to hurt. She hadn't worn heels in months. Would dinner never be served? She had only eaten half an omelet at lunch.

"Alone at last." A deep voice interrupted her thoughts and she looked up into large dark eyes more than half a foot above her—in those painful heels.

"Have we met?"

"Not yet." He laughed. "I'm alone tonight and Clayburne wouldn't have the nerve to introduce you to me. He couldn't stand the competition. Jean-Claude Daumière. In the U.S., it's Jack."

"You're American?" His accent was definitely British.

"My mother is half American and half English, but my father is all French. Crêpe suzettes with French fries and plum pudding, that's me." He laughed again.

He does love his own humor, Rosalind thought as she appraised his dark wavy hair and straight, firm nose. His eyes were the darkest blue she had ever seen and his teeth were white and even. He's almost too handsome, she decided, but he was certainly livelier than anyone else she had met so far.

"The combination also makes me a lover of beautiful women, a driver of racing cars, a marvelous businessman and an unrivaled breeder of horses."

Something about the way he emphasized the word *breeder* made Rosalind shiver. "Is that all?" she flipped back.

"It's more than enough for me and most of the worthwhile women of the world. Doesn't it make you curious?"

"How can I possibly become curious if you tell me about everything that might intrigue me before I can ask?"

"Touché! But they say you cannot truly know Jean-Claude until you have tried him."

Rosalind found the repartee with the sexual overtones exciting, like playing with a special brand of X-rated matches. Jean-Claude put his finger to his lips and led her over to the round tables where he switched the name cards around.

Clayburne could not understand why he was the only guest not seated beside the lady he had escorted. "There must be some mistake, Miss Connolly. I am certain that I should be seated on your right."

"Oh, don't cause a stir, Clayburne." Jean-Claude grinned. "Somebody made a simple mistake."

Clayburne sat down across from them and glared as Jean-Claude patted Rosalind's thigh conspiratorially.

"How is your dear mother, Lady Eileen?" Clayburne looked down his nose at Jean-Claude. "I hear she had an unusually difficult winter."

"He's trying to get my goat, as you Americans would say," Jean-Claude explained to Rosalind. "Well, dear Clayburne, Mummy dear has spent the last year in a lovely sanatorium in Switzerland, paying exorbitant sums bribing the staff to sneak in the brandy from which the good doctors are trying to wean her. But she is finally at large again and as delightful and promiscuous as ever. Does that bring you up to date?"

"Your mother is a beautiful Englishwoman with great charm and breeding. If her father, the former Lord Chamberlain, were still alive, things would be different. It is my belief that only a decadent French reprobate could have led her to her present state of overindulgence."

"Careful, Clayburne." Jean-Claude's grin turned ugly. "I should hate to ruin your evening by challenging you to a duel."

"Such a challenge would be suicidal, Daumière. It is only fair to warn you that I am a Grand Master."

Rosalind was fascinated. It was so feudal. Although the challenge was ostensibly over the insult to Jean-Claude's father, Rosalind felt an inner satisfaction that she was the real issue. It was a modern Camelot in a way, with lords fighting for her favors.

"I have been told," Jean-Claude countered, "that native ability and superior reflexes can outweigh years of rigid training that dulls the wits, especially if the wits are dull to begin with."

The arrival of the sherried tomato soup saved them, although

Rosalind felt a bit disappointed that her swains had not retired to the green for combat.

She was soon diverted by Jean-Claude's tales of his yacht *The Wilde Carde*, and his revelries on the continent. Hand on her arm, he punctuated all his stories with soft squeezes. "If you had only been with me." She wasn't certain how much was true, but he was a vivid storyteller and he definitely had animal magnetism.

Lord Clayburne ate a silent meal, dourly noting Jean-Claude's every touch and pat.

The surveillance heightened Rosalind's awareness of Jean-Claude's advances. Even when she thought he was getting out of line, inching his finger along her inner thigh as he described romantic Mediterranean breezes, she didn't pull away. She was enjoying young Clayburne's discomfiture.

The dessert had flambéed and the dishes had been cleared. Couples were dancing on the polished parquet floor beside the windows. Jean-Claude pulled Rosalind to her feet, ignoring the custom that demanded she give the first dance to her unhappy escort.

Jean-Claude pressed her breast close to his chest.

"Jean-Claude," she gasped. "It's so public."

"You are absolutely right." His smile was charming. "It must be time for me to take you somewhere private." He waltzed her through the small crowd of dancers and out into the hall. "I shall take you home with me."

"You can't! Lord Clayburne has the claim ticket for my coat!"

Jean-Claude laughed and headed for the cloakroom to unleash his charm on the young woman guarding the wraps. A minute later, Rosalind's deep red evening cloak draped across his arm, Jean-Claude sank to one knee. "Your wrap, m'lady."

Rosalind was charmed; she slipped her arm through his, feeling grand and beautiful as they crossed the elegant Savoy lobby.

Comfortably ensconced in plush high-backed lobby chairs, T and Colin frowned at each other as Rosalind swept by, playing the grand lady. The switch in escorts rang the alarm bell for both of them. When Jean-Claude patted Rosalind's rear as they reached the outside doors, both agents went into action.

Outside, the mood changed. Jean-Claude ordered the doorman to bring his car. Rosalind protested that she only wanted some fresh air; the Boulders would worry if she didn't return with Lord Clayburne.

Jean-Claude nibbled at her ear. "Don't be a baby. It will be a beautiful night of love."

She looked up into the smiling dark eyes. The man was a stranger. She didn't want to make love with him. "No!" she cried. "I'm going back inside."

His hand tightened around her wrist. "What are you?" he hissed. "Miss Prim-and-Proper all of a sudden? You led me on like a pro and now you think you can just turn your snotty little back on me? No way. You have a lesson to learn."

In the shadows by the door, less than fifteen feet away, T watched Colin for the go-ahead to move. Colin raised his hand to signal silence. Jealousy was eating into him like acid, but he had to see if Rosalind could handle this on her own.

"You'll teach me nothing," Rosalind said angrily. "If you think it's fun to coerce people, you have a lot to learn. You better go get yourself a good doctor, because I think you're crazy, just like your mother."

Jean-Claude saw red. The question of his mother's sanity haunted him. His hand shot out and lashed at Rosalind's cheek.

The reprisal was just as rapid. Colin sprang from the shadows and decked Jean-Claude with a left to the jaw. T moved in from behind, catching Jean-Claude before he went down and cracked his head on the marble.

"Wow!" Rosalind's eyes saucered. She had forgotten about Colin and T.

Colin brushed his hands together. "I guess that's about it for the night for that bastard."

"Thanks." Rosalind grinned with relief.

A low groan emerged from Jean-Claude as T leaned him against the building. "I don't think your friend is feeling too well at the moment." T chuckled.

"He's right about one thing." Colin turned to Rosalind. "When you play the tease, you're asking for trouble. You must have been leading him on to get this far—and that's pretty lousy."

"I couldn't agree more. I think teasing and leading people on is lousy. It can hurt." She returned his gaze. "And it can lead to trouble."

T frowned at the two of them, aware of the personal overtones he didn't understand.

"You are absolutely right," she continued. "It can lead people to play games and do things they wouldn't normally do out of frustration, if you know what I mean. But maybe you have a very high tolerance level for frustration."

Her chin was raised as though it were waiting for a punch of its own. Colin noticed the soft swell of her breasts below the soft rose silk as she breathed heavily, revealing her emotion. Only the dim awareness of T standing beside them prevented him from going to her. "Not very."

"Then . . . Colin?" Her voice choked. She glanced at T, took a deep breath, and closed her eyes.

Colin took a step closer. "Relax. Everything's going to be all right, I promise."

"You mean that?" She opened her eyes. "Like before?"

He did not look away or drop the curtain behind his eyes. He was tired of fighting himself. "No, like now. Better."

Lord Clayburne appeared in the doorway. Colin's back blocked his view of Rosalind. "I say," he snapped at the doorman. "Have you seen a girl in pink come out with a tall gentleman, so to speak?"

"Oooh . . ." Jean-Claude groaned and opened his eyes, fighting for focus.

"Jean-Claude!" Young Clayburne's smile at seeing his adversary down on the marble sidewalk was spontaneous. "You seem to have had a go at it. But tell me, old man, what happened to Miss Connolly?"

Jean-Claude shook his head, not ready to try speaking.

"I'm right here, Lord Clayburne." Rosalind dimpled sweetly. "Safe and sound with my agents."

"I couldn't understand what had happened. You disappeared and I became concerned. Lord Henry would never vote my way again if anything happened to you here." He looked from Colin to Jean-Claude and back to Rosalind. "I say, what did happen?"

"Oh, Jean-Claude became a touch . . . pushy, you might say . . . and Agent McReady taught him a lesson."

"Good show. I'd say he's been asking for it for a long time. I almost gave it to him myself a bit earlier. Sorry I missed out on the fun. Looks like the poor old thing had a glass jaw. I do a bit of boxing myself, you know. If either of you gentlemen would like to join me at my club this week, I would be delighted to spar with you. I'm quite keen on it, actually. New blood is always good for keeping the edge on one's game."

"Thanks just the same, but I only fight when on duty, for professional purposes," Colin said dryly.

"And I'm big on paper work, myself," T added.

"Too bad. If you change your minds, do take me up on it."

Jean-Claude staggered to his feet, lurching toward his Jaguar which was now waiting at the curb.

"Hmmm." Young Clayburne glanced at him. "Doubt if he's in any condition to drive home. It would be a pity if anything happened to that fine automobile. I suppose we should play the Good Samaritans and get the old thing home safely."

"Do you know where he lives?" asked Colin.

Lord Clayburne nodded.

"Then I suggest you drive him home in his car and Smith will follow in your car. Then you can drop Smith at his flat on your way home. Meanwhile, I'll see Miss Connolly back safely to Boulderdash."

"That sounds reasonable to me," Rosalind said quickly. Her eyes were shining.

"Hey—" T scratched his head. "Why don't I drive the dude home in his car and you follow us in our car?"

"Because, my friend, we don't know where he lives. And I'm not certain he knows at this point."

"Your plan does seem the most practical." Lord Clayburne nodded soberly. "Please give my regards to Lord and Lady Boulder, Miss Connolly, and accept my apologies for not seeing you home, but I am certain you shall be perfectly safe with your Secret Service agent."

As they maneuvered Jean-Claude into the passenger seat of the sports car, T wished he could echo the sentiment.

かが かか かか

"You were jealous." Rosalind spoke with satisfaction.

"Very." Colin carefully drove three blocks from the hotel before he pulled over to a curb and spent a good long five minutes kissing her thoroughly. It left them both wanting more.

Rosalind lobbied for them to go directly to Colin's flat. She was eager to see their new pied-à-terre.

Colin reminded her that Lord Clayburne would surely see Lord Henry on Monday. The pious young lord was the type who would check on Rosalind's arrival time, if only out of courtesy. "Is there any way you can sneak out and meet me at twelve-thirty?"

"No problem." Rosalind grinned. She had worked out the escape route one optimistic afternoon weeks before. Agents stood guard at the front and the back of Boulderdash, but not at the sides. Rosalind's second-floor bedroom window faced a single-story wing whose roof led to the lower roof of a storage building a few feet from the side alley. "It's the proverbial blind alley," she promised.

ᔿ ᔿ ᔿ

Rosalind regaled the Boulders with her adventures. She toned down her participation in the Jean-Claude flirtation, stating she had only agreed to "step out for a little air."

Lord Boulder, wearing green striped cotton pajamas topped by a maroon satin smoking jacket, puffed on his rosewood pipe and chuckled. "It's a good thing your agents were on their toes. These are the new agents, aren't they?"

"Yes, and they are much, much better than the last pair. Colin McReady and Thelonious Smith who's called just 'T' by everyone."

"No wonder, with a name like that. Well, bring them to dinner soon. I'd like to thank them personally."

"Just remember to tell Cook." Tulip smiled, tightening the belt around her fuzzy yellow robe; she had been getting ready to retire. "But you are very good about keeping Cook informed, my dear."

"She's good about any number of things, dear Tulip." Lord Henry pecked a good-night on his wife's pink cheek.

Rosalind sat and chatted with Lord Henry until shortly past midnight. Her adrenaline was racing. If she went upstairs, she would only stew and count seconds. With Lord Henry, she only counted minutes.

"Well, Rosebud, I know you're still wound round like Big Ben, but this old man has early meetings tomorrow. Affairs of state. So much drearier than those of the heart." He chuckled. "But I am delighted to see you cheerful again. Now run along and tuck yourself in bed with the dullest book you can find. You'll be asleep in no time."

Rosalind gave Lord Henry a big hug and kissed his cheek. "Thank you for being so wonderful."

"Oh, tommyrot. I'm not all that wonderful." He beamed at her nonetheless. "What did I do to deserve this?"

"You exist. That's all you need to do to be wonderful." She waved a good-bye and lifted her skirt to dash upstairs.

Lord Henry was still smiling as he opened his briefcase to review his remarks on accelerating the denationalization of industry. Rosalind was taking a place in his heart beside his favorite daughter, Katie. No one was being crowded out. He had lots of room there.

᭼ ᭼ ᭼

Upstairs, the rose silk gown lay forgotten, heaped across the dressing table's chair. In jeans and a T-shirt, Rosalind carefully molded her pillows into the semblance of a body. She tucked blankets around her goosedown proxy and examined the effect. Not bad for a fast glance. Besides, Boulderdash wasn't summer camp and there weren't any bed checks.

The window was one of the old floor-to-ceiling variety, with only a short drop to the first-floor roof. She slid the wide window up, stepped outside and pulled it down, leaving an inch so she could reopen it later. The gravel on the flat roof crunched. She was walking over the library. What if Lord Henry were still there? She could see the dark Secret Service car on guard across the street from the entrance. Could the agent see her? She crouched lower, tiptoed the last twenty feet and jumped down to the roof of the shed, a loud four-foot drop. Where was Colin?

"Pssst!" came the reply to her unspoken question.

She peered down at Colin's upturned face. "I'm still ten feet off the ground. I only came this far before."

"Okay. Roll on your stomach, facing away from me, and ease your legs over. I'll get you the rest of the way."

It was awkward, but it worked. Her stomach suffered a few scratches from a brief skirmish with a drainpipe, but she felt brave and accomplished. "Maybe I should apply for CIA work."

"I think you would be miscast for undercover work." He smiled. "Unless it's my covers you're talking about."

She inched closer to him. Without question, he was taking the first steps this time.

In the privacy of his flat, he admitted how much he had missed her and how she had filled his thoughts and fantasies during the rigorous weeks in Washington.

She felt shy. It was almost like a new relationship. In the

old one, she had begged, pleaded and pursued. Now that he was saying all the things she had wanted to hear for so long, her tongue tied. It was easier to touch him and melt into him than to articulate the long weeks of hopes and hurts.

Colin sensed her mood and fell silent, letting the BBC and Bach fill the quiet, and letting their bodies communicate for them. Skin next to skin. Not just any skin. Her skin and his.

Rosalind wrapped her arms around his strong back. "I can't get close enough. I want to melt into you and come out the other side."

"I can get closer," he whispered.

A moment later she could feel him inside her as she never had before. Each stroke evoked rising sensations centered deep inside her. His tongue found hers and echoed the tempo of their lovemaking. She was part of him. They were one creature, throbbing with prehuman cadence, with one nucleus building and building, moving, thrusting, pushing toward . . ."

"Oh, ooh, ooh!" Rosalind heard her voice escape as the world trembled for her, reaching up inside her with uncharted sensation. A powerful ripple ran through her, then another. "Oh," she breathed.

Colin, although limp from his own long-awaited explosion, could feel the shudders inside her.

"God, Colin," she whispered. "I didn't know it could be like that. I thought I had come before."

He kissed her gently. "Miss Connolly, I can testify that you are even teaching this old dog new tricks."

"You mean you're going to start paying me?"

"What trash have you been reading, talking about that kind of tricks? All right. I'll pay you in services, but what will you pay me?"

"Services, of course."

"Then I guess we'll be well serviced."

"Service by the Secret Service. That does have a nice ring to it."

"Like ring around a rosy?"

"Truce. I'm starving. Lovemaking always makes me hungry, if you recall."

"How about an omelet?"

"You must have a kitchen." She bounded out of bed, flipping on lights as she searched the spacious flat. Quickly she found the kitchen, frying pan, eggs, ham, cream and spices. "I'm going to cook!" she called.

Colin wrapped a towel around his waist and followed.

"You look like you should be the centerfold for Hugh Hefner's version of *Good Housekeeping*." He laughed. "Would you like an apron?"

"Why? I'm a neat cook." She glanced down at the dark patch of hair inches away from the eggs. So strong was her sense of freedom and well-being, she had forgotten that she was nude.

"I'll get you something from my couturier's closet." He brought her a white undershirt large enough to serve as a mini-dress.

Happiness can stimulate all appetites. They polished off the omelet in minutes and Rosalind toasted more muffins for the impromptu midnight supper.

∾ ∾ ∾

In New York, Dianne reached for her robe and slipped it on before she looked back at Dave. They had made love twice in less than an hour. The first time had been embarrassing. She had wanted to burrow under the chinchilla cover and never come out. As warmly as she had responded to his kisses and his touch, she had completely frozen the moment he tried to enter her. He had withdrawn, immediately aware of the physical retreat that signaled psychological withdrawal.

"What's wrong, lady?" he asked softly. "Am I being too rough?"

Tears welled in her eyes. "I don't know if it's fear or guilt or outright Irish stubbornness. I've made such a point of being faithful while screaming at Tony for his unfaithfulness."

"You haven't made love to anyone else just so you could pour on the moral indignation? That's a pretty lousy reason for depriving yourself of any close relationship. Sounds awfully lonely to me."

Dianne did not comment. Dave was right and wrong. She had her fantasy to protect, the image of Tony crawling back as the penitent who recognized that she was better and purer than he was. And then she could make him pay and pay in a million ways.

But unshared fantasies can give way when confronted by

the force of shared realities. Gently Dave led her back to forgotten levels of feeling as he teased and stroked, refusing to accept a wooden doll for a playmate. The second attempt was given a warmer welcome. And although she could not let go and completely lose herself in his lovemaking, she felt her own body moving with him, straining and building to find its own release. She came with him.

Tony had only been able to make her come with his insistent tongue and hands, but she had never come with him inside her. In the beginning, light-years ago, she had come with Bill. But now the memories of the long, passionate bridal lovemaking were shadowed by those of Bill's frequent five-minute down-and-done sessions with her leaden responses, distanced by the images of his other women. All smudged memories of love.

With Dave, she wanted nothing more than warmth and communication. Hardly money. She guessed that her monthly allowance was more than he earned in a year. Certainly not power. The man had absolutely no political or business ambition. And not glory. She wanted to stay out of his columns, not appear in them.

Dave rubbed his cheek against her shoulder from behind. She could feel his afternoon beard stubble through the soft blue butterflies woven into her silk robe. It felt good, homey. She couldn't help comparing her reaction with her demands that Tony shave immediately before approaching her.

She smiled and turned to run her fingers through Dave's hair. It felt soft and fine between her fingers.

"Nice." He smiled into her eyes. "Lady, you can be nice."

"What have you done to me?" she murmured. "I must look a wreck. You've chewed away half my makeup and my hair must look like a Maori's."

He viewed her soberly. "Yes, I did manage to rub away all your makeup." He looked at her pale, smooth face, framed by equally pale curls. "And Bardot and Raquel would turn green at the sexy things your hair is doing right now. You look sensational, as though your blood has been stirred."

"Perhaps it has."

"Lady, you have to learn to properly appreciate the true, unfettered joys of life."

"I'm willing."

"It could take a lot of practice."

"My schedule is flexible."

" . . . and time," he added.

"I've got time these days."

Dave had to think of what this relationship might mean. She was accustomed to "21" and Orsini's. Dinner on Steak Row was his idea of a big night out. His beach houses were rented by the season in good years. Hers had come with the territory.

"Speaking of time . . ."—she glided to the dressing table to inspect the damage—"it must be getting late."

"A little before eight," Dave noted. "Dinnertime. After that exercise, I'm getting hungry. Want to go out for a steak?"

Dianne put down the hairbrush and turned her head away from the mirror to smile at him. "No, let's stay in. Marie can do steaks right here. Do you mind?"

"Mind? I'm as comfy as a flea on a collie. But I must warn you, a good meal could regenerate my lust." He walked over and lightly kissed the top of her head.

She grasped his hand and pressed it against her cheek. She didn't want to think about where the affair might lead. She was only deeply grateful that she had allowed it to happen.

He traced his free hand along the stretch of her neck. "Soft, sweet, pretty lady. Who would have thought it?"

"Ah, well, reporters think everything has to be proved to them." She punctuated her remark with a fast kiss. "I'll be right back," she whispered.

She returned in three minutes, carrying a dark blue silk robe. "I hope you don't mind if it's you-know-who's." She spoke shyly. "It's all I could find . . ."

Dave's brows knitted together. "If it's all the same to you, I'll just toss on my slacks and T-shirt."

"If you would rather. . . ." Dianne momentarily felt at a loss. "Want to play some backgammon before dinner? It will be at least forty-five minutes. Marie refuses to just 'throw steaks on.' I think she likes your looks."

"I can make a mean omelet myself."

"You'll have to get to know Marie a lot better before she allows you in her kitchen. Rosalind is the only person with open access so far."

"Not even you?"

"My talents in the kitchen are limited to pouring milk and finding cold beer."

"A nice cold beer sounds good right now."

Marie raised a mental eyebrow as Dianne padded barefoot into the kitchen, poked around in the refrigerator until she found the beer, opened the bottle herself and left with a cheery, "Marie, darling, the sooner you can have dinner ready, the better. We are absolutely starving."

Good Catholic French lady that she was, Marie could not find fault in her heart for any "carryings-on" that made her mistress so happy. It was a rare thing to see these days. She added two more tournedos for the visiting gentleman in case he was especially hungry.

Dianne set up the backgammon board in the den.

Dave was amenable to the game, but he admitted he only played occasionally on the beaches of Long Island and never seriously. "If you turn out to be too good, I'll have to find a new game," he warned.

"Don't worry. The twins beat me all the time."

Dave proved to be competitive, but Dianne's rapid calculations of odds and positioning soon left him far behind.

"Give me a break, lady!" he protested as she rolled double fives to sweep her last four blots off the board.

"I'm beginning to think I should stick to playing with Leda." He glanced at the big dog sleeping under the desk.

Dave quickly set up the board for a rematch. "Okay, let's see if you can repeat the performance." He gave her a wry smile. "I'm big on repeat performances."

The phone rang. Dianne ignored it; Ardyth or Marie could answer. The ringing persisted. It was her private line. She shrugged an apology to Dave and answered.

Lady Boulder was on the line, obviously upset. Rosalind was missing. She explained that Rosalind had come back from a party, chatted with them and gone to bed. Lord Henry had stayed up in the den for another hour, working. When he started upstairs to bed, he noticed Rosalind's purse on a chair. He had stopped by Rosalind's bedroom to quietly slip it on her dresser—and she wasn't there. Should they call the Secret Service inside or what?

Dianne could hear Lord Henry in the background sputtering for Tulip to get off the phone. He interrupted Tulip midsentence, obviously taking the phone from her. He apologized for the call, saying it was premature. The hadn't even checked the house or the greenhouse. She had probably wandered off in search of a glass of milk. He would check things thoroughly and call back.

She put down the phone and looked at Dave. "I can't seem to have one untarnished day in my whole life. Why? Why must she do this to me?"

"Rosalind?"

She filled him in. His advice was not to worry. It was only two in the morning over there and teenagers like to try their wings.

"Dave, you know what trouble she's been in there already. And if she came back from the party and is sneaking out to another, she's just asking for trouble. I don't like it."

"There's nothing much we can do until Lord Henry calls. We might as well finish our game."

Dianne couldn't concentrate. She kept glancing at the phone, waiting for an update on her delinquent daughter. She watched Dave hit her blot and lifted it to the bar. "I've about made up my mind to bring Rosalind back to New York. How can I be comfortable after that last fiasco? And now this."

"Aren't you jumping to conclusions about tonight? You've sold me on the fact that Lady Boulder is a dizzy broad and you said Lord Henry didn't seem terribly upset."

"Lord Henry would not sound upset if a firing squad marched into his house with their rifles raised. Stiff upper lip and all that."

"Stiff upper lip, stiff upper crust?" Dave rolled double threes and hit another of Dianne's blots.

"Veddy, veddy." She stared at her two blots stranded on the bar. "I concede."

"A tie! Now for the tie-breaker!"

"How would you like to play the tie-breaker in London?"

"What? Lady, my paper doesn't give me the same sweet, flexible schedule you have."

"I think I'd better fly over and get her organized to come home."

"Calm down, Dianne. I know a great therapy for jittery nerves. I start on the toes and work up very, very slowly."

"Please don't try to distract me, Dave." She brushed the blots off the bar and slammed the case shut. "I have to handle this tonight."

Marie's gray head appeared in the doorway. "Dinner is

ready, Mrs. Marino." She noticed that Dianne's lighthearted glow had faded. She withdrew silently. Leda yawned and exited, following Marie and the smell of the steak.

"My stomach is in knots. I don't think I can eat anything."

"Well, I can. You have left me ravished and famished, lady."

"Oh, Dave, I have to bring her home."

"Put it on the shelf for a while. There's a lot to be said for your own privacy with the kiddos away at school."

"That's a terribly selfish way to look at it. If we want . . . privacy . . . there are other places." She turned warm as she met his look.

"The lady has a blush left in her." He spoke with delight. "Methinks it bodes well. Let's eat."

The sight of Marie's sizzling steaks awakened Dianne's taste buds. She had not eaten anything all day except a muffin at breakfast.

Dave paused halfway through his second tournedo and watched Dianne eating with pleasure. The phone rang before he could comment and Dianne was on her feet. "Lord Henry," she whispered.

When Dianne returned ten minutes later, Dave was cheerfully applying his charm to Marie, assuring her that an apple tart and coffee would make him the happiest man in the world. "Well?" He turned to Dianne.

"Marie, bring me coffee, black, and send Ardyth to my room to help me pack."

"Is Rosalind all right?"

"I don't know. I hope so, but it doesn't matter right now. That was Tony's secretary, Gil. Tony was in some kind of accident on an offshore oil rig in the Gulf of Mexico . . . just a couple of hours ago. He was knocked off the thing and almost drowned. Gil said they were lucky to find him, but it was worse than that. Fractures, concussion, internal injuries—they don't even know what yet. He's in a hospital in Mexico City, unconscious." She was dazed. "I can't believe it. They're getting a plane ready for me right now. It happened just a few hours ago." She looked at Dave with a new kind of horror. "It was just when we . . . when you and I were . . ." She couldn't finish the sentence.

"Dianne, don't get crazy." Dave was on his feet, arms around her, supporting her. "What we did had nothing to do with what happened in Mexico."

"I don't know what to think," she said dully. "But why did it have to happen at just that moment? At the very same time?" She rested her head on Dave's shoulder and thought about crying. "They may move him to Dallas."

Marie padded in with the coffees and the apple tart for Dave. Whatever the problem was, it did not seem to be between Mrs. Marino and her new friend. That was good. Whatever else was upsetting her could be handled. Things always worked out, one way or the other, but Marie was glad that her lonely mistress had found a shoulder worth leaning on.

◆ ◆ ◆

It was well past 3 A.M. London time when Colin returned Rosalind to Boulderdash, but lights beaconed from every window of the great stone house.

"They're probably looking for you. I told you it was a good idea to get back tonight," Colin whispered nervously.

They worked out an alibi they hoped was plausible as they drove into the side alley. The engine sounded like a roar. Both hearts were pounding. The door creaked when they opened it and refused to close without a slam. Then Rosalind lost her footing on Colin's shoulder and pulled a section of drainpipe loose.

"We've got to find a better escape route," she whispered.

Colin put a forefinger to his mouth in warning, blew a kiss and mouthed "Good Luck" when she had reached the roof of the shed.

He held his position and his breath as Rosalind inched toward the bedroom window, reached it, slid her finger under the crack and pulled up. The window didn't budge. Pushing harder, she lifted it up a quarter of an inch before it caught again. Her teeth bit into her lower lip as she stared inside. The lights were all on, but the room was empty. She slipped off her right loafer and used the heel as a wedge, forcing it into the crack and twisting. It moved. She gave a final push and the window slid open with a resounding scraping noise.

She quickly slipped into her nightgown and robe, grabbed *All's Well That Ends Well* from the bookshelf and tiptoed into the empty hall. So far, so good. She moved down the back stairs to the kitchen where she cut a piece of cake and poured a glass of milk, gulping and gobbling to create telltale signs. She crept into the main hall and heard voices in the library as she slipped into the music room and positioned sheet music on the piano. She took a deep breath and casually walked into the library.

"Henry!" Lady Gillian stared at the specter in green flannel.

Lord Henry swung around from the group beside him. Rosalind recognized one of her agents, the butler, the gardener, four maids and Margot, the cook. Just about everyone, she thought. "Rosebud!" Lord Henry cried. "Where have you been?"

"Right here." She shrugged. "What's going on?"

"We couldn't find you," twittered Tulip. "Where were you?"

"I was just wandering around a bit. I couldn't sleep. So I read in the greenhouse for a while. Then I came in, fiddled with the piano and had a snack." She opened her eyes in the most innocent look she could muster.

"I didn't see any dishes," accused Margot.

"They're in the sink."

"And we wouldn't have heard you in the music room because Henry had it soundproofed last year, isn't that so, dear?"

"There, you see, Tulip—I told you there was no cause for alarm. It was silly of you to call Dianne and upset her. This monster of a house is filled with nothing but niches and crannies to get lost in."

"You called Dianne?" Rosalind's innocence gave way to apprehension.

"Don't worry, Rosebud. Tulip called, but I took the phone and assured your mother that it could well be a false alarm, as it was." He beamed.

Agent Williams looked dubious. "We searched all the places you said you were, Miss Connolly. I don't see how we missed you."

"It's the old hide-and-seek trick." Lord Henry chuckled. "Keep moving. As you were looking in one place, she was heading for another. A game of coincidence, or lack of it, I should say."

"It did give us a terrible fright."

"I'm sorry, Lady Gillian, truly I am. I had no idea I was considered missing." That part was true enough.

Lord Henry glanced at the book in Rosalind's hand. "What

were you out reading to the orchids, my dear?"

She handed him the book with a smile.

"Marvelous. Let it be our motto for the evening. 'All's well that ends well.' "

"Do you think we should call Dianne?" asked Rosalind.

Lord Henry checked the ship's clock over the bar. "It's after midnight over there. No, I'll call her in the morning. Let sleeping mothers lie, that's what I always say." Lord Henry's mood was fully restored.

15

Why had it all gone so wrong? Dianne stared at the shrunken form, the focal point of a dozen bottles and tubes pouring futile fluids into it. He looked like an old spider caught in its own web. She tried to repress the revulsion she felt at the sight of spittle oozing from the corners of his parched lips. The jaw was slack. They had removed the bottom teeth, the ones he had insisted were real. Just as he had insisted on his true love for her—that, too, had turned out to be removable.

Her heart lay still, like a stone beside a rushing river. Why could she feel no pity?

Perhaps things had gone wrong because they had been wrong from the beginning.

"You'll never have to worry again, Dianne," he had promised. "I'll always be here to give you everything you could ever want or need." How could she have been so naïve? She had been in her thirties, surely old enough to see him for what he was. She looked back at that Dianne as an innocent, a dreamer, a fool.

Her head swung back to him angrily. What I don't need, she thought, is a shriveled-up old man who is dying on me. Even lying here like this, the man could roil her. He wasn't worth it. She, of all people, should know that he was what he was and had been exactly what he had been.

Tony's background, as he had painted it for her during the long intimate evenings of their courtship, had sounded so romantic, a real rags-to-riches story. When Dianne had whispered to him about the hurts and slights of growing up poor among the superrich, Tony had opened his soul to her, long ago when she had believed he had a soul.

He had shared his deep resentment against the Sicilian immigrant father who would play no games with the mob-connected cousins, the man who allowed his family to "grow up eating pride." First one must be able to afford one's pride, Tony had said. And yes, he had learned to deal with those cousins. Then he struck his first wildcat oil well and he created some terms of his own. From that first drop of oil, he scratched and pyramided his way to a vast fortune that he was compelled to expand again and again out of fear that it might all disappear someday.

Dianne had felt a thrill of delicious disapproval whenever Tony alluded to his ties with the mob. Bill had insisted that organized crime undermined the tax system and the Justice Department. Even involvement by association with Tony made her feel like a child poking her hand into a forbidden cookie jar, only Tony's jar was filled with green grown-up savories.

In those early days, Tony had been generous, even lavish. His planes were dispatched for friends of her friends. The favors for his yacht parties were done in 14-karat gold and real gems. And despite past resentments, he had provided generously for his parents until their deaths. He had even established generous trust funds for his ex-wife and children voluntarily. At that time, Dianne did not believe Tony had a stingy bone in his body.

But it turned out that the voluntary trust funds had been nothing but a clever tax dodge. It had taken five years of protracted and vituperative proceedings before the court determined that an additional fifteen million in cold, available cash dollars was more equitable.

Only later, when the two-year-old marriage held more vinegar than wine, did Tony bitterly compare her with his first wife, Helena. Both were useless people expecting something for nothing. That was the greatest sin of all for Tony—to give without getting. There had to be strings for him to pull.

And it was later still that Dianne learned that Tony, like Bill, had a lifelong habit of betrayal. Sitting under a hair dryer at the salon, she read in a movie magazine that Nicole Turrell had been involved in breaking up Tony's first marriage. How quickly he had returned to form—and to his tried and true French mistress. What a fool she had been.

And her daughter questioned why she insisted on checking people's backgrounds and being wary and slow to trust. Rosalind had to learn to protect herself if she expected to survive.

But survival is always defined in very personal terms. In Dianne's terms, a lioness's share of Tony's estate spelled survival.

The estate. The thought hung like a question in the sterile room, interrupted only by the muted rasps of the old man fighting to breathe. What had he done with his will? All her lawyers had was a file copy of a will drafted five years ago. If that one had not been altered, she could expect from thirty to forty million, probably a lot more now. That figure, based on twenty percent of the estate, had been calculated before the OPEC squeeze had sent oil prices skyrocketing.

The uncomfortable thought hit her that if Tony had spent days with his attorneys working on the separation papers she had torn up in Mexico, he could have easily drawn up a new will at the same time.

She glared at him. The bastard couldn't talk. She wanted to shake him and shake him until he opened his eyes and told her what he had done. Had he made the ultimate betrayal?

A nurse looked in and noticed the still figure in the cherry-red suit. She smiled warmly at Dianne and marched over to straighten the covers and check the tubes. Dianne nodded a silent greeting; she looked pale and strained.

"No change," the nurse said softly, half to herself. The prognosis was bad. The man had suffered a severe fracture in the back of the skull and there had been hemorrhaging. The emergency operation had relieved the life-threatening pressure, but the brain damage could be severe. A wave of sympathy flooded through her. "How old is your father?"

"My husband will be seventy next April." Dianne could not help feeling flattered.

"I shall say a Hail Mary for you and for him." The nurse padded from the room.

Dianne looked back at the shrouded figure of her so-called

husband. Nearly seventy. It sounded so old. He would have died soon anyway, but this was such an ugly way to die, sordid and decadent. It was nothing like the sudden collapse of Bill, which had been unexpected and clean, somehow more than mortal. Tony was confronting her with cloying mortality.

She gripped her arm, feeling her own flesh and muscles, which also would stop living and feeling one day . . . not so far away, perhaps. She was nearly fifty. In another twenty years she could shrivel up like Tony. Twenty years, the span of Rosalind's life. It seemed such a short time ago that Rosalind was two feet long and gurgling and blowing bubbles in her tiny bath. Life was too short, over too soon. You had to get what you could, while you could. I shall hate dying, she thought, and for the first time in her life, she believed it could happen to her.

She could watch Tony recover, hide the emotional scars and play the loving wife, but she could not stay and watch him die like this. Whatever he had done with his will was done, to be accepted or contested. Too much love had been publicly lost between them for her to need to pretend for the press.

Antonia, Tony's daughter and elder namesake, would be back in an hour with her red eyes and stringy hair. The husk of Tony would not be alone for long.

The dry antiseptic air felt stifling with a sharp, almost sweet odor. It's already like a morgue, she thought. Her arms were nothing but goosebumps. She had promised Tonia she would wait for her to return before going back to the hotel to change. But the death watch—the death smell—was unbearable.

An orderly carried in a huge spray of gladiolas, flowers Dianne always associated with wakes and funerals. She had banned them from all her tables—even in the White House. Her stomach heaved for a second before she willed herself to calm. That did it. She could take no more of this Tony, either.

∽ ∽ ∽

Tonia hurried down the hospital corridor carrying a vase of yellow roses, because she was in Texas and she deeply desired to remain the "light of Papa's life," even if he were comatose.

The stocky little nurse stood beside Tony's bed adjusting an IV bottle.

"Where's Dianne?" Tonia demanded.

"Who?"

"Dianne. My . . . my stepmother. The blond lady."

"You are the Marino daughter?"

"I am Antonia Marino, yes."

The nurse slid a note from her pocket, thinking that Dianne was much more pleasant than this younger, more demanding person. "This is for you."

Tonia grabbed the note rudely and skimmed it. Disgust deepened the lines etched beside her mouth. The nerve of that woman! Dianne was going to an island off the Florida coast for a few days because the vigil was too much of a strain. She promised to return if there was any change, for the better or worse.

Tonia crushed the note and aimed it at the crumpled florist's paper on the dresser. "Better or worse, my eyeball. She was a lousy wife to him living. I guess it's logical that she would be a lousy wife to him dying."

The nurse turned her head away.

Panic entered Tonia's voice. "What if the doctors decide to operate again? Won't they need her signature?"

"Mrs. Marino has talked with the doctors. And she has left phone numbers."

Tonia grappled for the crushed note. There had been numbers on it. Dianne would have to come back. Although Tonia had no affection for Dianne, she didn't want to be stuck by her father 's bedside twenty-four hours a day. Tony, Jr., had promised to arrive by evening, but that could change.

She poked at the flowers crowding the steel bureau and pulled a chair closer to her father's bed. The doctors had to be wrong. He had to recover. But what would that matter to her own life? She rarely saw him. Since the day he had moved out of her mother's house more than twenty years ago, she had only been the very occasional "light of his life." She jerked a magazine from the bed table to divert her thoughts. The six-month-old *People* featured Dianne and Tony on the cover—Dianne in New York and Tony in Paris with a solid black line running between them down the center. "Continents apart— are Dianne and Tony talking?" asked the headline.

Tonia stared at the photographs. The one of her father was flattering; it made a powerful contrast with the cocoon lying beside her now. She grudgingly conceded that the picture of Dianne taken at some formal affair was exquisite. All the old jealousy of the woman she blamed for taking her father away surfaced. It had been impossible to hate the entire collection of stars and beautiful young women with whom Tony had consorted. And as long as there had been numbers, there was always the possibility that Tony would come home to her mother and to her. But she could, and did, focus her hatred on Dianne, making Dianne the target of two decades' worth of hurt and resentment.

The nurse stepped back into the room. "There are reporters here, asking to see Mrs. Marino."

Tonia's eyes narrowed and a sly smile turned up the edges of her full lips. "Yes? Tell them that Mrs. Marino is not here, but Miss Marino will be happy to speak to them."

∽ ∽ ∽

Dianne rang for a bellman. When her personal demons had driven her from the hospital room, getting out of town seemed the only thing to do. Now she was torn. It would look bad for her to desert a dying Tony, but what earthly good would it do to sit and watch him die an inch at a time? Anything they might have done for each other should have happened years before.

The phone rang. Lord Henry reported that all was well. Rosalind had been in the greenhouse. London was a false crisis, but so was Tony's accident in its own way. Alive or dead, they had little left between them.

Cameras flashed as she followed the bellman through the lobby to the waiting limousine.

"Mrs. Marino, do you have any news on your husband's condition?"

"Dianne, are you leaving Dallas?"

"Dianne! Look this way!"

With Pavlovian instinct, she turned and smiled defensively as the flash went off, simultaneously upbraiding herself for getting caught. She stared stonily ahead to complete her getaway.

∽ ∽ ∽

The sand had molded to the curves of her body underneath the velvety beach towel. The sun seemed to be pouring strength into her, warming every cell of her body. It was the third afternoon she had devoted to the solar ablutions as if she were trying to burn apprehension, guilt and despair from her system forever.

The Conways, the friends who had responded with gracious

alacrity when she called to borrow their island off the west coast of Florida, had the guesthouse in order and the sweet-faced Cuban maid seemed eager to please her.

She called Dave every evening, urging him to join her, but she was secretly pleased with his stubborn refusals. She still felt some guilt about the coincidental timing of their lovemaking and Tony's accident. It was fading as her tan deepened, but she didn't want Dave with her on the island if Tony died in Dallas—if she didn't make it back in time.

She spent her days in sunlit solitude, reading historical romances and temporarily closing the door on personal concerns. And on Tony. When there was a change, she would be called. The plane waited in attendance on the private airstrip, two hours from bedside.

She found her lack of anxiety curiously out of character. Perhaps she had anguished, feared, regretted, questioned and hoped too much in her life. Now the emotions had all poured out of her, leaving her open only to the healing sun. At that moment, she wanted to feel nothing else.

"Señora! Señora!" The little maid scampered across the beach. "Teléfono! Importante, she say!"

Dianne mopped at her face with a hand towel and moved leisurely toward the house, refusing to speculate on the nature of the call.

She ignored the sand trail she made on the handwoven carpets and picked up the phone to be greeted hysterically by a distraught Antonia.

"Dianne! I've been holding forever! I thought the stupid maid had forgotten to get you. She barely speaks English!"

"Calm down, Tonia, and tell me what the crisis is."

"Dianne." Tonia's voice choked. "You have to get back here now. He . . . He's asking for you."

"He's talking?" That was a miracle. "He's asking for me? Are you sure?" That was more than a miracle. It was unbelievable.

"He's not coherent, but we've caught 'Mama' and something like 'Nicole' and he keeps saying, 'Dianne, Dianne.' It's distinctly 'Dianne.' Why did you leave without saying a word? You could have waited."

Dianne could not be bothered to explain. "I'll be there in less than three hours."

Her placid mood remained. She felt inured to Tonia's hostility.

Tonia obviously still wanted to hurt her, even now. The girl had to mention Nicole. She was probably heartbroken that Tony hadn't muttered "Tonia."

Why was Tony asking for her? Had he one last cruel word or was some ancient love bubbling up from a covert well deep within his subconscious?

She would never know. By the time she arrived at the hospital, the priest was chanting to the accompaniment of the slow beeps of the heart monitor. Tony's pulse was weakening inside the body now swaddled by an ominous new plastic cocoon, mechanically forcing air into his laboring lungs.

Dear Lord, she thought as she crossed herself, it's a rubber torture chamber. Again, the sweet antiseptic odors sent spasms to her stomach. She pulled a perfumed handkerchief from her pocket.

"Surely not tears," Tonia said caustically. "You are too late, as usual. He's gone back into a deep coma."

"Oh." It was so anticlimactic—hurry up to wait.

"Don't you care?" Tonia rose from the bedside. "No, you don't care about him, do you? It's just his money. Well, you have had plenty of that, so why don't you go away and sun yourself on another island? Why don't you just stay the hell away from him? You've never given him anything but grief from the moment he met you."

"Tonia." Tony, Jr., a tall slim man in his early forties, grabbed his sister's arm and looked at Dianne with an apologetic smile. "You can see how upset she is, can't you? She didn't mean it, did you, Tonia?"

Tonia jerked her arm free. "You've always sided with that witch. She put a spell on you as well as on Papa."

Dianne paled beneath her tan and turned toward the door.

"Please." Tony, Jr., dropped Tonia's arm and hurried to Dianne. "Please don't go. Tonia's crazy with grief."

"Yeah, Tony. I'm just a crazy Italian. Thanks for sticking up for me like a good Italian brother." Tonia spat at the floor beside Tony, Jr. "I'm going out for a while. I don't like the company around here."

Dianne, Tony, Jr., and the priest stared after her. Then the priest crossed himself and continued his soft chant.

"I returned because she asked me to." Dianne spoke quietly,

factually. The brief outrage she had felt at Tonia's outburst passed.

"Dianne, I'm really sorry about her press conference. It really wasn't fair, was it?"

Dianne looked blank. "I haven't read a paper since I left here. I don't know anything about a press conference."

"Oh, dear." Tony, Jr., looked uncomfortable.

"She can't have said anything worse than she's already said in print before." She gave his hand a gentle squeeze.

"Tonia was upset and the press picked it up like vultures. Those bastards can't even respect a deathbed, can they?"

"No, especially not deathbeds." Dianne's thoughts flashed back to another death that had been surrounded by more press than this would ever have.

"It's the uncertainty that's maddening, isn't it? The doctors said brain damage is certain, but they were amazed when he whispered names. They seemed to be questioning their own diagnoses. They say it could be over anytime or he could last months. Even years. All we—and they—can do is wait."

"Odd, isn't it? Your father never liked to wait for anything." Tony, Jr., nodded. "And now he has no choice, does he?"

Dianne rubbed the hinge of her jawbone, feeling the muscle tension. She had thought she was unaffected, but she realized her dissociation was superficial.

Months. Dianne closed her eyes. She hadn't been able to sustain the empty vigil for a day. She looked through the thick plastic at the distorted outline of the rasping form. Tony wouldn't want to live as half a man when he had tried to be a man and a half all his life.

Why didn't the doctors pull the artificial life systems' plugs and let him go? Let him go, she prayed to somewhere. Let him go. Go where? If there were a heaven, was there a special section for those who had lusted for power and fame? With a flash of wry humor, she pictured Tony and Bill meeting on a cloud to discuss their mutual earthly wife. "Outrageously extravagant," Tony might say. She envisioned Bill shaking his head with a sparkle in his eyes. "True, but what the hell, Tony," he might say with a chuckle, "we didn't take it with us."

"Dianne—Dianne?"

She opened her eyes to see Tony, Jr.'s concerned face. It was nice to have one Tony Marino concerned about her for a change.

"Why don't I take you back to the hotel for an hour's nap? I can pick you up for dinner later and then we can stop back here afterward. All right?"

Tony, Jr., still hadn't lost the habit of phrasing things in questions, Dianne noticed. It was almost as though the senior Tony Marino had used up the family's quota of statements. Perhaps when Tony, Sr., was gone, Tony, Jr., could alter his punctuation.

"That sounds lovely, Tony."

Their exit was quiet. Tony, Jr., fended off a small pack of reporters in the hospital lobby and Tonia was nowhere to be seen.

Too rested from the beach days to nap, Dianne called Dave with her daily update. She brazenly related her imagined conversation between Bill and Tony by the pearly gates. Dave laughed and begged to use it in his column someday. He promised to quote Saint Peter as the source.

"Not a word, you bastard." She laughed. "Or I'll send you to join them!"

She was humming as she opened the door to Tony, Jr.

න් න් න්

Dinner was a downhill slide. Tony, Jr., wanting to play the mediator, had pressed Tonia into joining them. Flashbulbs burst among the candles as they entered the hotel dining room. The known presence of reporters at adjacent tables added constraints to the already strained conversation.

Tony, Jr., floundered on his update of Marino Enterprises. It sounded too much like appraising the spoils the three of them were destined to divide.

Dianne tried fashion, but Tonia made it clear she wasn't interested.

The food was undistinguished, but it gave them a safe subject for mutual criticism while it lasted.

Then Tony, Jr., returned to the crisis at hand. "Do you think we should discuss who stays and for how long? Like family shifts? What do you think?"

"I think it's a teeny bit premature for that," Dianne replied. "If he holds his own for a few days, we can talk about it then."

"Papa would despise being like this if he knew!" Tonia spoke passionately. "If he doesn't get better soon, I'm going to make the doctors turn off the machines."

"Tonia!" Tony, Jr., looked as though he had been struck. "Have you forgotten that we're Catholics? You know you're talking about a mortal sin, don't you?"

Dianne held her tongue, not wanting to openly agree with Tonia's sentiments. She needed Tony, Jr., for her own support system.

"How long can we stand looking at him that way? He's like a great, decaying premature baby."

Dianne looked down at her demitasse to hide a smile. Tonia's simile was graphic and accurate.

"Tonia, aren't you forgetting that Father spoke this morning? He's still in there somewhere. The shell isn't empty yet."

"He moaned nonsense," Tonia snapped back. "Nothing but trash." She looked at Dianne.

Dianne ignored the slur. "Tony, dear, I could use an after-dinner drink. Amaretto would be nice."

But the Amaretto was too sweet for Dianne, too reminiscent of the nauseating hospital smells. She pretended to sip as they toasted Tony's recovery.

৶ ৶ ৶

Their toasts were short-lived. Tony stopped rasping forever in the first moments of dawn.

Although Dianne felt a kind of morbid relief, she realized she also felt a genuine loss. There was no one left to lecture her when her charge accounts ran too high, no one to play the martyr for and no last resort no matter what the terms. It left her with a hollow feeling.

At breakfast, Tony, Jr., complimented her on her composure while Tonia bombarded her with dark, tearful glares. "After the last time, when Bill died, people will expect you to maintain composure, won't they?"

Dianne almost laughed aloud. Tonia's lack of tact was just like that of Tony, Sr.

She had called her New York attorneys first thing in the morning before joining her stepchildren for breakfast. Jordan March III, the youngest and most attractive of the senior partners, was on his way. She had been concerned about her allowance and the continued availability of the Marino aircraft. Wait and see, she was cautioned. Some things depended on the goodwill of those running Marino Enterprises, especially her stepson.

At forty-three, Tony, Jr., still had an air of adolescent uncertainty. Divorced three times, the equivocating heir to a large portion of Tony's estate was still ripe for the plucking. Dianne toyed for a moment with the idea of marrying the son to retain the father's empire and laughed at the total folly it would be. Two Marinos in one lifetime would be grounds for commitment—clinical commitment.

Tony was talking about the funeral plans, asking perpetually, "What do you think, Dianne?"

What did she think? She didn't care what they did with the shriveled shell that had once held Tony Marino. For this funeral, there would be no riderless horse, no caissons and no heroic tears to shed with the nation and the world.

It seemed to her that politicians were much better at dying than the rest of the world. There was so much more to work with—traditions to follow, rotundas to drape and mourners to gather.

She would invite none of Bill's family or friends to this burial, not even Sean. He had never approved of Tony, anyway.

Her mother would come. Jane would be calmly supportive and outclass all the Marinos, looking twenty years younger than seventy. Jane could still make Dianne feel young and uncertain sometimes, but not simply because of Jane's youthful appearance. Somewhere in the life Jane had carefully sculptured with Uncle Herbie, she had come to peace with herself. Dianne envied that, because she had never been able to do it for herself and Jane had never been able to do it for her.

"Dianne?"

She returned to Tony, Jr., and Tonia. "I think the Tony I knew would want to be buried in the quaint little cemetery in Oklahoma where his parents are buried. He showed it to me years ago."

"Wrong," snapped Tonia. "He wanted to be cremated."

"Did he make any stipulations about it? Do you know what he put in his will?"

"Not much for you. That much I know." Tonia smiled.

"What are you talking about? Dianne is entitled to as much as we are, isn't she?" Tony, Jr., asked the question for Dianne.

Breath bated, Dianne waited for Tonia's reply.

"Papa told me last month that Dianne would get what she deserved—next to nothing."

255

"Tonia, can you hear yourself talking like an idiot?"

"Tony, I think you should check with your father's lawyers about the will to find out what his wishes were for burial. Then we can discuss all this intelligently."

It turned out that Dianne was correct and Tonia wrong about the burial. But Tonia was close to the mark regarding the provisions for Dianne. Her allowance was to continue at the same level until she remarried or died, Tony, Jr., reported in a state of shock.

Tonia was ecstatic. She and Tony shared equally in an estate estimated at nearly a billion dollars while Dianne would receive only about half a million a year.

"Does that seem right to you?" asked Tony, Jr.

Dianne smiled, tight-lipped. "Jordy, my lawyer, will be here soon. We can talk then."

"Don't worry, Dianne, I'll make sure you have everything you need. That's only fair, isn't it?"

"Papa put what he thought was fair in his will. That's why people have wills." Tonia fully intended to block Dianne from receiving any further benefits, even a free ride home from the funeral if possible.

"Tony," Tonia said to her brother, "what about the island and the yacht?"

He glanced at his scrawled notes. "I think we have an equal share in them."

Tonia smiled. She could talk Tony into taking the yacht so she could have the island for herself.

"They're split three ways—you, me and Dianne."

Tonia's smile dissolved.

Dianne's smile replaced it. At least she would have a few bargaining points.

Tony, Jr., worried his notepad. "What do you think about notices, Dianne? How shall we handle things?"

"Darling, Gil is the best person to deal with all that."

"But I think we should do something, don't you?"

Yes, Dianne thought to herself, she and her lawyers would definitely do something. Poor little Tony. Dianne smiled at him. He's lost his compass. Perhaps she had been lucky that Tony, Sr., had never gained that type of control over her. She was accustomed to handling things without him. Yes, this husband's death was different. There would be no major moves this time. It all boiled down to a nasty funeral to attend and the postmortem legalities. She resolved to handle both with quiet grace, a shadow in the background.

"Oh, my God." Dianne started. "I haven't called the children. I don't want them to hear it on the news."

"Yes, they'll be *so* upset, won't they?" Tonia spoke with venom. "We all know how close they were to Papa."

∽ ∽ ∽

Billy and Timothy were no problem. They eagerly volunteered to join her. Timothy dryly promised to make the great sacrifice of missing an English test and Billy said he would weep over missing an oral French exam. Both expressed sympathy, but neither sounded upset. Dianne decided they would be the perfect escorts for the funeral, her matched pair—if they didn't pull any of their tricks. She would have her mother give them a warning lecture on the flight down.

Then she called her mother. Jane, ever ready to do the correct thing, promised that she and Herbert would pick up the twins and continue west as a foursome. Dianne was relieved. She would have her own civilized contingent to ward off the Marino histrionics.

Next Rosalind. Should she insist that her daughter come? Rosalind would be an unwilling griever.

Dianne glanced at her watch. She would call after lunch. Her stomach rebelled at the thought of food. She wanted Tony's remains, his funeral and his family gone from her life. No more old men for her bed. She thought of Dave. Would he come to Oklahoma if she asked? She laughed. Jane would have a heart attack on the spot and Dianne wasn't ready to test Dave. This was hardly a crisis.

∽ ∽ ∽

Dianne reached Rosalind with the news at seven P.M. London time. Rosalind carefully expressed sympathy. "How do you feel, Mummy?"

"Oh, darling, I'm fine and . . ." Dianne caught herself before she expressed honest relief. "It's difficult here. We must have him moved to Oklahoma. And Tony's family is here."

Rosalind didn't want to interrupt the even keel of her London life, now that Colin was back—especially not for Tony, alive or dead. But if Dianne needed her . . .

"I sure could use my bestest friend right now." The maternal sigh echoed in Rosalind's ear. "But Grandma Jane is coming with Uncle Herb and the twins."

"And Uncle Sean?"

"Tony was never one of his favorites. I may ask, but I won't be disturbed if he can't come. I'm really feeling rather calm about all this."

Rosalind caught the subtext. Dianne wouldn't be upset if she didn't come. "Our second big production opens this weekend and I'm stage manager, remember?"

"It would be difficult for you to get away, wouldn't it?"

Rosalind nodded into the receiver.

"One more thing, darling. What kind of flowers shall I have sent in your name?"

"Carnations." Rosalind hated carnations and Dianne knew it.

"Don't be nasty." Dianne chuckled softly. "I think a nice spray of pink rosebuds would be appropriate."

"Fine."

"How do you want it signed? Rosie, Rosebud, Rosalind, the mystery guest or what?"

"Rosalind Connolly is fine, Mummy." Even at his funeral, Rosalind wanted to maintain the greatest possible distance from the man who had never made it to "Papa" for her.

"I'll say good-bye to him for you," Dianne whispered as her throat thickened again with the thought of death.

A small cloud of guilt passed over Rosalind's head. There was still time to catch a Concorde and rush to Oklahoma—to be snubbed by Tonia and fussed over by Tony's loud-mouthed friends. She glanced at her watch. Rehearsal began in forty minutes.

ᗡ ᗡ ᗡ

Dianne slowly walked back into the living room of the hotel suite, analyzing the feeling of relief that Rosalind was staying in London. She had needed Rosalind's constant presence and support—a lot to ask from a five-year-old—to bury Bill. But Rosalind was too volatile these days and Dianne needed no unwanted scenes if she were to get through the affair in the gracious, passive style she had chosen. The twins, albeit high-spirited, could still be controlled.

Lists in hand, Gil was sitting beside Tony, Jr., obviously well on the way to staging his boss's last event.

Tony, Jr., looked up at Dianne helplessly. "I miss him already and he's barely cold."

Dianne nodded silently. She would never again be able to think of Tony without seeing the tubes. She wished she had never responded to the call or left New York until it was over. But that would have been impossible; too often, reasonable actions seemed impossible.

"We'll all fly to Tulsa tonight at seven." Gil spoke crisply. "How many rooms will you need, Dianne?"

"Two suites and two rooms. Mother and Uncle Herb are bringing Billy and Timothy. And we'll need rooms for their agents."

"Mmm." Gil tried to be tactful with his next question. "You did pack black, didn't you?" He had noticed that Dianne was wearing pale blue.

She frowned at him. No, she had not packed black. It had never occurred to her that Tony was capable of dying, at least not until she had seen the clay figure in the plastic tomb.

"I'll take care of it, Gil." Jane could stop by the apartment and pick up the black Chanel and whatever else looked appropriate. Dianne's smile swept from Gil to Tony, Jr. "I'll be ready."

16

It was dark when Rosalind finished at the Academy and climbed into the front seat of the Minor, pushing Colin into the middle against T.

"Isn't this cozy?" T muttered.

"The three musketeers are heading for the Dover Pub tonight, remember?" She snuggled against Colin's arm. A week before, T had stumbled into Rosalind making herself at home in Colin's flat. He had at last become a reluctant party to the arrangement.

The trio had established a norm for the evenings when Colin and T were on duty and Rosalind wanted to go out to a show or restaurant. They went together.

Rosalind found the arrangement comforting. She had spent the greater part of her life as the female member of a younger trilogy.

Habitually, the triple dates ended on a forgetful note. Colin would forget to bring along a book Rosalind wanted to read; Rosalind would forget a sweater she had left in Colin's flat. T became accustomed to reading a magazine on duty in the lobby until they "found" the missing item several hours later.

"I'm not sure the Dover Pub is a good idea for tonight." Colin looked serious. "A stray reporter might catch us."

"You mean with Tony's funeral today?" Rosalind laughed. "Shall we stay at the flat and have a private wake?"

Rosalind's high spirits disturbed Colin. "Is Dianne all right?" he asked.

"She sounds fine. She didn't press me to fly over, which means it isn't upsetting her much. I wouldn't be much of an asset over there. I wasn't very fond of the Marino connection, you know."

"We know." T spoke flatly.

"What's that supposed to mean?" she demanded.

"Sometimes I think you forget how long we've been with you. We've seen some of your brattier moments with Tony."

Rosalind turned back to Colin. "Okay, no Dover Pub. So what do we do?"

"Go to the flat and cook spaghetti. We still have some sauce left from this weekend," Colin suggested.

"All three of us?" T looked interested. "I've heard about that sauce—loaded with sausage and pepperoni."

"Why not?" Rosalind grinned. "And this time if anything's lost, you can look for it in your own flat."

"What's lost," T muttered, "is my mind. I've completely lost my mind."

∽ ∽ ∽

Rosalind's week continued smoothly. An unidentified reporter called Boulderdash to speak to her, but the butler headed off the inquiry.

Dianne called and reported that the funeral had been tolerable and that she hoped her gracious behavior with Tonia and Tony, Jr., would ease the negotiations regarding the estate.

"Didn't Tony write a will?" Rosalind asked.

"He wasn't in his right mind when he did. He practically left us paupers."

"I can come home and go to school in New York. I don't mind."

"Don't be silly. It's costing next to nothing to have you in London, thanks to Lord Henry." Dianne sighed. "We aren't poor-poor-poor, perish the thought, but it's not what we should have. Jordy promises that the current will won't hold up in court, but it could take forever to settle things. But don't you worry about it. You just worry about staying out of trouble and doing well in school."

Rosalind did worry about it. She cut back on her lunches and magazines and tried to save.

Noticing Rosalind's new parsimonious bent, Colin tried to assure her that even if Dianne didn't get a cent from Tony's estate, Bill Connolly had left her enough to be comfortable forever. Still Rosalind worried. "You don't know how important money is to Dianne."

"I've heard."

The subject changed to Ian, Colin's son, expected for the weekend. Rosalind was apprehensive about the visit. Ian was too close to her own age. Would it seem strange to meet her lover's nineteen-year-old son? Would it make Colin suddenly seem old? One thing was certain. The weekend would be platonic with Ian lodged on the couch.

෴ ෴ ෴

The visit was a success. Rosalind's fears lost substance when Ian insisted on staying with friends in Notting Hill. "They're really friends of friends at the University of Dublin," he explained. "But I promised to drop some books and things there so I might as well sleep there, too. They have an extra bed."

Colin protested, but he conceded that his couch couldn't compete with a real bed. The arrangement suited everyone.

Ian bore little resemblance to Colin. The boy was blond, slim and of medium height. His curly hair and wide grin gave him an elfin quality. But in repose, he looked unformed, young and uncertain. Rosalind found it reassuring that he seemed younger than her brothers.

The father-and-son weekend passed amicably with no secrets shared and no feathers ruffled. On Saturday afternoon, Ian and Colin toured art galleries and in the evening, back on duty, Colin took them all—Ian, Rosalind and T—to see *The Merry Wives of Windsor*.

During a scene change, Ian observed that his father and Mr. Smith had a cushy job.

"We like to keep a close watch on Miss Connolly, right Mr. McReady?" T responded with a wink for Rosalind.

Colin and Rosalind laughed. Ian joined in the merriment.

The next morning, Ian joined Rosalind and his father for a ride in Hyde Park. The expansive grounds were crisscrossed with riding trails.

Lord Henry's stables beside the park were well maintained,

always ready for family or friends' pleasures. Months before, Rosalind had singled out a strawberry roan, conveniently named Strawberry, and Colin had his own love affair going with Shindra, the sleek black pride of the stable. Ian opted for a chestnut mare named Dahlia, one of Lady Gillian's gentle favorites.

The day was crisp and dry. The sun had burned off the last of the mist before they rode from the stables into the park.

"All right!" Rosalind shouted against the wind as she turned back toward Ian. "Welcome to the real London!" They rode until noon before lunching at Boulderdash.

Ian was impressed that his father was treated with respect by Lord Henry. The peer seemed to value Colin's opinions on subjects ranging from parliamentary bills to horseflesh. Across the table, Lady Gillian hovered over Ian like a long-lost son, coaxing him to eat more mutton and have a bit more of the cream sauce. Only Lord Henry shared Tulip's awareness that Ian looked much like their own son, Roger, who had died of viral pneumonia twenty years before.

෴ ෴ ෴

Back in Dublin, Ian's cronies were properly impressed by his tales of London and his father's job. As Ian embellished the stories with greater detail, it occurred to him that his father and Rosalind seemed very close. He heard himself wondering aloud if something was "going on" between the two. The thought bothered him. He and Rosalind were almost the same age.

Then Ian continued the narrative and described Boulderdash in detail. He looked at the dark, brooding graduate student who was concluding a ten-year quest for a doctorate in Irish history. "Lloyd, you would not believe some of the woodcarving in the place. I should take you along next time, just so you could date the stuff!"

Lloyd looked up, drawing his thick, dark brows together to make a solid line across his forehead. "I just might make me a visit like that with you. It all sounds most intriguing."

෴ ෴ ෴

"What you need, rich lady, is a job, right here in New York."
Dianne laughed.
"I'm serious. All your kids are away at school. You don't even have to get up to eat breakfast with anyone anymore and you're getting lazy."

"Oh, Dave." She leaned her head on his shoulder. "There's nothing I can do." She didn't need a job, she thought. She needed only a man to lean on, to be there, like this.

"Ridiculous!" He bolted upright, knocking her away. "There are a million things you can do."

"Name one," she challenged. "Other than marrying the most notorious and perverse men in the world."

"Cut the crap. That's dead and gone." He grimaced at his phrasing. "But it's true. You need a positive project to keep yourself interested."

"Such as . . . "

"If other politicians' wives can be successful lobbyists, you could be fantastic. You could even have fun competing with Sean for clients."

"Dave, what do you think I am? I am not going to run around Washington shinnying up to mealymouthed politicians I can't stand—or use Bill's friends to further someone else's purpose. It's all right for Sean, but I would rather scrub floors like the Irish washerwoman I'm descended from."

"I thought you were elegant old Dutch, founding family and all that."

"My maternal grandmother was from County Down and was known to have scrubbed a floor or two in her time."

"That's Northern Ireland, you know. Was she Protestant?"

"Having been raised a good Catholic girl, I never asked me mum. Hey, I'm hungry. The thought of scrubbing floors works up an appetite."

"No food until we settle this job issue. My mind is fermenting and I feel a vintage idea coming on."

"What am I supposed to do? Consider it or drink it?"

"I'm being serious, lady. Okay. Here it is. You are going to become a publisher. With your connections and money, it would be a cinch."

"Not quite, I don't have the money you think I have. Bill's estate is tied up in trust funds and I can't touch any of the principal there. Tony's is still in litigation and there's a chance I could come out of it with only a pittance for an allowance."

"You might really need a job then." Dave grinned. "Why don't you get your husband's family to back you?"

Her blue eyes sparkled with amusement. "Which husband?"

"I don't know." Dave laughed. "Try both. Make it a joint venture of the pirates and the politicians."

"But which is which?"

"Either-or," he retorted. "The politicians with the clandestine pirate roots or the pirates with the covert politicking."

Dianne's laughter died as she traced a well-chewed finger along the shoulder seam of Dave's plaid shirt. "Seriously, Dave, I would love to be involved with books and authors and literary things, but I don't want all that responsibility. What if the children should need me or what if I decided to take a long trip?"

"Yes, we must make concessions to your wandering soul and vagabond spirit. But publishers do travel."

"Only on rigid business schedules."

"Then what about being an editor?"

"That sounds like too much work for me, working and reworking manuscripts; I don't think I have the discipline."

"You could if you wanted to."

"I don't want to. I'd rather be involved with concerts or ballet, theater or fine arts . . . if I have to get a *real job* to make you happy."

"It's not to make me happy, Dianne. It's for yourself."

"Perhaps you're right," she sighed. "But I still don't know what I could do."

"Let's think logically. Your interests are in the theater and the stage, but you don't want heavy responsibility. Okay. You could be a cultural consultant for a major theatrical agency, arranging international tours for plays, concerts, operas, dance troupes . . . things like that. You could bring back the Moscow Circus and make me a happy man." He grinned.

"Do you really think I could do it?"

"Is the pope Catholic? You have great State Department connections here and easy entry into high levels of any other government, especially for cultural matters. You'd be perfect. Do you know anyone at William Morris well?"

"No," she shook her head. "I mean I know people there, but I think they're too commercial. I need something small and elite." She stopped to think. "Lady Eleanor has a friend in London, Lisbeth Mark, who has a booking agency that does that sort of thing. It's called Goldmark, International, I think. And they have a New York office. Goldmark. It has a nice sound."

"Yeah," Dave spoke dryly. "That's important for your image."

"As if you cared about my image!"

"I don't, but I care about you."

∽   ∽   ∽

Within a week the announcement was released to the papers. Dianne Connolly Marino had become an active associate of Goldmark, International's New York office.

To celebrate her new job, Dianne insisted on a week of sun and games first. Since it all had been Dave's idea, he had to come along. No excuses were acceptable this time.

Dave capitulated. He was ready for a late November tan, but he stood firm on one thing. He was paying their expenses. Dianne sweetly agreed, knowing that the Marino planes, thanks to Tony, Jr., were still at her beck and call and that the villa in Aruba, complete with staff and larder, would also be gratis.

∽   ∽   ∽

The press hounded them from the moment they deplaned in Aruba.

"What is your relationship with Dianne, Dave?"

"Family friend."

"How long have you been having an affair?"

"It's not an affair," he protested. "It's . . . it's a vacation."

After listening to a few of his lame comments, Dave decided that the "no comment" he detested on other lips was the only reasonable reply for himself.

Dianne found it all very amusing. "It's very Christian, in a way, darling." She laughed. "You get to turn the other cheek and feel what it's like on the other side of the cameras. It's such a marvelous role reversal! I just love it."

It was a double role reversal. With Tony and Bill, she had been the one to rail at the press.

"Dating you is like dating the Goodyear blimp," Dave growled on the return flight to New York. "I'm not sure which one is harder to miss."

"But we are tan and beautiful and I'm all ready to go to work."

∽   ∽   ∽

Although Dianne had carefully outfitted herself in subdued slacks and simple pullovers, she couldn't avoid the intense interest of the small Goldmark staff. Pique paralleled amusement

266

as she noticed her personalized memo pads disappearing along with her privacy.

She solved the problem by staying home except for planning sessions, which she insisted be held in quiet restaurants away from Goldmark's elegant but busy east side townhouse.

But maintaining her privacy was one thing. Feeling competent was another. Angus agreed to two weekly sessions until she felt stabilized in the new situation.

"You've only just started, Dianne." He tried to be supportive. "If you never arrange a single tour, you're worth ten times what they're paying you simply to have your name on the letterhead."

That was the problem, she stormed at him. Goldmark only wanted her name, that's all she had to give. She was a fool to think she had any talent for arranging complicated international events.

But within days of that session, she sailed in on a pink cloud to her meeting with Angus at Lady Eleanor's. She had been wrong. Goldmark was perfect for her. She was arranging an American tour for the Yugoslavian ballet company and the Belgrade symphony together, something that had never been done before. Everyone at Goldmark was amazed. Her ego was soaring.

A week later, the project was shelved. The high technology trade agreement between the U.S. and Yugoslavia that Sean was advocating was voted down in the House. And the Yugoslavian cultural attaché suddenly had no time or interest in Dianne's project. Her spirits plummeted.

Angus was getting worried. Dianne was too volatile. Smiles and tears were part of life, but Dianne was riding a roller coaster between them. He required that she call daily, just to check in.

Desperately, Dianne looked for projects to prove her worth.

_ॐ_ _ॐ_ _ॐ_

As far as Rosalind—in London—knew, Dianne loved her new position. On transatlantic calls, Dianne was nothing but breathless excitement about working with Goldmark. Content with the comfortable relationship with Colin, Rosalind was delighted that her mother was involved with something that kept her from worrying about what she, Billy and Timothy were doing every moment.

Ten days before Rosalind was scheduled to fly home for

Christmas, the peace was shattered by a call of whispered suspicions from Dianne.

Rosalind was confused. What did Dianne mean? Had she somehow gotten wind of her relationship with Colin? "What are you talking about?"

"The reports," replied Dianne. "They look too good. Lord Henry insists you are being a perfect young lady and I know you better than that."

Rosalind laughed. "You're joking."

"I'm not. I know you are sneaking around doing something. But we can get into all that at Christmas in East Hampton, like old times." Dianne's tone was acid.

"Mummy, are you all right?"

"I'm fine, just fine. It's you I'm worried about. You had better make certain you stay out of trouble, damn it. I can't take any more problems from your direction."

There was no point in arguing. It was obvious to Rosalind that Dianne was drinking again. Something must be going wrong for her. Rosalind's anticipation of the family holidays was colored with new apprehension.

❧ ❧ ❧

Later that evening, Rosalind heard herself snapping at Colin for no reason. She apologized, sensitive to the fact that the conversation with Dianne had left her on edge. She shared her anxiety with Colin, who promised to be on hand this Christmas.

In the past few months, without emotional barriers between them, the relationship had reached an easy rhythm. If they no longer made passionate love every night, they were close in other, deeply satisfying ways, discussing topics from missed cues at Academy performances to the psychology of friends and family to global politics. The only untouched subject was the future of their relationship. Both had fears, neither had answers; both had wants and needs the other filled like missing puzzle pieces. For the moment, their individual pictures were complete.

"You really are my best friend in the world, Colin."

"Everybody needs a best friend."

❧ ❧ ❧

All the cousins except Rosalind had brought a friend to the East Hampton Christmas Bea-hive. Even Billy and Timothy had

268

dragged along a friend from Andover to help pack the old house. Only Laura was conspicuously missing. No comment was made, but Sean seemed intent on being merrier than usual.

Sean focused his attentions on Dianne, also without a partner for the Christmas weekend. He was maturing wonderfully, Dianne realized. With his square jaw and wonderful physique, he looked so much like Bill had toward the end. For one whimsical moment, she speculated on whether Sean would ever divorce Laura. Then she could marry him and "tidy up the family." She curtailed the thought with a private laugh. One Connolly man was enough for a lifetime. Sean was as much of a ladies' man as Bill had ever been.

Turkey, cranberry sauce, oyster stuffing, roast beef and cloved ham, sweet potatoes and mashed potatoes, green beans and asparagus, plum pudding with hard sauce, pies and cookies— the sideboard groaned. It was Christmas Eve dinner, with twenty-two present and accounted for.

Crystal and sterling sparkled beneath the chandelier, while candles at the windows sent out beams toward the beach. The Connolly clan and friends did justice to the feast.

As brandies were passed out to the adults, the younger folk hurried to the upstairs playroom to inspect the tree and rattle presents one last time.

Downstairs, the adults wandered through the warm, rambling rooms of the old Victorian beach house, seeking spots to settle back and digest in peace.

Disguised in one of Dianne's old wigs, Rosalind sneaked away from the buzz of the Bea-hive for a private drink with Colin in the old inn nearby. Colin chortled at her appearance. She threatened to take off the wig and create a scene. But before she could make good on her threat, he placed a small jeweler's box in her hand.

She froze. What if it were an engagement ring? She wasn't sure what she would do. Gingerly, she opened the box, stared and looked up at her lover. "It's perfect!" She examined the finely wrought miniature gold rose with the tiny diamond chip dewdrop sparkling on one petal. She turned it over. "Eighteen karat, no less."

"Good eyes, love. I asked for twenty-four, but they said it would be so soft it would melt away in the rain. I didn't want it to fall apart."

269

"I don't want us to fall apart, either." Without the feared diamond to force her to deal with commitment, sentiment felt safe.

"Now that Santa's come and gone, we'd better get you back before you're missed and you get your agents in trouble."

"I certainly wouldn't want to do that." She reached under the table and produced a large shiny red rectangle. "But not before you get your turn."

"Ah! This is a surprise." Colin attacked the paper. Inside was a mellow leather attaché case from Dunhill's London store. "Hey, this is fantastic. I really need this. You noticed that the old one was on its last legs, didn't you?" Then he frowned at her. "I thought you were poor these days."

"I saved my allowance for weeks."

"More like months, I'd say." Colin knew the precise amount of her allowance. She complained about it constantly.

"Of course, I peddled my body on Marylebone Street Sunday afternoons when you weren't looking. That helped." She wasn't going to tell him that she had sold the butterfly pin Dianne had given her from Tony; she still had over £500 stashed away under her scarves back at Boulderdash. She knew Dianne would be furious if she ever found out, but Rosalind didn't care. It had been her pin and it certainly couldn't upset Tony anymore.

Colin dropped her at the edge of the compound, reminding her that the Secret Service car was parked at the rear entrance. "Go in the side," he whispered.

Rosalind tiptoed around the side toward the porch facing the beach. That seemed safest. As she neared the porch, she heard Dianne's and Sean's voices drifting out into the cold night.

"Dianne, I can understand your temporary difficulties with Tony's estate up in the air, but you will have to talk to Henry directly. He handles all matters dealing with the Connolly trusts. Are the twins and Rosie okay?"

"For now. Tony prepaid their school fees through the end of the school year and they still get their five hundred dollars a month allowance sent from Marino Enterprises—thanks to Tony, Jr., I think."

"Really?" Rosalind whispered. Sixty-five pounds hardly translated into $500. The dollar hadn't fallen that far! Any guilt she had felt about selling the butterfly pin vanished.

The voices lowered. Dianne's tone sounded sad and Sean's voice was comforting. Rosalind decided to try the side door rather than walk in on Dianne and Sean.

The screen door at the side of the house was latched. "Damn!" She jiggled the handle, trying to shake it loose.

The sound carried to the front parlor and Sean called, "Hello! Who's there?"

Rosalind jerked off the blond wig and tossed it on the ground behind a green garbage can. "Just me, Uncle Sean."

She ran around to the porch, up the stairs and into the front parlor. "Hi, Mummy. I took a walk on the beach. It's so beautiful tonight. And I didn't realize that the side door was locked."

"Oh, Rosalind, how could you? All alone like that." She looked tragically at Sean. "Sean, she was out walking alone on the beach. Can you just imagine the headline if there had been a photographer hiding out there? 'Lonely Rosalind Connolly Walks the Beach on Christmas Eve.' When will you ever learn discretion? Why must you do this to me on Christmas Eve?"

Sean squeezed Dianne's hand. "Come on, Dianne. She's okay. And *all's well!*" he shouted. "Now, I have to get upstairs and count noses. Good night, Rosie."

" 'Night, Uncle Sean. And thanks."

Rosalind was in no mood for a fight. She still felt a warm glow from knowing that Colin's precious gift hung around her neck just above her father's baby ring. Quietly, she sat on a chair and attempted to block out Dianne's ranting about maintaining Connolly privacy and not leaving herself so vulnerable.

"Well?" Dianne confronted her. "What do you think?"

"I think I'm ready for bed. Good night, Mummy. Merry Christmas."

"Merry Christmas!" Dianne echoed. "Merry Christmas. Is that all you have to say for yourself?"

"I'm sorry. I didn't think a little walk would upset you. Please, let's not argue on Christmas Eve."

"Yes . . . Christmas Eve at the Bea-hive. There have been so many of those here." Fading memories surfaced to divert Dianne from her irritation with Rosalind.

"Have you seen the upstairs tree yet?"

Dianne nodded. "That one has lots of presents under it. It doesn't need Santa. Now this one . . ." She waved toward the ten-foot pine beside the parlor fireplace. "This one is the real

271

one where Santa will leave his presents. That's because it's right next to the fireplace."

Somewhere in the shadows of her own memory, Rosalind remembered Bill Connolly saying that a million moments before.

"Don't you think we should put out some milk and cookies for Santa before we go upstairs to bed?" Dianne spoke with a soft smile. "Like we always did?"

"Oh, Mummy, we're all grown. Terry's thirteen—and she's the youngest."

"But it's always been part of our Christmas here. I know we haven't been here for several years and everyone's older now, but . . . it's part of this place for me."

Rosalind caved in to the tears welling in her mother's eyes. "Do you think we could find the stockings?"

"Cook might know." Dianne sniffed happily. "She's been here forever."

Dianne led the way into the warm, spacious old kitchen to enlist the cook in the search for Christmas past.

"I can't remember them being down here, Mrs. Connolly. Maybe they're in the attic."

Dianne looked up from the big drawer she had been rooting through, ignoring the cook's error. "Here they are!"

Rosalind leaned over Dianne's shoulder to see the old red felt stockings. Names had been carefully embroidered in green wool on the white cuffs. Wordlessly, Dianne tucked the BILL stocking back in the drawer and handed the one marked LAURA to Rosalind. "Terry's full name is Teresa Laura. She hadn't been born yet when these were made. I don't think her mother would mind if she used it. Poor Laura, she isn't here to mind. I hope she isn't having too bad a time. At least she isn't getting piles of terrible publicity—yet."

"Let's go!" Rosalind wanted to stave off any return to melancholia. "But not without the milk and cookies."

Cook shuffled over to the cookie jars. "We have sand tarts, rum bars, lemon, snickerdoodles and chocolate mint—those were Mr. Bill's favorites." She chuckled. "I had a hard time keeping that jar full. Molly, over at Mr. Bill's house now, was my assistant and I kept her baking day and night."

"Sand tarts and rum bars for Santa. And I'll have a chocolate mint right now." Rosalind munched reverently as she looked around the quaint old kitchen where her father had trailed after Cook, hoping for treats.

"I have the stockings." Dianne moved into the hallway. "You bring the Santa supplies."

By the time Rosalind had arranged the cookies and milk on a tray, Dianne had the bright stockings in place.

Rosalind admired the effect. Her small packages from London would fit nicely in the toes.

"Oh, dear." Dianne looked dismayed. "What about the guests? We don't have stockings for them."

"You already have presents for them waiting under the upstairs tree." Rosalind placed the milk and cookies on a small table beside the fireplace. "There."

"You're right, darling. This will be our special family tree, because my little family is here again with the big, big Connolly family for a wonderful family holiday." She gave Rosalind a hug. "It's roots time, my darling. It's time to get back to your roots."

Rosalind looked carefully at Dianne's bright eyes. The pupils were pinpoints. Was her mother taking drugs?

"And for New Year's we'll be with Grandma Jane and Uncle Herb. All our roots. Roses must have roots to be strong."

"Well, this rose is going to wither if it doesn't get some sleep. Aren't you tired?"

"I just want to stay here for a while and admire the tree and the stockings and the season."

"Are you feeling all right? You seem . . . hyper."

"Oh, maybe a little edgy from my new diet pills. I just couldn't seem to drop five nasty pounds I gained from munching Danish in my office. So Angus gave me some wonderful pills. My size six is perfect again and they really do give me extra energy."

"You should be careful of those things, especially with all the wine you've been drinking."

Dianne patted her daughter's cheek. "Still the little mother, always concerned. That's sweet, but I'm not even taking the prescribed dosage. Just one or two now and then—when I feel like it."

"Please be careful, Mummy. If they're amphetamines, they could give you a heart attack or stroke if you mix them with liquor."

With a shrug, Dianne laughed.

As Rosalind drifted off to sleep, minutes later, she did worry for a moment. What would she do if something terrrible happened to her mother? Who would be left, besides the twins, really? But in the comfort of the Bea-hive, with the Connolly clan on all sides, the thought did not hold great terror. Her hand curled around the tiny ring and the rose and she slept soundly.

∽ ∽ ∽

The next morning Dianne was up with the birds, munching sand tarts and lemon cookies as Santa's proxy while Rosalind tiptoed outside to retrieve the wig before it could be found and questioned. She returned to the parlor with her small presents in time to see her mother eat the last cookie. "Aha!"

Dianne whirled around and eyed Rosalind with her pile of bright boxes. "A Christmas elf—caught red-handed!"

"A charlatan Santa caught with her hand in the cookie jar!"

"All right, I won't tell on you if you won't tell on me. Now, let's get to work." Dianne picked up a pile of parchment paper. "I wrote everyone a poem to put in the stockings. I wrote one for each guest, too. Those we can roll into little scrolls with a red ribbon and put them on the mantel above the stockings."

Rosalind picked up a sheet. The careful lettering was interspersed with small, charming illustrations done in ink and water color. They must have taken hours to do.

"You did these last night?"

"Of course, my darling. They didn't take long."

"Only all night, I'd think."

Dianne ignored the observation, her throttle open wide, as she chattered about the presents. Two hours later, by eight A.M., the old house had surrendered to total chaos. Ribbons, boxes and wrapping paper were scattered everywhere.

Grandma Bea chirped about, begging everyone to be careful not to mix up cards and tags for the thank-you notes to come. Then everyone trooped off behind her for Christmas Mass before returning to the Bea-hive for another feast.

Dianne waxed more exuberant with each course. The Connollys were accustomed to soft murmurs and quiet witticisms; today, she seemed out of character as she raised her voice above the normal Connolly din. She applauded having "the family reunited," toasting the "true spirit of Christmas and dear, dear Grandma Bea and the wonderful comfort of the Bea-hive."

With the advent of the Beef Wellington, she cried out in sudden anguish, "If only Bill were here today to see how his children have grown."

274

Rosalind glanced at her brothers. They looked as uncomfortable as she felt.

ᑭ ᑭ ᑭ

After dinner, Dianne held court in the front parlor, regaling Sean, the cousins and their guests with exaggerated tales of moving Tony's body from Texas to Oklahoma and of dealing with the Marino relatives. Timothy and Billy avoided further embarrassment by whisking their friend upstairs for a game of darts in the playroom.

"How can we stop her? She's really out of control," Rosalind whispered to Sean.

"I don't know. She went through the same sequence when your father died. She held up, totally under control, for weeks and weeks. Then suddenly she bottomed out and went through a bad period, a lot like this."

"I didn't think his . . . his going . . . would affect her all that much."

"Neither did I," muttered Sean as he watched Dianne dramatically throw her hands in the air and laugh hysterically at one of her own remarks.

"Maybe it's the pills," Rosalind whispered.

"Pills?"

"Last night she said the doctor had given her some diet pills. They could be amphetamines or some other kind of upper. She said they give her extra energy."

Sean nodded. "And they could also drive her right through the ceiling when mixed with holiday wine." Sean was clinically informed. Laura's doctors had warned him against serving Laura wine along with the mood elevators the doctors had prescribed for her deep clinical depression. Sean had not told anyone, not even his mother, that Laura was spending Christmas at Payne Whitney in New York where some of the best psychiatrists in the country were trying to find the cause of her depression—chemical, psychological or both. He refocused on his niece. "Maybe you should give Dianne's shrink a call and let him know what's going on."

Rosalind gave Sean a peculiar look. He was treating her as an adult capable of handling a difficult situation. "Thanks, Uncle Sean. I'll do that."

Sean looked at his niece with a frown. Why was she thanking him for handing her a rather unpalatable chore?

"She'll be okay." He tried to sound reassuring. "I guess she's made it through worse."

꿈 꿈 꿈

The next day the worst seemed over. Dianne was openly exhausted. She had recognized that thanks to the tiny pink pills she had not slept in three days. She hadn't taken any pills the night before and had slept for twelve straight hours. She had awakened feeling low, but decided not to take any more pills for a few days. Perhaps Rosalind was right about the dangers of mixing them with alcohol. Dianne opted for wine and melancholy.

Since Dianne had calmed down and did not resume her frenetic activity for the rest of the holiday vacation, Rosalind did not bother calling Dr. Benninger.

꿈 꿈 꿈

The vacation passed too quickly for Dianne. After Rosalind and the twins returned to school, she felt at loose ends. Goldmark did not require a rigid work schedule from her, so she accepted an invitation for a winter cruise in the Mediterranean. The sun was always her best therapy and she hoped it could bake out her discontent once again. But she didn't want to go alone.

She waited for an opportune moment in the afterglow of lovemaking to broach the subject with Dave.

He protested that he had neither the time nor the inclination to repeat the circus of the last trip. "Look, lady," Dave said, simmering, "it's about time you learned that I will not come or go at your every whim. Contrary to the impression given in some of the articles I've read lately, I have not yet rolled over and become your lapdog."

She fought to keep it light. "Surely you don't believe everything you read in the press? Besides, with all the overtime you've been putting in lately, you must have weeks of comp time coming to you."

"Maybe, but I don't have a wardrobe full of elegant yachting clothes and extra hundred-dollar bills to tip the hungry little porters. Lady, I'm beginning to think I can't afford you—in time or money."

Dianne gnawed at a hangnail. She needed him. She never would have gotten this far past the winter blues without his support. "Dave! Where are you going?"

"To get a glass of milk. My stomach feels like shit."

"You're acting like one."

"Keep pushing, lady, and you won't have to worry about it."

She smiled sweetly. "Don't you think you should put on a robe? Just in case Marie is looking for a snack, too?"

He grabbed the robe from the chair. "All right, but I am not going along on some artsy-fartsy cruise."

◆ ◆ ◆

Dianne went cruising alone, halfheartedly dabbling in the idle merriment and the shopping forays at the ports.

Twelve days later she returned tanned and emotionally exhausted. She couldn't dredge up enthusiasm for anything. Not even Jordy's report that they were a week away from a hundred-million-dollar settlement with the Marinos sparked her mood. She would have to sign over any interest in the island and the yacht, but everything else was settled. That was fine, she told him. As long as the final figure was one hundred million after taxes and legal fees, she was satisfied. Jordy protested that her casual "after taxes and legal fees" made it all a new issue. She didn't care. Whatever it took and however long, she wanted that magic number—one hundred million dollars. Perhaps when she had it, she would snap out of the black-and-blues forever.

◆ ◆ ◆

The key for reviving her spirits turned out to be a sixty-three-year-old historian, a second cousin once removed of Kiki's husband, George.

A longtime professor of history at City College of New York, Brooks Wendt was writing an in-depth study of Lily Langtry and her times. Kiki was pushing him to expand the study into a book for the general public. She cajoled Dianne into reading a few trial chapters to see if Dianne thought Goldmark might be interested in representing the book, since Lily Langtry was a theatrical subject.

The first two chapters flowed with style and whimsy based on solid research. Dianne realized that Kiki was not just gilding cousin Brooks' Lily. She looked forward to meeting the man.

With a sober manner that belied the humor of his manuscript, Professor Wendt enjoyed teaching. At CCNY, his students across a forty-year span had included World War II veterans, neophyte communists, Armenian and Polish refugees, militant blacks, ERA proponents, children of McCarthy's blacklist targets and Vietnamese boat people—to name a few. Not every student who sat in Professor Wendt's classes followed in his academic footprints, but each one experienced at least one moment when another time in history came as alive as the present. The professor could make Julius Caesar as real as Richard Nixon, and Patrick Henry was viewed as a young liberal politician struggling against conservative forces much as a present-day Ted Kennedy did. Professor Wendt had a gift for anecdote and psychological analogy. And it all came through in the pages of *LILY, aka Lady Hugo Gerald de Bathe.*

Dianne sent a copy directly to Lisbeth Mark in London, who wired within the week that Goldmark would be delighted to represent the work. She insisted that Professor Wendt sit down and outline the complete book. Decades of lectures interrupted by spontaneous questions had inclined him to wander tangentially. Dianne soon recognized that *Lily* could be the first of many fine popular histories by Professor Wendt if he could only learn to structure his ideas.

She was surprised and delighted when he not only followed her suggestions but openly appreciated them. "I never could find anyone who was honest enough to say, 'Stop there. Don't write that. It's irrelevant.' I need you, Mrs. Marino. Thank you."

She thanked him.

ᵍ ᵍ ᵍ

A month later, Lisbeth Mark sold Professor Wendt's book to an established London publishing house and personally flew to New York for a celebration party staged at the Waldorf in Victorian splendor.

In the afterglow of the celebration as Dave toasted her success in the privacy of her bedroom, Dianne announced that she needed another break. "It will be at least a few weeks before the professor has the next chapter ready for review, so let's go celebrate in the sun!"

"Damn it, lady! How many times do I have to tell you that I am not a card-carrying member of the jet set. I happen to need my job."

"And I suppose I don't need mine," she snapped back.

278

"Not the same way I do. Lady, this is all getting very old . . . and I'm not sure I can deal with it—or you."

She sighed. She really didn't want to fly away for a lonely week with acquaintances who would coddle her like a three-minute egg.

Later in the week, when Dave asked her why she had canceled her great celebration in the sun, she fabricated a story about having to make some last-minute changes in the first chapters of *Lily*. She didn't want to admit that he was becoming so important to her, perhaps too important. Half the things she had cared about all her life were his scoffing grounds. Charities were unemployment agencies for their staffs. He believed that all inherited wealth should be abolished and that every child should be given an equal grant at the age of eighteen. The man was a populist. But he never bored her and most of his outrageous opinions were articulated with humor. Sometimes she wondered if he took anything seriously. But he did sound serious when he questioned whether he could afford her.

She made it a private game to arrange invitations to events in a way that would cost him no money. For charity balls and affairs she wanted to attend, she would have Kiki send a money order with a request that the tickets be sent to Dave at his home address. When he questioned the constant flow of on-the-cuff tickets, she told him that he had been placed on the very best of complimentary mailing lists. She knew she was playing an emotionally dangerous game, but it kept her properly entertained without offending her lover.

She was not entirely happy with the arrangement, which she knew was a time bomb. If Dave ever discovered the truth, he would be livid. She did not mention anything about the game to Angus. It would be too embarrassing to explain.

෴ ෴ ෴

Professor Wendt's book needed photographic plates from the period. Although the English publisher's editor could handle the search in London's museums and photographic archives, Dianne wanted to work on it personally. She wanted to remain close to the project and she consulted Lord Henry, who assured her of access to the royal family's personal collection.

Professor Wendt urged Dianne to fly to London. There might be a gem of a photo of Lily with Edward VII taken at a royal function, or, better yet, at a family function. "Bertie took photos himself," the professor said with excitement. "Imagine a candid shot by Bertie of Lily and Alexandria! Dianne, we know Bertie insisted that Lily be considered a friend of the family. You must go."

Dianne was touched by the professor's enthusiasm. She wanted to take him along, but he insisted that he couldn't desert his students. Besides, he had absolute faith in Dianne's ability to spot any choice photographs.

The enthusiasm was contagious. It was also an ideal project to share with Rosalind. If only Dave would join her for a week or two, it would all be perfect.

The more she prodded to come, the more he resisted, and the more Dianne smoldered. She had thought Dave was different from the other men she had known, free from the ego-strangling fear of public opinion. But in his perverse way, his determination not to capitalize on their relationship was as maddening as Bill's insistence she grant interviews and Tony's blatant usury.

"Look, I have a seminar series to give at the University of London in May." He tried to find a position of compromise. "If you wait until then, we can go together."

"I can't wait. I need the illustrations now."

"Don't give me that shit, Dianne. The professor's only halfway through the draft manuscript. There is no rush on the photos and you know it."

"But if I find a few gems for him, I know it will inspire him. Besides, I'd like to spend some time with Rosalind."

"You saw her at Christmas. We both did. She's doing fine. I was surprised she's such a level-headed kid."

"What do you mean by that? That her mother isn't?"

"No." Dave leaned forward and lit Dianne's cigarette. "I meant that considering the blackmail incident I expected someone less certain and, to be truthful, someone much less happy. She's a delight. She actually glows."

"I see." Dianne inhaled slowly, feeling jealous of the sparkle Dave saw in Rosalind. "It's nice to hear my daughter get such rave reviews."

"Hey, lady. Her mother already has my rave reviews, inside and out."

"But no youthful glow. And she evidently doesn't carry enough weight for you to spend one lousy week in London with her."

Dave's lips narrowed. "I don't think we should discuss that anymore."

"Fine. Then you can also stop discussing our plans for skiing this weekend, because I'm leaving for London on Monday and I'll need the weekend to pack and organize."

"Right. You have to itemize your sixteen suitcases and your ten makeup boxes, don't you? And it takes time to make sure you have matching shoes along for every outfit and to decide which precious jewels to take out of the vault in case the queen asks you to dinner. Just forget the cozy little ski weekend I had planned for us. How can it possibly compare with the joys of classifying your wardrobe?" He paused, breathing hard. Then he picked up his cigarettes and rose.

"Where are you going?"

"Packing!" he flung over his shoulder.

On Sunday morning, Rosalind opted for an early ride in Hyde Park. The weather was brisk and bright, rare for London in February. Rosalind didn't notice. Her mind was on Dianne's unexpected visit, scheduled for Tuesday.

"Everything's going along so wonderfully," she said to Colin as they waited for their mounts. "I almost hate for her to arrive and break the spell. We really do better these days at a distance. Divided we stand; united we fight. It should be the family motto."

"Don't sell yourself short. I think you've developed more insight lately. She can only get your goat if you let her."

"I suppose, but I can't help wondering what marvelous new surprise she might be arranging for my life."

"No point in worrying about mother's milk that isn't out of the cow yet."

Rosalind laughed. "If Dianne could hear you calling her a cow, she'd have a fit! You'd be fired in a second."

"I only have another month to worry about that. You'll be twenty-one next month—and on your own."

"I don't even want to think about that." She tried to laugh.

"I thought I would applaud the day when I was free from my 'men in gray.' Colin, what are we going to do?"

Colin was saved from replying as T emerged from a stall leading the old mare Rosalind called Mollywaddle.

"What's wrong with you dudes?" T grinned from under a wide white cowboy hat as he fought to mount his horse. "Let's get moving."

"Tallyho!" Rosalind shouted at him.

Mollywaddle took that as her cue. She galloped off, veering away from the bridle path and speeding down a small hill toward a cricket field to send players scattering out of position.

"He needs help!" Rosalind laughed.

Colin echoed her laughter as they watched Mollywaddle cross the playing field and skid to a halt beside a pond, sending T lurching forward. Graciously, the old mare lowered her neck to facilitate T's slide into the pond. The cricketers laughed and applauded as Mollywaddle trotted around the pond and disappeared into a thicket.

"To the rescue!" Colin announced as he mounted Shindra. "Go get a towel," he added, "and catch up."

Rosalind ran toward the stable.

"Psst," a voice hissed as she reached the door.

"Ian!" She stopped short as she saw her lover's son peeking around the corner. "I thought you weren't coming until next week."

"It's all a surprise visit. I have to talk fast because I don't want Dad to know I'm here yet. I want to give him a surprise party and I need your help."

"What's the occasion? His birthday's in May."

"Just a party. A group of us are here working on a research project. And he's been bugging me about wanting to meet some of my friends. So I thought we'd have a party for the hell of it." He spoke quickly. "Here's the plan. You slip away and make Dad think you've disappeared. Then we'll call up, innocent as lambs, and say, 'The party you're looking for is at such and such an address.' Can you sneak away to meet us?"

"Any time I want to—if I want to."

"Please, you've got to. It'll be a great lark." He handed her a slip of paper. "Here's the address. Eight o'clock tonight." He studied her face. "You won't fail me, will you? You'll ruin my whole surprise if you don't show."

It seemed silly and overdramatic, like a joke the twins might have plotted years before, but she didn't want Ian to think she was stuffy. "All right. I promise I'll be there. But it seems awfully compli . . ."

"Great," he interrupted. "I've got to run. T's coming."

Rosalind turned back in time to see T stop beside the stable gates and dramatically drop the once-white cowboy hat in the trash barrel.

"Hallooo!" Colin called as he rode up the hill, Mollywaddle in tow.

"Ready to try again?" Rosalind laughed and pocketed the note as T reached her.

"This ol' agent has been taken for his last ride by you two maniacs."

Rosalind appeased T by insisting that he and Colin come to brunch at Boulderdash to dry out in style.

The pleasant repast extended past tea and two games of billiards. As Colin turned over the official duty to the four o'clock shift, Rosalind avoided any questions about an evening rendezvous by announcing that she had to read three plays for a test the next day. Colin swallowed his hopes for a more stimulating evening as he and T thanked the Boulders for a delightful afternoon.

Lord Henry said he would dine at his club. Tulip would have Margot fix a light salad and leave it in the refrigerator for herself and Rosalind to eat at their leisure. She wanted to give the "dear girl" an early evening.

Rosalind was amused. Margot, the "dear girl," was at least fifty years old.

෴ ෴ ෴

At seven o'clock, an olive drab slicker shielding her green jeans and T-shirt against a cold, pelting rain, Rosalind hurried across Grosvenor Square toward the Marble Arch subway station. The streets were empty. The only sign of life was an elderly man leaning over a sodden poodle who was sitting stubbornly beside a fire hydrant. "Please, Heathcliff, raise your leg," pleaded the man.

The wet blocks seemed very long and the fifteen-minute wait for the subway was interminable.

As Rosalind emerged at Notting Hill Gate station and turned

north, the rain was coming down in torrents. She considered turning back, but a promise was a promise. She pushed herself into a soggy jog.

It was eight-fifteen as she sighted the Midland Bank on the corner of Colville Terrace. The third house from the corner, 371 Colville Terrace, the note had said.

The rain and gloom could not disguise the peeling paint and ill repair of the old row house. She double-checked the address. This had to be it.

She didn't have time to knock before Ian jumped out on the small rotting porch. "Great! You made it!" He quickly led her into a narrow hall, typical of Victorian design.

To the left of the hall was a dusty parlor. Four men of varying ages were draped about the shoddy furniture. None rose as she entered.

Ian took Rosalind's slicker and tossed it on an old dirty chair in the hall. His companions watched silently. Then he stumbled over introductions, using first names only.

Kiernan, a tall, thin man in his late thirties, sported a bushy red mustache below a wide upturned nose, cool very, pale blue eyes and thinning reddish hair. Rosalind wondered if he had grown the mustache to compensate. He looked like the type that could have dimples, but he only nodded curtly in response to her smile.

Lloyd, short and dark, seemed over thirty, too. He grunted a greeting and left the room.

Harry and Kerry were introduced as a duo. They were the same height, about five feet nine inches tall, with soft brown hair and matching eyes. When Rosalind asked if they were brothers, Harry replied in a soft brogue, "In a special way."

"I meant blood brothers."

"And brothers who have been blooded." Kerry laughed.

Rosalind perched on a worn footstool. It was a strange collection of friends that Ian wanted Colin to meet.

Kiernan smiled and pulled at his mustache. He did not have dimples. "I guess it's time to put you in the picture, as it were."

Harry and Kerry laughed.

Rosalind felt uncomfortable. "What do you mean? Isn't this a surprise party for Colin—Ian's father?"

"Oh, it's that," Kiernan nodded. "And more. You are also being given the honor of attending a cell meeting of the Irish

Republican Army, a noble group we believe you might wish to join."

"What?" Rosalind was speechless. Why would anyone think she would support the IRA? All she knew about the IRA was that they bombed everything from lords to railroad stations and were generally crazy and dangerous. Adrenaline surged through her, as much from excitement as fear. "Ian, are you a member?"

Ian nodded.

"Does your father know?"

"He wouldn't understand—at least not yet. He hasn't spent months studying the situation in Northern Ireland."

"But what about the violence—the killing?"

"The press blows that out of proportion," Kiernan said softly. "It only occurs when absolutely necessary."

Rosalind's throat felt dry. "Oh. . . . Do you have anything to drink?"

Lloyd returned to the parlor and gave Kiernan a short nod. "On schedule." Then, without missing a beat, he answered Rosalind. "We have white wine."

White wine for an IRA meeting—not whiskey or ale. It seemed odd. "Fine." She gave Lloyd a weak smile.

Kiernan waved Lloyd off to the kitchen and turned to confront Rosalind. "Have you ever heard of James Connolly?"

"*James* Connolly?" Rosalind drew a blank. "No. Is he well known in the U.S.?"

Kiernan spat on the floor. "You should hang your head in shame. Your father, God rest his soul, publicly praised his cousin James Connolly on the floor of the Irish Parliament. Things might have been different if your father had lived. We might have gotten support from your government rather than have to scratch out hidden contributions from Irish-Americans. Blood money, I call it, because they haven't got the guts to support us openly." He glanced at Lloyd returning with the wine. "Tell Miss Connolly exactly who James Connolly was, Lloyd."

Lloyd stepped forward reverently, holding a gallon of cheap wine. "James Connolly was a leader of the 1916 Easter Rebellion. *Sinn Fein*, meaning 'we ourselves' in Gaelic, was his battle cry as he and his brave men holed up in the Dublin Post Office and held off the British for a week. Connolly was wounded in the crossfire, captured and carried before the firing squad in a chair. His wounded leg was too gangrenous to stand on. He would have died from the gangrene within a week, but the Brits couldn't wait. They wanted to make him a public example." Lloyd stopped and laughed. "But it backfired. The cruel executions sickened even the British Parliament. James Connolly became a martyr and it was the true beginning of the Irish Free State.

"But the dream James Connolly died for will not be realized until the British are gone from a new united Ireland, an Ireland controlled only by the dictates of its working classes."

Rosalind was fascinated. She realized she was seeing a true fanatic for the first time in her life.

"Lloyd is a Marxist." Kerry looked at Rosalind for a reaction. "He says Connolly knew Marx."

"Connolly and Marx wanted the same thing," Lloyd growled as he poured wine into mismatched tumblers, "a society in which the opportunities are the same for all."

Rosalind couldn't stand the polemic. "You can't believe that communism creates equality. What about the special privileges for party members and the military?"

"No country has yet reached Marxist equality. But when we have gained control and the industries are nationalized, then you will see."

"Pour the wine and be quiet, Lloyd," Kiernan said mildly. "Sometimes our historian tends to think in extremes. Connolly was a celebrated writer and editor for socialist papers. He even lectured and wrote in the U.S., although I doubt if he visited your Connolly grandparents, since they were members of the class he was working to overthrow. But he was a nationalist first and socialist second. Lloyd likes to tint him pinker than he was."

Lloyd grunted a denial. "Don't sell our Marxist origins short. It's thanks to them that you get your extra material and training."

What was Lloyd talking about? Rosalind wondered. Who was supplying them—the Russians, the Chinese?

Kiernan shot Lloyd a warning look. Lloyd seemed to deflate and retreat to the other side of the room.

"For centuries, the penal laws of the ruling Protestant English prohibited Catholics from owning property, attending schools or holding office." Kiernan's eyes blazed. "The English have been confiscating Irish lands and giving it to the their Protestant lackeys in the north of Ireland since Henry the Eighth broke with Rome. We have been abused by the British for over four hundred years! The common laws of England have an unwritten exception—the rights of all men, as long as they are not Irish Catholic."

Rosalind could not help admiring Kiernan. She could visualize him holding an audience rapt with his fervor. But while she admired his passion, she recoiled from the cruelty she sensed behind the chill blue eyes. "But how can the northern Protestants be held accountable for what their ancestors did hundreds of years ago?"

"They are carrying on the great traditions of their illustrious ancestors," Kiernan answered with acid in his voice.

The room had become hot and smoky. Her throat was parched and the sweet wine wasn't helping. "Ian, could you open a window, please. It's getting stuffy."

Kiernan lifted a corner of his thin wide mouth in a half smile. "Sorry, they're all nailed shut."

"Is this neighborhood dangerous?" Rosalind asked nervously.

Kiernan's strange smile remained fixed. "It depends on your perspective. Locks work both ways—to keep people in or out." His eyes glittered with a peculiar humor.

Rosalind's eyes sought Ian. He stared guiltily at the shabby floor. But guilty of what? Why wouldn't he look at her? She fought the tension she felt. "Ian, isn't it about time we called your father?"

"I think you can be forgetting Mr. McReady for the evening, Miss Connolly."

She rose in panic. "Well, if the surprise party is off, then I'm ready to go home. I've heard about all I can digest in one night. But I will do more thinking about all this, I promise." She heard herself rattling on as she fought the fear rising in her. "I'll ask Lord Henry to explain the English position. There are always two sides to things, don't you think?"

Everyone seemed to be frozen, like wax effigies at Madame Tussaud's. Then Kiernan broke the tableau by pulling a gun from his shabby tweed jacket. "I don't think you're going anywhere for a while."

"Why?" She gasped. "What does it matter? This is hardly a formal meeting."

"Tell her about it, Ian," Kiernan whispered through his slanted smile. "You've earned the right."

Looking over Rosalind's left shoulder and focusing on the dirty lace curtains, Ian quavered. "A message to your mother has already been delivered to Boulderdash." His voice leveled. "When we have been paid one million dollars as instructed, you will be released." He looked at her defiantly. "If your father were alive, he would support us. It is only right that part of his estate should be appropriated to help unite Ireland. And a million is a drop in the bucket for you," he added.

Rosalind suddenly felt detached. She noticed for the first time that Ian's temples were splattered with pale freckles. Colin didn't have any freckles.

She felt as though she were sitting way above in a balcony, looking down and watching herself as part of a scene. She remembered reading in a psychology textbook that an almost cinematic detachment was one way people coped with extreme shock or terror.

She heard Ian clear his throat. Had he known or thought about all the possible consequences before he had brought her here? It didn't matter. Stupid or aware, he had set her up. And she had trusted him like a blind fool because he was part of Colin. But she saw now he was a different breed, a mutant.

"So." She folded her arms across her chest, seeking to calm the trembling. "What happens next?"

Kiernan waved the gun at her. "You sit down. And we continue our discussion." He noddded at Lloyd. "I'll bet she doesn't know about the great Irish American, Eamon de Valera."

Rosalind sat down on the footstool, her terrified eyes fixed on Kiernan's gun.

"Eamon de Valera was born in Brooklyn," Lloyd intoned, "but he came to Ireland to fight for Irish independence as a young man . . . like Ian. But de Valera must have been tainted by American influences, because he stood back like a coward while Connolly and others were shot and hanged. Then, when public sentiment forced the Brits to negotiate, de Valera, as one of the few surviving leaders, was made head of the provisional government . . . such as it was . . ."

Lloyd's diatribe continued. Why was she getting this slanted history lesson? Rosalind wondered. Was this the way the radicals started with Patty Hearst? Ideological brainwashing. Was this how it was done? The room was closing in on her. The dust and smoke were suffocating. Stop it! Stop it! Stop it! Her mind shrieked while she pressed her lips tightly together. She could not imagine herself as another "Tanya" wielding a submachine gun outside a country store, demanding supplies.

Lloyd droned on. They had caught the young queen bee and she had been royally screwed, rhetorically speaking.

∽ ∽ ∽

Dianne slipped on soft blue silk pajamas and nibbled at the mint the maid had left on the pillow. She felt uneasy, wishing she hadn't called Lord Conklin to meet her at the airport for a drink earlier. But after the huge row with Dave, it had seemed important that an attractive man be on hand for her London arrival.

She had flown using her own name and had casually told a couple of her less discreet friends when she was leaving. It was so much simpler to assure that the press would be on hand than to be certain of avoiding them. She was hoping that both the photos and speculations on a new romance would reach American newspapers—and Dave.

Unfortunately, her little public tryst with Lord Conklin meant that she had arrived at Claridge's too late to call Rosalind with the news that she had arrived early.

She was too keyed up to sleep. If only she had Tony's explosive temper, she thought. Tony could blow off steam and forget it. Her anger always lay like smoldering coals in the pit of her stomach, burning slowly into the fires of revenge. She had to distract herself before she got an ucler.

The *Lily* files were piled neatly on the Queen Anne desk. She glanced at them but didn't have the patience to deal with them at that moment.

She looked at her watch. Early enough in New York, but close to one A.M. here. It was far too late to call Boulderdash, but she could check with the Secret Service about Rosalind's schedule in the morning. Somewhere she had the London numbers of Rosalind's agents that she had wheedled out of General Madison's secretary.

She found the listing in her address book under "A" for Agents. Mendelson, McReady, Smith, Williams . . . who should she call? The handsome one, she decided.

"McReady, here," a sleepy voice answered.

"Mr. McReady, this is Dianne Marino. I am so sorry for

waking you, if I did, but I thought you should know that I arrived this evening instead of Tuesday. And I do need Rosalind's schedule for tomorrow."

Colin became instantly alert. "Tomorrow she has a nine-thirty A.M. scene design class at the Academy and I think she has an evening rehearsal, too."

"How is she doing? I do miss her so much, you know. I mean, how does she seem, generally? Content? Happy?"

"She's doing fine," Colin answered warmly. "This morning we all went riding in the park and then played a rousing game of billiards with Lord Henry."

"How *en famille*," Dianne purred.

Colin could have kicked himself for using the "we." "Of course I'm not with her all the time, but I think it's accurate to say that she is enjoying London."

"It's so reassuring for me to hear you say that, Mr. McReady. Having you on hand is such a comfort to me. Nothing ever goes wrong when you're on duty. I really don't know what we're going to do come March, when we lose you. She'll be twenty-one then, you know. I've been thinking about hiring protection for her privately. Would you and the other agent who works with you, Mr. uh . . ., the nice dark man . . ."

Colin rescued her. "Mr. Smith."

"Yes, that's much too easy a name to remember." She laughed. "You don't have to give me an answer right this minute. Maybe we can sit down and talk about it later this week. I really do have to think about it soon."

Colin was at a complete loss for a response. He realized that he had to deal with the same subject soon, himself. Dianne's casual offer hit him like simultaneous salvation and damnation. But it might be worth considering, at least until June. The current nest was a comfortable one. In fact, if Colin had had his druthers that night, Rosalind would have been beside him when Dianne called. He shuddered at the thought.

"I suppose it really is too late to call Rosalind, isn't it? Do you think she's still awake?"

"I doubt it. She said she wanted an early night. And Lady Boulder does turn in early." The statements sounded intimate to Colin's ears, but he didn't want Dianne waking the Boulders at this hour.

Dianne sighed. "Then I'll call her first thing in the morning."

She paused. "Mr. McReady . . . ?" The words hung softly in the night.

"Yes?"

"Thank you for being so helpful. Good night." Dianne quickly poured herself another glass of wine. She had come a breath away from asking him over for a nightcap. He had sounded so helpful—and masculine. She could have discussed Rosalind with him. He obviously spent more time with her than Dianne did these days. She pictured Agent McReady's clear blue eyes and tall, well-conditioned body. He was much better looking than Dave. Dianne, Dianne, she chided herself. The man couldn't be forty yet. And Dave wasn't far past forty, she added to herself ruefully.

She had found herself recoiling from Lord Conklin at the airport. Tall, silver-haired and distinguished, he photographed beautifully. But the pictures didn't reveal the liver spots on his hands. Thanks to Tony, she probably had developed a deep-seated fear of watching another old man die. She made a mental note to discuss it with Angus.

She had consumed too much coffee and was brimming with far too much nervous energy to sleep. She kept rerunning in her mind the stormy exit scene with Dave.

What inner compulsion kept making her push him over the brink of anger? She was well aware that she liked to control her own schedule. That's all Dave seemed to want for himself. But something compelled her to want him to be everything—protector, lover, companion—on cue and at her convenience.

Did she really want to turn him into a lapdog? She would hate it, she answered herself.

Then why did she prod him, knowing he would resist? Part of it was honest, she decided. She liked having him with her to lighten her dark moods with his incisive black humor. But she opened her eyes in the dark bedroom to the reality that a perverse part of her was trying to mold him into her own images, from moment to moment.

She reached for a cigarette, giving up on sleep. She had fought against Bill's priorities and emerged scarred from that marital bout. Then she had poured her energy down a dark hole trying to carve Tony into a tractable Uncle Herb type. Pushing against the grain always left splinters.

What did she want? She didn't want promiscuous, lying

bastards. She wanted someone who honored his commitments. Dave always honored his word. Like for this trip, she thought. His "no" meant no. Honest, but stubborn. Bill and Tony had been stubborn, but dishonest. There was no question in her mind which was preferable.

But there were other problems with Dave. He had achieved in an area that gave rewards in reputation rather than dollars. He couldn't compete with her world in terms of mobility and buying power. And he wouldn't allow her to openly use hers for him. He said he didn't want to feel like a gigolo. He had also said one wine-filled night that the only way he would marry a rich woman was if she gave all her money to charity first. Yes, there were problems with Dave. She hadn't spent over twenty years putting up with Tony's and Bill's garbage to toss away the few benefits she had gleaned in the process.

When she had waved good-bye to New York less than twenty-four hours earlier, she had told herself she was also saying "good riddance" to Dave. But now, in the hollow silence of Claridge's spacious suite, the thought rang false.

Despite the problems, Dave had given her something beautiful and rare for her, an up-front, honest kind of love. If she wanted to save that good and sensuous communication, she realized she would have to control her destructive conditioned responses, the insistence on having her own way, the prodding and second-guessing. She had to respond to Dave rather than the ghostly images of Bill and Tony. Besides, those techniques had never worked on Bill or Tony either.

She gave herself ten points for insights. Angus would be proud of her, she thought.

She reached for the phone to call Dave and tell him she wasn't upset with him, that she understood. She would even apologize, if necessary.

ᔕ ᔕ ᔕ

Colin padded into his compact kitchen, hoping the milk supply was still good. Dianne's call had banished sleep. What had she meant by *"en famille"*? The phone echoed again in the narrow hall. Was Dianne calling back to third-degree him? Reluctantly, he answered.

Agent Ira Mendelson, lead man on the midnight-to-eight shift, was on the line. "Sir, I don't know if this is a sick joke or what, but we just found a ransom note on the front door of Boulderdash. We haven't seen anyone come in or out and we haven't alerted the household yet. The note was in a large white envelope addressed to Dianne Connolly Marino, in care of the Secret Service of the United States."

Colin pictured Rosalind creeping across the roof. What if she had decided to surprise him tonight? She had done it a number of times in the past few months, despite his protests. And what if someone else had intercepted her? It was an ugly thought.

"Shall I read the note to you?"

"I'll be there in ten."

He was already buzzing for the lift before he remembered that Dianne was in town, itching to talk to Rosalind. He raced down the stairs. It was faster.

LET THERE BE NO MISTAKE. ROSALIND CONNOLLY HAS BEEN KID-NAPPED IN THE NAME OF HER ILLUSTRIOUS ANCESTOR JAMES CON-NOLLY. HAD WILLIAM CONNOLLY LIVED, HE WOULD HAVE APPLAUDED AND SUPPORTED THE GREAT CAUSE OF IRISH UNIFI-CATION. NOW, THOSE WHO SURVIVE HIM, MUST CARRY THE TORCH FOR HIM. IN RETURN FOR ONE MILLION AMERICAN DOLLARS, IN SMALL UNMARKED CIRCULATED BILLS, MISS CONNOLLY WILL BE RETURNED UNHARMED. YOU MAY EXPECT A CALL AT EIGHT THIS MORNING GIVING YOU FURTHER INSTRUCTIONS.

THE SONS OF THE EASTER REBELLION

"What do you think?" asked Mendelson.

"We go in and find out." Colin led the way to the door.

Rosalind's bed was empty and her window unlatched. Colin rifled through her closets and drawers. All her suitcases were there along with the outfit she had worn that afternoon. But her favorite green jeans with the print lining and the slicker she wore for her window exits were missing. He hated revealing how intimately he knew her wardrobe, but they needed a description. "She's wearing green jeans and a drab olive slicker," he told Mendelson and Lord Boulder, trying to sound normal about it.

Lord Henry tried to be helpful. "The chief inspector of Scotland Yard is an old friend of mine from Cambridge. Could have him here in a flash, if you like."

"Thank you, sir, but my superiors are already calling in the CIA and MI-6."

Lord Henry nodded. "Only trying to help, my boy."

"We are really going to need you to get ready for the eight A.M. phone call. Our guess is that the call will be made to Boulderdash, since the note was left on your door rather than wired to Dianne in New York."

Lord Henry's back straightened and he regained his air of brisk authority as he explained the switchboard with the open line to his office at Parliament.

Colin knew little about phone lines, but he figured correctly that it would keep both Lord Henry and himself busy until the experts arrived.

∽ ∽ ∽

Less than twenty minutes later, Sam Graham, CIA chief of the London station, a white-haired man with a youthful face, arrived to take charge. He was followed within minutes by E. E. Wattle, a stocky middle-aged MI-6 senior operative.

Technicians from MI-6 were already at work inserting wires and monitoring devices into Lord Henry's phones.

To Lord Henry's delight, considering the circumstances, Graham and Wattle quickly determined that Boulderdash would do for a temporary communications center. The rumble of introductions and pleasantries hushed as they examined the ransom note. Then notebooks were unsheathed as battle plans were drawn.

Rosalind's movements during the preceding week must be checked and double-checked. Any unusual contacts must be analyzed. Interviews had to be coordinated. Everyone agreed that Rosalind had not been taken by force. She had been the victim of a decoy operation.

"Or party to the plan," Graham softly postulated.

Colin felt duty-bound to describe the "possible" escape route across the roofs. Sam Graham watched Colin carefully as he explained how it was feasible.

Colin continued by outlining Rosalind's past week, coloring slightly as he reported Sunday's activities with the Boulder's. Graham's silent surveillance made him nervous.

Graham continued to cosolidate control. Everyone would report to him.

Before anyone could ask any questions, T ushered in Dianne. Graham had insisted she be alerted immediately. He didn't want any special hassles from Washington because Dianne felt left out of anything or shunted aside.

"Oh, Mr. McReady, how could this have happened?" Dianne spoke in a lost-little-girl voice. "You can't just let them kidnap her like this. You have to get her back."

Graham eased the moment by making introductions and assuring Dianne that everything possible was being done. Agents were already scouring the streets in London, Dublin and Ulster, searching for rumors of any kidnap plans. Activities files of all known IRA activists were being cross-checked in CIA and MI-6 computers. He also assured her there would be no publicity unless absolutely necessary.

No publicity. For a moment, Dianne wished the story would make headlines worldwide. That would teach Dave a lesson for not coming along.

"If it were to become public," Graham continued coolly, every kook and fringe organization in the world would come out of the woodwork to confuse things. Keeping it quiet is to our benefit as well as yours."

Dianne's eyes narrowed. Was Graham trying to tell her that she warranted no special privileges? He had better find Rosalind fast or he could be sorry. She still had friends in Washington who could turn the screws inside the CIA.

She turned to Colin. "I would like to see the note, Mr. McReady, since it seems it could cost me a million dollars."

Colin walked to the library table and stared down at the note, examining it once again as he said, "It's over here. We can't touch it because the lab hasn't finished with it."

She slowly crossed the room and stood beside him. "It's so . . . so juvenile looking."

"I know, it looks like my son printed it when he was five." Colin smiled ruefully. The crossbars on the T's had the same peculiar slant that Ian's first attempts at letters had had. Ridiculous. There were probably a million kids who started printing like that. He brushed the thought aside and studied Dianne's reaction.

"One million dollars." She gave her head a little shake. "Just like that. Do they think I have a safe full of cash just sitting around?" Suddenly panicked, she turned to Graham. "Doesn't the CIA keep piles of cash around for emergencies?"

"Not for paying off kidnappers." Graham shook his head. "I don't know what the policy would be if your late husband, I mean President Connolly, that is, were still in office, but I doubt if the present administration would finance this operation. I'll check, but don't count on it. You better work on it privately. We'll make every effort to recover any ransom, I can promise you that, but we can't make guarantees."

"How reassuring," Dianne said sarcastically.

"I should think your first concern would be for the safety of your daughter, Mrs. Marino. If they really are hard-core IRA veterans, they are dangerous men. And we might have no other way to get a line on them except by making contact when we deliver the money."

Dianne held back tears of frustration. She didn't want to give Graham the satisfaction. "Is there a phone I can use to make a private call?"

As Colin led Dianne into a small study off the library, no one mentioned that all the lines were tapped.

Colin returned to find Graham quietly enjoying his pipe and a cognac. The aroma of the cherry tobacco was strong.

"Have a drink, McReady. Relax." Graham waited for Colin to pour himself a scotch before he picked up the thread of the earlier discussion about Rosalind.

Colin began cautiously, then warmed to the subject. Talking about her in action helped dispel the torturous image of her in confinement.

"You seem to know her much better than the other agents do," Graham said and waited.

"Well, sir, T and I have been with her for over seven years. You get to know someone pretty well in that time."

"You like her very much. Very much indeed." It was a statement.

Graham sent up small puffs of smoke, like irregular signals. "Maybe seven years is too long for one assignment."

Colin's fur raised. "If you're implying that I'm getting lax, forget it. This did not happen on my shift. When I'm on duty, I know exactly where she is every minute."

"I don't doubt that." Graham looked past his pipe directly at Colin. "I've seen my own fieldmen get into trouble by becoming too close to situations, too emotionally involved. I don't have to spell it out for you, do I? You might consider requesting reassignment."

"I've already tried that, sir, and was turned down." Colin's professional self felt miserable. His career could be on the line. But that wasn't important at the moment.

"Try again. I'll back you up next time."

"But not until she is safe and this thing is over." Colin leaned forward, intense. "I've got to see this through, sir. No one knows her better than I do. I know I can help."

"Then stay cool and don't try any grandstanding. Check with me before you even sneeze. I want your word on that, Mr. McReady."

"Sir, there is no way I'm going to go tearing off on my own. I am right with you at ground zero. I don't have the slightest idea of where to find a vipers' nest of IRA radicals in London."

Dianne entered the room and focused on Colin. "And only last night—this morning, really—I was thanking you for taking such good care of my . . . my . . . Rosie. . . ." Her voice cracked.

"We'll find her," Colin spoke from between his teeth. "On my mother's grave, we'll find her."

"But how? And when? Can you find her before I have to hand over a million *borrowed* dollars to revolutionaries? And what if they kill her first?" She asked the question of her own soul as well as of them.

Sam noticed Colin's jaw harden. Dianne was pushing too hard. Everyone had to remain rational. "There is nothing more we can do until the phone call in the morning."

E.E. Wattle yawned from a quiet corner by the fire. "I'd better go check on my men."

Dianne stared after him. "He is the most unlikely intelligence agent. He looks more like a grocer."

"That could be one of the reasons he's the best. No one knows more about the IRA than E.E.," said Graham.

"One would never guess it." Dianne grimaced.

Sam went on the offensive. "Is everything worked out on your end? You got through to your attorneys all right?"

"What you mean is, have I arranged for the one million dollars?" She emphasized the amount. "My attorney is personally flying over with the money, for which I had to pledge my jewels as collateral. But none of it will be worth anything if she's dead."

Lord Henry entered the room in time to catch Dianne's last two words. He went pale. "Dianne! What did you say?"

"I said I will never forgive any of you if anything happens to my daughter. I trusted you, Lord Henry, and I trusted the Secret Service. Now whom can I trust?"

"Dianne, you know I would have done anything in the world to prevent this from happening. And I will do anything in the world to help. In fact, I would be honored if you would let me arrange the ransom money for you. Please, Dianne."

It was tempting. It would be nice to have Lord Henry's money in jeopardy rather than her own, but it wasn't worth allowing him to salve his guilt that easily.

"No, I have taken care of it for *my* daughter."

"Well . . ." Lord Henry was at a loss.

Dianne fidgeted in her purse, looking for a new pack of cigarettes. "Just do something to find her now . . . do something!"

Graham studied her. The body language was clear. Nothing would comfort her at the moment. "Lord Henry, why don't you find a bedroom for Mrs. Marino to rest in until morning?"

"I won't be able to sleep. I'll just lie there," Dianne argued like an angry child.

Lord Henry placed his hand under her elbow. "A nice hot bath will soothe the raveled edges, Dianne, my dear."

She started to pull away from him, but stopped as she glanced at his face, filled with genuine concern and pain. He really was worried about her, like a father. And he was there, waiting to be leaned upon. "All right. I'll try a nice hot bath and then I'll see."

"Tulip will find a warm nightie for you and Margot will make you a milk toddy. . . . " He soothed and kept talking as he led her from the war room.

The room was quiet for a few heartbeats before Colin moved. "I'm going to go back to the flat, shower and change. I'll be back by six A.M."

"Make it seven," said Graham. Then he waited until he heard the front door close and turned to T. "Think he'll be okay?"

"He's a rock, sir. Steady as she blows," he began with mixed metaphors, then stopped, realizing it sounded too glib. He tried again. "He's pretty much of a realist. I think he'll do whatever is necessary to help, whatever you think is best."

"That's not what I'm worried about, Mr. Smith, not his

willingness to help. Even wise men can make mistakes when they're too close to a situation."

"I wish I didn't know what you're talking about." T sighed.

∽ ∽ ∽

Dianne sat up in bed and pressed her forefingers into the sinuses beside the bridge of her nose, fighting the inevitable headache. Jordy would help with his well-tailored big brother attitude, but he wasn't enough. She took a deep breath and dialed Dave's number.

"Driver here," Dave answered sleepily.

"Oh, Dave, I'm sorry to wake you." Dianne choked. "This is serious. You have to fly over here right now."

"Wait a minute. First you call me last night to say you're sorry you pressured me to come over and now it's the same old tune. Are you losing your mind?"

"No, it really is serious. Rosalind has been kidnapped and they're demanding a million dollars' ransom."

"Whew!" He whistled. "I hope you're kidding."

"I wouldn't joke about this. The note is signed by the IRA."

"What a story. Does anyone else have it yet?"

"Oh, no. There can't be any publicity. Not a whisper. The CIA and British Intelligence are swarming all over the place. I'm at Boulderdash."

"Yeah, I can understand the hush-hush for the moment. How about an inside story after Rosalind is recovered?"

"Good God, Dave. Is that all you care about? A story? Well, I am not one of your slimy sources and I didn't call to give you a news update for general publication. I called because I'm falling apart over here alone. I need you." Her voice choked with a sob.

"I'm sorry, Dianne. It's Pavlovian after all these years on the paper. But if you have a houseful of agents around, you're hardly alone."

"Please don't be funny. Not now. I really can't handle it. This is a real crisis and if you care about me at all, you will be on the next plane to London."

"You are reverting right back to form, making everything black and white according to your own definitions. Dianne, I hope to God that Rosalind is all right, but I don't see what I can do over there to help. If you wanted to get all the newspapers and media involved in the search, I could be useful, but otherwise . . . Are you sure it's the IRA involved?"

"I'm not sure of anything. All I know is that Rosie's gone, they are demanding a million dollars and I am utterly alone."

"Bullshit. I would bet a million myself, if I had it, that you have one of your hotshot lawyers on his way over right now. Don't you?"

"That's not the same thing and you know it!" He was making her angry. "What kind of person are you, anyway? I thought you had a soul hidden under your wisecracks. I really thought you were a decent human being, one of the few I knew. Now it appears that when the chips are down, you are just like the rest, willing to hold hands when it meets your own selfish terms, period."

"Wait a minute, lady."

"God knows I've broken my back to meet your terms and protect your stubborn pride, to get you on the best invitation lists and even pay for the tickets myself to be sent to you 'gratis.' You owe me this one, David Driver."

"Well, I'll be damned." Dave spoke softly. "Paid for and delivered. And I thought I was eluding your manipulations. You are really something, lady."

"Dave," she gasped, aware that she had gone too far.

"I better get off the phone," he continued in the dulcet tones that signaled controlled fury. "I would hate to be further indebted to you by running up a monumental phone bill."

"Wait. Please wait. You know I didn't mean . . . "

"I know you aren't capable of giving a person space to do the human thing. You don't ask. You give orders. 'Fly over here right now.' You didn't even have the grace to explain the situation and let me offer to come. Damn it, lady, it's a terrible situation for you, but you've got to get rid of your bulldozer!"

"Then you'll come?" Her voice lifted.

"Let me try to work things out." Suddenly, he sounded tired. "I'll give you a call later and let you know."

"What time will you call?"

"I don't know. When I can check things out."

"What things? What do you have to check out?"

"Good God, Dianne. Ease up!"

"I'm sorry, Dave."

"I am trying to understand that this is a terrible situation and you are going through hell."

"Yes," she whispered.

"Then let me make my own moves and I'll get back to you."

She pulled back the satin comforter and crawled into the empty bed. She needed a willing comforter. She didn't have the energy to fight or bargain.

What had her mother said? "Never ask people for anything they can't give freely. It won't be a gift, only a chore." It was like Jane to dismiss emotional struggles as "chores."

Jane had always warned Dianne against expecting too much from people. "Hope is fine, but if you expect it and don't get it, you'll only be sadder for it."

"You have to demand things, Dianne. You have to stand up strong and say what you want. Then you'll get it." It was ironic that those had been Big Bob's words. He had ended up with so little.

She reached for another cigarette, angry at herself for falling back on her parents' clichés. She had not spent a small fortune on Angus to wallow in superego rationalization.

It seemed to her that the real problems in her relationships boiled down to personal terms. Bill's and Tony's terms had conflicted with hers. In different ways, Dave's terms were also incompatible.

Their terms, my terms, she thought. All she had ever wanted was someone to share life with, to come to "our" terms with. Perhaps she was past the possibility of finding everything she wanted and needed in one man, the way Jane seemed to have done with Herb. Perhaps she had held on to Bill and then Tony too long. Now her needs were a quarter of a century older and her life-style less flexible.

The quest for security that had given impetus to both marriages was over. She didn't need a man for financial security and she really didn't want any man who would let her become his financial security. She didn't want any more joint property in her life. And it was much too late to find someone to play a positive father role for Rosalind and the twins.

She shivered under the downy comforter, wondering if Rosalind would have been better off if she had not married Tony. But then Dianne would not have had the financial ability to bail her out. A million-dollar ransom would have created a real panic. Still, she might have remained closer to her daughter if

Tony hadn't been an emotional wedge. There might not have been the difficulties of the past year—and the present horror.

It seemed ironic. Dianne had married Tony, in part, to stabilize life for Rosalind and the boys, and the marriage had initiated a decade of turmoil between herself and Rosalind.

But she had tried, she told herself. She argued against the feeling of guilt for failing Rosalind, for not having been a good mother. She had always done the best she could at each moment, but it had always seemed a question of how to survive each crisis. And now it really was a question of survival—Rosalind's.

She brushed away a tear and padded across the bedroom to her jewelry case to get the rosary Bea had given her the day Bill's coffin had been placed in the Capitol rotunda, the old mother's gift to the young mother during tragic days. Dianne had not used it in years, but she always carried it with her.

Grasping the finely wrought gold, she held on to the first amber bead for dear life.

"Holy Mary, Mother of God, pray for us sinners now. Blessed art thou among women and blessed is the fruit of thy womb. . . ." Tears ran down her cheeks as she knelt facing the wall, counting and chanting.

If there were to be any help from outside the earthly plane, she prayed, it would have to come from the intercession of mothers. "Pray for us sinners now." She leaned against the Victorian-print wallpaper and murmured on. Ten. Twenty. Rosalind's age. So young and vulnerable. Truly too young to die. Thirty. Thirty-three. Her age when Bill had died. Forty. "Hail, Mary, Mother of God. . . ." Fifty. She was too close to fifty.

She stopped counting and praying, exhausted. The rosary had offered only momentary comfort. Images of Rosalind brutalized were waking nightmares. She sat on the carpet, back against the wall, chastising herself for everything she had not done and everything she might have done, replotting her life and her children's lives a dozen ways. But none of that changed the reality.

Dragging herself erect, she fumbled in her purse for the barbiturates. She needed help to turn off her mind. She could not do it herself. She was too alone. She railed at Bill and Tony for deserting her by dying and at Dave for deserting her while alive. Why didn't he call back?

Still clutching the rosary, she climbed back into bed. Dear God, she prayed, let my daughter live long enough to choose her own way to grow old.

Rosalind was too much her father's daughter, she mused, too impetuous, fearless and trusting. Bill had been stabbed in the back many times by fools he had trusted. She had warned him. But she had warned Rosalind about trusting people, too. Neither one had listened. On the other hand, the twins never got in trouble with outsiders. They had each other, she thought wryly.

Dave hadn't called back. If he didn't call back, it would be "Good-bye, Charlie"; she would never forgive him.

What if Dave were here right this moment? she asked herself. What good would that do? He'd probably be asleep. The man could sleep through anything. And he would probably want to make love; nothing seemed to divert him from that. The thought of Dave's hands sliding across her body trying to stimulate her made her shudder with distaste. Until Rosalind was safe and sound, sex was the last thing she wanted.

Maybe Dave was better off where he was. But she wanted him to hold her and make her feel secure. Maybe doing something alive and positive like making love would be the sanest diversion. She felt a sexual ache rising within her. Good God, she thought, the man is turning me into a horny old woman. She pounded the pillow back into shape, then plumped it up and laid her head on it, still too tense to sleep. Would morning never come?

"Wake up!"

In her dream, Rosalind felt something grip her shoulder and she struggled to break free. "No!" she screamed and came awake, knocking Lloyd away. "Get away from me!" she spat.

He laughed at the repugnance in her eyes. "What a little hellcat. You might be a challenge to tame, but we have better things to do with you right now. You have to get ready to make a phone call."

"Phone call?" she croaked. Her throat felt raw and swollen.

"Get dressed," he ordered. "It's time to call Mummy."

She scrambled into her jeans and sweater, trying to ignore Lloyd's all too human inspection. Then she raced down the stairs ahead of him.

"Here she comes," Lloyd called down to the others.

Rosalind hurried into the parlor and stopped short as she saw Ian laughing with Harry. The nerve of him, she thought. "Well, Mr. McReady," she rasped. "It's so nice to see you up and about. It looks like a lovely day for a kidnapping."

Ian reddened and looked away.

"A *perfect* day for a kidnapping," mocked Kiernan, making a mental note of Ian's reaction. Minus ten.

"Here's breakfast." Harry thrust a chipped bowl at her. Gray lumps of porridge lay congealed within.

"I can't eat it like that. Is there some cream and sugar?"

"My, my, m'lady can't stomach the simple fare of the Irish peasant," sneered Kiernan. "Then don't bother eating it." He took the porridge and set it on the desk beside a single sheet of type-written paper. "Here's your script for the phone call. You will read it exactly as written or you will learn a lot about pain very quickly."

Rosalind sat down at the desk and slowly read aloud. "I am fine. If you do precisely what you are instructed, no harm shall come to me. You are dealing with dedicated professionals who will stop at nothing to accomplish their aims, including murdering me if necessary." An icy chill ran through her. Kiernan and Lloyd seemed capable of killing her without a second thought. The heat from the cereal bowl contrasted with the cold fear suffusing her. She had to live. She began to eat, her mind racing as she chewed the gummy mess. If she could only somehow pass along a clue on the phone.

Kiernan smiled coolly. "Just don't try to get clever."

The porridge churned in Rosalind's stomach. Kiernan was evil, like a mind-reading Rasputin. She sincerely hated him.

✎   ✎   ✎

At fifteen minutes before eight that cold morning in London, the scene at Boulderdash was tense. Dianne, Lord Henry, Graham, Wattle, Colin, T and sundry agents encircled the bank of phones on the library table.

Tea and coffee grew cold in Wedgwood cups. The small talk had tapered off to silence. Dianne's hand rested nervously on a receiver. A tape machine was already rolling in anticipation.

At precisely twenty-seven seconds before eight, the phone rang. Dianne's knuckles turned white as she gripped the reciever.

"Answer it," barked Graham.

"Yes?" she whispered into the phone. "Yes?"

"You have been expecting our call." The touch of brogue was unmistakable. "You are ready for your intructions?"

Dianne nodded.

"Yes," hissed Graham, coaching.

"Yes," echoed Dianne.

"One person, alone and unarmed, at two A.M. tomorrow morning, is to take the money and drive west on the M4 motorway and get off at number four, heading north on Cowley Road. A car with a driver and additional instructions will be waiting exactly one quarter of a mile along the road on the left.

"If there is any sign of surveillance of any kind, the operation will be disbanded and we shall simply tell you where to find Miss Connolly's body."

Dianne gasped.

"Are the instructions clear? You do have tapes recording this, don't you?" The laugh was scornful.

"I want to speak to my daughter. I want to know if she is all right."

There was a fifteen-second pause before Rosalind came on the line. "This is Rosalind Connolly," she began.

"Rosie! Are you all right?"

"Mummy!" Rosalind quickly departed from the script. "How did you get there so quickly?"

"I arrived Sunday night. If only I had called you from the airport . . . but I had an appointment with . . . Rosie? Rosie, are you there?" Dianne stopped. She could hear sounds of an argument in the backround. Then Rosalind returned.

"I an fine. If you do precisely what you are instructed, no harm will come to me. You are dealing with dedicated professionals. . . ." She continued hoarsely through the script.

"You sound terrible! Your voice . . . what have they done to you . . . Rosie?"

There was a pause and more background mutterings before Rosalind replied. "I an fine. I have a cold, that's all."

The mocking voice took over. "We shall next be in contact with you along Cowley Road." The click was audible.

On line with MI-6's communications center, Wattle spoke immediately. "We have a fix on the address. Bury Street."

Graham and Wattle traded glances. It was too easy.

"Bury Street." Dianne's eyes welled. "Such a horrible name."

"*Yes? Yes?*" Dianne was startled to hear her own voice. Then she realized Graham was replaying the taped conversation. She and Colin both moved closer to the speakers.

"*This is Rosalind Connolly.*"

Colin's hands turned into fists as he concentrated on the tape, trying to drive the words and the sound of the voice into his memory bank. Her voice was stilted. Obviously, she had been reading a prepared text.

"Blast," Wattle said, looking at Graham. "The old phone

relay trick. The Bury Street house is vacant except for two phones rigged together. They called the first phone and someone waiting there used the second phone to call here, attach the phones and run out. It seems overcomplicated, but it explains why our kidnapper was in no great hurry."

"So they like to play games." Graham pushed a stray strand of hair from his forehead. "Okay. McReady and Smith, get working on Rosalind's friends at the Academy. Williams and Mendelson, you take the professors, custodians and anyone else around—shopkeepers, bums, everyone. Don't discount anything or anyone. We're looking for needles." Graham's glance pierced Colin. "Stay organized and stay calm."

Colin followed T outside into the frigid gray morning. Colin was oblivious to the cold. He stared blindly at the U.S. Embassy across the square, his mind still focused on the tape. "I an fine. If you do precisely what you are instructed, no harm will come to me . . . I an fine." What was peculiar? She sounded as though she were swallowing her *m*'s. But when she said "harm," the *m* was clear. Was the mispronunciation intentional?

A scene from Northampton flashed into his mind. The first time he had mentioned Ian to her, she had laughed and insisted it should be pronounced with a long *I*, making it "I-an" rather than "Ee-an." Was she trying to give him a clue and say "I-an" her way? He cautioned himself against desperate reasoning. Ian was in Dublin.

Dublin. A new warning light flashed. Although Ulster and Northern Ireland were the battlegrounds, Dublin was still a planning—and recruiting—center for the IRA.

"T." Colin grabbed his partner's arm. "Drop me off at the flat. I want to check if Rosalind left anything there—notes, phone numbers, anything. I'll catch up with you at the café."

"You better tell Sam you're pulling a switch."

"You want to tell Sam exactly why there might be clues in my flat?"

"I don't think he'd be surprised, do you?"

"Just give me an hour."

"Okay. One hour and no more."

ю ю ю

Colin didn't bother searching the flat. He'd done that earlier. He immediately dialed Ian's number at the university flats, hoping against hope that Ian was there.

A groggy voice with an Irish lilt answered. "Hello. Keith Malloy here."

"Keith!" Colin had reached one of Ian's roommates. "Sorry to wake you. This is Colin McReady, Ian's father. I'm trying to reach Ian. Do you know what classes he has today?"

The pause was leaden.

"Keith, it's vital that I reach Ian today. You might even say it's a matter of life and death."

"I'm sorry, sir, but I pro . . . is it something . . . is someone sick? Is his mother all right?"

Colin's mouth went dry. Why was the boy hedging? "When do you expect to see him?"

"Not until he's back from London."

London. Oh, God. "Are you sure he said London? I'm not expecting him in London until Friday."

"Yes, I'm sure," whispered Keith. "He said he had to go to London to work on a special project, but I swore not to tell anyone he's away." Keith's voice cracked with frustration. "I really don't know why he was so mysterious about it. He said it had to do with one of his courses, but that's all I know."

Colin believed the boy. Keith was too upset to be lying.

"Keith, don't tell anyone I'm looking for him. I don't want him to get worried until I have a chance to talk to him myself." If Ian were somehow involved, the wrong question from Keith could be dangerous. "Just forget I called. Okay?"

"Fine, sir." Keith sounded relieved. "And I'd rather you didn't tell Ian I told you anything either, sir."

"I won't, son." Colin hung up and stared at the silent phone. The call had eliminated nothing. The possibilities remained ugly.

He dialed his Dublin cousins. Jamie and Rose Ellen McReady had four children, two boys and two girls. The oldest, boys, were classmates of Ian at the university.

"Ah, Colin," Rose Ellen answered. "You are a fortunate man to find me in. I was on my way to the market."

Lucky to find one Rose, he thought as he explained his search.

"Ah, but it's hard to keep track of them. The boys are off a-larking on some project themselves. It's not like when Jamie was in school, sitting in class all day and studying all night. I remember that clearly, I do. Him studying and me working." She laughed.

Colin could picture his slim, green-eyed cousin by marriage, head tossed back in laughter. Despite four children and an endless managerie of pets, she had retained a coltish grace. Her candor and sparkle were refreshing if one didn't want fast answers.

"Do you know which professor was in charge of the trip?"

"I wouldn't be knowing if they are on the same outing or off on three." She chuckled. "When they are out of the nest and flapping their wings, they don't report in to mother hen. I hope it's nothing serious that you're wanting him for?"

"I don't know, Rose Ellen. I hope not. But there is a rumor I am curious about. I've read that the IRA has intensified its recruiting efforts at the university. It worries me a little. Have the boys mentioned anything about it?"

Rose Ellen's tone cooled. "I wouldn't be knowing."

Colin's next question sprang without forethought from some dark corner of his Irish soul. He had to know. "Where do you and Jamie stand on the IRA issue?"

"On Irish soil," she replied quickly. "Sinn Fein, as the elders say. But I have no time for discussing political philosophy this morning. I must be running off to the butcher, baker and candlestick maker, all of them! But if I see my boys, I'll tell them to have Ian call you—when they see him."

"I'd appreciate that."

"Now don't be worrying. He'll show up by and by. They always do—with jam on their faces and turtles in their pockets. The only thing that changes is the kind of jam and what they consider turtles." She concluded breezily, ordering him to come visit soon.

"*Sinn Fein.*" The phrase and what it represented lodged in Colin's mind. Colin had not openly challenged Rose Ellen's change in attitude at the mention of the IRA. If she and Jamie were involved even peripherally, they could trigger a defense before Colin even knew what he was attacking.

He pressed his palms against his eyelids, trying to clear his mind. Did middle-class citizens like Jamie foster the lawlessness of the IRA? It was unthinkable.

Go back to point one, he ordered himself. Everyone agreed that Rosalind must have known someone involved with the plot. Would she have crawled across the roof to meet Ian? Yes, came the self-mocking answer, if it had been presented as a lark or joke. The perverse conjectures had a clear logic to them.

Was Ian susceptible to the romance of a guerrilla group? How little he knew this boy he had sired one rash night in the back seat of an old Dodge. He knew the boy was bright, but he knew nothing about his values and ideals. He hadn't been around when the twig was nourished.

"Dear God in Heaven, let me be wrong," Colin breathed to the walls.

ᵛᵖ ᵛᵖ ᵛᵖ

Rosalind blew her nose on some cheap toilet paper Kerry found for her. "How in the world did you ever get involved with these people?" She looked into Kerry's mild brown eyes.

"If you have a conscience, you work to set things right. It is not right that Ireland should be divided."

"And you really think that violence and kidnapping help?"

"Come on, Rosalind. It's not as though you're a helpless two-year-old. Your kidnapping is only to get money to keep working for unification. There is no violence in it."

"What about the Mountbatten killing?"

"Personally, I thought that was dumb," Kerry said mildly. "It turned public opinion against us and made Mountbatten a martyr for 'English justice.' "

Harry looked up from a newspaper. "You better not let Kiernan hear you say that."

"He has no more time for that hollow institution—English justice—than the rest of us."

"You know what I mean—Mountbatten."

"Yeah, he does get touchy on that subject. It's enough to make a person wonder. . . ." Kerry trailed off.

For the first time in fourteen hours, Rosalind was distracted from her own predicament. "Do you think Kiernan had something to do with the Mountbatten killing?"

Harry shook his head. "Not for discussion."

"I wish we could take a run." Kerry stretched. "I miss our morning mile."

"It is stuffy in here," Harry agreed.

"Claustrophobic, I'd say," Rosalind added.

"How about some calisthenics? We'd better do something to work up an appetite for lunch. Old Lloyd the Marxist thinks porridge exemplifies the true spirit of the revolution." Kerry laughed. "Maybe we can slip out for a burger later."

"Where is everyone, anyway?" asked Rosalind.

"Kiernan and Lloyd had a meeting and they took Ian along for protection," Kerry answered.

"Protection?" Rosalind laughed. "Ian as a bodyguard?"

"The protection is for him, against your evil influence." Kerry leered theatrically. "Kiernan doesn't want the lad to feel any remorse."

"Kerry, you and your wagging tongue are going to get us in a heap of trouble one of these days," warned Harry.

"I don't see what harm it does for me to know Kiernan doesn't think Ian is as tough as nails. You two don't seem like seasoned warriors to me." Rosalind eyed the front door. If she could divert them, she could make a run for it. Maybe Kiernan or Lloyd had forgotten to lock the door. Trying, no matter how bad the odds, was better than nothing. "Were you serious about calisthenics?"

"Sure." Kerry grinned. "We don't want anyone to say we didn't give you adequate excercise."

"I'll watch." Harry remained sitting while Kerry pushed back the couch to make room.

"Push-ups?" asked Kerry. "Or are you soft and weak like most American girls?"

"I can do twenty without a break," she said with bravado, hoping it was true. She had done ten when Billy and Timothy had challenged her last summer.

The contest was on. One. Two. Three. Four . . . Six . . . Eight. Rosalind felt the pressure in her sinuses. The carpet was dusty and her throat felt raw. Twelve. She gulped for air. Peripherally, she saw Harry lean forward, with interest. Fourteen. She had to make it to twenty to prove herself. Sixteen. Prove what? Prove she could do it. Eighteen. In the bird's-eye view of her mind, she watched Kerry rising and falling easily while she struggled to lift herself from the dust. Nineteen. What did it matter? Who were they anyway? Cheap radicals playing stupid games surrounded by horror. The muscles of her inner arm trembled, resisting the command to elevate her body. Goddamn it, she would do one more.

Sweaty and panting, she sat up and pointed her chin at Kerry. "There," she gasped. "Twenty."

"Twenty-five," announced Kerry, grinning at her. "But you were terrific! I didn't think you could do it." He leaned over and gave her a hug. "Congratulations!"

312

Kiernan had quietly entered from the back hall and stood in the doorway, surveying the scene. "How very cozy."

Kerry scrambled to his feet, embarrassed. "She just did twenty push-ups!"

"Lloyd will take over the watch. You two fix lunch."

"Porridge," Lloyd instructed the chastened pair.

With Harry and Kerry gone, the atmosphere in the parlor palled. Lloyd shoved the ancient couch back into position while Kiernan leaned against the mantel and stared down at her, still sitting on the floor. She felt foolish and filthy.

"I'd like to wash up a bit," she said as she stood.

Kiernan nodded. "Lloyd, take her up to the loo."

She quickly walked into the hall and turned away from the stairs toward the door. Her hand grasped the knob before Lloyd could reach her. Locked. There had been no careless mistake.

She felt Lloyd's fingers dig into her arm and leaned against the flaking paint of the door, fighting against crying out and admitting his strength.

Lloyd twisted her arm hard, forcing her to swing around. She stared in hatred at him.

At that moment Ian entered the hall from the kitchen and froze as he saw Rosalind held captive by Lloyd.

"Ian!" she called.

Kiernan stopped him with an icy look.

"You want to go up to the loo?" Lloyd shoved her forward, knocking her down against the foot of the stairs. "Go." He kicked her hard on the side. "Move." His foot jabbed her again— and again.

Kiernan's eyes had not left Ian. "Thank you, Lloyd. We needed a loyalty test about now." Then he turned and watched Rosalind struggle to rise. "Lock her in the loo for an hour, just to remind her that it is dangerous to get cute."

"Move." Lloyd prodded the small of her back with his gun.

She swallowed back bile as her anxious stomach rejected the semi-digested lumps of breakfast porridge. She staggered forward, up the stairs, away from her tormentor. Swallowing hard behind clenched teeth, she lurched into the bathroom.

"Don't try anything clever," Lloyd sneered at her back. "We'll be right outside the door."

She heard the key turn in the lock and untensed. He was locked out. Then her stomach heaved and she sank on rag doll legs beside the toilet bowl and stared at the ugliness that had been inside her. Gray foamy lumps speckled with dark splotches and clots like blood. In her own way, she had been blooded. She heaved again, not caring if Lloyd could hear.

Water from the toilet and vomit splattered up on her neck and face. She grabbed frantically for the single frayed towel. She had to clean herself. A thread caught on the tiny petals of the gold rose pendant. She thought of Colin and a sudden rage erupted. She tore at the rose, breaking the clasp and sending the miniature rolling across the gummy linoleum to rest at the foot of the exposed sink pipes, the diamond chip catching the light.

Bill Connolly's baby ring rolled in the other direction to stop at the edge of the toilet.

"My father, my father," she half prayed as she scrambled for the tiny ring, ignoring the pain of her bruises. "I'm sorrry. Forgive me. Please, please, help me."

The Bill Connolly Rosalind knew best, the one she had created from photos and speeches and articles, would not have wanted his daughter groveling on the bathroom floor, not for all the terrorists in the world. The thought gave her strength as she fumbled for the ring.

And the rose, the gift from Colin, Ian's father, but also her lover and her best friend. Maybe Dianne was right. Maybe no one was safe for them.

Hesitantly, she picked up the rose and sat on the toilet seat to attempt to repair the damage. She had time enough.

ᔰ ᔰ ᔰ

Dianne sat in the greenhouse, half listening to Tulip chattering about the Boulder aphid. Lord Henry had told Tulip to entertain Dianne and keep her busy. The greenhouse seemed as good a place as any.

"I'm thinking that I should call Billy and Timothy, my sons. I haven't called them yet since I've been here. And it would be terrible if they heard it from their uncle Sean accidentally. After all, Rosalind is their sister."

"Do you think it's wise to tell them about the . . . the . . . terrible thing going on?" Tulip could not bring herself to say *kidnapping*.

"I don't know, I really don't. I hate to upset them, but they

314

get furious if they learn things they think they should have been told earlier. My children are quite grown up these days and very close . . . or they were."

Tulip looked sympathetic and murmured, "Do what you think best, dear. You know your own children best." She frowned at an orchid leaf. "Oh, dear, I must go get old Jack to take a look at this. I'll be back directly."

Dianne sat alone among the blossoms. Did she know her children best? The twins were becoming so adult. Their voices had dropped an octave two summers ago. Was it right to try to protect them? From the time they were three, an orphaned three, she added to herself, they had insisted that they would protect her—and Rosalind. Before she had sent them away to school, rationalizing that they needed to learn independence while she looked forward to new privacy, they had been so close. She realized they had gotten strength from each other. If they had to be different from other children and have Secret Service agents trailing behind them twenty-four hours a day, they were in the same predicament, together. Rosalind had played "little mother" for her brothers, especially when Dianne was out of town, according to Kiki's reports. Perhaps that had been too often, but they had always seemed content with each other. And Billy and Timothy had been Rosalind's personal court jesters, always able to bring her out of any temporary pout. Why had she insisted on separating her little family? All they really had for family was each other—and her. If she discounted the Eighth Street Theater incident, none of them had ever got into any difficulties when they were together. If only she had kept her children together, Dianne lamented, she would not be going through this terrible ordeal in London.

She decided to give her sons a call. Perhaps Rosalind had said something to them during the holidays that could give them a clue.

❧ ❧ ❧

Colin tossed aside his notebook, disgusted. He had been replaying the scene in his mind for the past ten minutes.

Ian had insisted on staying in Notting Hill with friends during his last visit. When Colin had asked for the address and phone number, Ian had acted as though it were an invasion of privacy. Colin remembered he had almost dropped the matter

315

before insisting out of paternal perversity. Then the picture faded. He couldn't remember where he had written the information.

The incident had occurred moments before they had left for dinner that Friday night. Where would he have written it?

The slant-top desk was crammed with notes scrawled on the backs of cleaning receipts, match covers and napkins. He made a mental note, hardly the first on the subject, to stop using scraps for notes. He forced himself to slow down and methodically examine each scrap with care. Unidentified phone numbers, shopping lists, reminders for T, notes for Rosalind— a collage of his life, without glue.

Twenty minutes later, the desk was clear and the wastebasket jammed, but he had come up empty.

What had he worn that night? The brown tweed. He remembered joking about it with Ian, saying Irish tailors liked to put pockets in their pockets and asking if Dublin was the center of the pickpocket industry. He rummaged through his closet with care, probing for the smallest piece of paper.

"Damn!" He hurled the jacket on the bed, then viewed the heap of tweed with guilt. It wasn't the jacket's fault, for pete's sake. He picked it up to hang it back in the closet over the vest. The vest. He had worn the vest that Friday night. He reached in to the left vest pocket and felt the small pocket watch there. Good thing he hadn't sent it to the cleaner's, he chided himself. The chain was caught inside the pocket. He gave it a tug and it pulled free, along with a small business card which fluttered to the floor, faceup. A restaurant he'd taken Ian and Rosalind to. Suddenly Colin remembered.

He had pulled out the card to check the address for dinner. When Ian had raced through the address and number, Colin had written it on the back of the card. He held his breath while he turned the card over. "371 Colville Terrace, London W. 11. 1-229-0715."

Should he call Graham before trying the number? But with what? Uncorroborated suspicions of his own son? He didn't need to lose any more points with Graham. Depending on what Graham decided to tell—or not to tell—the commander, Colin's position, along with all benefits and honor itself, was vulnerable. He had warred with himself about the affair with Rosalind for months, aware he was compromising his duty. But he had never thought it could destroy his career—or her. Now he rued the cold winter day he had treated their honor so lightly.

Sweat gleamed on his upper lip in the icy flat. His fingers trembled as he dialed the number. One. Two. Three. Four rings.

"Yes?" The voice was young and masculine.

At the last second, Colin reached back to his Dublin visits for a touch of brogue, playing it with caution. "I'd like to speak with Ian, if you please."

"One moment, please."

Colin strained to distinguish the muffled conversation in the backround.

"There is no Ian here. Are you sure you have the right number? What is this Ian's surname?"

"I'd be calling Ian Flannery at 1-229-0751." Colin reversed the last two digits.

"Wrong number. Wrong Ian."

It all rang false to Colin. Why say "wrong" Ian if there were no Ian there? Again, nothing concrete, but nothing disproved either.

He called the Arts Café. T was waiting by the phone.

"What's the good word, Mr. McReady?"

"I found an address written on the back of a restaurant's business card—nobody she's ever mentioned—but I'd like to check it out."

"Have you called Graham? Wattle's boys could run the address through their computers to see if there's any IRA connection. What's the address?"

"371 Colville Terrace."

"West London. Lousy part of town."

"Tell you what. You call Wattle and check it out with him while I grab a cab and take a run out there."

"Okay, I'll call Wattle and then meet you there to give you a ride back."

"Funny. You don't look like a Jewish mother."

"We're a team, remember? And while you're out grabbing at nameless straws against Graham's orders and my better judgment, let me at least cover the back court, okay?"

"Okay." Colin signed off quickly. He still hadn't voiced his suspicions to T. He needed facts beyond the sick gut feeling that he was on the right track.

By luck, a cab dropped a woman off in front of the building

and Colin jumped in before she had closed the door behind her.

He leaned back and took a deep breath, filling his lungs with the smell of old leather and forgotten cigars. He stared at the oblivious crowds, freely milling in and out of shops, hailing cabs and munching sweets while Rosalind was trapped, locked up God knew where or with whom. There were madmen in the IRA, with or without outsiders like the PLO. Wattle had said as much. They were men who blindly bombed offices and blew up cars and houses, innocents be damned. And Rosalind was truly that, a blind, trusting innocent.

But she had been alive that morning, he reminded himself. "I an fine. . . ."

～ ～ ～

Rosalind had not spoken a single word to anyone since Lloyd released her from the bathroom. She had nothing to say to any of them.

Kerry and Harry had cajoled Ian into playing gin with them. She tuned in on the game long enough to know Ian seemed distracted. Perhaps he wasn't having such a wonderful time as a revolutionary. He was too weak. He never should have been allowed to leave America. She wished she hadn't herself.

Why, why had she ever let Dianne push her into coming to London? All she had wanted was to finish Smith like Cynthia, like a normal person. Cynthia would never believe the whole thing when—if—she got back.

Her side ached. She had checked the nasty bruise in the bathroom—red, on the road to purple. Lloyd should be killed. If Tony were alive, she thought, he could have done it. He had been tight with the mob; she had read it somewhere. Dianne had insisted it wasn't true, but for all her sophistication, Dianne was more naïve than she. Dianne. Everything had to be cushioned for Dianne. Rosalind would have wagered that Dianne already had someone to lean on in London while her daughter was imprisoned in mortal danger.

She ran her fingers through her snarled hair, fighting the tangles. She stopped, feeling Lloyd's stare. She squinted at him through her lashes, confirming the eerie surveillance, and turned with a shudder toward the card players.

Kerry caught the motion. "Want to make a fourth?" He looked at Lloyd. "It's okay if she joins us?"

Lloyd grunted assent.

Rosalind realized that if she played she would have to break the silent treatment, but there would be a compensatory pleasure in physically confronting Ian with his duplicity, across the card table.

Harry pushed the deck at Ian. "We'll start from scratch. You deal."

If only she could start from scratch, Rosalind thought. Ian's eyes met hers as he finished dealing. He reddened and turned to Kerry. "You lead."

The last time she had played gin had been with Billy. Did he know she had been kidnapped? Probably not. Dianne treated them as if they were emotionally backward, hiding anything she thought might upset them until it suited her personal convenience, as with the sudden trips that preempted family events. She wondered how Billy and Timothy would handle being kidnapped. They would be sassier, of that she was certain. She suddenly wished they had all been kidnapped together. The thought of her brothers made her feel better.

She concentrated on the game. She wanted to win at something.

✍ ✍ ✍

"It's not even that heavy!" Dianne lifted the valise and looked at her attorney, Jordan March III. "Jordy, open it. I want to see." She leaned forward, tongue caught between her teeth. She had never seen one million dollars in cash.

It lay in neat, banded rows, 25,000 twenties and 10,000 fifties. Dianne picked up a stack of fifties and fanned them slowly as she turned to Graham with a hurt look. "Why do we have to give them my real money? You're supposed to have vaults full of counterfeit money."

"It's rarely that good and we don't keep million-dollar inventories," Graham answered.

"Mrs. Connolly"—Wattle slipped without notice or correction—"if the kidnappers even suspected the money was counterfeit, it could be signing a death warrant for your daughter. The IRA is more sophisticated than you seem to realize. I can assure you the money will be subjected to scrutiny."

"Our first concern is returning your daughter to you safely." Graham spoke flatly. "That is your paramount concern, is it not?"

"How dare you suggest otherwise?" Dianne's eyes misted. "Nothing else matters. If anything happens to her . . ." She straightened the pile of fifties and solemnly positioned them in the valise, like putting a rose in a coffin.

Graham half expected her to lean down and kiss them good-bye.

"Are they marked?" She turned to her lawyer. "Jordy?"

Jordy patted her hand. "There wasn't time, darling."

"They might spot that, too," Wattle added. "It would be a futile and dangerous exercise."

"It sounds as though the thought of any recovery is a futile exercise." Dianne's eyes blazed.

Wattle adjusted his dark wool tie which looked absurdly narrow against his portly middle. "Since the kidnappers obviously desire only money, not publicity, I believe it is likely your daughter will be returned unharmed and then we can pull out all stops."

"Only money," Dianne mocked. "It's 'only money' when the money is mine. Jordy, shut the case. I can't stand looking at it."

Jordy snapped shut the case. Graham wished for a handful of dirt to throw on top before it was buried in the numbered accounts of the Irish Republican Army.

Dianne gripped Jordy's hand tightly. "Jordy, how could she do this to me?"

"I hardly think Rosalind was at fault for being kidnapped."

"She runs wild," snapped Dianne, irritated at Jordy for defending Rosalind. "She leaves herself vulnerable."

Lord Henry entered the library carrying a tray of Bloody Marys. "A touch of afternoon refreshment," he said at large. "Any progress, E.E.?" he asked, turning to Wattle.

"We're going after every known IRA sympathizer in London. The Bury Street operation indicates that at least some of them are here."

Wearily, Lord Henry reached for a glass. "Perhaps it's just as well not to stir up any hornets until our little Rose is safe again."

Dianne felt too drained to react aloud. Rosalind had been stolen from under this very roof. It was partly Lord Boulder's fault. And she was not *his* little Rose; *he* had not just turned over one million dollars for her.

"Dr. Symons is here," Lord Henry told Dianne gently.

"Would you like a sedative? We all have a long wait until tomorrow morning."

"Yes, I would." Dianne wanted to sleep and sleep and wake to discover it was all a bad dream. She had felt that way after Bill's death a lifetime before, but then she had resisted sedatives and forced herself to stay awake and hurt publicly so the nation would suffer with her. Now there was no nation to suffer with her, only Lord Henry and the bumbling idiots from U.S. and British Intelligence. There was no need to pose for them.

"Dr. Symons is in the breakfast room," Lord Henry said.

Dianne rose. "Come with me, Jordy, and bring that along."

There was no question about what she meant. Jordy picked up the valise and followed her into the hall.

Graham watched her exit with relief. He didn't like the way that woman kept pushing him and Wattle, worrying about her damn money. It didn't dampen his determination to recover the girl, only the money.

"Sam!" Wattle sounded excited. "The 371 address is leased by Megan Higgens. I seem to recall she was a former girlfriend of Tom Corcoran, one of the men still in custody for the Mountbatten affair."

෨ ෨ ෨

Dianne stopped in the hall beside the carved panels and turned to her friend and attorney. "Oh, Jordy, what did I do wrong? I have tried and tried with her. Was I wrong to send her here? I only wanted to broaden her experience." She giggled suddenly and dropped the martyr's tone. "But I didn't want to broaden it this much." She giggled again, hysterically.

"Dianne, you need rest. I think a sedative is an excellent idea."

Jordy never had had a sense of humor, she thought as they reached the breakfast room, but she fought to remain serious. She needed Jordy's total sympathy. "I'm so afraid," she whispered as she noticed that Dr. Symons was under forty and attractive. "She sounded so terrible on the phone. . . ."

"Dear lady, don't torture yourself with conjecture." Dr. Symons spoke in a soothing voice. "I'm going to give you a shot to calm your nerves and let you rest."

"Jordy?" Dianne's little-girl voice wavered. "Will you sit beside me until I fall asleep?"

"I promise, Dianne, whatever you want." He had known

from the beginning that hand-holding went along with the position as Dianne's attorney. He relished the extra assignment while emphatically denying his estranged wife's accusations of infatuation. Dianne was an important woman; to be needed by her was an important trust.

"Jordy, get me a picture of Rosalind. The agents have them."

Dianne waited quietly until Jordy returned with one of the glossies the CIA had printed for their agents' search. Jordy looked at it for a long moment before handing it to her. "She's matured since I saw her last. She is lovely now."

Dianne felt a pang of jealousy. "She photographs well."

"I'd like to see her again," Jordy said, unconscious of the irony.

"So would I," Dianne snapped.

"I'm sorry, Dianne. You know I didn't mean it that way. I certainly didn't want to upset you."

Dianne's tone softened as Jordy's attention focused totally on her again. "Jordy, I want to look in Rosalind's room. I want to touch her things. I need to feel close to her."

Jordy thought about Bill Connolly's cuff link. When the president collapsed, a cuff link had been knocked loose from his sleeve. The papers had reported that Dianne held it in her hand for twenty-four hours, refusing to put it down or to sleep. But this was different, he hoped. As far as they knew, Rosalind was still alive.

៚ ៚ ៚

Rosalind fought to stay alert and play cards, but she was dead tired. Her eyelids felt swollen and her side ached. The slightest movement of her left knee was painful.

"Rummy!" Kerry grinned.

She looked at her cards. "Twelve points." After winning the first game, fatigue had won out over her desire for blood. Besides, Kerry and Harry's banter provided a peculiar brand of normalcy. "What time is it?" She yawned.

"It's about . . ." Kerry began.

Lloyd interrupted. "She has no need to know. Her time will come soon enough, one way or the other."

Lloyd was the most repulsive person she had ever met, Rosalind thought.

Three sharp knocks sounded on the front door. Kiernan hurried into the parlor from the back entrance.

"Hello!" a deep voice called followed by a louder knock.

Kiernan gestured to Lloyd. "See who it is. And the rest of you stay quiet, especially you." His hand gripped down on Rosalind's shoulder. "Or you'll think the hour in the loo was a picnic."

Lloyd pulled out his gun and opened the door a crack.

During the long ride through snarled traffic, Colin had decided to play it straight when he arrived. Graham was right. He was too emotionally involved. His anxiety was feeding his imagination. The most he could hope for was a lead in tracking down Ian.

"Hello," Colin said to the shadowed eye he glimpsed through the crack. "My name is Colin McReady and I'm trying to find my son, Ian."

Rosalind's mouth flew open in surprise only to taste the soot and salt of Kiernan's palm. Instinctively, she bit down hard.

Kiernan's face twisted with pain, but he neither moved his hand nor made a sound. "Pillow," he mouthed at Harry.

Ian froze, white knuckles gripping the deck of cards.

"There's no Ian here," snarled Lloyd.

Colin pushed, forcing the door open a few more inches. "He stayed here with friends a couple of weeks ago."

"You must have the wrong address."

"No, the address is right. Three seventy-one Colville, three doors down from the Midland Bank."

"You stupid son of a bitch," Kiernan hissed at Ian.

"Do you live here alone? Is anyone else around who might know Ian?" Colin glanced past Lloyd into the dingy hall. An olive-green slicker was slung across a chair.

"Look." Lloyd tried to block the crack. "I am the only one here and I don't expect anyone else."

Colin knew that there were thousands of drab green slickers in the world, but Rosalind had been wearing hers and this man was lying. Colin had distinctly heard muffled voices as he approached.

Lloyd tried to pull the door shut but it was stuck on something. He looked down and saw Colin's foot blocking the door.

"I'm sure I heard voices inside. Maybe someone just came in the back." Colin shoved the door hard.

Lloyd reacted instinctively to bar the doorway. His trigger finger tightened.

The shot echoed into the parlor.

"Colin!" Rosalind's scream was muffled.

Colin heard the cry as the impact of the bullet knocked him backward. He fell, striking his head on the edge of the small porch. He heard the door slam shut as he struggled to rise.

Inside, Kiernan dropped the pillow and ran into the hall. Rosalind started to follow, but Harry grabbed her arm. "Let me go!"

"Shut up!" Harry slapped her across the cheek, hard.

She turned on Harry. "You're all alike. You pretend to be nice, but you're all devils—including Ian." She looked at Ian staring glassy-eyed at the door. "Oh, God." She fought back tears. She had to stay alert. Ian would just sit there while they killed his father.

"What happened?" Kiernan demanded of Lloyd. "Christ, you're a trigger happy bastard."

"It was an accident. He pushed the door and the gun went off, but I hope it killed him."

"Kerry, check the window," Kiernan ordered. "See if there's anyone else out there—cars, trucks, anything."

"Nothing," Kerry reported. "No one has even come out to check on the shot. And I don't see Cousin . . . I don't even see the man Lloyd shot."

"He must still be on the porch. We could be lucky. He might have been fishing alone. We better bring the bastard inside before someone finds him."

Hope churned in Rosalind's heart. T would have to be nearby. Her optimism faded quickly. By the time help arrived Kiernan would have two hostages—if Colin were still alive.

Her emotions wavered. If it had not been for Colin, she would never have met Ian and gotten into this mess. But for all she knew Colin was lying dead on the stoop. Her first love, her agent, her friend, dead like her father. Tears streamed down her face, soaking the dirty pillow Harry now held over her mouth.

"He's staggering across the yard," Kerry shouted.

"Lloyd, go bring him back," Kiernan ordered.

Kerry continued watching. "Wait! A black man is running toward him!"

Lloyd was already outside.

Rosalind's heart skipped a beat as she heard another shot. Then she saw Lloyd run back into the hall and slam the door.

"I missed," he snarled.

"And now they have us located, asshole," Kiernan snapped.

"More cars are pulling up," reported Kerry.

Lloyd raced to the back door. "Car pulling up in the alley!"

"Everyone in the parlor!" Kiernan shouted. "Now, take a deep breath and relax, because we have Madame Trump with us. As long as we have her, we can walk out the door smiling."

"A man's coming up the walk, holding a white handkerchief," said Kerry.

A loud rap on the door was followed by a deep voice. "We know you're in there. We want to talk."

Lloyd fired at the door.

"Who's running this show?" Kiernan turned white with fury. "I just might be in the mood to talk about now."

"The only good Limey is a dead one," Lloyd growled as he reloaded his gun.

"Lloyd didn't hit him," Kerry called. "He's running back to a car. Another guy seems in charge—about fifty or so, short, bald and round. A queer-looking copper."

"Forget the commentary." Kiernan tossed some nylon cord to Kerry. "Tie her arms. We may have to use Q-Z."

"Q-Z?" croaked Ian. "What's Q-Z?"

Kiernan ignored the question. "I don't like those bastards breathing down our necks! Lloyd, write them a note. Quote. Clear out and follow the original instructions or start planning the Connolly funeral. You have five minutes. Unquote." He laughed without humor. "Watch that get the bloody Limeys moving."

Lloyd opened the door and flung the response onto the porch.

"Let's take a look now." Kiernan pushed the curtain aside and watched men swarm around the small note. The short, bald man nodded and one by one the cars pulled away. Kiernan pointed at Lloyd. "Check the back."

"They're clearing out," Lloyd reported.

Kiernan continued staring out the front window. "A gray van just pulled up, two doors down. Smells like coppers to me."

"So. We have a trump card. You said so yourself." Harry double-checked the cord biting into Rosalind's wrists.

She felt numb and detached again. She would die here, she thought. Lloyd would turn and fire and it would be over. Would

Dianne care, really care? Uncle Sean and the twins and Grandma Bea and the cousins would care for a while, but they'd get over it, just as they had gotten over her father's death.

Colin would be devastated by guilt, but that was all right. In a way, he would have helped kill her. But none of that would matter to her. She would be dead. A chill of emptiness surged through her. She didn't know what that meant. Her icy fingers clasped behind her back. They had no warmth to share with each other. Please, dear God, let me get out of this alive. Let Colin and T find some way to break into this house. They were so close . . . and so far. She had a sudden terrible cognition. Colin had been looking for Ian; he must have gotten her clue, "I an fine." In a way, she had brought this latest confrontation on herself. "Shit," she whispered, unnoticed for the moment.Lloyd joined Kiernan by the front window.

"The London SWAT teams have too many balls for their own good," Kiernan said softly. "I think it's time for Q-Z."

Lloyd's eyes narrowed as he followed Kiernan's gaze to Rosalind.

Kiernan nodded. "There are lots of ways to get money. Bunko games in West Dublin, banks to rob in Ulster."

"You mean—?" a delighted smile lifted Lloyd's face.

"I ordered them to clear out or plan the funeral. Honor is always more important than money."

"Q-Z included taking her along," protested Kerry.

"It's more important to teach those bastards a lesson." Kiernan gestured toward Ian. "Come here."

Ian moved toward Kiernan like a sleepwalker.

"Take my gun and kill her," Kiernan ordered.

Ian's eyes darted to Kerry and Harry. Their sober faces told him nothing.

"No." Rosalind stepped back. "No!" she gasped.

Harry's arms closed around her upper arms, giving her false assurance.

"Go on, Ian. Go on, brave soldier boy, Irish hero," mocked Kiernan. "You have five seconds before Lloyd thinks about shooting you instead. One."

Trembling visibly, Ian lifted the gun and turned toward Rosalind.

"Two," Kiernan counted.

She stared at him, speechless with terror.

"Three."

Glass shattered on the floor above them and Rosalind screamed. The gun resounded as Ian dropped it to the floor.

"Lloyd, finish the job and get out. Q-Z."

"Ian, too?"

"I don't care just make it f . . ."

Something crashed against the outer windowsill and bounced on the porch. Lloyd ran to the window. "It's gas! And they're aiming for the windows."

"Move!" barked Kiernan.

It was all happening so fast. Rosalind glanced at Ian. His face was buried in his hands. Then she saw Lloyd level the gun at her.

The next second the front window shattered and a small metal ball hurtled across the parlor floor.

Harry and Kerry dashed for the hall on Kiernan's heels. Kerry shoved down on Lloyd's shoulder as he ran past at the moment Lloyd pulled the trigger. The shot rang out.

"My foot!" screamed Lloyd.

"Lloyd! Move it!" Kiernan shouted from the kitchen.

Lloyd limped down the hall, tracking blood, moments before a second object shattered through the front window.

Gray smoke filled the room in seconds. Rosalind's and Ian's stomachs heaved and bowels gave way.

Dimly, Rosalind heard someone retching in the back hall as she felt cold air sweep into the room from the jagged holes in the window. Then the front door caved in with a crash and two aliens with steel-gray faces shaped like giant ants entered holding guns.

One ran toward her while the other pounced on the dark metal ball hissing beside her.

"It didn't detonate completely and the other was a dud." Rosalind heard the unfamiliar voice, hollow through the filtered mouthpiece. Then she felt herself being lifted.

"No," she choked. She didn't want to be touched. Her jeans were wet and soiled. She felt shamed, vulnerable. She pulled away and collapsed down on the hall chair, gasping for air.

The alien lifted off his metal head to reveal a square-jawed man in his late thirties.

E. E. Wattle entered the doorway at the head of a second,

larger invasion force and pulled off his gas mask. "All safe already?"

"Yes, sir. Technical problems. They didn't blow the full charge. But we only found the girl and an unarmed kid."

Quickly Wattle dispersed teams throughout the old house. "Check the basement. That's where sewer rats hide." Then he turned to Rosalind. "Are you all right, my dear?"

Rosalind felt anger surge as her head cleared. "Great, just great," she snapped. "What was that stuff?"

"Nasty, isn't it?" E.E. chuckled and glanced in the parlor where Ian was still heaving. "Developed by your people for Vietnam. They call it a 'barf bomb' for short. Instantly hits the gastrointestinal system."

"Well, it missed the others. The killers." She began to tremble uncontrollably.

"Mr. Wattle!" A youthful agent ran down the hall from the kitchen. "We've found a tunnel in the cellar that connects with the sewers. They could be anywhere!"

"You're right. It's a labyrinth. You'd better go get the dogs."

The young agent dashed out, narrowly missing crashing into Dr. Symons and Colin as they entered.

Symons kneeled beside Rosalind, checking her pulse and asking her brief questions.

Standing in the doorway, his right hand gripping the left shoulder of his overcoat where a dark red stain marred the fine fabric, Colin stared past Rosalind at Ian sitting dejectedly on the parlor floor, head bent while tears streaked his grimy cheeks. Colin saw a stranger.

"That your son?" Wattle asked quietly. During the short siege, Colin had briefed him on the convoluted relationships.

Colin nodded, muted by his own guilt.

"The official word is that we've uncovered an IRA bomb factory. The block is cordoned off, but I think you better get her out of here before the press arrives."

"What about him?" Colin nodded toward Ian.

"Never saw him here. I certainly don't expect to see him in my IRA files, especially if he's on the other side of the Atlantic. Of course, I intend to have a lenghty private interview with the lad."

"I appreciate the courtesy, sir, but I don't see how we can keep him out of a public trial."

"Public trial? Perish the thought. This was hardly a public

kidnapping. It's best to keep a lid on these things so radicals don't get any extra . . . inspiration."

"There may be another problem, sir. I suspect Ian's cousins are involved."

"Yes, it could get complicated, but I'm sure we can work things out." He looked from Colin to the doctor. "Symons, take a look at his shoulder."

"It's only a graze," Colin protested.

Symons stood and probed gently while Colin gritted his teeth, unmindful of Rosalind looking up at him, now aware of his presence. "Nasty," muttered Dr. Symons. "Looks like a broken clavicle. You're bleeding like a stuck pig, my man. We'd better get you to a hospital."

"No. I'll hold out until we get Rosalind back to Boulderdash. Then we'll see."

"Yes." Rosalind glared at them all. "I want to get out of here. I have been here nearly two days, two of the longest, most horrible days of my life." She choked, fighting for control.

Colin looked down at her, unsure of his feelings at the moment.

"Colin, I could have been killed. Kiernan ordered Ian to shoot me. Ian had the gun pointed at me and then the window shattered and he dropped it. But then Lloyd took his gun to shoot me himself but Harry or Kerry bumped into him and he shot his foot," she rattled on hysterically. "But he would have killed me. He already had kicked me and hit me and I was dying from fear and I called and I called for you, Colin, in my mind, but you didn't hear because it was all your fault. . . ."

Colin saw red as bright as the blood oozing between his fingers. "I got your little clue and I found you before you were really hurt and they got their bloody million. But it was your stupidity that got you into this, not me. I don't remember your asking to take a moonlight trek into the worst section of London to play footsie with the IRA."

"I didn't know," she gasped. "It was supposed to be a joke on you. And it *is* your fault because he's your son and you should have known what he was into." She rubbed her red-rimmed eyes still stinging from the gas. "Can't you see that, you stupid fool? It's your fault!"

Colin released his shoulder and slapped her across the cheek, leaving a bloody trail among the tears.

"That's enough!" Colin barked. "You're getting hysterical."

"Easy, Colin." Wattle put his hand on Colin's shoulder from behind, then reached for his handkerchief. His wife would complain about the bloodstains, but those went with the territory.

Rosalind sobbed uncontrollably and Dr. Symons busied himself calming her and giving her a mild sedative.

It was at that moment, when Rosalind turned on him, too self-involved to notice his bullet wound, unwilling to accept one iota of responsiblity for the situation, that Colin finally realized he could not sacrifice his life and career on any terms for her emotional and physical well-being.

Rosalind pushed Dr. Symons aside and looked up at Colin, her anger spent. "Colin, help me."

Gently, Colin took her hand like a child. "Wipe your face. It's a mess." He released her hand to reach for his handkerchief.

She sniffed, obeying, then reached out for him again.

"Dianne is waiting for you at Boulderdash." He gripped Rosalind's hand, trying to give her strength to remain calm, then looked at his son, still sitting in the parlor. "Ian. You're coming with us."

"I'm sorry," Ian muttered and walked, head lowered, toward the door.

As they walked outside, T ran toward them, his hand lifted in a victory sign.

Colin watched, expressionless, unmoved by the Pyrrhic victory. Then the cold air hit him like a solid wall.

"Ah!" Rosalind inhaled the cold air greedily. "Oh, Colin, I'm sorry I was so awful to you. I didn't mean . . ." She felt his hand release hers and turned. He wasn't there. He lay crumpled on the sidewalk beside her.

Dr. Symons knelt beside Colin, feeling for a pulse. Colin moaned and tried to rise. "Lie still," said Symons. "You've done enough."

Wattle was already reorganizing the exodus. An agent paramedic was assigned to go with T and take Colin directly to the hospital. Two other men were designated to accompany Rosalind and Dr. Symons back to Boulderdash.

The cars had squealed away from the curb before E. E. Wattle noticed Ian beside him. "Good Lord, boy, I forgot about you. Now what shall I do with you?"

"If it's possible, sir, I'd like to go to the hospital. I'd like to know if my father's all right."

"Would you now?" Wattle looked at him.

"Yes, sir." Ian chewed his lip, still fighting tears.

"Very well. I'll take you over myself in a bit. We can begin our little chat on the way, in fact. But first, you had better go clean yourself up as best you can. You are beginning to stink, my boy."

19

Irish breakfast tea. Dianne could hardly believe the irony of Lady Gillian calmly pouring Irish breakfast tea while they waited for Rosalind. It seemed the wrong time to support the Irish. Nonetheless, the tea was delicious—full-bodied and spicy.

Dianne's emotions were mixed—relief that Rosalind was safe, delight that her one million dollars remained intact, irritation that it had taken Intelligence so long to find Rosalind, and anger at Rosalind for getting herself into another sordid situation.

Graham had said Rosalind had gone willingly to meet the radicals, although it had been some kind of setup. Somehow, Colin McReady's son was involved. She had burned when she heard that. She had trusted McReady. But Graham had also said Colin was responsible for finding Rosalind and that he should be thanked for that. To her way of thinking, it was a wash.

"I really don't understand how she could do this to me." Rosalind spoke as much to her teacup as to Lady Gillian.

"To you?" Tulip's pencil-line brows rose.

"She seems to attract these horrible situations like a honey pot—no, it's more like a money pot. That's what everyone seems to think we are."

"They're on their way." Lord Henry entered, speaking. "She should be here in minutes. Symons doesn't think a hospital visit is necessary. He says a good bath and some rest are all the medicine she needs!"

"Thank goodness," Dianne whispered, although in the dark corners of her heart she had been half hoping that Rosalind would be injured, not critically, but enough to punish her and make her eternally wary. Dianne felt a surge of anger that once more Rosalind had managed to come through untouched. Somehow, she had to get through to Rosalind, to make her understand once and for all.

Lord Henry outraced Ronald to answer the doorbell. "Rosie!" His voice echoed in the paneled hallway. "Rosie!"

Dianne stepped into the hall in time to see Rosalind collapse into Lord Henry's arms and hear her daughter's sobs on his shoulder. I should be there. I should be the one doing the comforting, Diane thought.

Rosalind raised a tearstained face to Lord Henry. "Colin was shot. He's in the hospital."

"A nasty shoulder wound, sir, but he'll be all right," Dr. Symons added from behind Rosalind.

Jordan emerged from the library and steadied Dianne's elbow. "It will all be fine now, Dianne. You'll see."

"Oh, Jordy." Dianne's eyes filled with tears. She suddenly felt inadequate and uncertain.

Lord Henry looked up and saw Dianne. "Rosie, your mother's here."

Rosalind wiped her eyes with the back of a grimy hand. "Oh, Mummy. It was a nightmare."

"But . . . you really are all right, aren't you? They didn't do anything to you, did they?"

"What do you mean by 'do anything'? They kidnapped me and beat me. Isn't that enough?"

Dianne nodded mutely. She was sorry she hadn't opened her arms and shared the relief and sympathy she felt at the sight of Rosalind's swollen eyes, stringy hair and general dishevelment.

"Aren't you even glad I'm alive and safe?"

"Oh, darling, of course. Of course I am, but I have been through so much myself, waiting and wondering and arranging the money and everything. It was a terrible night, darling."

"And it's all my fault, right? You've been blaming me because I walked right into it, right?"

"Damn it, Rosalind, you twist things before they are even said."

Lord Henry moved between them. "I think the best thing about now would be a nice hot bath and one of Margot's hot milk punches. Then you can tell us all about it, Rosie."

"Come along, dear," Tulip chirped. "I'll have the milk sent up and Rodney, dear, you come along, too."

"Yes, I would like to check that side again, Miss Connolly. It is a wicked-looking bruise."

"What happened?" Dianne's eyes sought the doctor.

"She was kicked," he replied tersely.

"Kicked! What kind of creatures were they?"

"Kidnappers, Mummy," Rosalind called down from the stairs where Lady Gillian was herding her upward.

Dianne stared after them. These people were taking her daughter away from her, swooping her away. Ever since Rosalind arrived here, there had been nothing but problems. She had to regain control of the situation, but she knew from past experience that getting angry wouldn't help. It would only drive Rosalind away. "Rosalind!"

"Yes?" Rosalind halted on the stairs.

"Rosie, didn't I always tell you you were worth a million dollars to me?"

Rosalind had to smile. "Yes."

Dianne reached deep and pulled out a mischievous grin. "Well, it looks like I just proved it to you, didn't I?"

Rosalind's laugh rewarded her. "Guess so, Mummy. Why don't you come upstairs while I take a bath?"

ഗ ഗ ഗ

Rosalind lay back on the cool, clean sheets, aching but relaxed. Dianne sat on the edge of the bed and ran her fingers through the short fine hair at Rosalind's hairline.

"Ours can be a crazy kind of life," Dianne said softly.

"Clinically insane, I'd say." Rosalind half smiled.

"You do get yourself in the worst fixes. I swear you'll be the death of me one of these days."

"I don't mean to. You know I don't mean to."

"I know, I know." Dianne's hand moved gently in the silence.

"Sometimes I would really like to know, Rosie. . . ."

"Know what?" Rosalind yawned.

"Oh, I don't know exactly. I'd like to know what you're trying to prove, what you want."

"Nothing special. At least I don't think so. I want to have ordinary fun like ordinary people. It was all supposed to be an ordinary practical joke, you know."

"Thinking that way is what gets you in trouble, my darling. You are not living in an ordinary situation. Ordinary people don't need the Secret Service to protect them. And we are much richer than most people and when Tony's estate is settled we'll be even richer.

"It makes us targets. You have to learn that, Rosie. You are a prime target and you can't march out on the shooting range and pretend that you are something else. Please, please get that through your head or you'll get yourself and me and the twins and everyone around you hurt—again and again and again."

"I don't want it to be that way."

"And the ordinary people you try to involve in your life will get hurt even more than you, because they won't have the money and the connections to bail themselves out."

"I'm not sure what you're talking about, Mummy."

"Maybe I'm not entirely certain myself," murmured Dianne. Was she talking about the Cindys of the world and the time Rosalind and Cindy were caught sneaking wine into their room at Smith? Cindy would have been expelled if Diane had not intervened. Or was she just talking about the Lydias and Ians—the weak and the greedy—the obvious threats? Or was she talking about the Daves in her life as well, the people who lacked the freedom of whim that money provides? Perhaps. She hadn't called him to tell him Rosalind had been found. He simply hadn't seemed relevant. And she hadn't needed him to lean on—Jordy had been wonderful. Different men for different purposes. With financial security, she didn't need to turn a good lawyer or lover into a bad husband.

"Rosie," she said to her daughter's closed eyelids. "Your agent, Mr. McReady . . . Were you . . . involved with him? Something Mr. Graham said made me wonder."

Rosalind's eyes remained shut. "I'd rather not talk about that, Mummy. Not now. Not until I sort things out."

"I see." A pang of envy silenced Dianne as she visualized the attractive agent with her daughter. She really didn't want details.

"I wish I did." Rosalind drifted toward sleep. She felt too drained to talk, but it felt good to have Dianne there, stroking her hair. Colin seemed far away, like the past or future. Now, she was content to have her mother beside her.

≈ ≈ ≈

"Oh, Rosie."

A hot, wet tear splashed down on Rosalind's cheek. Dianne was crying. Rosalind reached for her mother's hand. "How long have I been asleep?"

"Less than half an hour. I'm sorry if I woke you."

"I'm the one who's sorry, Mummy, really I am. You are my best friend in the whole world. I know that now."

"I try to be."

"Did you say the twins are on their way over?"

"They'll be here in a few hours."

"I could use my big little brothers with their crazy sense of humor about now." She smiled.

"We will be together more, I promise." She said it to both of them.

"It's all so open-ended now, isn't it?"

"What?"

"Our lives."

"Oh, I don't know. Life is so simple. You grow up and then you fall in love with the knight on the white horse and you live happily ever after. Isn't that how it goes?" Dianne held her daughter's hand tightly. "And then you have wonderful little princes and princesses who grow up and meet knights and ladies and fall in love and . . ."

"And you know it doesn't work that way, Mummy."

"Mmmm. But it should. We have to find a very special knight for you, because you seem to need protecting."

"What about you?"

"I seem to have run out of knights."

"Maybe we'll have to protect each other for a while."

Dianne laughed, suddenly feeling good, ready to plan again. Rosalind could take some courses at Columbia and finish up at Smith her senior year. And Rosalind could help with the Lily

Langtry research. She would take her to the islands and then back to Manhattan for a new wardrobe, haircut, the works. Dianne reined in her flight of fancy. The haircut would be a battle. A new look would be the old fight. There had been too many battles between them. If the catharsis of the kidnapping was to have any positive effect, she had to accept her daughter on her daughter's terms. Somewhere between London, New York and the rest of their world, Dianne had to find some common ground for them.

"Mother?"

"I thought you were asleep."

"Almost. But I want you to get some sleep, too. You've had a terrible day."

"I'm not alone in that." Dianne smiled. "No, I'm not alone."

Jordy appeared in the doorway. "Phone call, Dianne."

Dianne patted her daughter's hand. "I'll be back, darling."

As Dianne hurried from the room, Jordy took a hesitant step inside. "Can I get you anything?"

Rosalind gave him a sleepy smile. "No, just stay and talk to me awhile. I think I'm waking up again."

∽   ∽   ∽

Dianne was surprised by Dave's phone call from JFK airport. In the excitement of the past few hours, she had forgotten to worry about him.

"Okay, lady, you win this time," Dave announced. "It's taken me a day to arrange things, but I'll arrive at seven o'clock tomorrow morning. I should be there by eight."

"Darling, that's wonderful!"

"How are things going over there?"

"Rosalind's a little bruised, but it's nothing serious. I've been trying to get her to go to sleep."

"She's there! You mean it's all over? They have the kidnappers?"

"Rosalind's safe and sound. I'll tell you everything when you get here."

"Let me slow down. The crisis is over. Thanks a lot for calling me with the news," he said caustically. "How long have you known?"

"Only a couple of hours. I'm sorry, Dave. I was so relieved to have her back, it didn't occur to me to call."

"And I was just supposed to waste my time and money by flying over so we could all fly home together—'and then they all went off to the seashore.' Isn't that how the story's supposed to end?"

"What a wonderful idea. Come over and we'll all go to the Bahamas for a week as soon as Rosie feels up to it."

"Thick or thin, you just never give up, do you?"

"And I hope I never live to see the day I do—on anything that matters."

"I don't consider the beach a high priority matter."

"Then you don't consider me very high priority either."

"Lady, you have just pushed me one step too far. Give me a call next time you're in New York—if it occurs to you."

"Goddamn you, Dave," she sputtered into the dead line. Then she turned from the phone in irritation and looked into the clear gray eyes of Rodney Symons.

"I'm sorry, I didn't mean to eavesdrop."

"That's all right. It was just another change of plans." She sighed.

"I was wondering if you would like a sedative to help you sleep tonight."

"Do you play bridge?"

"Passably."

"Then let's get Lord and Lady Boulder to play a rubber or two."

The good doctor smiled. "That sounds boring enough to put us all to sleep."

"And just what the doctor ordered." She managed a smile. Different men for different needs.

∽ ∽ ∽

By the next afternoon, Rosalind was up and dressed in a becoming green and gold plaid wool dress. She still felt fragile.

She wandered through the rooms of Boulderdash, enjoying the freedom of movement. Tulip reported that Dianne was out shopping and Lord Boulder was at his office. A few MI-6 agents were working on the phones, returning them to normal. Otherwise, the large house seemed calm. She headed for the library, looking for something to read.

"Hello," Jordy said from the leather couch where he was reading the *Times*. "You're looking remarkably well this afternoon. I'm not sure what I should say. How are your bruises doing?"

"The physical ones are turning nicely purple, thank you, but the ones to my pride are still pretty raw." She smiled.

"Sit down and have some tea. I've managed to restrain myself so there are still a few pastries left."

"Thanks." Rosalind perched on a chair and munched a tart. "Jordy."

"Yes."

"Could you take me over to the hospital?"

"What's wrong?" His brown eyes filled with warm concern. "Do you feel sick?"

"I'm okay," she said softly, "but I'd like to visit my agent who was shot." She nervously looked at Jordy for a reaction. "I'd like to know if he's all right."

"I can give the hospital a call and find out. Do you know which hospital he's in?"

"The University of London." She had gotten that much from Williams. "But I feel perfectly well enough to go in person."

"Is it that important?"

"He is my agent and he got shot trying to rescue me. I think that's important, don't you?"

"Yes." He paused. "Is that all there is to it?"

"I'm not on the stand, counselor. Either take me over or don't. I don't need the third degree."

"Okay, okay, I won't probe. I'm just not certain that your mother or Dr. Symons would think it's a good idea."

"I think it's a good idea and I'm fine. Please, Jordy, just for a ten-minute visit."

"I give up. You're as persistent as your mother."

"Stubborn. I don't mind being called stubborn."

He laughed. "Guess it's the Irish in you."

She winced. "I'd rather not be reminded of that right now."

"I can't imagine why," he said dryly.

"Guess you don't have much imagination." She laughed.

∽ ∽ ∽

"You would have to get shot in your left arm, since you can't hit the side of the barn with your right one. You really will go to any length to get a month's leave, won't you?"

"Thanks a lot, friend." Colin paused. "Seriously, T, thanks.

If you hadn't followed up on the double, I might not have made it this far."

"Strictly in the line of duty, as they say. Now, let me get your order straight. Two double-burgers, fries and a chocolate shake."

Colin nodded.

"What you want, you get. I'll be back in twenty."

T grabbed his jacket and turned toward the door, stopping inches from Rosalind who had been standing in the doorway. "Well. You're looking well, Miss Connolly. Been standing there long?" he asked coolly.

"T, I didn't do anything wrong," she began in protest.

"Better to let bygones be bygones," he said quickly. "Nice seeing you." He gave a nod to Jordy and hurried down the hall.

"Jordy," she whispered. "Could you wait in the lounge or somewhere? Just for a few minutes."

"Sure, Rosalind." He gestured at a red couch at the end of the hall. "I'll be there with your agents."

"Thanks."

Colin's face brightened for a moment as she moved toward the bed, then became controlled, sober.

"Hello."

"You seem to have survived remarkably well," he responded.

"I'm pretty tough for a young thing."

"Tougher than this old man, that's for sure."

"You're okay?"

He glanced ruefully at the cast confining his left arm and shoulder. "Just dandy. Give me a month or so and I'll be back swinging on trees."

"Colin."

He waited.

"Colin, I'm sorry I said all those things yesterday. I really didn't mean them. I was just so . . . so terrorized."

"You did and you didn't. In some ways, it was my fault. More than just the involvement with Ian. An agent can't remain objective if he's emotionally involved. I was walking blind, letting you run wild around the streets of London."

"You didn't let me sneak out to Colville Terrace," she interrupted.

"But I let you sneak out other times, crawling in and out

of windows and slithering through back alleys. It was the same thing. Dangerous."

"Colin, that's absurd."

"I was behaving pretty absurdly for quite some time."

"But we had so much going for us. We had so much fun. . . . " She smiled and blushed. "And so much more."

"Maybe right things for the wrong reasons."

"Is it so wrong to care about someone, to . . . love?"

"I am nineteen years older than you are, Rosie. I could be your father. And I really think that's half the attraction for you. You're still looking for the father you lost. And you are not grown up. A grown-up wouldn't go crawling out of a window on a lousy night on a harebrained scheme, joke or no."

"Well, I, for one, would hate to grow up old and stodgy."

"Yes." He paused and studied her. "I'm afraid by the time you are grown up, I'll have grown old." Colin leaned back against his pillow and closed his eyes for a moment.

Rosalind's anger drained away and was replaced by concern. "Should I get you anything? A glass of water? The nurse?"

He shook his head and opened his eyes. They were clear. "Rosie, our relationship was too incestuous. And I have finally realized that I have been parenting the wrong child. I'm afraid both you and I have suffered from that."

"Colin," she said softly. "You know there was more than that between us."

"Yes, perhaps there was, but somehow it was all twisted up with these other things."

She stared down at her hands. The nails were broken and cracked, which she hadn't noticed before. She folded her fingers in loose fists, hiding them. "Well," her voice cracked. "Where do we go from here?"

"I go back to the States as soon as I get the medics' okay. Then I'll see. The commander is probably going crazy deciding whether I deserve a merit award or a terminal citation." He chuckled. "But you'll be agent-free in March, anyway."

"Colin. I'm never going to be rash again."

He reached for her hand and unfolded it. "Never is a long time. Start be being careful, especially about people."

"You sound like Dianne." She gripped his hand. Even here, she could feel the physical attraction, the warmth flowing into her from his hand.

"Rosie, I care for you a lot, too much. But we are never going to make it together, not in this lifetime."

"Never is a long time."

She felt his hand squeeze hers for a moment. "Not if you stay busy. It goes by in no time flat."

"Very funny."

"I like to think of myself as lighthearted. Especially"—he paused and stroked her hand—"especially when it hurts."

She didn't try to blink back the tears. "I expect I'll be going back to New York. You could give me a call in a week or so . . . to let me know how you are."

"Rosie, Rosie, please don't cry. I can't be everything in the world to you. And I can't make it all the way up to your world. There are more wrongs than rights between us."

"But I love you," she whispered.

"Don't do this to us. You've got to grow up a little. How much more do you want to hurt yourself?"

"Rosalind." Jordy spoke from the doorway.

Colin released her hand and looked up.

"Agent Williams just reported that Dianne is back at Boulderdash. We'd better go."

"Duty calls." Colin smiled weakly.

Jordy nodded at Colin. "And agent McReady looks pretty pale. I don't think you should tire him out."

Rosalind looked at Colin's face, drained of blood. She realized that he was hurting inside as well as physically. "I'll come back if I can," she whispered.

He handed her a tissue. "Be a good girl and blow your nose before you go."

She obeyed dutifully.

"Now skedaddle and let an old man get some sleep."

She stood and leaned over to brush his lips with hers.

"Mr. March, take this young lady home and make sure she gets some rest."

"I'll do that, Mr. McReady." Jordy approached the bed, hand extended. "And I want to thank you. Without your personal courage, things might not have ended so well."

Colin gave them both a tired grin. "Once a hero, always a hero, I guess."

"You know one of the things I liked best about London, Mother? I could go public places as a private person—nobody ever recognized me. I liked that."

"Maybe you're finally beginning to understand why I value my privacy so highly. I get so little of it. That's half the reason I always wanted to travel—to get far, far away where I wasn't affected by what strangers around me expected me to be. Or maybe it was the constant question in my own mind about what they might expect me to be. There have been times I have been so concerned with what people might be thinking about me that I didn't do any thinking or feeling for myself.

"Rosie, I'm afraid that it's too late for me to feel free and private in public, as you phrase it. My freedom can only be found in private, controlled situations. Your only chance of being unhassled is if the press, and thus the public, finds you very boring. And leaving yourself vulnerable for kidnappings or public displays—like acting—is not boring stuff. So far, we've been lucky to emerge with minimal attention."

"No." Rosalind gravely looked into her mother's eyes. "It wasn't luck. It was you. Thank you, Mother."

Dianne blinked back tears. "I know I haven't always been

easy. And I've been selfish at times. I know it. But all I've really wanted to do is to give you and your brothers a chance to live your own lives, to let you grow up and pick your own ponds, large or small. I wanted to give you a financial and emotional security that I never had. If I seemed to control too much, it was only so you could have freedom as adults."

Rosalind smiled softly. She knew Dianne was speaking truthfully on one level, but she also was aware that Dianne's desire to control and manipulate was not always high-minded or simple.

"Let's make a pact, Mother. If I promise to do it quietly, will you give me the freedom to make my own mistakes and bail myself out in my own way?"

"What does that mean?" Dianne frowned.

"I'll be twenty-one in less than a week. I've decided that I don't want to go back to Smith. I'd be a year behind Cindy and my class and I feel a thousand years older, anyway. I think I'd like to finish college at Columbia—and get my own apartment."

"Oh, Rosie, I don't know about that."

"You don't approve of Columbia?"

"Columbia's fine. I'm just not sure you're ready for your own apartment."

"Mother, you need privacy as much as I do. You don't want to play Magic Mummy twenty-four hours a day, do you?"

Dianne smiled at the phrase. "No, I think I've grown up enough not to need to play that role all the time—just now and then."

The sounds of bedlam erupted from the direction of Dianne's bedroom. She and Rosalind raced down the hall toward Leda's barks and the shouts of the twins, home for the weekend. Rosalind and Dianne reached the bedroom in time to see a wet Leda escape the towels brandished by the twins and leap to safety on top of Dianne's chinchilla spread.

"Oh, no! Is nothing sacred?" Dianne attempted not to laugh.

"Nothing, absolutely nothing." Rosalind did laugh.

Timothy climbed on the bed and yanked at Leda's chain while Billy pushed at the stubborn beast from the rear. Leda sat her ground, not yet ready to trust the twins who had inflicted the bath on her.

"Look at my poor spread!" Dianne protested.

Rosalind joined the would-be dog groomers in an attempt to save the chinchilla.

Outnumbered, Leda squirmed out of their grasps, plopped from the bed and ran from the room, leaving a trail of wet paw prints on the white carpet.

"Idiots!" Dianne laughed in spite of herself. "I pay the dog groomer an arm and a leg to give that creature baths!"

"But she rolled in some garbage in the park," Billy explained.

"It was really foul," added Timothy. "So we thought we'd give her a bath and surprise you."

"And we did," Timothy concluded.

"You better go find her before she soaks the rest of the place," Dianne said sternly. "And take her outside to dry!"

"It's getting dark," Billy objected.

"Too bad. You started it, kiddos. So get moving. You have to leave for your party in an hour."

"All right. All right." The twins scurried from the bedroom to escape a full-fledged lecture.

Rosalind turned to her mother, chuckling. "If you let me get my own apartment, I'll take Leda with me for protection."

"Rosie, the only way that old dog would stop an intruder is if she drowned him to death with one of her sloppy kisses. Besides, as much as I hate to admit it, since you all went off to school and left me with that ridiculous beast, I've gotten attached to her."

"Okay, you keep Leda, but what about my apartment?"

"I'll give it some serious thought, I promise. But there is one thing I would insist on for your protection. You would have to have private security guards to replace the Secret Service. No matter how quietly you live your life, there are still kooks around."

"If you insist, I guess I can live with that, as long as they are there for my protection and not your information."

"Rosalind! How can you say that!"

"As Grandma Jane says, 'People may grow up, but they never really change.' She also says you were born nosy."

Dianne laughed. "You are as wicked as Dave and as deft at attack with long-lost phrases. Maybe you should take up journalism."

"I don't think I'm going to take up anything long term right now," Rosalind said seriously. "I think I need time to catch my breath and catch up with myself. It's been a long year."

"A very long year," Dianne agreed.

The doorbell chimed.

"Oh, dear," Dianne murmured. "I'll bet that's Dave already and I haven't checked my makeup. We're going to the Gauguin opening at the Met. I'm sorry. I didn't even ask if you were interested in coming along."

"I couldn't anyway. I have a date."

"Oh. With whom?"

A sparkle entered Rosalind's eyes. "Jordan March the third."

"Rosalind! He's married!"

"Divorced as of last week. You didn't hear?"

Dianne brushed aside a faint shadow of jealousy and shook her head with mild motherly disapproval. "He is forty if he's a day."

"I like older men. Maybe when I'm older like you, I'll like younger men." Rosalind glanced up at the doorway to the den. "Hi, Dave."

"My daughter is a very wicked young woman," Dianne said with a laugh in greeting.

"Then I'd better get you away from her evil influence." Dave winked at Rosalind.

Dianne was amused, but not too amused to remember to call to Rosalind from the hall, "Rosie! What time will you be home?"

"What time will you two be back?"

"Before midnight," Dave called back.

"I'll tell the boys to stay out until two," Rosalind shouted after them. "And I promise not to be back before one thirty—at the earliest."

Dave's and her mother's laughter echoed in the hall before the elevator doors closed it off.